Undeading Bells

UNDEADING
BELLS

Drew Hayes

Edited by Erin Cooley (cooley.edit@gmail.com)
Edited by Kisa Whipkey (www.kisawhipkey.com)
Cover and Book Design by
Ashley Ruggirello (www.cardboardmonet.com

Paperback ISBN: 978-1-675068-15-1

This one goes out to all you wonderful readers who made this possible. Thanks to everyone who's been with Fred and the gang on the journey, and rest assured that there is still more to come.

Special thanks to my beta readers who are always here offering outstanding feedback to make these books better: E Ramos E, TheSFReader, and Priscilla Yuen.

PREFACE

I ALMOST CERTAINLY DO NOT KNOW YOU; however, I shall assume you are a lovely person, and it is my loss for not having yet had the opportunity to meet you. Still, I must assume you and I are connected in some way, for the works you are about to read are selections from a journal of my memoirs. I compiled these not in the belief that the stories within are so compelling they must be told, but rather because I found my unexpected life transition to be so shockingly uneventful—at least initially. I place the blame for my aggrandized expectations

1

squarely on contemporary media, filling my head with the belief that a ticket to the supernatural also put one on an express train toward coolness and suave charm.

This is simply not the case. Or, at least, it was not my case. I recorded my journeys in the hopes that, should another being find themselves utterly depressed at the humdrum personality still saddling their supernatural frame, they might find solace in knowing they are not the only one to have felt that way. Given the lengthy lifespan of many of the people with whom I associate, there is no guarantee they will have passed on by the time this is read. Therefore, names have been changed as I deemed necessary.

So, dear reader, whom I suspect is a wonderful person merely in need of a bit of reassurance, take comfort in my tales of uneventful blundering. One's nature is hard to change; sometimes even death is insufficient to accomplish such a task. But be assured that, while you might find yourself still more human than anticipated, you are far from the only one. You will eventually discover that under the movie stereotypes, imposed mystique, and overall inflated expectations, each and every one of us is at least a touch more boring than our images would indicate.

And that is not a bad thing.

- Fredrick Frankford Fletcher

SOMEWHERE OLD

1.

THE WHINE OF THE ENGINES SLOWED AS OUR turbulent travel neared its end. Even without the ability to lose my stomach, after being batted around the sky by heavy winds, I had to rise from my seat with care.

My fiancée, Krystal Jenkins, looked unbothered by the flight to East Texas. Admittedly, that was par for the course with her. Unlike myself, Krystal had a natural air of composure, like no situation was too much of a challenge. Despite the late hour, her brown eyes were electric with excitement and worry, occasionally darting down to the gun stored expertly on her hip. As an agent of a more or less unnamed secret government organization dedicated to the policing and peacekeeping of parahumans living in America, she was quite familiar with the firearm, to say nothing of the skills she boasted when things got truly dangerous.

Ah, but perhaps I should pause briefly, lest that last paragraph has you think me mad. My name is Fredrick Frankford Fletcher, but most everyone in my life calls me Fred, and I am a vampire. By this point in our tale, I'd been one for several years and had dipped enough toes into the parahuman world to have met other supernatural beings. Technically, Krystal wasn't in that group, as we'd known each other back during our human days, though her work for the Agency had brought her into the fold as much as her relationship with me. Most of the other parahumans I'd met were friends, or at least people who felt neutral toward me. Regrettably I did manage to pick up a few interested parties who weren't so cordial.

My sire, Quinn, was the least predictable. I could never be sure if he was insane or brilliant; except, the mere fact that he was able to avoid the Agency's pursuit proved the latter attribute had to be at least part of the equation. Of course, he'd also thought I'd go wild and kill countless humans, so he certainly wasn't infallible. Aside from Quinn, my largest issue to date was another vampire clan that had moved into my town of Winslow,

Colorado: the House of Turva. They were crafty, coming at me through the treaties and systems of our kind, staying within the law to ensure the Agency couldn't help.

The final faction I now had to keep track of wasn't technically an enemy—not yet, anyway—however, they were in my life due to the Turvas. The Blood Council, the ruling body which governed all vampires living in the United States under the secret treaties signed at the nation's founding, had taken an interest in me. Originally, they'd done so to see if I was competent enough to lead my own clan, the House of Fred. After they learned I was immune to silver as a consequence of dragon magic, their interest became far more piqued.

Tender fingers ran along the back of my scalp, soothing my active mind and nerves. "You okay in there? That was a quiet flight, even for you."

"Still nervous," I admitted. "I know there are checks in place—that's why we're meeting them here. I understand that the town is safe, cut off from the rest of the world, and I believe you when you say the security here is up to the task. Rationally, I mean. It's just hard getting it to sink in. I mean… you know how powerful Deborah was. There's going to be her *and* another member of the Blood Council present. It's hard to imagine someone could stop them from taking me if they pleased."

"Freddy, I'm not going to lie to you." Krystal's hand guided my head, pointing my own eyes toward hers. "Badass as I am, I'm not sure I could beat a member of the Blood Council. I also don't think they could beat me. I could probably wrangle us an escape, or some sort of stalemate, but that's not really the point. I definitely wouldn't be able to defeat two of them working together."

It was a strange mix of reassuring tone and expression, paired with words that promised failure. My confusion must have been evident. I caught the sly grin tugging on her lips, a sure sign I was following exactly where she wanted.

"Now, ask me if Sheriff Thorgood can beat them."

"Could Sheriff Thorgood defeat—"

"Yes." Immediate and certain, there wasn't a quiver of doubt in her. While I had no idea what Sheriff Leeroy Thorgood actually had in terms of parahuman abilities, I did know he'd trained Krystal when she first discovered her true nature. She held the man in high esteem, true, but Krystal was also exceptional at her job, which included the ability to assess potential threats and allies accurately. If she was sure, then it was warranted. I didn't need to know the specifics; I trusted her.

That didn't mean I wasn't still at tad curious, however.

"Does it even matter who I was going to ask about?"

"In theory, sure. In practice, I'm pretty sure you only know one parahuman who would be able to even fight in the sheriff's league, and I highly doubt you were about to guess Gideon." Krystal let go of me, stepping over to the luggage that was tamped down in the plane's rear.

I was glad for her timing, because I've no doubt the dumbfounded expression on my face was quite ridiculous. Gideon was an acquaintance of ours, sometimes even an ally, who also happened to be an ancient dragon and the King of the West. His magic was technically the reason I was in this mess, since helping him was what cured my silver allergy. Gideon was also what I used as the ceiling of my parahuman power scale. In every situation we'd encountered, save only for the time another dragon was involved, he was utterly unassailable: a being of seemingly near-infinite power, masquerading in the form of a child, who conquered every foe who dared offer even the slightest challenge to his authority.

And he was only in Sheriff Thorgood's *league*?

Had I possessed more time, I might have actually taken a moment to sit and ponder the implications of that. How much higher up did the power scale go? What other potential demi-gods should I steer clear of?

Sadly, I did not possess such free time. Krystal and I had flown to Boarback, Texas with a purpose. Multiple purposes, in fact.

The first was the far more pleasant one: the planning of our wedding. Given that Krystal's job often led to her interacting with a wide variety of parahumans, we'd decided to hold the event in one of only three towns built specifically for supernatural creatures. Boarback was a hidden hamlet, a place where creatures of all shapes and powers could live openly, without the pretense of being human. This also meant they had the food and facilities for almost any type of parahuman, which would make things easier on our different kinds of guests. Of course, since we didn't live in Boarback, a trip had been necessary to handle the details and in-person touches. That was originally why we'd planned the outing.

Unfortunately, the Blood Council had somehow found out about it, and decided to send representatives for what they were referring to as a "comprehensive condition evaluation," which was apparently code for testing me six ways to Sunday to see if my silver immunity offered any other perks. I didn't even have the option of saying that this was unlikely: I'd already discovered one such side effect when Quinn tried to dominate my mind via his bond as my sire, only to fail completely. Much as I'd like to claim strength of will, I'd never even felt the compulsion. Whatever connection he'd been trying to use was either broken or gone, and the only explanation for something that crazy was good old dragon magic. The experience had shown that the request for further

testing was not only reasonable, it was actually the sort of thing I should have done for myself years ago.

Finished with freeing her bags, Krystal tossed mine over as well—much stronger than her slender form betrayed. "Take it easy. We'll get settled in before sunrise. After I grab a nap, we can use the tunnels to go do our wedding stuff, then deal with the Blood Council tomorrow. You've got a whole day to be anxious, so don't use it all up tonight. It's a marathon, not a sprint."

Even as she teased, Krystal stepped back across the small expanse of the plane and took my hand. "It'll be okay. They don't have any grounds to take you. Between the treaties and the deal we hammered out for you, you'll be safe. If the Blood Council makes an aggressive move, they'll do it knowing they call down the full wrath of the Agency. The higher up someone is, the more serious it gets if they break the rules. And if the Blood Council did something that dumb, we'd *have* to drop the hammer just to send the message to everyone else that we don't take that shit. They know it, and we can both agree that Deborah isn't the type to make sloppy moves."

In an odd way, my former bodyguard's competence was reassuring. If she struck, it would be hard and swift, and likely from an angle I'd never see coming. Which meant that something this obvious was unlikely to be her method... unless that's exactly what I was supposed to think.

At that moment, I realized Krystal was right. Wrapping myself in knots wasn't going to make any part of this process smoother. Granted, I continued to be anxious, because fear isn't quite that reasonable or easy to dispel, but this understanding did help ease my nerves—albeit slightly. If nothing else, I had a day with the woman I loved to look forward to, exploring one of her favorite places in the world. On the off chance the Blood Council was planning to kill me, I could think of few better ways to spend my final day. There was no reason to let them taint what was supposed to be a happy, relaxing weekend.

I held our bags while Krystal opened a heavy door at the front of the cabin and leaned in, speaking briefly to the pilots I hadn't met. Seconds later, a loud hiss sounded as the plane's door unsealed, opening slowly from the top. I was fairly sure these kinds of small-propellered planes didn't normally have such complex security or automatic features, but that was a perk of flying on Agency transportation. They took their security quite seriously, and not without good reason.

Unlike the last time I'd flown to Boarback, the door didn't open to reveal an empty field surrounded by trees. The field was still there, as were the trees, but what differed was the presence of people. Our arrival must have been better timed today, as I could already see the beat-up truck Sheriff Thorgood used to navigate the rough terrain. Except, that wasn't the only vehicle present. There was also an SUV, an expensive-looking one that I knew at a glance had an array of extra features. I'd seen enough like it by this point to catch the signs—not to mention, I was keenly aware of Deborah's preferred taste in transportation.

"Those motherfuckers," Krystal muttered over my shoulder, clearly reaching the same conclusion.

There was nothing for it, so I made my way down the stairs. No sooner had my feet touched the grass than the doors on both vehicles opened. From the truck came Sheriff Thorgood, looking casual and unworried despite the odd circumstances of our meeting. From the SUV emerged Deborah, one of the five ranking members of the Blood Council. Her official title was Prudence: she dealt with strategy, long-term planning, and everything else where it paid to have someone with a cool head and a knack for seeing the bigger picture. Whether it was an act of teasing or friendship, I didn't know, but Deborah was wearing a large, puffy sweater, something I'd only seen her don during her time as my guard.

The person accompanying her was one I didn't recognize. He was plainly a vampire, with hair shaved close to the scalp and a long, thin frame, like he'd been stretched out just a tad more than was wise. His ensemble was unremarkable save for his jacket, which was somewhere between the bastard child of a lab coat and cargo shorts. The pockets were located in almost comically awkward locations, except there was nothing funny about his determined approach as he strode up to meet me. Deborah got ahead of him, fast as always, though she seemed a tad put off by his sudden charge.

"Fred, Krystal, good to see you both again. I'd like to spend more time on pleasantries and catching up, but I think it best we kick this off with an introduction. I'd like you both to meet Claudius, acting Wisdom of the Blood Council, and a man who was quite insistent upon making your acquaintance."

I turned to the advancing form, putting on my best professional-networking face. "Hello there, Claudius, pleasure to meet you."

"Yes, yes, era-appropriate greetings to you, too." From one of his seemingly innumerable pockets, Claudius produced a blade that, when pulled free of its sheath, gave off the unmistakable scent of silver. "Now then, if we can get down to business, I would very much like to stab this through your chest."

2.

IT WAS CERTAINLY AN UNUSUAL GREETING,
even by parahuman standards; however, there were two
positives to take away from the encounter. The first
was that, low a bar as it may seem, Claudius was at
least trying to get my permission before he stabbed me.
Several of the vampires I'd met would have stabbed first
and perhaps offered up a half-hearted apology after, if
even that.

The second point of encouragement was that
Deborah clearly recognized the insanity of such an

introduction and hurriedly jumped in to smooth things over. I'd hoped that having the one Blood Council member I sort of knew act as a diplomat would make finding common ground with this new person easier—or that she'd at least keep him from killing me by accident. I felt reasonably sure that none of them wanted me dead yet; not when my condition was such a promising find.

"Sorry about that," Deborah said, laying a firm hand on Claudius's shoulder. "Before turning, Claudius was a mage, the kind who did better with studies and theories than his fellow human beings—habits that have only been reinforced over the centuries. He doesn't actually want to murder you, Fred."

"Of course not. I want to prove this entire enterprise to be a waste of my impossibly valuable time." Claudius was a man who spoke with absolute confidence, as if even the notion of his wrongness was unfathomable. "Mr. Fletcher, while I applaud your skills in pulling the wool over our Prudence's eyes, you'll find that I am not so easily flimflammed. No vampire is immune to silver: it flies in the face of our very understanding of magic. Once I jam this in your sternum, the pain will be too great to use your trickery, and we can be done with this nonsense."

In an odd way, his accusation was a relief. It was encouraging to hear that not everyone on the Blood Council even believed my ability was real; the fewer people who were interested in me, the better. Not to mention that this was one test I had no fears about passing. Although it had brought me, overall, more trouble than aid, I really was immune to silver. Now that the secret was out, I had nothing left to hide.

"I'm sorry if this is a silly question—Deborah can speak to my lack of vampire knowledge—but that won't count as being staked, right? My understanding is that said stake needs to be wood, but I want to make sure that a knife doesn't count."

Claudius looked even more ready to knife me, but Deborah mercifully took the time to explain. "Usually, it does need to be wood, but there are some enchanted objects that can surprise you, so the general rule is don't let anything hit you in the heart when you can help it. As for the knife, no one said anything about a heart. Just jam it on the right side and show Claudius its effects."

"Very well, then." I could have pushed back, asked if this was an official order, kicked up a fuss about them coming early—there was no shortage of methods for stalling—but frankly, I had too much on my plate as it was. This was clearly happening, so getting it out of the way would make the rest of the trip easier. Besides, I didn't appreciate being called a liar.

With minimal flair, I lifted the blade from Claudius's hand, raised it a few feet into the moonlight, and thrust downward, plunging the blade into the right side of my chest. Only after I had made the cut did it occur to me: I should have removed my sweater vest and button-down shirt, both of which were now stained by the small amount of thick blood that came from a vampire's wound. It didn't matter, as seconds later, Claudius leaned in and casually tore through the garments around the stab point, permitting him to examine it closely.

At first, he looked from me to the knife, clearly waiting for me to scream or whimper and admit it was all a hoax. After a minute, he touched the knife itself. Wiggle here, slight pull there; with every twitch, he looked back, expecting me to break. It took nearly ten minutes before Claudius stood straight once more.

"I must say, whatever trick you have come up with, we'll need to discuss. How you've managed to dull the pain of the silver, I cannot even begin to fathom; this method holds tremendous promise for our people. The charade, however, is at an end. Dulling the pain is one thing; no amount of self-control will hide the simple truth of our bodies. Wounds inflicted from silver heal slowly, and often leave scars when deep enough. Sorry, Mr. Fletcher; this was always the limit of your lie."

That was all the warning I had before the knife was yanked out of my chest. I made no movement, keeping my torso turned toward Claudius. No one else looked as closely; the majority of them had already seen this show before. The wound knit back together in the span of seconds, a full belly of blood fueling my unnatural healing. After a minute, my skin was as smooth as it had been before the blow.

To a vampire, this should have been a mundane sight. Claudius, conversely, appeared as though he'd just taken a cannonball to the head. Eyes wide, swaying on his feet, he poked at my skin, then grabbed it, fingers probing the flesh, looking for a scar, a rune, some sort of prosthetic, anything that would explain this seemingly impossible thing.

"Show me again. On your hand, this time."

From behind me, Krystal stepped forward. "Okay, Freddy's been a damn nice sport about this, but we have shit to do. The Blood Council has its testing time tomorrow, so how about we satisfy your curiosity boner then?"

"Agent Jenkins, what Mr. Fletcher is showing me uproots some of the fundamental understandings of magic upon which everything we know is built. Forgive me if I'd like to see this experiment repeated a few times before accepting such a revelation at face value."

To his credit, Claudius hadn't stabbed me. Reeling though he was, he still waited for me to give the nod, which I did. In an odd way, I felt for Claudius. I'd been where he was more recently than anyone else. Going from human to vampire meant coming to grips with a lot of "truths" that turned out to be comforting lies humanity told itself. I'd had my world uprooted less than a decade ago, and I could still remember the feeling of having the ground fall out from under me, the desperate need to grip onto anything real or true. If this got him through it faster, then that was better for all of us.

Once more, the knife bit my flesh. I didn't even bother rolling up the sleeve. With half the shirt gone, I was counting this one as a loss already. Once more, it didn't matter, as Claudius tore it off to check the wound. This time, he didn't leave the knife embedded as long. He required even less time with the next wound to my shoulder, and after that, stabbing my foot was mostly just formality. Each time we repeated the results, Claudius appeared to grow more stable.

Well, perhaps "excited" is more accurate than "stable" in terms of overall mood. Whereas I'd expected a researcher whose work was just invalidated to be upset, Claudius was practically vibrating by the end, his eyes alight with possibility. After a final leg wound, he sheathed his blade, satisfied.

"Mr. Fletcher, I owe you an apology. While I'm not quite prepared to call this a full immunity until I've gone through a few more tests, even if those fail, the undeniable fact remains that you are closer to it than any other vampire outside of myth. Your assertions were truthful, and I am sorry for doubting you."

To my surprise, he bowed deeply to me, a gesture I returned out of habit. When meeting new people, mirroring body language is generally a good method for matching their energy and staying polite. People have different forms of greeting in both the human and parahuman world; reflecting the motions they offered rarely went over poorly.

"And with that, I think Claudius and I have some work to do before our official meeting tomorrow. Fred, thanks for being such a good sport. I'll find a way to make this up to you. Agent Jenkins, always a pleasure." Deborah grabbed Claudius by the arm and essentially dragged him across the field, back toward the SUV.

She paused only when passing Sheriff Thorgood, who greeted Deborah with a friendly smile. For a fleeting moment, she stiffened before offering a cordial expression of her own. An hour prior, the idea that Deborah might be afraid of Sheriff Thorgood would have been outright preposterous. I'd seen what she could do when barely trying. At her peak, Deborah was among the most feared vampires in the nation, if not the world. That said, I was fairly certain she wasn't as powerful as a dragon, which meant that, according to Krystal, Sheriff Thorgood was substantially more dangerous than she was.

Much like Claudius, my own head threatened to swim under the assault of new information. Every time I thought I had a handle on the parahuman world, some new piece of the puzzle revealed how little I actually knew. I pressed a hand to my temple and moments later, felt a warm presence at my side.

"How you feeling?" Krystal asked. She didn't bother whispering, since around this crowd, it wouldn't do any good.

"Exposed," I replied, motioning to my destroyed shirt and sweater vest.

"I kind of like the torn shirt look. Reminds me of the old bodice-rippers my mom kept around the house." Krystal kept smiling, tossing in a salacious wink, but I caught the flicker of pain in her eyes. Generally speaking, Krystal didn't talk about her parents, especially her mother. They'd never known about the power passed down through their bloodline, had no idea that until the prison of their devil was passed from mother to daughter, the owner was almost unkillable— a feature that her mother might have wanted to hold on to once she got sick.

None of this needed to be talked about at this particular moment, especially considering the company. Instead, I threw an arm around her and did my best attempt at impersonating what I imagined that sort of romance-cover charmer to sound like.

"Hold fast, ye lovely... strumpet... lest I must stroke, er—cuddle, um—"

The laughter wasn't necessarily what I'd been aiming for, but the pain was gone when she looked at me again. "I am absolutely going to make you keep doing that when we get to the room. I hope you have a lot of material prepared."

Together, we made our way over to Sheriff Thorgood's truck. I went to work on the luggage, while Leeroy swept Krystal up into a giant, rib-crushing hug. She let out a squeal of glee with unabashed joy, giving him a hug around the neck that looked like it would choke a lesser being.

After a long embrace, Leeroy finally set her back down. A moment later, he started toward me. Too late, I realized what was happening—not that I would have had the presence of mind to dodge, anyway.

"Seeing as you're about to become family, it's time I started greeting you that way." Sheriff Thorgood scooped me up, pressing down on my body with the same affection he'd shown Krystal. Ours was at least a shorter interaction; he set me down after only a brief squeeze.

Slapping the hood of his truck, he motioned for us to climb in. "Let's get headed back to town already. I know you two have a wedding to plan, and only so much time to work with."

My eyes darted to the taillights of the SUV driving off toward Boarback. Not bad for a first meeting, but that had been proving my condition was real. From this point on, I had no idea what their testing might entail. I moved my vision from the fading taillights to Krystal's smile.

Whatever the Blood Council had in store, we'd deal with it when the time came. Until then, we were in her favorite place, planning our wedding. If there was one piece of advice older parahumans kept giving me, it was to enjoy the good times while I had them.

Pushing the thought of tests out of my head, I joined Krystal at the truck, intertwining my hand with hers as we headed off toward the curious town of Boarback, Texas.

3.

IN THE YEARS SINCE I'D LAST VISITED,
the Bristle Inn—Boarback's sole hotel—had undergone
some slight renovations. New wallpaper and carpets
mostly, though I did note a hot tub filled with bubbling
green liquid installed by the pool. What that was, or
whom it was for, I had no idea, nor any inclination to
find out. Between planning a wedding and being stabbed
repeatedly, I had enough to keep track of for one trip.

Getting there was smooth, at least. Sheriff Thorgood
and Krystal spent the time catching up, and while they

did their best to include me in the conversation, it wasn't a dynamic that was easy to slip into. Not that I minded; a little time to process what had just happened was actually helpful. Besides, it was nice to see Krystal so joyful. Sheriff Thorgood had been there to teach and train her at her lowest point. She'd just lost her mother, then learned about her powers, the parahuman world, and where she fit into it. He'd been the one to start her training, and listening to them chat, it was plain she'd missed her mentor.

By the time we arrived at the remodeled hotel, they were largely up to speed on recent events, and Sheriff Thorgood dropped us both off with another round of powerful hugs. Check-in went smoothly—we were given a room with enchanted glass so we wouldn't have to choose between keeping the shades drawn and me turning into ash—and we unloaded our bags and turned our attention to the itinerary.

"Okay, let's break this down. Primary objectives are venue, catering, and transportation. These are what we need to lock down for a wedding to occur and must be secured while in Boarback. Secondary objectives are decorations, cake, entertainment, basically anything that would be essential to the event but that doesn't necessarily *have* to come from Boarback. We *should* aim to source locally for convenience, if nothing else.

Tertiary objectives are anything we think up that isn't wedding essential."

As much as I loved Krystal, it was easy to forget that under the devil-may-care attitude was a highly respected agent with countless missions under her belt. Just because she usually chose to let me handle "boring" things like logistics didn't mean she wasn't more than capable of doing it herself. Looking at the bullet-pointed list she had produced, I found myself impressed by the step-by-step planning.

"Venue is out, for now," she continued. "We're too close to sunrise; better to get a fresh start tomorrow. In theory, we could scout enclosed options, but when you're dealing with a large number of parahumans, it's always best to have indoor and outdoor space. Things can get messy otherwise."

I wasn't sure how to interpret that particular brand of messy, so I opted not to ask for clarification. "Looks like catering comes next, if we're skipping venue until tomorrow."

"That it does, and this is a big one. Part of why I suggested Boarback, in fact. The range of food options we need is insane. The only option is to use a caterer who specializes in wide-range parahuman events." Krystal moved her finger along the paper to a boxed-in section with three entries. "One does that weird molecule gas cooking thing we see on shows sometimes, another runs more traditional fare, and the third is the diner we ate at last time."

I was knocked a bit off course by the diner being on the list, but after a moment's consideration, it all fell neatly into place. Obviously, an operating diner in a city for parahumans only would have both the supplies for and practice in meeting a vast array of dietary needs. Perhaps not the best food for such a formal event, though.

"I must admit, I am curious how one applies molecular gastronomy to parahuman cuisine." A brief glance at Krystal's expression gave me all the feedback I needed on that front. "But I've watched your reactions when we see that genre presented, and I know you're not a fan. Plus, a wedding might not be the optimal place for culinary experimentation."

Krystal produced a pen and marked off the first item in the box. "That's a very good point about the experimenting. I'm not against trying new stuff, just maybe we should aim for food that looks like actual food, not three bird eggs in the shell being devoured by snakes made out of deconstructed enchiladas or whatever."

That was more or less how it went as we went down the list, prioritizing our top pick destinations, with some backups just in case. It was something we could have done back at home, and had I been on my own, we'd already have a spreadsheet of destinations in descending order of priority. But I was learning to be a bit more spontaneous, just as Krystal was meeting me halfway on planning. While it was not the most efficient way to plan out our day, it *was* a lovely bit of decompression with the woman I loved. Efficiency couldn't hold much of a candle to that.

By the time we were heading toward the shopping district, there was only a couple hours left until sunrise. We strolled through the grassy lands, along one of the cobblestone roads winding over the landscape, staying aboveground until the sun forced us to the tunnels. Boarback had a few roads, but for the most part, it was made to be walked, a feature I admired. Dearly as I loved our town of Winslow, there was potent appeal in never having to fight traffic.

The most interesting thing about this town wasn't the walking paths, however. Nor was it the secluded nature, or secret existence, or even the population of parahumans. What I found most fascinating about Boarback was the effect it had on Krystal. She visibly relaxed more than almost any time at home, and was at peace in a way that was fundamentally different. I wanted to ask her why that was, yet I loathed to pry.

For a change, that was not the end of my thought process. Yes, I did loathe to pry, but a place that meant so much to Krystal was something I should at least try to understand.

"Much as I hate to spoil the lovely silence of our walk, I was wondering something. Perfectly all right if you don't want to answer, but I couldn't help noticing how much more at ease you are in Boarback. This place relaxes you more than it seems like just a change of scenery would."

"Don't knock a good change of scenery; helps shake the cobwebs off." Krystal leaned in closer, resting her head against my shoulder. "The reason is simple, Freddy. Like I told you last time we visited and I left my gun in the room: this place is safe."

I was willing to let it go at that, giving her hand a gentle squeeze. Krystal, on the other hand, continued to explain. "Maybe it's a little more than just that. It's like… I'm finally off the clock. I love my job, I love that I get to make a difference, and I love kicking the ass of people who deserve it. But being that powerful comes with duties, to those you serve and those you love. Part of why I enjoy being in Boarback is because—and yeah, I know how this sounds— I'm *not* the strongest one here. Not by a longshot. If something goes completely wild and chaos breaks out, Sheriff Thorgood can more than handle it. You and I would just get in the way. I don't get to feel like that very often: just a normal person on a walk with her guy."

When she put it like that, I almost felt silly for having asked. Just because Krystal didn't show the burden she carried didn't mean it wasn't there. I knew there was virtually nothing she wouldn't do to protect the members of our clan, our family. I just hadn't considered how being the one who would actually have to *do* virtually anything would be a constant, heavy boulder of worry.

"Do you ever wonder what would have happened if we'd found romantic ground in high school?" I asked. "If there's another world where we ended up together as humans? Well... one human and one woman-with-a-devil-she-hadn't-activated-yet. I try to picture it sometimes, the two of us living normal, happy lives."

A poke to my ribs caused me to jump. "Like those versions better?"

"No. That's what I was getting to." I was tempted to rub my ribs, except that would have required letting go of Krystal's hand. Besides, it was more habit than need, anyway. "My point was, I 'try' to picture it, but I never really can. It's hard to imagine the younger versions of ourselves pairing up to begin with. More than that, I just can't see a version of you that's content without being all that you currently are. I've known human Krystal, and I've known agent Krystal. Anyone with that perspective can easily tell which of you is happier."

My hand jerked as Krystal stopped moving. I turned, worried I'd said something wrong, only to have her mouth meet mine in a sudden, passionate kiss. We lingered there, under the falling moon, for perhaps longer than I feel proper recounting. When we finally broke apart, she drew me in close, laying her head against my sternum. Were I still alive, she could have heard my heart beating.

"One of the things I hate about all of this is that when I got my powers, I stopped being Krystal to almost everyone. I was an asset, or a threat, or a tool. People in the know see the job or the monster, and I have to lie to everyone else, never letting them into my real life. You don't know how lonely I was after Tem betrayed me. For a long time, I was just the job. I gave everyone what they wanted... until I remembered what it was like to have someone see me as Krystal again. Do you want to hear something I don't think I've told you?"

"Always," I replied honestly.

"When we were first dating, before Quinn attacked, I was terrified of what would happen when you found out the truth. I kept wanting to tell you and finding reasons to put it off. But then, after everything went down and you saw me partially transform, you didn't run. Instead, you did the most Fred thing I can imagine: you sat with me while I still had red eyes and claws to have a frank discussion about our relationship. Because... you still saw me, still knew I was in there, no matter how the outside changed. That was the night I realized just how far this relationship had the potential to go."

We kissed again, more briefly this time, and when we broke apart, it was my turn to speak. "Given our current agenda, I hope that's a decision you're happy with."

"Have to wait and see," Krystal shot back. "Sure, the love and support are nice, but we all know a wedding is really about the cake. Feels like that's going to be a deciding factor on whether or not this was a smart call."

"Well then, seems we will have to sample quite the wide array. I wonder if they have any parahuman-specific flavors."

The sharp peal of laughter from Krystal was music to my soul. "Freddy, brace your stomach. You are in a for a wild-ass ride."

4.

OVER THE COURSE OF THE NEXT FEW HOURS, Krystal and I proceeded to look at an array of stores, all open despite the late hour. Our first was a flower shop run by a lovely woman with leaves growing out of her hair, whose wares included tulips that sang a soothing melody and several gnarly looking plants with what certainly appeared to be working mouths. Krystal quickly steered us toward some flower I'd never seen before whose petals gave off a gentle, shifting glow. It was lovely, and I agreed to the choice, only to be shown ten more before we settled back on the original selection.

That was, in essence, the theme of the day. Krystal was a woman who knew what she wanted—that had always been the case—yet she was also open to the idea that there might be options she hadn't considered. In effect, it meant that we knew within the first five minutes of arriving at each shop what her choice would be, but then had to do a full circuit before actually making the selection. It was a day of wasted time, a truly inefficient way to handle our tasks.

And I loved every minute of it.

In my time away from Boarback, I'd almost forgotten how it felt to not be... different. Here, everyone was parahuman, from the naga waitress slithering to her shift at the diner to the crow-like man resting atop a nearby roof. No one gave either a second glance, nor was a mere vampire enough to draw attention. It wasn't that I changed how I was acting or behaving—more that I no longer had to affect the constant effort of being aware of what I did so that I might ensure none of it betrayed my true nature. Outside of being at home, or around only loved ones, this was one of the few times I felt that sense of awareness fall away. I didn't need it. Not here.

Spending such time with Krystal doing incredibly mundane tasks only made the day better. We weren't an agent and a vampire, with all the worries that entailed.

We were a normal couple shopping for a wedding: having deliberations, reeling at prices, imagining how the day we were building would ultimately shape out. I deferred to Krystal on most items because, as the sweater vest demonstrated, I was not renowned for my sense of style. We did meet halfway on a few items, though, including a color scheme with substantially less red than Krystal advocated for. She loved her signature color, but I convinced her that a vampire wedding festooned by crimson was a little passé.

It was hard not to think about vampires as our day wound down. After the initial cake-tasting, in which we were shown around by what seemed to be an array of small creatures working as one, we offered some feedback and were told to come back the next day. Evidently, this was their process, as Krystal took the dismissal without umbrage.

With that done, we returned to the hotel, where Krystal grabbed a quick nap while I caught up on work. So far, Lillian was holding down the fort quite well, but there was no way I could take off the duration of our trip entirely. We were slammed, scrutinizing more and more prospective clients weekly. It was an excellent problem to have: word of our reputation was spreading, especially among parahumans. Unfortunately, we simply didn't have the staff to keep up. While Lillian had proven an apt study over the years, and could now handle everything of intermediary difficulty and lower, I was still taking on the harder cases. We needed more people; that had become clear long ago. The problem was that I had yet to even hear about another parahuman accountant who wasn't already spoken for, such as those who kept books for the Agency.

Recruiting was an option, presuming I could find someone trustworthy, competent, and actually interested in learning the occupation. It was a slower route, certainly, but Deborah had gotten me thinking about longer-term solutions during our time together. I could hold out for a perfect new accountant to fall into my lap, or I could lay the groundwork now, so it wouldn't be a problem in the future. I knew my luck and had no question which path I should bet on. Slow, steady, and reliable won the day every time.

Until then, I was stuck keeping the plates spinning. By the time I got to a solid stopping point in my work, Krystal had woken up, grabbed a shower, and dressed for the less enjoyable outing on our agenda. This time, I noticed she didn't leave her gun in the room. Maybe because she'd be acting as an agent, or perhaps she just wanted to send a message. I truly hoped it wasn't because she planned to use the thing. Fine a shot as she was, it was going to take more than a mere pistol to stop a member of the Blood Council.

Stowing my laptop, I took the time to adjust my current outfit, though I saw no reason to change. Deborah knew what she was getting, and besides, they'd already ruined one shirt and vest so far. I certainly didn't intend to have my formal wear shredded.

Krystal was waiting by the door, no longer quite so at ease. I hated that Deborah's assessment stole that respite from her, even briefly, but it was better than my being taken in the night and locked away in some secret testing cell. We had to play nice. That was the only way this situation stayed viable.

"You ready?"

If I said no, that I wanted to bolt, I knew she would back me. We'd have to suffer the consequences, but this *was* still my choice. I could flee, if I really wanted to.

"Ready as I can be." Running was a final option, a bell that couldn't be unrung. So long as the Blood Council was upholding their end of our deal, this was the better tactic. Should that change, I'd reconsider my options.

Together, we left the Bristle Inn through the front door rather than the tunnels, a new night coating the sky. Finding the Blood Council would be easy, at least: Sheriff Thorgood had shown us where they were staying on the drive over. It was a substantial manor resting atop a modest hill, fenced and fortified from every angle.

This was not, as I'd initially suspected, some holding the Blood Council owned in case of random trips to Boarback. Rather, the estate was the equivalent of a floating embassy, the sort meant to house those of high stations: people too important to put up in the town's hotel, yet who still required lodging. The manor could be rented, albeit only by specific parties and with a fair amount of red tape, principally to discourage anyone from dropping by. Sheriff Thorgood had been quite open about that last part; he had no inclination to let Boarback become a tourism spot. It was a community first and foremost, one he intended to keep intact.

We could have called for a car, but we enjoyed the walk. Both of us could easily outpace a human, so the trip didn't take too long. Mostly, it was an excuse for another moonlit stroll through the city. The Blood Council might be able to force themselves into our getaway, but that didn't mean we wouldn't make use of every moment they didn't own.

Sadly, the walk eventually came to an end as we arrived at the manor's gate. I was expecting some sort of guard to be waiting, and in a way, I was right. Only, we got a far more dangerous guard than I'd thought would be assigned to handle the front gates.

"Glad you both found the place." Deborah stepped out of the shadows, the large metal blockade behind her grinding into action as she moved. Whether she'd hit a switch, or someone inside had incredible timing, I couldn't tell, but it did make for a lovely display of coordination.

"Hard to miss," Krystal replied. "You two get settled in nicely?"

"I did; Claudius has been on a tear since last night." Deborah chuckled under her breath. "Despite everything I told him, he didn't truly believe in your condition until he saw it for himself. Sent the man into a tizzy. He's been devising other aspects to test, now that he knows there's something to investigate."

I bristled slightly, wondering what fresh horrors my previous compliance had unlocked. Deborah caught note of my stiffened back and continued. "Don't worry. Unlike Claudius, I *did* know we were coming here for real work, and I made sure the tests we have planned are the most vital ones. For all his excitement, he hasn't presented one experiment that was important enough to bump another off the list. I appreciate that you've given us this time, and you should know that we respect it."

Uneasy as I felt about working with the Blood Council, Deborah's approach did relax me somewhat. Then again, that was no surprise. She was a vampire of untold age who'd spent weeks getting to know me and my friends; she knew exactly which technique to use on me at any given time. Still, if I had to have a handler, it didn't hurt to have one who was good at her job.

The smile on Deborah's face dimmed. "On that note, I thought you should have a bit of say in how the night goes. I won't lie to you: some of what's coming will be very unpleasant. We can scale up or down, depending on your preference. Start small and work your way up, or complete the hardest exercises first and let things grow progressively easier."

For some people, I suspect it might have been a difficult choice, but I knew myself too well. The anxious, worried nature I was born with would go wild if every test I had to take was more challenging than the last. I'd certainly get in my own head, imagining more and more dangerous tasks still to come. Handling the hardest task first, on the other hand, would let me know that I could take on whatever came next. I already had enough people to watch out for; I didn't need to work against my own brain, as well.

"If it's not too much bother, I'd like to start with the more difficult side of the spectrum."

That earned me a nod. "I had a feeling. Follow me, and I'll explain."

Perfectly on cue, the gates finished opening. Had she controlled the pacing of our entire conversation? I wanted to dismiss the idea as ludicrous; however, spending time with Deborah had taught me never to assume that anything was impossible for her, especially when she had a chance to plan. I didn't ask about the gates as we followed her into the building, since she was busy telling me how the night would begin.

"Fred, what you need to understand about tonight is that your immunity to silver represents more than a neat trick. What we are, as vampires, could be described as cursed corpses. We're dead bodies, with the soul bound and flesh animated solely thanks to magic. It's why silver hurts us: it disrupts the spell that keeps us sustained. For you to be completely immune to silver means that something fundamental in the magic that makes you a vampire has changed."

We strode through a large marble entrance that was beautiful and also surprisingly generic. Then again, a rented space probably did better by keeping the decor neutral. The loud snaps of our shoes on the hard flooring echoed around the empty house, announcing our presence to what I hoped was still a limited number of company.

"Or just dragon magic," Krystal added. "Let's not pretend their shit doesn't regularly break the few rules of the arcane we kind of understand."

To my surprise, Deborah agreed. "Precisely. Everything I've said is based off our understanding of magic, most of which is little more than theory. It very well could be some unexplored side effect of sustained draconic magic that's run through an undead body. But you can see why that is a distinction we need to make, and soon. Between being immune to silver and resistant to a sire's compulsion, there's a very real chance that Fred is a new form of vampire. We can't assume any of the standard abilities, outside of blood-drinking, work as normal."

I almost asked about the blood thing before realizing that Deborah had seen me drink from an dead mage and temporarily gain the power to see magic, so that was one she already knew about. We kept walking—down a hall, toward a beeping noise that was gradually edging in through my selective attention. As soon as I paid it my full attention, I knew what it was and stopped in my tracks.

"You can't be serious."

"Deadly serious, and I'm not talking about you," Deborah shot back. "You wanted to start with the hardest task, Fred. Where did you imagine that would lead?"

Krystal was looking between us; her hearing couldn't catch the shrill beeps through the walls. "Freddy? What's going on?"

"I know what the first test is. They want me to try to turn another human into a vampire."

5.

"OPENING WITH MURDER IN FRONT OF AN agent. That's a bold damn move." Krystal didn't reach for her gun just yet, but her hands didn't exactly stray from her belt, either.

Deborah, unbothered as always, produced a stack of pages from her back pocket and handed them to Krystal. "First off, we do get a set amount of legal turn-attempts per year; that's part of the treaty. Secondly, if you'll look through this, you'll find everything to be on the up-and-up. We knew who was coming to this, Agent Jenkins, and all legalities have been observed. Lastly, Fred, will you at least hear me out? Listen to the full situation before you reject it."

They were asking me to kill someone. Dressing it up as a turn-attempt might sound nice, but the odds of success were so low, this was like betting a life on a roulette wheel. That assumed I even *could* turn people: as Deborah had just pointed out, my vampire abilities weren't quite right. My guts twisted at even the idea of it, and on my own, I might have taken a stand right then and there.

Until I heard the slight gasp that escaped Krystal's throat. She looked up at Deborah, eyes narrowed. "This is bald-faced, emotional manipulation."

"If it's that obvious, can you even call it manipulation? I prefer to think of it as presenting a palatable option to an ethical man," Deborah countered. "Fred, I know you. I know your limits, and I am telling you, this is one you should at least consider."

I looked to Krystal, who was still glancing down at the documents. "Be careful, Freddy. I don't like the way this was set up for us, even if I can't say they broke any rules. But... maybe it is worth a listen."

It was rare for Krystal to be unsure about anything. Whatever she was reading must have rattled her. Much as I still wanted to reject the idea outright, it was clear there was more at work here than I was yet grasping. Better to understand things fully, and then make my choice.

"Okay, Deborah. You've earned that much trust. I'll listen to what you propose."

She motioned for us to continue, and we arrived at a simple door. Stepping through, we found ourselves on the viewing side of a one-way mirror. In the adjacent room lay a woman hooked up to dozens of tubes and machines—body thin, eyes sunken, though there was still a slight sparkle in them. She wasn't gone entirely. Sadly, it was clear from the context that she wouldn't be around much longer.

"This is Sherilyn—Sheri to her friends and family. Advanced cancer, as you can probably guess. Hell, you'd be able to smell it if you went in there. Sheri has three kids: two boys and a girl. Her husband died of a heart attack last year. As things stand, she'll likely be dead before the end of the month, if not the week. She leaves behind a grand total of five thousand dollars to provide for her now parentless children."

It was heartbreaking; however, I wasn't sure that killing her sooner was really the right thing to do. That said, staring into the room, it was hard to feel as secure in my position as I had been before. Would a wild swing at undeath be worse than slipping away? Were I in her shoes, would I risk it?

"If I try to turn her and fail, her kids lose even the chance to say goodbye."

"They've already said their farewells. Her family thinks she's been taken off for a last-ditch, experimental treatment, which, in a way, she has," Deborah explained. "Besides which, no, that's not all that changes if you fail to turn her. In exchange for her participation in this experiment, Sheri's children will receive trust funds and access to custodians and legal advisors to help them until they come of age. Even if you fail, you'll be giving her peace of mind that her kids are provided for."

No wonder Krystal had called this emotional manipulation. Deborah was cutting off all my objections before they could even be properly raised. Given that her entire job was planning and anticipation, it was to be expected. That didn't make it fun to experience, though.

"I see. So, if I succeed, she becomes a vampire, presumably with a better support network than the one I started with. Should she perish, her children are provided for. The only circumstance in which nothing improves for her is if I refuse to even try. Is that about the cut of it?"

There was no shame in Deborah's face as she shrugged. "You're a kind person, Fred. You care about people, even those you've never met. In a lot of your life as a vampire, that's been a boon, but it also makes you incredibly easy to handle—assuming one has the gall to be straightforward about it."

I could hardly accuse her of playing it subtle; that was overwhelmingly true. She'd even chosen the same disease that had claimed Krystal's mother, meaning that there was no way my fiancée could stay truly objective. Even as Deborah and I talked, Krystal was looking hard through the glass. The sight was no doubt stirring up old memories; it was amazing she could stay so composed.

Following her lead, I looked in, as well. So many tubes and machines… this barely seemed like living anymore.

Taking a mental step back, I tried to examine my hesitation. Was I afraid that turning her successfully was a curse? No… thanks to my friends and my life, I'd learned that being undead wasn't some unbearable sentence. It was just one more way to exist among countless other options. The larger part of my fear stemmed from the more likely outcome: that I was about to kill this woman. No matter how many ways we twisted the situation, that was what would most likely happen.

But was it really all that noble to leave her to those machines? I wasn't saving her from anything, only refusing to dirty my own hands with the deed. At least with turning, there was a chance, no matter how uncomfortable it made me. It was a tangled snarl of a question that I wasn't sure how to start wrapping my head around.

Finally, the simple truth dawned on me: I was talking to the wrong people.

"Can I speak with her?"

"We pumped her with some meds to provide temporary energy, so I'd say now is the perfect time to have a discussion." Deborah nodded to the door. I noticed that it had no lock—nor, I realized, was there any reason for one. No one was locked in or out. Everyone had chosen to be here, a point she was driving home at each opportunity.

As my hand closed on the door, I felt Krystal's touch at my shoulder. She was checking to see if I wanted company, but I gave her a reassuring nod. Just seeing this must be hard enough; she didn't need to come in. Besides, no need to overwhelm Sherilyn.

I stepped into the hall, taking a moment to gather myself, and then moved into the makeshift hospital room.

What hit me first was the smell. I'm not sure I'd have recognized it as illness without Deborah's prompting, but once inside, it was impossible to miss. From the bed, I heard a voice.

"Debbie? Is something happening?"

In all honesty, it took me several seconds to realize that she was calling out for Deborah. My eyes darted to the glass, but I kept my focus largely on Sherilyn. She was the one I needed to talk to.

"Sorry, no. My name is Fredrick. However, most people call me Fred." I stepped around, putting myself in easy view so she could see I was no threat.

As it turned out, such movements were unnecessary. At the sound of my name, what little mass she had animated. Her eyes burned with hope as she struggled to rise higher in her bed. "You're Fred? You're the one who is going to... save me?"

The gasp of air as she labored to finish her sentence cleaved deep into my heart. Every word, every act, was a struggle. Extra meds or no, she was fighting to have this talk. I had to make it worthy of her efforts.

"I don't know, Sherilyn. They want me to try, but you understand that, by the odds, that would make me your executioner."

"Never tell me the odds." Her half-cocky grin lasted for several seconds before she turned serious. "Didn't they explain? Even if that happens, you're helping my family."

I kept waiting for some trick, some deceit of the Blood Council to reveal itself: a lie they'd used to keep Sherilyn in the dark, a trap they were looking to spring. None were coming, however. I knew then what I was truly looking for: an excuse I could use not to face the real ethical dilemma they'd put me in. This was my predicament, and it ended only when I made my choice.

"Are you scared?" A simple, silly question, yet it popped out all the same.

To my surprise, Sherilyn laughed, which turned into a cough shortly thereafter. "Absolutely terrified. Vampires and magic. Death. Even if I live, I know it won't be the same." Her sentences were getting choppier as she worked to fit in breaths. A casual conversation was taxing her this much, while I could throw a fridge across the room with minimal effort. For the first time, I found myself wondering what it would be like to give that strength to someone else.

"Are you *sure* it's worth it? What's happening to you is tragic, but it's part of the human condition. If you go down this path, assuming you somehow survive, you'll never truly be part of that world again. It's forever on the other side of the glass, visible and always out of reach."

To my shock, Sherilyn jammed her arms down, slowly tilting forward, moving herself into a sitting position. The simple act had her sweating, but she was able to straighten her back as she looked me in the eye.

"Fred, let me be clear. I'm not dead yet. I'm grasping. At life. At something to leave my kids... at anything. If I can't be there... I can at least provide for them. You're scared... own it. Don't put it on me. I know where I stand. I don't want to die. Only one of us could change that. So give me your fucking blood already. *Please.*"

A forceful personality. A fighter. On top of everything else, my former bodyguard had selected a candidate I was sure to see Krystal in, a person I'd inherently want to help. Deborah was right: this was so overt, I couldn't even call it manipulation.

In the end, none of that really mattered. It was all just set dressing for the situation, not the predicament itself.

What mattered was that I had the chance to help Sherilyn, slender as it might be. There was nothing good or moral about holding back due to my own hang-ups. She wanted to take the chance, knowing that, even in failure, she'd have something to leave for her children. The only obstacle she had was my inflexible nature, and that wasn't near a good enough reason to deny her probably final wish. This was Sherilyn's choice, a terrifying one she'd made wholeheartedly. Time for me to get out of the way and help.

"Deborah, would you mind coming in here, please? I've never attempted a turn before, and I think, for Sherilyn's sake, it's best if I have guidance."

Her tired form collapsed back against the bed, but she managed a weak smile and a few quiet words. "My friends call me Sheri."

6.

IT WAS STRANGE TO SEE DEBORAH INTERACT with Sheri. Had I known the elder vampire only by title, I might have been shocked by the amiable, outright kind demeanor she displayed. The two had clearly formed a bond over however long they'd been at this. While Sheri was too exhausted to spit out more than a word or two after the effort of lifting herself, Deborah filled the silence with gentle banter as she adjusted her patient's position.

"Here we go. Let's get you nice and cozy. The process takes a few hours for someone in your state, and let me tell you, going down in the wrong position will give a crick in the neck that lasts ten years. It's why most new vampires are so grumpy." Deborah shot me a wink, then motioned for me to draw closer. It was nearly time.

"Pay close attention to this, Sheri. It'll save me from giving you the same instructions in a few years." Despite knowing the odds, Deborah was clearly putting on an optimistic front. Given the situation, it seemed the only viable option, at least for anyone with even a semblance of bedside manner. "To turn someone is to make them into what vampires are at our core: a corpse animated by magic."

Her hand slid down, raising Sheri's rail-thin arm. "Normally, we accomplish that by draining our selection down to near death, and then having them drink our blood. Inside our veins lies a potential fountain of youth, one that contains the magic to sustain the undead. You are, in effect, killing someone, and then trying to activate a curse or enchantment, depending on your viewpoint, before their soul leaves their body. This is all theory, mind you. We understand our own natures about as well as any other magic, which is to say, barely. But it's a theory that bears fruit, even if not as much as we would like."

From the bed, Sheri chuckled lightly. She was nervous, with extremely good reason, yet I caught not so much as a whisper of hesitation from her. This was her course, and she was set upon it.

"In this case, I don't think you'll need to take that much blood to get her there. No offense to Sheri, but this is more akin to turning someone on a battlefield while they're bleeding out. You don't need much blood: if the mortal is already on death's door, then focus on expediency."

That seemed as good a cue to get started as any I could expect. "I'm worried about trying to hit a vein with my teeth, given her condition. Perhaps we should draw blood with a syringe to be safe."

To my surprise, Deborah looked momentarily confused. "Right, sorry. I should have prefaced with this: you have to drink from them directly. I don't know why—part of me suspects some mage put it in play to keep us in check—but turning only works if you take the blood yourself. There are currently zero known successful turn-attempts recorded where another method was utilized."

Much as I wanted to protest that such a stipulation made no sense, enough years of dealing with magic had taught me better. Magic made as much sense as it wanted to, and the more powerful it became, the less it seemed obliged to any sort of logic or reason. Bickering about it would accomplish nothing, save for wasting time—a truly precious asset in this particular room.

I looked down at Sheri's arm and knew it was a lost cause even as Deborah laid it back at Sheri's side. The neck. It had to be the neck. That was where my fangs would find their way to her blood. My instincts, so often a nuisance than anything else, would ensure I didn't miss the mark. This was how it was supposed to be.

Leaning in, I looked at Sheri one more time, wondering if this would be the face that haunted my dreams for the rest of my immortal days: the face of the first person I killed. "See you on the other side."

No words, just a wink. That was all she had left. I dared not close either of my eyes as I moved in, tracking her pulse, the chugging movement of that essential liquid. In no time, I was there, fangs piercing easily into her thin flesh.

The blood came fast and hot, racing down my throat. There was a time I wouldn't have been able to do this, to handle taking blood from a living being. Deborah had been the one to push me past that hindrance, the one who taught me to drink without having to kill. It was a thought that gave me hope in that mad moment; so far, she'd steered me in the right direction.

Pulling away after a few moments, I licked Sheri's neck to close the wounds. Still, I could see her shaking. She wasn't in a condition where suddenly being light on blood was something her body could shrug off. With panic, I suddenly realized that I had no idea how I was going to give Sheri my blood. Should I get a cup? Did it need to be taken in person, too?

Luckily, Deborah kept a cooler head than I, her hands falling firmly on my shoulders. "It's okay. She's not gone yet. Bite lightly into the palm of your hand, cup it like you're holding water, and let her drink."

By this point, I was working robotically, following her directions because I had no idea what else to do. My movements were slow, but precise. I sank my fangs deep enough to start the blood moving—though, even after having just fed, vampire blood is a tad too thick to be called flowing. Thankfully, enough soon gathered for me to hold it to Sheri's lips. That was as far as I could take things. The rest was up to her.

I'd barely gotten my hand in place before a ragged slurp rang out. She clumsily tried to choke down the viscous liquid. Deborah rubbed her sternum, leaning over and whispering encouragement I was too distracted to hear. All of my focus went into holding my hand steady, matching Sheri's movements, ensuring that not a drop was lost. Of all the ways this could go wrong, I wouldn't let something as simple as not providing an adequate amount of blood to be our failing point.

After roughly a minute, I realized my wounded palm had healed. As I opened my mouth to bite once more, Deborah caught my arm. "That's okay. She's gotten enough. It's started."

To me, Sheri looked much the same, only with stains of red along her mouth. "How can you tell? If I'm learning to do this, that seems like something I should know."

"Her heart. Listen to it."

I trained my ears and found that I could easily discern the sound of blood pumping, albeit weakly. It was strange: there *was* something off about it, yet try as I might, I couldn't discern what. Only that there was a wrongness that itched at the edge of my senses.

In the end, Deborah saw my struggling expression and took mercy on me.

"You can tell she's under the enchantment because her heart's fallen into a perfect rhythm. Normal hearts can't sustain that; their rates go up and down constantly in response to stimuli. All blood flows to the heart, and that's where our change begins. Now, her heart rate will drop, until it halts entirely. That's when we find out."

Seconds later, Sheri had a spasm that rocked her body. When it ended, I listened once more and noticed that her heart's rhythm had shifted to a slower tempo. How long would it take? How long had it taken me?

Looking at her like this, my mind flashed back to how I'd been upon waking. Alone, abandoned, unsure of what had even happened. Everything I'd learned was pieced together from movies, lore, and general experimentation. It had been a hard way to start a new life. I was glad that Sheri would have a better experience—if she woke up.

"A more brutal wound spurs the change on faster as the body fails, but with chronic conditions like these, it tends to last for at least a few hours," Deborah informed me. "You should be done with Claudius before we know. I'm going to be here waiting, so if we find out earlier, I'll come tell you."

Right. I'd nearly forgotten that this was only the *first* of my tests scheduled this night. Tackling the hardest first had seemed like a sound strategy at the outset, yet after the turn-attempt, I wanted nothing more than to crawl into a bed and lock out the world. No one to blame but myself; I was the one who'd chosen this order.

Before I left, I took a towel from a nearby station and wiped the blood from Sheri's mouth. She was unconscious, though whether that was exhaustion or part of the process, I had no idea. Without the force of her personality, she looked even more frail, like one good shock would break her to shards.

"How do you do this?" I asked, gently mopping Sheri's face. "How do you roll the dice on people's lives? I've known this woman for all of ten minutes, and I'm hoping with every fiber of my being that she makes it through, odds be damned. If she were a friend, a loved one..."

"The answer is an easy one: experience," Deborah replied. "I've stood by, helpless, while people I loved died. Live that once, Fred, *once*, and you'll understand.

To be so powerful, and so useless, as the life slips from their eyes; it's the worst kind of hell. There's debate about what the successful turn rate really is—we don't exactly have great data to work with. Some say one out of a hundred; others, one out of a thousand. There are even optimists who push the one in ten theory. The real truth is this: it doesn't matter. Because when you see them fading, any shot becomes better than giving up. One in ten billion wouldn't pause me for a moment, because I know with absolute certainty what happens when I do nothing. I've had an immense sample size to assess on that front."

"That's not going to make burying her any easier." I finished cleaning and set the towel back down.

From her pocket, Deborah produced a phone and began to scroll. "Maybe, maybe not. But how many people get to die with sincere hope in their hearts? When the majority of humans take their final conscious breath, it is in terror or fear. Sheri closed her eyes knowing that they might yet open again. I like to think that matters, if only to us. Now, go back to the other room. I'm sure Claudius is climbing the walls waiting for you, and I've got a book to read."

"I'm surprise he didn't just barge in." Claudius hadn't struck me as the especially restrained sort.

"He would have, if he were allowed through that door." Finding the correct app on her phone, she pulled up a wall of text, only then throwing a quick glance to the mirror. "As her caretaker, only I decide the ones permitted in here, by the order of the Blood Council. I wanted to make sure Sheri had some peace."

If nothing else, those words reiterated the fact that Sheri was in safe hands. I couldn't do anything else here, and there were still more tests to get out of the way.

Moving with more speed than usual, I cut a brisk path back to the other side of the mirror. Time was of the essence; there was a chance I could get the other tasks handled before Sheri's change was complete.

Aside from a spark of hopeless optimism, I didn't expect her to make it. Life just didn't play that fairly; the ones who deserved the breaks rarely got them. Which was all the more reason why I should be there. No matter how we dressed it up, I was responsible for taking her life tonight. I was fairly sure I could live with the fallout, knowing it was what she wanted, but that didn't lessen my responsibility. I should be there at the end, if possible.

That was the very least I owed to the first person I'd killed.

7.

I FELT AS THOUGH I WAS SLEEPWALKING through the remainder of the tests, so it was a good thing they required minimal participation from me. Claudius was indeed waiting, along with a shaken but still composed Krystal, both of whom had witnessed the entire turn-attempt. I was thankful, actually, for Claudius's brusque nature; there were scarcely any words of greeting as he dragged us to a new room in the house.

It was a vast space, most likely used as a ballroom under normal circumstances. On this occasion, it was filled with various tools and equipment, giving it the air of a makeshift science lab combined with a medieval weaponry store. Taking me over to a large table, Claudius sat me down and began to poke my arm with different materials. A moment of thought was all it took to discern that he was trying to see if my silver weakness had been replaced with something else, the way fey were wounded by iron.

In truth, this didn't quite seem like the second-to-hardest test, but I entertained the idea that they were giving me a bit of recovery time—that, or it was *really* going to hurt if Claudius found something. As he prodded one arm, the other found itself being gripped by Krystal. We said nothing as Claudius ran through his sample list, muttering to himself; we just held hands, feeling the other's presence.

None of the samples produced a reaction, baffling Claudius further, so we soon moved on to the next experiment. That was the pattern for most of the night, in fact. Claudius would test some aspect of my vampiric nature, from checking basic strength and speed to finding the limits of individual senses. Some exams were more exacting than others, but after the one we'd started with, I barely registered anything. My mind was in another part of the house, with a woman whose heart was slowly failing.

After what felt like hours, Claudius made a checkmark on his large clipboard and didn't immediately rush us off to the next part of the room—not that we had any unexplored areas left to be ushered into. "Hmm. It seems all that remains is the sunlight examination. We'll need you to demonstrate the effect of sunlight on a finger once dawn breaks. Don't worry. We've stocked blood with exceptional regenerative properties to mitigate any damage done."

Checking my watch, I noted that we were still a couple of hours away from dawn. Hustling as the time had seemed, Claudius worked quickly and efficiently. "What should we do until then?"

"I don't especially care. There are spare rooms if Agent Jenkins wants to nap, food for you both, if needed, and plenty of space to explore. Just be here thirty minutes before dawn for the next test. I've got data to input until then." Claudius turned from us to the laptop he'd clacked away on as each test ended, diving back into his work.

Not even I could miss those social cues, so we headed out into the hall, leaving Claudius to his work. Another night, the food and rest might have tempting. We could have stolen away for a few hours of peace; no doubt, I'd have been fretting that there was some final, secret test awaiting me, because the rest had been too easy. That wasn't a concern on this occasion: the first test had been far more taxing than I imagined any ambush could hope to match.

"How're you holding up?" I put an arm around Krystal as we walked. Neither of us needed to name the destination; it was never in doubt. "I'm sorry that they used your past like this."

"More or less okay. She's been dead a long time now. It still hurts, just not in the same sharp way it used to." To my surprise, Krystal looked down at the floor, her voice subdued. "Actually, the truth is, all of this has me thinking about my dad. The period when Mom was sick was the last time we were close. Not long after that I had my accident, and he... didn't respond well to the supernatural stuff. He'd just lost his wife, so he probably wasn't in the best frame of mind, but it went over pretty poorly. The kind of poorly where we haven't spoken since."

Growing up, I'd known Krystal's father in the same way I'd known many parents of people in similar social circles: as a presence at large events and milestones, perhaps even at the occasional extracurricular outing. Her dad had appeared nice enough, a bit on the stern side, albeit nothing concerning. She'd never talked about him after our reconnection, and I hadn't pushed the issue. We were so different from our old lives, it seemed irrelevant at the time.

"If you decided to reach out, I'd be there with you for as long as you wanted." It was an admittedly strange conversation to have while walking the luxurious halls of a rented mansion, surrounded by potential enemies, but it was rare that Krystal felt comfortable opening up like this. She needed to talk, and this was the time we had to work with.

"I do reach out, every few years. A call, a card, none of it goes anywhere. He did… he did send one response. I sent him an early RSVP form, letting him know about the wedding. Got it back with just the 'No' checked and nothing else."

A flash of anger lit my chest as I saw the pain in Krystal's eyes, followed by a wave of sadness for both of them. It must have been hard enough for them to lose Krystal's mother. Losing each other immediately afterward made it all the worse.

"Part of me secretly hoped that this would be enough. That no matter how things with us were, he'd show up to walk me down the aisle. It's dumb, and I know that—I do. Especially given what we just saw someone else going through."

"Krystal, you never need to apologize for being hurt," I told her. "Sheri has her struggles, and you have yours. Besides, I'd say you're handling the news extremely well. I never even caught a blip of anything until you mentioned it."

A squeeze pressed my hand as we drew near Sheri's door. "I've had enough time to realize blood and family are not inherently the same thing, and it's not like I'm hurting for people who give a shit about me. When we get married, it'll be surrounded by the people I love. If he doesn't want to be part of that, it's sadder for him than for me."

Strong words, but they didn't fully hide the pain in her eyes. Then again, she didn't especially seem like she was trying to conceal it. Tonight had forcefully pulled away several layers of defense, and for the moment, Krystal appeared content to stay that way. As for me, I wasn't quite sure how I would fare. Hard as the act of turning Sheri had been, I expected what came next to be umpteen times worse.

Not waiting for a reply, Krystal yanked open the door, pulling me inside and ending our brief discussion. Deborah glanced up from her digital book, eyeing the both of us.

"About time. I was going to come get you out of the hall. There's not long left."

It took actual effort for me to hear Sheri's heartbeat now; in addition to slowing, the pumping had also weakened. She was barely alive, hanging on to life with the thinnest of threads. Tempting as it was to sit at her side, it felt presumptive to do for someone I'd just met. Instead, I hunkered down next to Deborah.

Krystal held no such compunctions. She grabbed one of the spare chairs and dragged it over to the bed, taking Sheri's hand carefully in her own. No one made any effort to move or stop her—not that I liked either of our chances if we did.

"The good news, Fred, is that everything has gone entirely as expected. Steady rate of decline, heart transitioning through the normal stages; so far as we can tell, your turning ability works the same as the vast majority of your other vampiric talents. Couple that with the data Claudius has been emailing over, and it looks as though we can rule out other abnormalities. We're starting to get a handle on your condition."

"Great." I didn't mean to be rude or flippant. It was just so hard to care about such things when I was watching a life fade before me—a life that might have been near its end, but that wouldn't necessarily have reached it tonight without me.

I wasn't prepared for the gentle pat on my back that came next; I was so accustomed to vampires acting aloof that I had forgotten Deborah knew how to be comforting. "I know it's hard. I do. This is part of the process, though. We have so much power to give, and it can be tempting to try to bring our favorite humans into this world. So tempting, in fact, that some vampires think to play the odds and make the turn before it is absolutely necessary. Seeing your attempt fail and living with the consequences is harder when it's one's first turn. At least you get the comfort of knowing you made a difference. When this is over, I can show you some of the schools I've been looking at for Sheri's kids."

That was something. While they'd no doubt prefer their mother, if nothing else, I'd helped to make what came next easier. Maybe I could pitch in, if that was permitted. It didn't feel right to kill her, and then trust everything to the Blood Council. Being Sheri's executioner, I owed her more than that.

As with most things, Deborah proved to be right. There wasn't much time left at all. Less than ten minutes after we returned to the room, Sheri had another spasm. When it ended, I could only just make out the faintest of heartbeats. Deborah closed her phone and rose, a gesture I quickly mirrored. Only Krystal remained seated, holding Sheri's arm in a reassuring grip. No matter what, she wouldn't spend her final moments alone.

"The next shudder will be the last. She's nearly to the end." Deborah laid her hands on the edge of the hospital bed, smoothing the covers. "Tonight, I, Prudence of the Blood Council, do hereby bear witness to the attempted turning of Sherilyn Devereaux by Fredrick Frankford Fletcher. Since time unknown, the blood has chosen who will join our ranks and who must return to the earth. We pray the blood should see wisdom in our selection and grant you the gift of immortality. Should you perish, we honor your efforts and bravery. Few have the courage to walk the sunless path. May the blood raise you from the shadows."

There was an instant aura of ceremony the minute she began to speak. I felt like a child sitting in the pews again. How many times had she given that speech, or something like it? The answer was probably uncountable in a very literal way. The room came alive as Deborah spoke, though none of the energy made its way to Sheri, who was only with us in the most technical of senses.

Deborah stood there, poised and waiting, I had no idea for what. It wasn't a long mystery, as soon, Sheri started to spasm once more. This time was different. Less violent, and shorter, the last gasp her body could manage after all that had come before. Try as I might, no degree of straining found her heartbeat any longer.

It was done. Sheri had become a corpse.

I waited, hoping despite myself to see her spring back up, defiant of the odds. No such jolt came. She merely lay there, lost forever. Because of me. Because I'd played a part in taking her before it was time. I lowered my head, unsure of who would even be appropriate to pray to in such a moment.

"Come on, Fred. I'll show you that school info we talked about. We've got some staff who'll get her ready to go home for the funeral. Krystal, you're more than welcome to join us." Deborah started for the door, almost managing to conceal the flash of pain as she looked to the bed.

"I can't," Krystal replied, something strange in her voice.

"I assure you, our staff will be very respectful and thorough. There's no need to worry."

"No, I mean I literally can't." Krystal held up her arm, showing Sheri's hand tightly gripping Krystal's own. "Sherilyn just grabbed on to me."

8.

IT WAS HARD TO SAY WHO WAS MORE SHOCKED between me and Deborah. Who recovered first is far less in question; she snapped into motion seconds later. Appearing at Sheri's side in a blur, Deborah produced a flask similar to my own, enchanted to keep blood at the proper temperature, and pressed it to the apparent corpse's mouth. No reaction at first, so Deborah pulled Sheri's lips apart, getting a few drops onto her tongue. That was enough to stir something. Sheri swallowed, albeit not without intense effort.

The moment she did, a change rippled through her entire form. Bone-thin appendages swelled, sallow skin tightened. Her whole body seemed to (ironically enough) come alive at those meager drops of blood. After a few seconds, her eyes opened once more.

"Debbie?"

"Well, well, well, look who's back from the dead. Took you a little longer than normal. Some people just *have* to make an entrance, I suppose." Deborah tapped the flask against Sheri's lips once more. "Open up. You need to keep drinking. I went to all the trouble of getting you something special for your first meal. The regenerative properties in this will have you up and around in no time."

As it all unfolded, I fought the urge to collapse into a chair. Somehow, despite the odds being overwhelmingly against it, Sheri had come through. I'd had the impossibly good luck of my first turn-attempt being successful, a record I had no inclination to test anytime soon.

It was the outcome I hadn't dared let myself hope for, which made it all the more confusing that Krystal was visibly nervous. As Deborah fed Sheri, Krystal made her way to my side, leaning in close. No amount of whispering would keep our words from Deborah's ears, but some habits were more powerful than reason.

DREW HAYES

"Freddy, I am really happy to see this outcome, both for you and for her. But you *do* understand what just happened, right?"

"He doesn't, and I don't have time for the slow walk," Deborah butted in. "You just successfully turned the first human you tried to change. I won't say that this has never happened in the history of our kind, but as a man of numbers, you can appreciate how unlikely it is. In any other case, I'd write it off as a lucky break. With you, we have to consider other options."

"Before this goes any further, I'd like to remind you that at his current station, Fred is entitled to two legal turn-attempts in a single calendar year. As the officiant—you—just declared, he's already used one. So if you're planning to line up a string of toadies for turning, expect the Agency to object." However much the events of the day had been hitting Krystal emotionally, she was still an agent, and damned good at her job. I hadn't even considered that possibility, whereas she'd already planned against it.

Deborah didn't respond right away, though that could have been because she was feeding Sheri, who looked healthier with every passing moment. "You make a good point, Agent Jenkins, except the Blood Council does have the right to reallocate attempts by those who give them up to interested parties. With the passing of

72

a few measures, Fred could legally change hundreds per year."

"Pass the measures, and we'll talk. For now, just be aware that I know the limits of what you can ask."

Coughing came from the bed. Sheri sat forward, waving off the flask. "Is anyone going to explain all of this to me?"

"Eventually. I'll tell you everything," Deborah promised. "For now, you need to relax and let your new body settle. I can walk you through the basics for the rest of the night. Fred, after you finish with Claudius, you can be done, as well. While Krystal is right that this isn't over, we don't have to tackle it all at once."

Sheri blinked, looking at me closely. "You're Fred? Sorry, I could barely make you out before." She smiled— the first time I'd seen the expression on her filled-out face—and I felt the stress of the night fall away. "Thank you, Fred. This is so much more than I dared to dream about. Thank you for giving me a second chance."

Her words hit me hard, especially on the heels of Deborah and Krystal's points. It wasn't often that I got to play any sort of hero, nor was that a role I particularly yearned for to begin with. Rare was the time I ever got to really help, let alone save someone. Tonight was an exception to the rule. Looking at Sheri as she moved so easily, I remembered her struggle to sit up and stare me in the eye. Krystal was afraid of what this successful turn could mean for me, and I understood why. If my turnings were more likely to succeed, the Blood Council might be tempted to put me to work changing their loyalist humans and expanding the number of vampires overall. But there was a flip side, as well: a world of people who needed second chances.

"You are more than welcome, Sheri. I'm proud to be your sire."

"Speaking of, there is one quick formality we should probably get out of the way. Sorry, but this will probably sting." From her pocket, Deborah produced a small box, from which she drew what appeared to be a nail with the bottom covered in rubber. I could smell the silver as soon as it moved through the air, striking Sheri's arm briefly before Deborah returned it to the box.

Sheri let out a sharp curse and a hiss at the red mark now stretched three inches across her skin. "Sweet molasses, that hurts."

To my surprise, Deborah appeared relieved as she tucked the box back in her pocket. "That was silver, something you're going to want to avoid for the remainder of your days. The good news is that most parahumans are weak to it, so you'll rarely see it used by other supernatural entities." Her eyes fell hard on me during that bit, not that Sheri noticed.

With the glance, it snapped into place. Deborah was seeing if I made normal vampires, or ones who were like me. The slowly healing strike to her arm was all the proof needed that my silver immunity didn't carry over, which was a very good sign for Sheri. I had Krystal, some standing as the leader of a clan, and a myriad of allies to help protect my free will. She was entirely in the Blood Council's hands; it was hard to imagine her situation being as favorable. Then again, I'd yet to hear anyone else get away with calling Deborah by a nickname. Maybe Sheri was more protected than I thought.

"All right, you two, time to clear out. I'm going to walk our new member of the undead through the basics, as well as get her something more fashionable than this hospital gown. Fred, you did good work today. I won't say it gets easier, but they won't all be this hard. They also won't all have a happy ending."

"That much, I was already braced for." Making sure Krystal was ready with a quick glance, I moved on to goodbyes. "Deborah, it's always an experience. Sheri... I honestly don't know what to say to someone newly changed. It will be difficult at times, a new kind of living, but it's a life worth holding on to. Take things a step at a time, and remember that much like humans, parahumans can be more than reputation and appearances suggest."

"Thank you again, for everything," Sheri called back.

"And make sure you listen to Deborah about the rules," Krystal added as we headed for the door. "You'll find out that the people who enforce them are some scary motherfuckers."

Not quite the ending I'd have chosen to depart on, but it was certainly a fitting one for us.

With roughly an hour left until sunrise, we opted to head back toward Claudius's lab, giving me the distinct feeling of being a ping-pong ball. In truth, though, my spirits were high. This was an outcome I hadn't dared picture, let alone expect, yet for once, things had gone well. Ignoring the possibility that I might have a higher turning success rate than others and how that could impact things long term, of course.

"Out of curiosity, if it turns out I am better at making new vampires than everyone else, how do you think that would play?" I assumed we were being listened to as we walked, but I doubted Krystal would suddenly offer some bold new plan they hadn't already been considering. Mostly, I just wanted to know what to brace for in case they made a play tonight.

"Not totally sure," Krystal admitted. "Depends on how high the chances are. If it's coin-flip good, I expect more overt manipulation like tonight: placing people in your life who would be good vampire candidates and finding ways to push you toward turning them. If it's better than coin-flip—say, three out of four go well—they might risk having you attempt to turn some high-value human assets. Those are tricky, though. Kill one, and the consequences are severe. Much better than that, anything in the ninety percent range, and it gets sticky. A near-guaranteed turn is something the Blood Council would do almost *anything* to possess, and use."

Krystal drove that point home, squeezing me a little to make sure I caught the inflection. The ability to choose who could become a vampire was a potentially game-changing one, and not necessarily in a good way.

"Luckily, you've only got one attempt left this year, and if you think human governments move slowly, you should see the pace an immortal one cuts. No way they'll reallocate those extra attempts any time soon. It'll be a decade at least before they have enough samples to calculate a success rate for you—years we can spend getting you ready."

"How about we do the wedding first, then start preparing for an assault from the Blood Council?"

That earned me a poke in the ribs. "Some of us know how to multitask." Moments later, I was snared by a kiss on the cheek. "But fine, I guess we can prioritize."

We turned the discussion to our upcoming nuptials, moving away from thoughts of changing humans and long-term implications. There were much heavier issues worthy of consideration, but we had both reached our limit for the evening. Living a life like this, compartmentalization became paramount. Rough as the night had gone, this was still our mini-vacation/

wedding-planning trip, and we intended to make use of the time, intrusive Blood Council or no.

Although, I had a feeling the events of this night would result in one more name being added to the guest list.

9.

THE SUNLIGHT TEST PASSED WITHOUT ISSUE, as we'd known it would, after which Krystal and I returned to the Bristle Inn, this time driven over in one of the protected SUVs. For what I imagined was a plethora of security reasons, there were no tunnels to the mansion. Barely instants after she'd stumbled into bed, Krystal fell into a solid sleep while I went to work, running the office as best I could from a remote location. She awoke that afternoon, grabbed some lunch, and soon stole me away from the laptop as only Krystal could.

By the time evening arrived, we were raring to go, a list of venues in descending order of priority clutched in Krystal's hands. This leg of the journey would require transportation, however, given the remote locations of some options. Walking out of the Bristle Inn, it was a tad surprising how glad I was to see Sheriff Thorgood waiting for us. He looked so innocuous, a simple small-town lawman with a wide frame and a hefty stomach, I'd have easily believed he was a former football player post career change. What he actually was, I still had little clue; all I knew for sure was that he was on Krystal's side. I'd been parahuman long enough to realize that was the point that mattered most.

Krystal grabbed him in a hug and, accepting the inevitable, I gave a quick embrace as well, getting only partially crushed in the squeeze for my trouble. "Glad to see you both up and kicking! I take it there was no trouble yesterday?"

"No more than we expected, and less than we could handle." Krystal slapped the bed of the truck, causing something unseen to rattle. "Now, let's get cooking. Got a lot of places to see tonight, and our plane leaves a couple hours before sunrise."

"About that," Sheriff Thorgood began, motioning for us to hop inside the vehicle, "I was curious if you'd be interested in touring an extra spot tonight. Something special you might not have known about."

The excitement in Krystal's eyes threatened to light the cab on fire with its intensity. "Did Cragrulth finally get his underwater glass enclosure working?"

"For about three months. Then a big fish hit a fracture point, and it all went back to square one," Sheriff Thorgood informed her. "But this is something different. Think of it as a hidden gem of Boarback."

"I thought you showed me all the hidden spots." There was a thread of playful accusation in Krystal's tone.

If he heard it, Sheriff Thorgood chose not to engage, his cheerful energy unwavering. "I showed you all the ones I could when you were here. Things change, even in spots as remote as this one. Just trust me, you're going to want to see this."

There were a lot of ways I'd noticed Krystal and Sheriff Thorgood were close, but even if I'd had no prior knowledge whatsoever, the fact that she actually sat back and relaxed when around him would have spoken volumes. Krystal was not the type to "just trust" anyone, especially when it came to dealing with new things. She led the charge and loathed being kept in the dark. The level of faith she put in Sheriff Leeroy Thorgood was almost unmatched. I only hoped he lived up to it.

Puttering through town, I took note of the bustling evening. Therians in their semi-shifted form, small green creatures moving as a mini-mob, a hunk of what looked like living clay hauling a keg to the diner, where I could see Yenny, the naga waitress, serving what appeared to be an ogre, if I were to take a guess. All in all, it was a slice of Americana swirled together with the most ambitious parts of Halloween. I understood why Krystal loved this place. If I'd wound up here before putting down roots in Winslow, leaving might have proven too great a task.

We wove up through the town, past the outskirts and into the forest. This was a different direction than the one we took to the airfield, and while Sheriff Thorgood seemed to have no trouble navigating, I was immediately lost once we left the proper road. That wasn't to say we were tearing through brush—there were tracks here and there—but this area was far less traveled than anywhere I'd been so far.

As we ascended, the truck began to grind, until Sheriff Thorgood slapped the dash once. With that, the grind vanished and we pressed forward. I resisted the urge to shoot a look over to Leeroy, chiefly because I knew there were no clues to be found from his form. Whatever he was, it wasn't something I'd knowingly encountered before.

A steep bump sent me hurtling up, banging my head briefly on the ceiling. Looking down, I was shocked to find my seatbelt had come unfastened. Attempt after attempt to latch the safety device ended in failure, until finally, Sheriff Thorgood noticed my struggle.

"Sorry about that. The whole area is coated in... well, let's call it a discouragement field, something to keep wandering souls from moving in this direction. The closer you get, the more things go wrong. One of the same ways we keep cars from accidentally finding us."

"That's going to make bringing people in tough," Krystal pointed out.

"Not so much. I'll turn it off for the wedding; didn't seem prudent to leave this undefended in the meantime." The ground leveled out suddenly, just as Sheriff Thorgood's voice faded. Before us was a clearing bordered by a *massive* grove of trees.

I mean that in the sense that both the number of trees was massive and that the trees themselves were enormous. Even from a distance, I could see they were four times as thick as the trees we'd been driving through, and those were the ones on the fringes. Deeper in, I could see larger pillars of wood spearing the sky.

Krystal and I were both dumbstruck as the truck puttered along. For a moment, it seemed as if Sheriff Thorgood were going to plow right into the first trunk, until he slowed just as we drew close. A branch scratched the window, and to our shock, Sheriff Thorgood rolled it down.

"Evening, Douglas. These are the two we talked about. Bringing them around to see what they think."

In life as a parahuman, it is often tempting to get jaded about the existence of magic. When anything is possible, one would think the extraordinary would lose its shine. Those sorts of ideas tend to fall away when faced with the mind-warping sight of ambulatory foliage moving out of the way, however.

I stared in open-mouthed shock as the massive trees rumbled, the ground rippling like waves as they slowly parted to reveal a path forward. Glancing over to Krystal, I expected her to be nonchalant as always, but instead found eyes as wide and awestruck as my own.

To his credit, Sheriff Thorgood didn't make us ask. He was explaining even before his foot hit the gas, lurching us forward once more. "Few months back, had an old fey friend reach out with a problem. She'd been tooling around and created something unexpected: a living grove. Not the first of its kind, but you don't see many popping up. This one came out small, not strong enough to survive in the wilds of the fey lands, and she didn't have the heart to put it down. We haven't had much use for this area since a mage accidentally tainted the soil, so I offered to take Douglas in. Works for both of us: he's slowly purifying the corrupted dirt and gets a nice place where no one will bother him."

As we rode, the trees continued to part, often just in time. It was like racing down a tunnel, straight at a wall, only to have each obstacle fall away at the very

UNDEADING BELLS

last moment—which is to say, the drive was *incredibly* stressful. Knowing that I could survive a car accident does not make them any more appealing.

Then, without warning, we were in a new clearing. No one spoke while the last sputters of the truck died. Silence was the appropriate reaction to what we saw.

I felt like I'd stepped into another world. High, interwoven branches blocked off any sign of the sky and moon overhead, yet there was no shortage of light. That was thanks to the countless white flowers growing along the trunks and branches, each emitting a gentle glow that collected to form ambient lighting. Huge, rolling plains of perfect grass formed the floor. Dozens of animals darted about, already they were clearing out quick; no doubt, they could sense a vampire had invaded their space. A large lake lay at the far east end, next to what appeared to be a rough structure, one that I genuinely could not believe was truly there.

Upon exiting the truck, I was able to confirm that my eyes were not playing tricks on me. There was a building growing from the ground. Quite literally growing, at that: it was formed of a dozen smaller trees, all growing and interweaving to form an actual structure. Amazing as it was, all of it, one thought did keep echoing in my head.

If this was too small a grove to survive the fey lands, what sorts of creatures roamed that world? It was a question I very much hoped I'd never discover the answer to.

"Now, there's obviously a lot of work to do," Sheriff Thorgood said. "We only had a few days to get started. Douglas will grow you a proper hall by the ceremony, and some smaller buildings, as needed. Whatever your wedding colors, he'll have flowers to match. The branches can move if you want a moon overhead, or can stay in place if you were thinking of getting married in the day. There's lots of stuff like that, but first, let's you show you the big appeal. Douglas, please draw the curtain."

More trees parted, farther back along the line this time, away from the truck. As they moved, new lights could be seen. One by one, I caught them, and as I did, I realized what we were seeing: Boarback, laid out below, the flickering lights of the town. No wonder the truck was straining, if this was how far we'd climbed. Not that I complained—Sheriff Thorgood's instincts were certainly on the money so far as views went.

"It's perfect." Krystal was at my side, gazing out at the town she loved so dearly. For a moment, her eyes met mine, making sure we were on the same page. I was happy to nod my agreement. Even if it hadn't been lovely and perfect, the joy on Krystal's face was. That was all I cared about, so far as venues went. Well, that and coverage from the sun, obviously.

"Not perfect yet, but with some time to work, I bet we can fashion something magical for you." Sheriff Thorgood chuckled at his own joke, though his eyes kept scanning, looking for things to improve.

To my surprise, Krystal's face pinched. "You're right. Not perfect yet. I'll have a man I want to spend my life with before me, friends I truly love at my side, and now, an amazing place to hold the ceremony. But there's something missing."

As she turned to fully face Sheriff Thorgood, I realized it was probably not the first time I'd seen Krystal nervous, but no truly comparable occasion sprang to mind. She was fidgeting, shuffling her feet, holding one arm with the other, all the body language that tended to be more in my wheelhouse than hers. This moment scared her, *actually* scared her, and there were tremendously few things that could accomplish such a feat.

"Sheriff Leeroy Thorgood, I was wondering if you'd be willing to help out with the ceremony itself. Even if it's silly, I always liked the traditional wedding setup. Except for that, I need... I'd like someone to give me away. With me and Dad on the outs, I can't think of anyone I'd rather have in the role."

His response was one I should have seen coming, knowing the man even cursorily as I did. With seemingly no effort, he hefted Krystal up from the ground in a mighty hug, squeezing her like she was unbreakable. "I would consider it one of the great honors of my life to walk you down the aisle."

That earned a sharp, joyful squeal from Krystal as she hugged him back. I tried to sidle out of the picture, but a rogue hand snatched me into the embrace. Sheriff Thorgood's strength was something else, though I suppose I might not have struggled quite that hard to resist the communal embrace.

It seemed I was going to have to get more accustomed to this sort of thing. After all, Krystal clearly regarded Leeroy Thorgood as family, which meant soon, he'd be the same to me. Best to build up a hug tolerance now; once we came back, there was no telling how many joyful embraces might be coming.

And we *would* be coming back. Looking around at the unnatural forest, out onto the flickering lights of the town, and back to Krystal's joyful face, there was no doubt to be had on that. We'd found our venue. Now, we just had the rest of a wedding to plan.

SOMEONE NEW

1.

IN THE COURSE OF LIFE, THERE ARE TIMES when a truth, no matter how unpleasant, can no longer be ignored or denied. Such was my predicament a week after returning from Boarback, as my team and I readied for an essential task that I was nevertheless dreading. However, there was no bucking the obligation; it had to happen, and I was the only one who could see the job through. After all, it was my company, so I was the one who made hiring decisions.

Despite Lillian's rapid education in the accounting field and my own constant dedication to work, Fletcher Accounting Services was simply growing too fast for us to keep up with. I could have turned down new clients, and had on several occasions, but it was hard to say no when parahumans reached out, given that I knew they had greatly limited options. It was my own wedding—or, more specifically, the subsequent weeklong honeymoon that had been promised—that pushed me to finally accept the inevitable: we had to hire more staff.

Ideally, we'd start with one or two new employees, the sort who could be carefully trained up as I had done with Lillian. Once everyone was competent, it would be simple to hand off more complex tasks to Lillian and trust the new help to support us until they were up and running on their own. Had those been our only considerations, it would have been a simple matter, but there was another complication to consider. Given how many of our clients and staff were parahuman in nature, we needed to hire another parahuman for the role. Getting a human clearance in the parahuman world was a huge pain, to say nothing of how clients might react. Asha had managed her position thanks to a deep well of ambition and resolve; it didn't seem fair to ask that of someone showing up for an entry-level accounting position.

Of course, I was assuming we could even find parahumans who were interested. I hadn't met many with a penchant for numbers, but I remained optimistic as I scanned over the application paperwork. Normally, much of this process would have been done online, except that parahumans tended to be more analog on the whole. While some would have undoubtedly figured out digital applications, I didn't want to limit my potential candidate pool. It didn't matter what they came in knowing, so much as what they were willing to learn.

"Conference room is ready," Lillian reported. She was clad in a business suit that I felt reasonably sure dated back to the '80s, thanks to the shoulder pads, with some creative tailoring added in to keep the ensemble in style. It worked to create a professional image—at least as respectable as my sweater vest, if not more. We had to put our best foot forward, especially on unfamiliar terrain.

The essential nature of parahumans, even those of us who weren't deathly allergic to tans, meant that we preferred the shadows to the light, which was why our interviews best served the applicants by being held at night. Unfortunately, that also limited our available locations to use for the event. Charlotte Manor had been ruled out, as she wasn't fond of untold strangers suddenly traipsing around. Besides, Arch had called the idea of opening our stronghold a "security non-starter," and then left to smoke, effectively ending the discussion. My next choice would have been renting space in Richard Alderson's building; however, we didn't want to compete with the club scene that comprised most of the downstairs—too many ways for applicants to get lost and things to go awry.

In the end, I'd settled on signing up for one of those shared, cooperative office spaces that were starting to catch on. The price to rent a conference room felt a touch high, though not exorbitant, and they were designed to accommodate a rotating array of strangers, often in situations just like ours. The one complication was that no such facilities were entirely run by parahumans. The best we'd found was what we were using: a facility that was human-owned, but where the graveyard shift was staffed by one of Richard's therians. He was a nice young man named Hank, who'd barely raised his sleepy eyes from his computer when Lillian, Amy, Bubba, and I strolled into the building: a perfect fit for the night shift.

"Wards are done. I still think you're being just a tad overly cautious, but they're set." Amy entered from another doorway, dusting chalk from her hands. Tempting as it was to have Krystal or Arch around to keep things in hand, agents had something of a fearsome reputation among parahumans, and not one that entirely unearned. Asking some less terrifying friends to help out seemed a better way to ease our applicants into the situation.

"I'm not sure those words ever apply when dealing with groups of parahumans, even ones as small as what we'll be getting," I replied. "And if there is a ruckus, the wards will at least ensure we don't bother the neighbors."

Between Amy's skills, Lillian's raw power, and Bubba's clout, I was really hoping to keep the evening peaceful, but I'd been a vampire for much too long to not plan for chaos. In truth, that was almost something of an optimistic outlook: having trouble would mean that I had enough candidates to cause some, and part of me suspected Bubba would return with reports of a fully empty waiting room. Having spent years as an accountant in the parahuman world, I'd gotten a sense for the value placed upon those skills, and it generally wasn't high. Certainly, there were those who saw the importance of balanced books, but on the whole, paperwork didn't appeal to many living the supernatural lifestyle. My choices for employees would likely be limited, and I had to be at peace with that.

"Okay team, once Bubba gets back with a headcount, we'll start things off. Amy, pass out forms, pencils, whatever they need. Lillian, help those who have questions, and keep an eye out for anybody that seems to get it right off the bat. Send them back to me as they finish, and I'll handle the interviews. Bubba works security to make sure we don't have any incidents, and hopefully, we're all done by midnight. Should we do a 'go team,' or wait until Bubba returns?"

Lillian flipped through the stack of single-page applications—standard, boilerplate forms stripped down to only the most essential pieces of information. "Let's wait and see how good his news is. Be a waste to cheer only to realize we didn't have anyone to go out there for."

It would be disingenuous to say Lillian was the pessimistic sort. A truer assessment would be to say that life had gone out of its way to prove what a bastard it could be to her, and she'd merely taken the message. Still, despite her tendency to brace for the worst, she didn't sound entirely doubtful.

"You never know. I might not be the only weirdo willing to take a chance on a new career."

The sound of an opening door drew all our attention to Bubba. He looked quite different than he had minutes prior, when he'd left our prep room for the first time in an hour to go check the lobby. His eyes were wide, a trickle of sweat was on his forehead, and tension radiated off his entire being.

"Good news: you definitely ain't the only weirdo. Other news… well, maybe it's best if y'all just come with me." He motioned for us to follow, which we did. Bubba wasn't a man of overstatement. If he said we needed to see this for ourselves, then it was true. Besides, it wasn't as if he was taking us far.

We wound through the shared office building, into the floating desk section and the modest kitchenette area where workers no doubt took their meals during the day. We continued past the public bathrooms to where a robust door with a pane of clear glass separated the building's inner workings from the world at large. Together, we clustered around the window, peering out into the lobby.

For a moment, I sincerely thought Amy had enchanted the glass to play some sort of television program, except that I'd definitely have heard about any show like this. The lobby had transformed from a simple empty space with ten chairs lined up into the sort of carnival people would pay millions to witness. There were the usual telltale, hulking shapes that denoted therians— several of those, in fact—along with a grumpy-looking fellow in robes I presumed to be a mage. Things got more exotic from there.

A satyr was arguing with a centaur about some sort of slight, both growing visibly more worked up by the moment. Something that had to be fey-adjacent, like a green version of the brownie I'd seen June call upon, was darting around between legs, while a creature unlike anything I'd ever seen before was casually chewing on the top of a chair. Tentacles whipped past the window, their source outside my field of vision, and I had just enough time to catch sight of Hank, no longer sleepy-eyed, darting to deal with some emergency before the tentacles flitted past again.

"What the heck is going on?" I barely dared even to whisper the words as I slowly backed away, fearful the full attention of that room would fall upon me.

"Near as I can figure from chatting with the room, they're all here to apply for the job."

"The *accounting* job?" My eyes darted from Bubba to the room and back in rapid alternation. "Richard said he was going to put the word out, but not to expect much response."

I felt a gentle patting on my shoulder as Amy came around to my side. "Looks like he didn't realize how strong the siren song of finance is. Or something weird is going on."

Oddly, Amy's words halted the mounting panic in my mind. Right. Of course, something was up. That was always how these things went. We just needed to find out what the issue was and take care of it; then, we'd be able to get down to the business of making a new hire.

"No helping it, I suppose. New plan is the same as the old plan, except everyone starts poking around to find out why these people are really here. In the meantime, if they want to pretend to apply for the job, that just presents an easier way to ask questions and assess their real goals. You three head out there and see if you can get things settled down before Hank blows a gasket."

"What about you?" Lillian asked.

I pointed back to the conference room we'd just left. "Off to make copies of the application. We're going to need a lot more than expected to deal with that crowd."

2.

AFTER A QUICK RUN TO THE COPIER, I headed back toward the packed lobby, head still spinning. What could have drawn everyone here? The most obvious answer was that this was an attack by someone like Quinn or the Turvas. The problem with that theory was the sheer variety of parahumans in the lobby. Outside the House of Fred, millennia of supernatural infighting had made the parahuman community surprisingly segmented. Coexisting was one thing, but for all those creatures to be working in unison would take diplomacy and connection well past anything I'd seen my old threats display. Deborah, perhaps, could have pulled it off, except this was nowhere near her style.

I was so lost in thought I nearly plowed into a tall, broad man lingering in the hall. His attire was dark, well-tailored to his thick frame, and professional. Exactly the sort of ensemble one hopes to see on applicants at a job interview. A heavy brow and dense features adorned his squat head. It was curious; I'd never seen a man so large appear to be so densely packed in. Probably a therian of some sort. He certainly had the bulk for it.

No sooner did our eyes meet than he gave me a curt nod. "You are Fred. I am here for the position."

"Fantastic! Are you my first interview?" I checked his hands for a completed application, only to see the stubby fingers completely empty. "Whoops, looks like you missed the lobby. Have you talked to Amy, Bubba, or Lillian yet?"

Slowly, his head turned, signaling no. There was an ember of confusion in his eyes as he made the motion, yet he asked not a single question.

"Nothing to worry about. I've gotten turned around a few times in here, myself. Come on. I'll walk you there, and we can get you started." We moved down the hall together, a heavy silence immediately descending. While normally, I'm fine with a lack of conversation, the context of this situation made it appropriate to get to know my candidate. "What's your name?"

He took his time in answering; we were nearly back to the lobby when he finally spoke. "I am Gregor, of the Slate-Claw clan. First in my cracking, first in the fang and the fist, initiate in the—"

The loud buzzer that sounded when opening the door to the lobby cut Gregor off, which was actually helpful, since I was about to have to part with him, anyway. Much as I wanted to learn about my applicants, I also had a chaotic crowd to deal with and interviews to conduct. We'd pick things up again once his turn came back around.

To be polite, I waited a moment to see if Gregor would resume his speech. After several seconds with no words, there was little choice but to press forward. "I look forward to reading all of your titles. Please, fill this out fully, then let one of my staff know and they'll get you slotted for an interview. If you have any questions, they'll be glad to help."

Despite accepting the application and moved to a chair, Gregor's face was still creased with confusion. Not the greatest signifier of a competent future accountant, but perhaps he was the sort to gain momentum once he grasped the material. There would be time enough to find out later; until then, my concern shifted to the still spiraling room.

In fairness to my people, they had managed to calm the worst of it. Almost everyone was seated, though the centaur really didn't have that option and a few folks preferred to stand. For the most part, conversation had dimmed in volume, if not intensity. There were still fierce whispers being traded, as to whether they were barbs or questions, I lacked the focus to discern. My mind was busy scanning the room, clocking who was doing well with the applications, who was struggling, and most importantly, who I thought our biggest troublemakers would be. With some purposeful scheduling, we could theoretically churn through the ones causing the most chaos, get them interviewed and out the door.

The problem with that plan became immediately evident when Lillian ran over with a slender stack of applications. "Looks like we had three who understood what we wanted on the forms and got them done properly, so these are going to be your initial interviews. We're helping everyone else, and they'll slot in once they're ready."

Right. Of course, the more competent ones would be first. They would have come in prepared, ready for a real interview, not a clusterfudge in a coworking space. Mentally readjusting, I decided to lean into the task at hand. I would get the most promising candidates processed before things inevitably went crazy. Hopefully, when the dust settled, I'd have some prospects and the night wouldn't be a total bust.

I probably should have been more concerned, given the factors out of my control, except that, by this point, mysterious happenings and people potentially trying to kill me were becoming par for the course. Besides, knowing the strength of who was with me, I didn't feel especially vulnerable. Technically, I should have also had a new bodyguard, but I was in no hurry. Despite the last one turning out to be okay in the end, there was little compulsion in me to replace Deborah soon.

I took the pages from Lillian and gave them a perfunctory scan. They were all completed properly, but the first application had a strange smear of color at the top, like something had been written and erased. Probably grabbed a red pen by mistake and started the application; it could happen to anyone when improper supply labeling was allowed to run rampant. Since the rest was in order, and quite good order at that, I checked for the name.

"Al?" No last name, which was more common among parahumans than I'd initially suspected, though the moniker's brevity had me wondering just how many of the assembled crowd might respond. As it turned out, only a single candidate was waiting to hear that name called.

"Here!" She popped up into view, previously hidden between the heft of the two therians hunched over and scribbling on their applications. Al was on the short side, a couple of inches under Arch, and was one of the few people who had dressed to interview. I'd known to expect a casual air from the start—parahumans and formality go together about as well as vampires and garlic bread—so it was a pleasant treat to see another someone in appropriate garb: a sleek, simple suit, the sort one might see among cubicles in any corporation. Al's wide smile, enthusiastic eyes, and cheery demeanor certainly didn't hurt, either. Working with happy people made the environment better for everyone.

"Come on back. Let's talk about your application." I held the door as she darted through, quick on her feet despite her short legs. We had a brief walk to my temporary office, chosen purposefully to make it easy for candidates to find. Interviews would happen here, whereas the conference room was for regrouping with my team. Given what we were now staring down, we'd need a place to work and strategize away from prying ears. Even if things were spinning out of control, we had to appear competent. That was the employer's part in this hiring dance.

The office itself was simple: blanks walls, a simple desk with one comfortable chair on the far side and two lesser ones closer to the door. It lacked a computer, but

I'd be using my own laptop anyway, so it was hardly an issue. Aside from those basic accoutrements, there was only my own stack of pages and a bowl of plain diner mints. I'd had enough interviews where anxiety over things like breath had set in, so I thought my applicants might appreciate an on-hand remedy.

No sooner was Al seated than she began to speak, forcing me to hurry across the desk to get in position. "Thanks so much for doing this, by the way. When word went out, I didn't even believe it at first."

"That an accounting firm would be hiring?"

Al made a disturbing noise in her throat, like a high-pitched hack. "Well, no, that part makes sense. But the fact that you made it open." Her already worryingly wide eyes expanded even more. "Wait, this *is* open, right? You know I'm not a vampire?"

We were only a few sentences into the interview and I felt like it had already taken several wrong turns. Still, if I'd accidentally done something unique, that might explain the gathered crowd. "I didn't want to be rude and ask, but yes, I noted you lacked the traditional hallmarks. I'm not interviewing for vampires, though. Only accountants, or those interested in learning the trade."

Relief swept through her, and for a moment, I could have sworn the room smelled like honeysuckle. "Thank goodness! I knew the word was that anyone could apply, but... you know... some people just like to say that. They don't actually want *anyone*; they want someone who fits what they're already searching for. Especially in the parahuman world. Unless you've got a specialized skill set like therians and muscle, it's hard to find someone hiring outside their species."

Was that really it? Were the opportunities for career advancement in the supernatural so rigid that even a position on my staff, innocuous as it was, represented previously unavailable opportunities? It was certainly possible, and seemed to be Al's case, but I wasn't so sure it accounted for the rest of the crowd. Accounting wasn't really that exclusive an educational specialty, even more so thanks to the rise of online classes. Anyone with sufficient means and motivation could start down this path for themselves. The idea was a nice one, though, and I hoped it turned out to be the rationale for the vast turnout.

"I am happy to report that today's search is sincerely only about finding new accounting employees. Your particular parahuman nature is your own business, and you should feel no need to disclose it. The sole exception is if you have any specific requirements for a safe working environment, such as my obvious sun allergy. We can't make accommodations without a proper warning, after all."

Another wide-eyed stare as Al processed my words. "Seriously? You'd hire me without even knowing what I am?"

"Is there some reason I shouldn't? I presume that if your species had incompatibility issues with being around vampires, you wouldn't have come for this interview. You will have to be around a variety of different parahumans for the job; I do want to make that clear up front, in case it's an issue."

"No, that's no problem." Al reached into her jacket pocket. I caught a flash of color before she produced a white handkerchief and dabbed at her temples. She didn't appear to be sweating, so perhaps it was a nervous tic, the way I still made a habit of breathing, though it served no purpose. "I get along with everyone. Sorry, I know it seems silly to be nervous about all this. I guess part of me kept expecting the other shoe to drop; for the rumors about you in the lobby to be right."

My ears perked as my stomach dropped. Nice a delusion as it had been to think everyone was here to learn the trade, mysterious rumors seemed a far more likely clue to the explanation. "There are rumors about me?"

"I mean, not just you, personally," Al said, backpedaling quickly. "About the clan as a whole. You keep picking off top talent from other groups, making powerful alliances; I heard you even survived a visit from the Blood Council. It's just, there's some who think you might be, you know... gathering enough strength to kick around the old power structures. People see a chance to be on the ground floor of something new, so they're jumping at it."

Only my professionalism kept me upright and smiling, like this was nothing more than silly gossip floating around the office. It wasn't the first time word of our exploits had been warped in the retelling, but before, it had always been seen as a laughable delusion. If people were starting to take that silliness seriously, then we were in trouble.

Because if the masses thought I was preparing to revolt, then that meant my lobby wasn't stuffed with aspiring accountants. It was full of people looking for a fight, and when I didn't have one to offer, they might well choose to start a brawl of their own.

3.

UNWELCOME AS THAT NEWS WAS, IT DIDN'T fundamentally change the task before me. I still had to hire more help for Fletcher Accounting Services; the fact that my waiting room was staffed with people who had the wrong idea about what we were offering promised to make that more challenging, but it didn't remove my need for assistance. Especially with my honeymoon bearing down on us. Krystal had made it abundantly clear that if she was stepping away from work for a full week, I was expected to do the same.

In one stroke of fortune, Al didn't appear to fall into the bloodthirsty camp, and as I scanned her application, I noted an excellent history of self-motivated higher learning. She'd taken business classes, introductory accounting courses, even some freelance entrepreneurial offerings. No degrees, however; just lots of partial education. On top of that, she'd listed no relevant work experience, or prior history at all. Part of me wondered if that was in error, but aside from the smear of color across the top of the page, her application was flawless.

"Quite the number of classes under your belt."

"But nothing formalized to show for it," Al replied, answering my question before it was even spoken. "My family life growing up was complicated. Traditionally, these aren't the sorts of pursuits we go in for. I was able to grab classes here and there by making them seem like flights of fancy, and while the internet opened up more opportunities, a degree was never on the table. Not until I can get it on my own."

Earnest, straightforward, and with a strong personal conviction toward growth. But Al was squirming slightly, her confident tone not mirrored in her wandering eyes and fidgeting hands. While I'm far from an expert in body language, being uncomfortable in an office setting is my native tongue. We hadn't hit her most dreaded hurdle yet; although, I had a hunch where it would be.

If the curious education wasn't worrying her, then there was an obvious next step.

Rather than head there immediately, I decided to steer away first and get to know my applicant a little better. We couldn't linger for too long, what with the crowd, but there was no point in even holding these interviews if I wasn't going to do them well.

"Okay, Al, you can pick which of these next questions you wish to answer: why do you want to work here, or what are your greatest strengths?"

She looked back, frozen for several seconds, barely even daring to move. I thought I'd terrified her comatose until she let out a careful, steadying breath. I knew that expulsion well; it was a technique to manage nerves that I, myself, had been very fond of—back when oxygen still influenced my body. "That's a good surprise question. I wasn't geared in to having a choice; nearly threw me for a loop."

"It's partially born from having to muddle through terrible questions when I was on that side of the desk, and partially because I like seeing which questions applicants choose to answer. Says almost as much as the answers themselves." That was, perhaps, a much cooler explanation than the truth, which was that I'd seen too many poor answers sink entire interviews in my own corporate days. Offering options tended to put people more at ease, give them a sense of control. The rest of the bluster was just to make sure they took the choice, and subsequent answer, seriously.

Adjusting her jacket slightly, Al straightened up. Even if she didn't feel confident, she was powering through, a move I very much respected. "In that case, I'll take telling you why I want to work here. Truth be told, I do want to learn accounting, but it's not just that. I want to learn *everything* about running a business. All the nitty-gritty details, all the paperwork, all the boring aspects most people try to skip. Because one day, I want to start my own. Not an accounting firm; numbers are just one skill I'm going to need. We're talking years and years down the road, though—I don't want you thinking I'm just hopping in for a quick education. My kind live a long time, and I'm willing to put in however long is necessary to learn it all."

In the course of this interview, I'd learned several things. When let loose, Al could talk for a clip. Her internal drive was exceptional, and she either had an honest nature or had chosen a very strange stretch of lies to spin. My goal for today had been to hire someone with ambitions toward accounting, but there was no harm in someone who wanted further knowledge. The one major concern would be her clearly stated desire to eventually break off—but, then again, did I really expect these people to spend centuries with me? We weren't asking her to swear fealty to the House of Fred: this was simply a job. From that perspective, a multi-year commitment was perfectly reasonable, especially if Al worked as hard as she suggested.

Which, unfortunately, brought us around to what I suspected would be Al's biggest issue: the utter lack of experience. "I understand the desire to learn, and the yearning to strike out on your own. However, given what you've just said, it does call into question why you haven't tried this route at other companies in the past. You seem the sort who would have a career plan, and I know I wasn't part of it, as we only put word out that we were hiring earlier this week."

"About that..." Her squirming hit a fever pitch; we'd definitely hit her stumbling point. "I actually have had jobs before. Some at mundane companies, some run by parahumans. But I once read that you shouldn't list a place if you didn't work there at least a week..."

It was my turn to wear a surprised expression. A job not working out was one thing, but how was she managing to get fired in the span of under a week? Multiple times, from the sound of it? Personality differences could certainly arise, yet Al seemed amiable and competent. Mercifully, she didn't force me to pose the question.

"Not because I showed up drunk, or stole, or anything," Al said, veering toward babbling as her nerves won ground. "But my parahuman nature has fairly...

noticeable displays, at times. Causes friction. Sometimes they fire me; more often, I'll just go once I see the warning signs."

While this interview was for Al, to my surprise, I found myself facing an unexpected test. She was, to the best of my gathering, a candidate who, while perhaps not fully qualified, certainly had the features I looked for in an employee: upfront, driven, and with clearly defined goals. The largest potential hurdle seemed to be her parahuman nature, which was plainly a factor to contend with. When we'd opened this interview, I'd told her there was no need to share what she was, and Al had taken me up on that. If I asked, my gut said she'd tell me. It would paint the full picture, telling me the entirety of what I'd be biting off in choosing Al.

I won't lie and say there wasn't a real temptation to do just that. My mind lit up with defenses and explanations, arguing that it was safer for the clan to know what we might be letting through our doors. But in the end, the application I was looking at made a concrete case for why I couldn't go back on my word. Based on what I could see, Al had the makings of an excellent employee; others in a hiring role had plainly seen that, too. Yet here she was, swinging at a wild chance of a job in the middle of the night, all supposedly because of her supernatural heritage. Maybe Al wouldn't be the best fit for the role. There was still a waiting room full of candidates to speak with. But whether she was or wasn't, it would be based on *her*, not her parahuman complications.

"Well, if you have environmental or dietary requirements, that is something we'd need to go through during the hiring process, should you get the job," I explained, setting up proper expectations, just in case. "Outside of that, what you are is your business, and we can deal with hurdles that arise as needed. I hate to keep this short, but as you've seen, there are quite a few others I'll need to speak with tonight. Is there anything else you'd like to say before we head back to the lobby?"

Al took her time, carefully considering the opportunity rather than spitting back a bland pleasantry. "I get that I'm selling an odd package here, one with obvious complications, even if you don't yet know what they are. All I can tell you is that what I am matters a lot less to me than who I want to be, and the kind of work I can do. If you give me a chance, I'll use it to prove that to you."

"Very well said," I noted, rising from my chair. Al followed the lead, wrapping up with a steady handshake as we headed out the door. "Originally, I was going to ask those with promise to linger for a second interview once we'd narrowed down our options, but that was back when I considered ten people showing up an optimistic pipe dream. Please feel free to take your leave, and we can schedule a follow-up via phone."

"If it's okay with you, I'd rather wait, just in case. I *want* this job, and I'm not afraid of cooling my heels to get it that much faster." I was fast growing to appreciate Al's straightforwardness. She said what she wanted plainly, in no uncertain terms, and worked steadily toward it. The dedication certainly didn't hurt, either.

Heading to the door, my eyes were struck by a splash of red on the desk. Momentarily confused, I quickly realized it was just my bowl of mints. Except... I was positive I'd gotten the plain kind offered in bowls at diners, not the round ones with red and white striping. It was a detail I'd have given more thought to, were there not more pressing matters to deal with.

When we finished the short walk to the lobby, I noticed a commotion coming from the other side of the glass. Shifting our positions, I moved so that Al was behind me as we drew near the door. Unless she was something truly special, odds were strong that I was the hardier of us. If anything was going to go wrong, it would hit me first. As I arrived, I found myself looking out at what was possibly the last thing I expected.

Standing around the lobby, nearly all of the applicants were singing, dancing, and generally causing very vocal merriment. On its own, that would have been concerning, but there was a larger issue catching my attention: Bubba and Amy were both belting songs with the rest of the room. They had their arms around each other's shoulders, both visibly relaxed, singing and swaying for all they were worth.

Whatever was going on, two of my helpers were smack dab in the middle of it.

4.

THE UPSIDE TO UNWILLING ADVENTURES IS
the benefit of experience. If I walked into a room and
saw everyone on fire or nursing bullet holes, I'd know
Krystal was on the scene. Lots of precise, deadly blows?
That meant Arch had come through. Giant smoking hole
with no sign of survivors? Well, that one I'd yet to encounter in person, but I had a hunch I'd know Gideon's
handiwork when I saw it.

As for a room full of people who looked to be in an
altered state of mind, one rarely had to look farther for

the cause than the master alchemist and revered mage named Amy Wells, whose specialties were known to revolve around the recreational side of mystic herbology. Need some horrific danger stopped dead in its tracks? Call the Agency. Need to get absolutely wrecked despite a parahuman metabolism or being a living corpse? That took nothing more than a text to Amy.

"Stay back," I cautioned Al. Peering through the window, I scanned the room, hunting for Lillian. Generally speaking, unless one of Amy's concoctions was made specifically for undead, we tended to be immune to them. She used elements that relied on traditional ingestion—in this case, my guess was on inhalants—and vampire bodies generally ignored such things. Unfortunately, the trouble with magic was that there were no universal rules. I'd once accidentally drunk from Amy's glass rather than my own at dinner and spent the next three hours watching the ceiling swim. Whatever this was, I couldn't be certain of my immunity, which was why my eyes hunted so fervently for Lillian. If she still had her head, then I could go in. Otherwise, I risked becoming as addled as the others.

Much as I craned my neck, I couldn't find her. That could be a good sign; perhaps she'd held on to enough mental clarity to flee while escape was still an option. Or perhaps Lillian's idea of a fun time involved racing through the night; I preferred not to think too hard on that possibility.

"Real shitshow in there, right?" I heard a voice ask from behind me—a voice that definitely wasn't Al's. Spinning around, my eyes locked on Lillian, standing at Al's side and visibly waiting for me to notice her arrival. "Also, we have got to work on your awareness, Fredrick. I wasn't even being quiet."

"What... how...?" Eloquence has never been my talent, and getting caught by surprise only exacerbated the issue as I floundered for mental purchase. After a moment to compose my thoughts, the next attempt at speech was thankfully more cohesive. "What's going on out there?"

"You can put the pieces together easily enough. The crowd started to get unruly not long after you left with our first candidate, here. Parahumans aren't great with patience, in general—not as many lines in our culture. Since we're not supposed to use force outside of extreme circumstances, Amy said she was going to fix the room's vibe. A few drops was all it would take; once they hit the floor, everyone would breathe in the good mood."

Lillian was right: this was more or less how I'd have imagined things had played out, which said a lot about my friends and my life, a fact that there was insufficient time to properly contemplate. "I'm guessing Amy miscalculated?"

"Dunno. It's possible her idea would have worked, except that whoever brought the tengatulon didn't train it well. Amy got whacked on the knee by a rogue tentacle while pouring and dropped the whole bottle. It had considerably more than a few drops in it. Good news is, it definitely doesn't work on vampires. I got a face full of it and feel fine, so at least one of us is sober."

The implied bad news was that we were now two sober vampires and one job applicant, pitted against an entire lobby of blissed-out parahumans. They appeared content and pliant, so that was something. And in all honesty, despite the strange scene, it was impossible to say that things hadn't calmed down. No destruction, no panic. Just a bunch of people singing along to what appeared to be four different songs coming from various people's phones. Looking out at them, a new, immediately relevant thought entered my mind.

"Wait, why are you back here? If you're immune to Amy's potion, shouldn't you be keeping order?" While I can appreciate how it might seem as though I was accusing Lillian of dereliction of duty, that couldn't be further from the truth. I'd worked with Lillian more than enough to know she was dedicated, as well as independently competent. She wouldn't have left the lobby without a reason, and said reason seemed the sort of thing I should probably be abreast of.

Sure enough, a cloud of worry flashed across Lillian's face, one she kept largely concealed from Al. "Because I'm not the only one who wasn't affected. There was a guy sitting in the corner, noticeably big, even in a room of therians. Didn't seem the sort to go in for an accounting job, but I know how you feel about preemptive judging, so I kept an eye on him, quietly. Not long after Amy dosed the room, he slipped out. I heard him going around back, and then..." Lillian's eyes darted around once, like she was afraid of being overhead. "Fredrick, it pains me to admit this, but I lost him."

"Sorry to interrupt, but given what that lobby looks like, you shouldn't be so hard on yourself for losing someone in the chaos." Al patted Lillian on the shoulder.

"You're sweet. However, it is not shame that worries me. It's fear. I am no newly turned prowler of the night. I have had time and training; within the Turva clan, my skills as a tracker were widely respected. For someone to slip even one of my senses when I'm paying full attention means that they have exceptional skills of their own. The sorts of skills an assassin might have trained."

I really, truly, dearly wanted to tell Lillian the idea was absurd, and was stopped only by the simple fact that I knew it wasn't. The Turva clan she'd just mentioned had already tried to take me out through various means, all of which had failed. The latest had involved bringing in the Blood Council, the final resort of our vampire ruling system. With that gambit gone south, it was entirely possible they would switch gears and attempt a more overt solution. There would be fallout, if that were the case—my clan had alliances with powerful people—but none of that would make me any less dead. The permanent kind of dead, too, where I didn't still get to enjoy time with friends and muddle through new experiences.

"That said, it's a long walk from seeing people lose their minds to being a secret murderer, so maybe our big man was just looking for the bathroom." It was hard to say how much of Lillian's optimism was for my benefit and how much was for the sake of Al, a stranger who likely wasn't accustomed to these sorts of issues. I also wasn't entirely happy with the realization that I clearly *was* becoming unfazed by them, another implication that would require proper time to unpack. "The real question here is what do should we do next?"

I looked back out through the glass. While the group was content, there were also several parahumans with unnatural features visibly on display. I didn't know how they normally blended in with human society, so I couldn't put those measures into place. Given their state of mind, it would be cruel, bordering on criminal, to turn them loose into the world without the capacity to care for themselves. And since the only person I knew who might be capable of reversing the effects was leading a drum circle using an overturned plastic wastebasket, it didn't seem like Amy would be a lot of help in curing everyone. Our only option was to wait it out, let people sober up enough to make their own way safely home. Maybe Amy would come around early and could help speed things along, but we couldn't risk digging about in her supplies. At her best, Amy considered labels to be suggestions more than tools.

"We keep going with the interviews," I declared. "It's what they're expecting, anyway, and I'm not sure this will fundamentally impact their ability to answer basic questions. Anyone who wants a do-over can have one, but if nothing else, this should let us weed through those interested in the position, rather than the rumors."

"Oh, sure, when you hold interviews with people who are fucked up, it's fine, but if I'd suggested having Amy whip up something to put us in a good mood, you'd have said it was unprofessional. You see what we're dealing with?" Lillian gave Al a good-natured elbow poke in the ribs, eliciting a sharp giggle that Al quickly cut off by covering her mouth.

"Sorry," Al said quickly. "I'm kind of ticklish."

"My fault. Apologies, and so noted." Lillian strode over to me, peering out through the window. "I still think I should be patrolling for our missing man. With Amy and Bubba out, it might even be time to call in backup. You're still down a bodyguard, you know."

"If we call in an agent, there's no telling how that crowd will react. Let's not add more dynamite to this powder keg just because we think someone out there has a match. Until we know for certain there's danger, we play things calm. Give him a chance to show us what he's up to. Once we know what we're dealing with, we can make smart choices."

Lillian nodded, though not without hesitation. "You realize that what you're describing is using bait to lure a target into the open. Except the bait in this instance is you, and if I'm running between the lobby and the halls, I can't promise I'll get there in time, should you need me."

I heard the rustle before Al spoke, telltale signs of straightening her back and smoothing out the skirt on her suit. "Perhaps I could help? The assassin is out of my depth, but it looks like all you need upfront is someone with basic organizational skills. Collect the applications, take the names, sit down those who are done and send back whoever is next."

"Much as I do love initiative, I'm afraid we can't ask you to go into the lobby," I replied. "There's no way to be sure that Amy's potion isn't still lingering in the air, and if it is, you'd become effectively useless once exposed."

"Yeah, about that. Mood elevators don't really work on me." Moving with surprising confidence, Al walked up to the door and took the handle. She waited a moment, allowing Lillian and me to step clear, before slipping past the barrier quickly and resealing it behind her.

We watched as Al stepped surely into the lobby, taking deep, visible breaths while she inventoried the situation. There was no loss of coherency or sudden slide into song. After a full minute, she flashed a thumbs-up sign at us before proceeding to collect the various applications that had been scattered along the floor.

"She's a fascinating one. Not many use magic to hide even their scent. Ambitious and thorough. Could make for an interesting new coworker."

"I suspect we do not yet know the half of it," I agreed.

Lillian leaned in, lowering her voice to a whisper, just in case. "What makes you say that?"

"For one thing, I'm almost completely certain that your jacket didn't have a glitter pattern woven into it when the night started."

At my words, Lillian jerked back, yanking off her suit jacket and staring at the twinkling depths that had suddenly appeared. A wild smirk pulled at the edges of her lips. "Well now, this night is turning out fun in all sorts of surprising ways."

5.

TO BE HONEST, I WASN'T QUITE SURE WHAT to expect at the prospect of interviewing spaced-out parahumans for an accounting job. It seemed the sort of situation that could go in any manner of unexpected directions filled with danger and mishaps. Instead, I got the outcome I truly was expecting the least: things went smoothly.

Turns out, whatever Amy was peddling came with minimal tolerance for, as Krystal would put it, "dealing with bullshit." From my second interview with a therian whose animal form was that of a bear, and who secretly held dreams of playing piano, it became clear that we were dispensing with the formalities and cutting right to the truth. Consequently, the interviews weren't just easy sailing, they were actually sort of... fun.

Not fun in the raucous sense, mind you. This was a blissed-out high, gauging from the outside, the sort of chill that ran to the bone. No, what I found fun was that, when stripped of their facades, most of the people I spoke with were quite enjoyable to hold conversation with. Ben, the bear therian, spent much of his time talking about the confines of the expectations upon him due to his size and strength; it seemed like no one had ever bothered asking where his own passions might lie. We ended things with a powerful hug—something I really should have expected given his name and nature—after which, Ben thanked me for listening.

That set the tone for the next hour of my life. Parahumans would come in, escorted by Al, who, I realized halfway through the proceedings, technically had no way to open the door from the lobby. The applicants sat, sometimes long enough for me to fire off a single question, before launching into a tirade about where they were in life versus where their ambitions lay.

The satyr worked a struggling farm handed down for generations, while he dreamed of using of the land and his skills to tap into the state's recent "green rush," even if the knowledge was beyond him. I had a mage whose talent for destruction magic was apparently top-tier, yet she wanted to pursue a simple life of research. It was impossible to ascertain the natures of some of the candidates—I couldn't for the life of me pin down why the tall gentleman with pale green eyes couldn't be a juggler, even after he lamented that fact for the entirety of his interview. Thanks to the drugged-up applicants, and Al's unintentional hint, a picture was starting to emerge in my head, an understanding of why so many had shown up for a job they clearly had no interest in.

It wasn't about me, or the clan, or even the job itself. We were a way to break free of the system. Every species had its own trappings, expectations, culture, and limits: structures that probably worked for the majority of those within them, but not all. The applicants tonight were those who felt limited by those systems, constrained from the paths they wanted to follow. I wasn't their goal. I was a way to get out, a way to learn new skills, meet people outside their own cultures. My job was a foothold toward something different that they were desperately trying to grip, and I didn't begrudge them that in the slightest.

However, that did mean the number of candidates I could seriously consider was deeply limited, even taking into account everyone's mindset during the discussions. A few of them did have skills that would mesh well with accounting work, and some possessed dispositions that I suspected would still be amiable when sober. Through it all, though, I must confess a twinge of disappointment. Even the best candidates, like Al, were not in it for the actual accounting; to all of them, that was a tool, a step toward something greater. Part of me wished we could find someone with actual love for the work itself, but companies weren't run on hopeful sentiments. We needed more staff; competence would have to take precedence over passion.

I looked up from my desk at the sound of noise, expecting my next candidate. Instead, I found Al there, a concerned look on her face. "Mr. Fletcher, there's something I wanted to bring to your attention."

My tongue nearly told her to call me Fred out of habit, but I resisted the urge. Formal titles were useful in professional settings, especially as we were still in the interviewing process. Besides, hers was not an expression that invited needless interruption.

"I've been out there talking to people, giving out water, generally keeping things steady. The mage woman—Amy, I believe—had a message for you. Said she couldn't find some of her vials. Apparently, she took a few out when hunting for the bliss potion and is no longer sure where they ended up. That seemed like something you should know about."

That was indeed a serious complication. While I trusted Amy not to have any *truly* dangerous potions outside of her lab, she and I had differing definitions of the word "danger." There was genuinely no telling what could be in any of her concoctions. One might turn tiles into tigers, while another would likely be perfect for removing old coffee stains. Amy was an artist, and for her, the act of creating something fascinating was more vital than what uses it had. The stuff she sold was just so she'd have the means to fund her experiments.

"Thank you for bringing it to my attention. That is indeed a factor I should be concerned by. How many interviews do we have left?"

"Six or seven, depending on if the sleeping dude in the corner wakes up. Oh, and I guess the centaur has been outside for a while. We think he had to use the restroom, and obviously, human toilets weren't going to work," Al continued. "We had a few people go out back to clear their heads, and I took everyone's keys so they couldn't get any ideas about driving off. Thankfully, I think someone already took the tengatulon out there, as well. Can't imagine all those whipping tentacles would make my job any easier."

"What was that thing, anyway?" I asked.

Al took a moment, tapping her chin in contemplation. When she did, I noticed something—almost like a flicker—run across her skin. It was interesting, albeit less so than it probably should have been, since I had no idea the significance of such a display.

"Sort of like a parahuman version of a bonsai, except it's alive and constantly working to kill its owner. I've heard some people keep them as pets, so they learn never to let their guard down, while others consider it a display of power. There are also a few who just like them. Can never discount strange taste as a factor."

My face must have betrayed my worry, because Al visibly read the concern. "Don't worry. They only go after their owner. Anything else they hit is just collateral damage. Besides, they aren't nearly strong enough to hurt a vampire; either of you could rip it apart."

I bristled at the image, though I did my best to hide it. The destructive reputation of vampires was far from unearned; if anything, most seemed to revel in it. Still, I disliked that such was the solution everyone expected of us. It wasn't Al's fault; she had no reason to expect anything different from me yet. Nevertheless, her casual words were a reminder of how the world would view me, unless I showed them something different.

"Let's hope it doesn't come to that. While I know that's how most vampires are perceived, I prefer non-violent solutions to my problems."

"I'd heard rumors to that effect. Didn't entirely believe them until tonight." Al shook her head, looking me over once more. "If we're being truthful, I do have a hard time believing *you* managed to stand against both the Blood Council *and* the Court of Frost."

Interesting. Not many people knew about the Court of Frost's involvement in my assessment with the Blood Council. Al was apparently more tapped in than I'd expected. As for her disbelief, that was a much easier aspect to mitigate.

"Good. You shouldn't believe that, because I didn't. Stand against them, that is to say," I clarified. "My clan survived their tests and judgment, nothing more. We didn't rebel, or strike back, or in any way buck the system. The Blood Council came to test me, and I managed to survive. There's no greater glory to tell."

"You say that, but Hellebore is famous for getting what she wants. Favors from the Blood Council are useful, sure; however, having an agent bound to a contract isn't something to sneeze—"

Al was cut off by the sound of a horrific crash coming from out in the hall. Crunching, snapping, and a sudden *thud* echoed throughout the entire building. She whirled around as I dashed to my feet, both of us looking out the doorway. What met our eyes was the sight of Ben, the therian, in hybrid form as he stomped atop the now crushed door between the lobby and the offices. A mighty roar pushed past his lips as he began to thunderously beat his chest. After a moment, I realized the crowd behind him was cheering.

"To the snacks!" Ben declared, showing more leadership than I might have expected from our interview. At his words, the bulk of the crowd surged forward, pouring into the halls and spreading throughout the shared office compound.

Behind him, wearing a look of forlorn loss, Hank stared at the needless destruction, no doubt wondering how in the hell he would explain this come morning. That was a concern to tackle later, as the immediate situation took far greater precedence.

"Al, go find Lillian. I don't know if everyone is getting better or worse, but they're clearly more energetic. We need experienced muscle on hand to keep the peace—or as much of it as we've got left. I'll hunt down Amy and hope she's come around enough to be of help. Also, stay safe. They look substantially less relaxed than earlier."

"You sure you want to go diving into all of that?" Al asked. "There's probably a decent place to hide while we sort this out."

Tempted as I was, it was an offer I had to decline. "Should you become my employee, you'll learn I'm not the 'above this' kind of boss. My idea of leadership is doing my best and trusting my people to do the same. It's the only real strategy I have, and I see no reason to abandon it now."

"I've dealt with much worse management styles than that." Al licked her lips once, smearing the gloss I was sure hadn't been there minutes ago. "Look, if things get really bad…"

"If things get bad, run." I jumped on the opportunity to finish that thought before she could gather her words. Al was in too deep as it was. She had no obligation to see this through to the end. "This is my problem, and in truth, I've already let you help more than an interview candidate should be imposed upon. Don't worry about us; this is sadly fairly expected for one of our clan outings. You've more than proven yourself already. I can say without hesitation that you're the current top candidate for the job and will definitely be getting a call back."

A blink of surprise, then a nod. "I appreciate the concern. How 'bout I still *try* to see if I can find Lillian before giving up and bailing?"

More crashing, this time from deeper in the building. "Good plan, but we should both hurry. Otherwise, there might not be much building left to save."

6.

SINCE I WAS HUNTING AMY, THE SIMPLEST method was to follow the crowd. It was an easy trail: a rambunctious horde of parahumans isn't the most careful of groups, to say nothing of the ruckus I could hear coming down the halls. After a brief jog through the newly scratched and dented walls, I arrived at the scene of the revelry, stopping dead in my tracks.

The kitchen area was ravaged. How they'd gutted it so efficiently in such a short amount of time was a genuine mystery, especially given their collective mental state, but every cupboard's door had been ripped away, the contents hurled toward the center of the room, where others were descending on the feast. Someone had similarly looted the refrigerator, a chip station, and what appeared to some sort of cereal cubby. All of it was being tossed about, devoured, and then thrown to the next person in a Bacchanalian event centered around cheap office food.

They were definitely getting more energetic. Part of me wanted to believe that meant they were also getting more sober, but Amy had products with secondary, even tertiary, waves of effect. This could just as easily be a new, more problematic version of their existing trip. As my eyes scanned, however, I did catch sight of a familiar face. She was ripping into a bag of mass-produced cookies with a dangerous look in her eye—though, I'd seen Amy do the same in many situations, so that didn't speak much to her state of mind.

"Hey! Amy, are you with us?" I was over in a flash, prioritizing speed above appearances. The longer this went on, the more the damage piled up. Carefully, I took her by the shoulders, trying to meet her eyes.

A few blinks, a long swallow, and then Amy was looking back at me. "Woooo, this batch is *potent*. I'd have sworn I've been at a music festival for the past few days."

"Your talents continue to amaze. Do you have any sort of antidote, maybe, on hand?"

Amy reeled like I'd struck her, an expression of naked disgust on her face. "Antidote? Fred, would you demand an antidote to a ten-course gourmet meal, or an expertly played symphony? The experience is the *point*. I would never create an antidote to lessen it." She finally tore into the cookie package, ripping it in half and wolfing down the food in mere moments. "Might work on including an appetite suppressant next time. Munchies come on hard with this mix."

That was more help than I'd expected from Amy in this state, and as she dived down for another piece of snack food, I made no move to stop her. She was, after all, just as influenced as everyone else, and at least I now knew not to waste time looking for a cure. My eyes scanned the room again, taking in the diminishing food supply and trying hard not to think about what would happen when it was gone. There were gas stations a few miles up the road that this cavalcade of crazy might very soon decide to march upon, and once a mass of parahumans descended on a civilian business, it would be a short walk to agents showing up.

Worried as I was about the ruckus, a flash of motion in a doorway caught my attention: someone big, moving quickly and surely away from our area. Seeing as the only non-drugged people were Al, Lillian, and myself, none

of whom were especially muscular individuals, that only
left our mystery man. Al and Lillian were elsewhere,
Amy was on the ground scrounging for more food, and
Bubba appeared to be in an arm-wrestling contest with
the aspiring juggler. With all my allies either occupied or
compromised, it was on me to see what this fellow was
up to. Part of me felt as if I should stay and try to control
the crowd; however, a quick look around demonstrated
how ludicrous that was. The crowd was too wild and too
large; I'd never be able to stand in their way. At the very
least, I could ensure they were in a safe area, with no
secretive figures stalking about planning mischief.

Using care to walk quietly, I made my way over
to the doorway where I'd seen the motion. No signs of
anyone, but a focused concentration of effort helped me
pick up the sound of talking coming from deeper in the
building. I crept along, fast as I dared, yet not giving
away my advantage just yet. There was a chance that
surprise could be useful—as a distraction, at the very
worst—and right now, we needed any help we could get.
As it was, I'd already started evaluating how much repairs
for this place were going to cost my company, and that
was in the most optimal of situations—assuming no one
got hurt, for example. Those sorts of damages were much
harder to square.

It didn't take long for the words to become clear;
only the absolute din coming from the kitchen had

drowned them out, and that faded as my position changed. I recognized the first voice quickly: it belonged to Gregor, the densely built man I'd met in the hallways, and our apparent intruder.

"Please move. This has already taken too long. I do not wish to harm you, but the job must be done." Calm, which was tempting to take as a good sign, except time spent with Arch had taught me well that "calm" and "peaceful" did not inherently go together.

"Look, Mister, I don't know who you are or what your deal is, but you have no idea how long I've been waiting for a chance like this. You are not gumdropping it up." This voice belonged to Al, though it carried a more forceful tone than anything she'd utilized so far. Something else, too: an edge of danger, a thread of warning. Spend enough time around people who hide their real power, you begin to catch the warning signs that the veneer is slipping. Since I had no idea what Al was, I also lacked any clue as to what form her "cutting loose" might take. Given the situation we were already in, it was hard to imagine it would make things better.

Saying a silent prayer that Lillian was nearby, I steeled my nerves and stepped into view. Gregor was halfway down the hall, maybe ten feet ahead of me. Another ten feet past him was Al, wearing a stern expression with her hands on her hips. Someone might have called it adorable, if they weren't smart enough to realize that tremendous power could live in unassuming packages.

"For reference, I do expect instructions given to an employee to be followed. I believe I instructed you to run if you came across any danger, Al."

"Until I sign a contract, this is an interview, meaning you're not my boss yet," she countered.

Gregor, on the other hand, completely ignored our banter. At the sight of me, his face pinched. "Too dangerous for you. Go back to the crowd."

Well... that sort of put a hole in our assassin theory. Gregor seemed more bothered by my appearance than intrigued or delighted; definitely not the behavior of a man whose target had just shown up. From a few rooms away, I heard a distinctive clatter, followed by thumps and thuds, like the sound of fighting. Apparently, I wasn't the only one, as the noise seemed to light a fire under Gregor.

"See? Too close. Go. I shall come for you after."

"Hang on, who is that?" I whipped through a mental tabulation, a rare chance where my talents with numbers was of use beyond activities that required a desk. Everyone was accounted for—be it in the crowd, or this hallway—save for Lillian. She would make sense as one side of a fight, but who was she against? It would have to be a totally new entity, someone completely unaccounted for. The idea that we could have an unseen intruder was tough to swallow, but there had certainly been enough chaos and confusion for a bit of stealth.

Another series of bangs, this time coming from much closer—a single room away, if that. Al let out a yelp of surprise, leaping to the far wall, away from the noise. Gregor, on the other hand, took a more direct approach. He started on a direct course for me, hands already outstretched.

"If I must move you myself, so be it."

I darted back, quicker on my feet than I'd expected—not that Gregor made much of a grab. By retreating, I was already giving him what he wanted. Unfortunately, from Al's perspective, it must have looked like he was making a real move. To my utter shock, the diminutive woman raced down the hallway and leapt atop Gregor's back, moving a hand over his face like she was trying to block off his nose and mouth.

"You waste your time, little one. I am not so easily fell—ACK!"

Whatever cool speech Gregor had planned was cut off as an explosion of rainbow glitter engulfed his head, a sizable amount of the material going into his open mouth. He hacked and coughed as the cloud spread, coating everything in a thin layer of sparkles. While Gregor struggled to regain his composure, Al slipped daintily off his back and raced over, taking my hand.

"Let's go!"

She tugged hard, finding my body unmoving as I planted my feet. "Thank you, Al. I sincerely appreciate the concern. Thing is, that sound is one of my friends. I have no idea if I'll actually be of any help to her, but I have to go try."

The response earned me a look of befuddlement and, unless I missed my guess, hope, strangely enough. "Not many bosses would dive into the fire for their assistant."

I laughed, which was more mirth than I felt. But if Krystal had taught me nothing else, it was the power of chuckling at the reaper. "Lillian is definitely not my assistant, though that's not really the point. I said it already, she's my friend. A member of my clan. Given the chance, I'd happily hand this off to one of the members actually suited for it; sadly, that's not an option. Better to be here and useless than to have Lillian need me while I'm running away."

It was one of the most cohesive, non-cowardly speeches I had managed. Unfortunately, the moment was cut short by a loud crashing sound as one of the nearby walls collapsed completely. I had just enough time to see Lillian whip by and slam into a door, knocking it clean off the hinges.

The thing that had thrown her was immediate and distinctive. Unable to properly fit in the building anymore, it undulated, slapping against walls and ceiling as it struggled to move in the tight space. The dark green hue was the first clue that something was off, as were the hissing mouths that had formed at the edge of every appendage. Near its base, I noticed the twinkle of glass cracked along what counted as a body. Just like that, it all fell into place.

In one fell swoop, we'd found our intruder, the missing tengatulon, and what I suspected to be the remnants of Amy's lost potions. The good news was they were all one. The bad news was that those hissing mouths had turned from Lillian to where Al and I were standing. In a flash of green, it came barreling toward us, countless tentacles snapping for our flesh.

7.

ONE OF THE MOUTHS MUST HAVE HAD A
taste for accountant, because it veered toward me as the
tengatulon rushed forward. This close, I could see the
bark-colored fangs dripping dark purple liquid, which
could be anything from poison to a drug that made
music *outstanding*. We were dealing with unknown Amy
potions, mixed with a creature who had distinctly non-
human physiology. Anything was on the table, a thought
I tried not to dwell on as I backpedaled.

Unfortunately, having already retreated from Gregor left me little room to work with. I should have probably gone back around the corner to the other hall, but when untold pounds of hungry monster are bearing down on you, directly back sure sounds like the best direction to move. I made it all of six steps before smashing my rear against a wall. One glance told me there was nowhere left to go in that direction, and by the time I turned back, that hissing mouth was nearly on me. It lunged, fangs out, striking for my center of mass.

Instead, the fangs struck and subsequently broke against the thick arm of Gregor, who'd managed to wipe some of the glitter from his face now that the coughing was under control. As the tengatulon mouth pulled away, I could see the shattered teeth, as well as the tears in Gregor's sleeve. It wasn't any sort of armor that had halted the bite, merely his skin.

"I see now why Gideon chose one of my station for such a task. You are troublesome to protect." Hand striking with unexpected grace, Gregor grabbed the rogue tentacle with the broken mouth, dragging it and the tengatulon back in the direction it had come. As he did, I caught sight of Al on the other side, easily dodging every strike the tengatulon sent her way. She was nimble as could be, waiting for us rather calmly as she avoided the attacks.

While Gregor dragged, the tengatulon took notice, sending more and more of its enhanced appendages whipping down on him. No matter where they hit, the result was the same: shattered fangs, torn clothing, and not so much as a scratch on the man himself. On one hand, I was still reeling from him having so casually dropped Gideon's name, but as I watched him shrug off the assault, I mentally replayed our exchange earlier that day.

"Gregor, please forgive me if this is presumptuous, but are you, perchance, my new bodyguard?"

The tengatulon was in a frenzy now, whipping Gregor with its already broken-mouthed tentacles, causing more damage to itself than to the man it attacked. Gregor seemed unbothered by the increase in effort, glancing over his shoulder to shoot me a distinctly sour look.

"As I told you before, I am Gregor, of the Slate-Claw clan. First in my cracking, first in the fang and the fist, initiate in the order of the Obsidian Talon. By declaration of his majesty, Gideon, King of the West, Savior of the Slate-Claw, Slayer of Traxmort, I am hereby bound to your service as protector. Until failure or dismissal, I will protect you down to my final nail and scale."

While he was talking, Gregor deftly grabbed another tengatulon tentacle and began tying it in a knot with the first one he'd grabbed. Watching the tengatulon struggle, snapping walls and leaving dents everywhere, I realized that this creature was still extremely powerful—it just couldn't stand up to Gregor's raw strength.

A moan from the doorway reminded me of Lillian, who I quickly dashed over to check upon. She was hauling herself up from the rubble, wounds already healed. As a rule, we both kept ourselves well fed, just in case, and especially on any night where we interacted with the public. Shaking her head, Lillian seemed to come around fully, hopping back to her feet.

"Where's that snapping bastard? I'm ready for round... two..." Lillian's voice trailed off as she noticed Gregor, who was already tying a third tentacle into the growing knot, his clothes turning to shreds as the tengatulon continued to struggle. "Huh, that's a surprise. Fredrick, any insight?"

"That's Gregor," I explained. "We haven't done a full sit-down yet, but I think Gideon sent him to be my new bodyguard. No idea if that went through the Agency or not, though."

"His majesty has had the proper forms filled out to appease the keepers, even if his word alone should be more than enough." Another snag; it was getting easier as he tied off more of the tentacles.

Lillian let out a sharp whistle. "Damn, that is strong fella. The tengatulon gained a lot of power from something; my cuts were doing crap-all to leave a mark.

Is he a therian who shifts into a gorilla or something? Hard to hear with this ringing in my head."

"He says he's of the Slate-Claw clan." Al wandered over, as there was no longer a threat to dodge. In fact, the tone of the room had become rather subdued while we watched Gregor handily clobber the charging monster.

This time, she didn't whistle. Lillian's eyes lit up as she looked Gregor over again, examining him with a fresh perspective. "That would explain it. Slate-Claw is a gargoyle name. I've never actually seen one in action, only heard the rumors. They're said to be among the hardiest parahumans out there. No known weaknesses— not even silver can get through their armor. Supposedly, they can go without food and air for weeks, if needed, and as you can see, they're strong as hell."

Given that we'd just watched Gregor tie up a monster capable of knocking Lillian through a wall, that part was certainly not up for debate. Having more or less immobilized the creature, Gregor wiped his hands on his largely tattered slacks; some of the tengatulon's blood (or its version of it) had gotten on him as it struck. Regarding Gregor himself, the man was completely unharmed.

"The bigger question," Lillian continued, "is why one agreed to be your bodyguard. They are legendarily closed off, even from the rest of the parahuman world. I can't imagine Gideon's paying what one would cost just to act as your protection. Dragons don't part with gold that easily."

"I would *never* sully the honor of the Slate-Claw by demanding compensation from His Majesty." Gregor actually seemed to rile a bit at that, the first emotional blip I'd really clocked on him so far. "Centuries ago, Gideon took mercy upon my ancestors in our darkest hour, saving our clan from extinction. He is our hero, our patron, the only king we kneel before. Since then, the greatest of us have had the honor to work in his service. His Majesty said you were useful to those who mattered to him; therefore, he wishes you to live, and it is my duty to see his desires made real."

It was a lot to take in, especially from someone who'd been fond of brevity thus far. The key points were fairly easy to shake out after a moment's consideration, though. Gregor had a deep, powerful loyalty to Gideon, who'd ordered him to act as my bodyguard. He clearly took any order from our local dragon-king seriously, and had already shown competence at the work. So far as sudden surprises went, a capable bodyguard wasn't the worst. And as a bonus, this one hadn't even come in threatening to kill me, so he'd already made a better first impression than Deborah.

Another series of crashes came from back toward the kitchen, causing all of us except Gregor to bristle slightly, ready for another attack. While one didn't come,

I noticed a rise in noise. The crowd was getting antsy; they must have finished all the food. I could already hear footsteps of them heading in our direction, no doubt in search of fresh grub or distractions.

"Glad to have you on the team, Gregor. I don't suppose you have any talents in dealing with a crowd of drugged-up parahumans, do you?"

"Not any you'd like." He slammed a powerful fist into his open palm, producing a serious *crunch* that was very disconcerting. Gideon must have briefed him on my attitudes toward violence. He hadn't killed the tengatulon, only tied it up.

From behind Lillian, Al stepped forward, gaze running from me to Gregor. "You really don't care what we are, do you? You know nothing about gargoyles, but welcomed him without a second thought."

"He's here to help, sent by someone I trust to not want me dead. The rest is basically just details," I replied. "I care a lot more about the fact that he jumped in to keep us safe than what his particular nature is."

"I'm going to remind you of that when the water cooler contents turn into strawberry lemonade." As she spoke, Al kept walking, past Lillian and Gregor, past me, putting herself at the hallway's turn, where we could already hear the thunder of the approaching horde. She stretched her arms out, interlocking her hands and popping the fingers in a slightly disturbing way. As she shook them out, sparkles of glitter and a few flower petals drifted to the ground. Her shoes tumbled through the air as she kicked them off, pressing her bare feet against the cheap carpeting and hunkering down into a sprinter's stance.

I glanced down and noticed that the shoes were fading, falling apart into strands of woven grass that in no way resembled their previous shiny black surface. "Al, anything you want to warn us about?"

"Warning wouldn't really help; I'd suggest you just enjoy the show. This isn't one I'm going to put on very often."

That was when the crowd came into view, the centaur and the pale man leading the charge. Al didn't waver for a moment. Already, she was sprinting toward them, moving quite fast despite her short stature. As she ran, the lights began to flicker. Not out, but to different colors, like someone was trying to start a rave indoors. Faster she went, right on course with the centaur, neither of them giving so much as an inch to the side, barreling toward one another at top speed. I felt sure Al would jump or dive at the last minute, do something to turn this to her advantage. It turned out, I was dead wrong. Al didn't do any sort of acrobatics or nimble attack.

Instead, she ran directly into the torso of the centaur and exploded.

8.

WHEN I SAY "EXPLODED," THAT'S NOT to imply that a bomb went off and a shower of viscera rained down upon the job applicants. However, I do stand by the word choice, because there truly was a blast as Al vanished. It tore out from where she'd been moments prior, a wave of light and sparkles that crashed over the entire crowd, momentarily stunning them. A flash caught my eye: something moving fast, too quick for even vampire eyes to properly track.

It was like a living trail of light weaving through the group, and as I watched, I realized it wasn't just zipping around. The light was binding everyone with chains of flowers, an endless rope of flora wrapped around every arm, leg, and near-approximation the parahumans had to offer. While that might seem like it would be entirely useless against such powerful creatures, to my shock, each person bound soon slid to the floor. Not in pain (rather the opposite, based on their expressions), yet completely incapable of rising to their feet. As the last of the flower chains was woven, only two people remained standing. Bubba and Amy had been spared the fastening; not that either looked particularly aware of that. Whatever Amy had cooked up, it was still hitting them hard.

The light zipped over then, stopping in front of us. Seconds later, Al reappeared, only her outfit was now quite different: a green dress that seemed to have grown on her rather than be donned, golden shoes like the first rays of sunlight, and giant gossamer wings that made quite a statement piece.

"For official purposes, my name is Alstroemeria. To answer what you must be wondering: I'm a pixie. Don't worry if the size threw you; not all of us can change our shape naturally and few bother learning the magical route, preferring to stay small."

Despite the bravado, there was a touch of nerves to her voice that hadn't been present before. She'd just shown us her power, and while it was very impressive, there was clearly more to her nature than had been spoken aloud. This did put the strange occurrences I'd been noticing into new perspective, however.

"Al, pardon if this is indelicate, just trying to make sure I properly understand things. Pixies are a species of fey, correct?"

"Summer fey," Al specified. "We're supposed to serve as messengers of joy and fun. It's why my magic always tries to shape itself like, well…" Jerking her thumb up, she pointed over her shoulder, past the gossamer wings, to the hall of bound parahumans. "Flowers, candy, glitter, rainbows; you get the idea. I'm pretty sure you've noticed, but it doesn't always happen by my intention, either. Kind of a residual aura I give off; if you bring muffins by my desk, there's a good chance you're leaving with cupcakes."

Now, at last, Al made sense to me. She was bright, eager, and clearly capable, yet with her track record, there had to have been some kind of issue. This was inconvenient, certainly, but nowhere near as vexing as it would have been in a more traditional work environment. I imagined glitter suddenly showing up on documents in my old corporate gigs and suppressed an involuntary shudder.

"But everything else I told you is true." Finally given a chance to speak honestly, Al was bursting, all of it pouring out. "I want to work, I want to learn to run a business, and I want... I want to learn to be serious. Boring. Normal. I have ambitions, ideas for pixie-industries that could offer whole new paths for my people. But everyone just sees bluebirds and rainbows when they look at us. Heck, even the name of my species is a derogatory term for women who show a little too much joy."

In a funny way, Al's revelation put me truly at ease. I'd spent a night worried about the crowd, a potential assassin, and the effects of unknown Amy-drugs, all on top of the fear that I might fail to find a single viable new hire. Hearing her situation, one thing became abundantly clear: Al was an outlier. Too serious for her own people; too pixie for the rest of the world. That was a mighty relief, because if there was one thing I could say for the House of Fred, it was that we had a knack for attracting oddballs.

"I can't promise to teach you all of that," I cautioned. "All I know is how to run an accounting business. If that's not enough, I fully understand, but if it is, then I will promise to show you all that I know. Over time, of course; there's a lot of groundwork and basics to knock out first, to say nothing of eventual certifications—"

"Does that mean I got the job?" Interrupting wasn't really good interview form, but then again, this had long ago ceased to be a normal interview.

I nodded, adding in what I hoped to be a reassuring smile. "Seeing as you're quite literally the only candidate still standing, it's a fairly easy call. Besides, after tonight, you've proven you can hang on when things go crazy. That is, sadly, also a part of working for me. If you're not put off by the possibility, then yes, the job is yours."

"Welcome to the team," Lillian added.

Al let out a squeal of joy. At the same time, three songbirds flew out from literally nowhere, and the entire hallway's lighting shifted to alternating pink and green. The birds let out several joyous notes before disappearing as suddenly as they'd arrived. Had they been illusions? Summoned animals? Fey magic was its own creature; one I'd had very limited experience with.

"Thank you so much! I promise you won't regret it. Just don't wear anything around me that you don't want turned sparkly."

"She's going to wreck my whole closet, isn't she?" Lillian looked wryly at her own outfit, a formerly dark, practical ensemble that now sparkled freely. As much as she'd left behind elements of herself when changing clans, Lillian's fashion sense still went solidly along the expected vampire color-scheme, if maybe a bit more stylish than some bothered with.

"Enhance," Al corrected. "I call it wardrobe *enhancing.*"

As the two new coworkers got acquainted, I turned my attention back to Gregor, who was attempting to fashion his remaining clothes into something cohesively covering. I noticed through a slice in the back of his shirt that there was a pair of large bumps on Gregor's back, irregular, yet somehow not unnatural. They were part of him, but what part, I could only conjecture, even if there were serious context clues to work with.

"I can't remember if I actually said this in the fray or not, but thank you for saving me."

A neutral gaze greeted my appreciation. "It is only natural. My life exists to guard yours."

Not quite as emotionally overflowing as Al, that was something I'd probably need to get accustomed to. Still, I did want to say thanks in a way that would register. The man had protected me from a mauling at the minimum, and that couldn't be something we treated as irrelevant. Thinking back on what little I knew about Gregor, there was one spot where I could see potential.

"Be that as it may, good work deserves recognition. I'll send a message to Gideon this evening, letting him know how well his selection has performed."

Now *that* got a reaction. Gregor's whole body went taut, like he was bracing for an unseen attack, before relaxing once more. I watched as his eyes bulged, silently scrambling for words, until he finally managed to produce a weak shrug. "His Majesty no doubt already knows his own wisdom in all decisions. But I am sure there is no harm in knowing others have recognized it, as well."

By the standards Gregor had set thus far, that was basically gushing. At least now I had some idea of how to show gratitude, though the trick might wear thin after a few uses. Something to contemplate for a later day.

Watching Gregor fasten his clothes together, a blink of light caught my eye. For a moment, I thought Al had shrunk down again, but when I glanced back, she was still standing near Lillian. Only, she wasn't alone any longer. Surrounding Al was a cluster of familiar zipping lights, lights she was whispering to in a language I couldn't understand. Not that I didn't grasp the meaning of the words, mind you—the words themselves were sounds that felt wrong to the ear, like my brain couldn't properly even fathom them.

"One thing I should warn you about, given how tonight played out: pixies don't do violence. Goes against our joyful natures. What you saw is basically my maximum in terms of conflict resolution." Al's outfit was changing as she spoke, reshaping itself to the suit she'd originally walked in wearing. "However, we do have a lot of other talents. Since I don't want my new boss on the hook for all these damages, I asked some friends to do a demonstration."

With a wave of her hand, the floating lights shot off into the building. A few stayed nearby, running along the wall and ceiling. Before our eyes, the dents popped out, and the scratches vanished as a new coat of tangerine-colored paint replaced the previously utilized dull gray. The door Lillian had shattered began to reform, pieced back together and solidified in under a minute. The pixies were working up a storm, mending the destruction like... well, forgive the phrase, but it is truly the most appropriate one to use... like magic.

"Uh oh. Charlotte's got competition in the convenience department," Lillian whispered.

I was more amazed by the overall display, as well as noting the visible style differences. Although the building would apparently be whole by sunrise, it would also have some very different aesthetics: much brighter, more energetic, and, unless my eyes deceived me, with a bit of glitter woven in at irregular intervals. There would still be some serious explaining to do, just not the kind that opened police files or lawsuits.

"What do you think?" I asked Lillian. "One accounting employee, one bodyguard, no deaths, and it looks like we might not even wreck the place. Best we could have hoped for?"

In the corner, Gregor had fastened his scraps of clothes into a pseudo-loincloth. Meanwhile, Al was commanding the pixies, as well as checking to make sure the other parahumans were still blissed out in their flower chains. Bubba and Amy were leaning against a wall, deep in discussion about the merits of cider versus beer. That was encouraging; they had the debate frequently, so hopefully that meant they were edging closer to sobriety.

"Shit, if you'd told me this was how it would end, I'd have called you optimistic," Lillian shot back. "Our little enterprise is growing. But you do realize that adding a gargoyle and a fey to your entourage isn't going to quell the rumors that keep popping up."

Despite the fact that my clan wanted nothing more than to live in peace, our exploits had the unfortunate outcome of attracting attention. Without proper context, some of the things we did could seem more grand or ambitious than they'd really been: saving Gideon, outfoxing the Turva clan, surviving the Court of Frost— and that was to say nothing of what people thought of my wide circle of friends. To others, it appeared I was gathering various parahuman forces, trying to amass power while bucking the system. The sorts of people who did that didn't tend to have positive outcomes in mind.

"At this point, I have resigned myself to the fact that no matter what we say or do, the whispers will continue. Our best move is to keep living openly, showing that there's nothing to fear, and hope nobody decides to test the rumors for themselves."

"That won't work forever, you know." It wasn't chiding, more a warning. Lillian was like Deborah, old enough to see things long term. I knew what she was hinting at; from an eternal perspective, sooner or later, we *would* face conflict.

Slowly, I gave Lillian a slight nod. "I know. But for as long as it holds, I want to use the diplomatic option. I much prefer these sorts of resolutions." Looking down the hall, I again took stock of the many parahumans drugged out of their skulls and the array of pixies feverishly mending the damage that had been caused. "Okay, maybe not these *exact* sorts, but you get what I mean."

That earned me a short laugh from Lillian, whose expression was unexpectedly gentle as she too stared at the scene. "Having spent a long time with the other kind of problem-solving, yes, Fredrick, I understand completely. And I agree: this is nice, for however long we can hang on to it."

We stood in silence, until a rogue thought struck me as I stared at the blissed-out horde. "Oh, crap. What are we going to do if they aren't sober by the time this place opens?"

A gentle clap on my back was Lillian's initial response as she turned to walk away. "Dunno. Sounds like a boss problem to me."

A PARTNER BORROWED

1.

AS MUCH AS I DEPENDED ON MY FRIENDS, their support of me was by no means a one-way street. Being part of the same clan, to say nothing of our social relationships, meant that I was frequently tapped for fiscal consulting, or to pitch in with general work where vampire strength was applicable. Some of the obligations went deeper, though, past the sorts of things that could be easily knocked out in a few hours.

When I'd helped Amy Wells renegotiate her debt to the mages that had initially funded her, part of that excess income was set aside to help other mages avoid her problem. She wanted to offer a better alternative than getting in bed with the existing power structure, a chance to give others a true starting point, rather than trapping them with debt. For a time after our renegotiation, little moved on that front, as Amy allowed the income to pile up and looked for potential new projects to fund. However, despite the initial hesitation to undertake such a role, she had been working hard behind the scenes.

With two weeks left before my wedding, it was time for my final work trip before I left for the honeymoon: a mage-scouting expedition with Amy. In truth, it was my last major task at all; the remainder of my energy would be spent supervising Al's training to make sure she could be minimally supervised in my absence, as well as giving Lillian any support needed to prepare her for being in charge. They had to be ready for my time off, and mercifully, their capability was one area where I wasn't feeling abundantly concerned.

Al was getting along well with the others, except, oddly, for Charlotte; those two treated each other with a curious coldness. Outside of that blip, Al had been pleasant and hard-working. Not everything about the job came naturally, and we discovered early on that Al learned a lot more efficiently with regular breaks woven into her schedule, but she was steadily picking up the trade.

Gregor, on the other hand, made no socialization efforts beyond the polite essential of learning everyone's names. He was constantly around, yet still had an unexpected talent for slipping into the background. There were times I genuinely forgot he was in the room until a rogue glance reminded me of his presence. So far, the person he seemed to get along best with was Arch, in that they would sometimes sit in the same room, saying nothing, for long stretches of time. The rest of us realized that he liked his personal space and gave it, as needed.

Much as I would have preferred to stay around the office and focus on training my new staff, my commitment to helping Amy came first. Even if I hadn't agreed to help her, she was a friend, part of my clan, and had come to our aid countless times through the years. I owed her more than a helping hand; she was entitled to the very best of my efforts in whatever the task demanded. On the upside, we'd decided to use the brief trip as something of a test case.

"Sure you don't want to look the schedule over one more time?" Lillian tapped the monitor, where her itinerary for the next two days was displayed.

"I think we've gotten it as smoothed out as we can. At this point, it's all about the execution, at which I have no doubt you'll be amazing." That wasn't mere bluster to reassure a worried friend, either. Lillian was an outstanding employee, dedicated and focused in ways

I'd never dared hope when she first joined me. The speed at which she was learning my profession attested to how capable she really was when self-motivated. It was a wonder to me, even years later, that the Turva clan had failed to recognize Lillian's true potential.

Pity she didn't share my certainty. Her pale teeth rested against her lips as she studied the screen. "You know, I used to go on covert operations for my old house, and I never felt this nervous. Not even when I was loaded down with artillery."

"Perhaps it's because this time, you actually care about doing well?" It hadn't taken knowing Lillian for long to realize that her heart had never been in the old role she'd been forced to fulfill.

"Or I just haven't had to do anything truly new in, like, a few decades," Lillian countered. She looked at the schedule once more, then clicked the tab away. "We'll hold the place together. Or I'll ask Al's friends to come patch Charlotte up before you get home."

A loud creak echoed through our office, the sort of noise one never heard from a magically animated house, unless it was intentional. My best guess took it to be something of a groan, although that was speculation in its truest form.

Lillian continued, ignoring the brief interruption. "How 'bout you? Got everything sorted?"

"Heading up to see Amy's potential investment today. Transportation is already arranged, and I've been assured it shouldn't take more than a day to look over the specifics. Took some doing to get a big enough vehicle with enchanted glass, but I don't have to worry about being defenseless."

Since this was Amy's money and project, she would of course be along for the assessment. Wanting a second pair of mage eyes, she elected to bring Neil along, too, which meant that Albert would also be attending. Adding in me and Gregor tipped the scale to five, except it counted more as six when adjusted for Gregor's bulk. For a seven-hour drive, that promised tight quarters in a normal vehicle. Thankfully, Amy assured us that she could get a hold of something with adequate room.

"I'm surprised Arch didn't tag in; he keeps a close eye on his pupils," Lillian said.

"Except when he wants them to get experience on their own. This is apparently one of those situations."

A slight cough announced Charlotte's presence, and she soon manifested in the form of a young woman wearing a gown from centuries past. This tended to be her default form when dealing with long-term guests, such as ourselves.

"Fred, I wanted to inform you that a new vehicle just pulled into my parking lot. Also, Krystal has begun to threaten violence if you take much longer."

I was tempted to peek out the window and see what Amy had procured; luckily, my relationship wasn't so young that I failed to recognize which piece of information was more important. Lillian waved me off, pausing just long enough for a quick hug. "Take care of yourself. I don't want to do this for more than two days, you know."

While I said nothing, I wasn't so sure I believed Lillian about that. As her competence in the subject matter had grown, so too had her interest. She was a far cry from the person who'd yawned her way through every scrap of paperwork when first starting out. It had occurred to me more than once that I might very well be training my eventual competition. In truth, that was a rivalry I would welcome. The parahuman world needed more people willing to do this work; we'd both drown in business, and more people would get help.

She wasn't there yet, however, and this would be her first time running things solo. Hopefully, it would go well, but much like my own task, only time would tell. Working in the parahuman world came with heaping helpings of uncertainty at every turn, even for those of us just doing the paperwork.

Making my way down the stairs, I arrived to find a grumpy Krystal waiting, tapping impatiently on her watch. "Bad enough you're skipping town right before the wedding, now you're not even giving me time for a proper goodbye where I threaten to beat up your ghost if you get yourself killed."

There was a time in my life—my actual, heart-pumping life—where I would have assumed that statement to be comical hyperbole. The thing about being a corpse animated by magic was that it didn't offer much refuge in the idea of the impossible. I'd met a residual spirit, so I knew firsthand they existed. I pushed these things out of my head as I walked down the stairs, into her arms. Such concerns might very well be relevant at some point, but not tonight.

"Given a Weapon of Destiny, two people trained by Arch, one of the smartest mages of her generation, and a bodyguard appointed by a dragon, I feel relatively confident we can handle anything this new mage requesting funding might be able to conjure." Saying it out loud, part of me wondered if we were showing up a little *too* strong. Granted, I understood everyone's purpose was either defensive or supportive, but from the outside, it could easily look like a gang of parahumans coming to cause trouble—especially with a vampire in the mix. Our ability to drink from other parahumans created a harsh, and historically deserved, reputation.

"I'd like an agent in there, as well, but Gregor does seem competent," Krystal admitted. "The Agency has only ever had a few gargoyles join through its history, so I've never gotten to see one in action. Based on the stories, they're some tough bastards."

"Let's hope I've seen as much of a display as I'll need to for a while."

Words fell away as we moved on to kissing goodbye, a shorter affair than either of us might have preferred, thanks in no small part to the humorous car horn melody that soon rose from the parking lot. It sounded like the first ten bars of some old song from the seventies, so faded and out of tune that the actual melody could no longer be discerned.

Krystal and I pulled away from each other, both looking to the door.

"Did you let Amy get the car for this trip?"

"She said she knew of one we could borrow," I supplied weakly. Only now, with a few spare moments to think properly, did I realize that the majority of Amy's friends outside of the House of Fred would be other mages. And mages tended to be a bit... eccentric at times.

Interlocking our hands, Krystal and I made our way onto the front porch of Charlotte Manor, where I found Gregor already loading bags into a van. It was certainly a large enough space to accommodate all of us, along with our luggage—that much had been delivered as promised—and I trusted that the windows would repel the sun once it began to beat upon us. But the giant, tie-dye swirls along the right side of the extra-large van gave the distinct impression the vehicle had just driven right out of Woodstock. In a way, it was impressive to see such a vintage machine running so smoothly; although, that was slightly mitigated when one realized the owner was likely employing magical maintenance.

"Great, right?" Amy leaned out the passenger's side window, dropping an empty potion bottle to the ground as rings of light began to ripple through her brunette hair. "Borrowed it from a buddy. Won't get stopped by any police, barely needs gas, and drives like a dream. I just chugged a Nectar of Navigation, so I'll guide the driver around any upcoming traffic."

"Great? It's awesome!" From around the other side of the van, Albert stepped into view, followed closely by Neil, who was wearing a far less amused expression. I hadn't even noticed them arrive, but the day had been busy as I prepared to depart. He caught sight of me and gave one of those big, enthusiastic Albert waves I'd grown to know so well. "Fred, you gotta come see this! There's a mural of giants fighting on the other side."

I forced a polite smile onto my face as I waved back, mercifully spared the need to come up with an immediate response by the distance between us. Krystal gave my other hand one last squeeze before letting go. "I was hoping she'd find a wild one, but this is better than

I dreamed. Damn, really should have set up a camera to record your expression."

A quick kiss on the cheek pulled me back from my shock. "Go on, and get moving. Sun will be coming in a few hours. Be smart, be safe, and be back here with me when it's all over."

"You're more worried than normal, given the job we're doing," I noted. Krystal didn't tend to be overly concerned unless my life was in immediate peril, which, admittedly, had happened a few times by now.

"Geez, Freddy, all those old movies you love, maybe work some classic action flicks in there occasionally. I'm more or less a parahuman secret agent and long-time loner on the verge of settling down with someone I really love, which means it feels like fate is just waiting for the chance to snatch it away. Of the two of us, you die a lot easier. It's hard not to worry the closer we get." To my surprise, she slipped in for a hug. Quick and tender, with none of the usual overt display Krystal favored. It wasn't part of any show; she'd just needed a moment of embrace.

I held her, too, considering my words. Promising not to die was a silly thing; if it were my choice, I wouldn't choose to, but I knew all too well the fragility of this undead life. "I'll do everything I can to come home safely. No needless chances, and if things smell funny, we'll pull back right away. Given that we're just going to see some mage's prototype, odds are it's going to be another boring business meeting."

"It's not this job that scares me. You pissed off the Turvas, the Blood Council has special interest in you, and there's always Quinn lurking out there somewhere. One thing this job has taught me, grudges have a way of coming 'round again." Letting me go, Krystal turned back to the van, where Gregor had nearly finished loading everything. "I'll feel a lot better once we're finally married. Some of the restrictions we've been dealing with get eased up, and you gain access to more protective services from the Agency. Until then, stick near Gregor and Albert if things get dicey. The other two can't protect and attack at the same time; you'd be slowing them down."

"I shall keep it under advisement." One last kiss, a quick peck before I headed into the night. "See you soon."

"You damn well better."

I left her on the porch, watching as we piled into the multi-colored van that smelled strongly of rock concerts and late-night munchies, if you take my meaning. Bracing myself for an odiferous next few hours, I made my way around to the left side of the van to pile in with the others. In doing so, I made quite the discovery.

Albert was right: whatever else I thought of the van, that mural of the fighting giants turned out to be exceptionally well done.

2.

WHETHER IT WAS THE VAN'S SPELLS OR Colorado's new attitude toward alternative recreation, our ride was shockingly uneventful for a road trip in a tie-dyed vehicle. No police pulled us over, thanks to the van's enhancements; no sudden, comically timed break-downs. Not even an attack from an overhead helicopter. Neil behind the wheel even proved to be a good choice, as the young man made a quite competent driver.

Looking at Neil, it was hard not to notice he was leaning more toward "man" than "young" in that equation. Over the years since we'd met, he'd undergone untold hours of training under both Amy and Arch, an effort that had shaped him from a scrawny megalomaniac into a sturdy fellow who wouldn't have looked out of place on a soccer or baseball field—far from Bubba or Richard's bulk, yet athletic all the same. The contrast was especially sharp when compared with Albert, whose only physical changes were whatever tricks they'd done to add more muscle to his frame. Outside of that, and some style updates, he looked the same as he had the night we met. The same way he would always look.

At least Neil wouldn't be aging into dust too soon, leaving Albert behind in the process. Mages lived extended life spans, and the greater the magics they commanded, the longer they could last. He'd already been considered a talent; under the tutelage of someone like Amy, Neil was probably on the path to serious power. But he wasn't my chief concern for this trip; that honor belonged to a newer mage.

"Walk me through this once more," I said, angling myself toward Amy in the front seat. Making sense of Amy's notes—really, most mages' notes—was a Herculean task, if not a Sisyphean one. Sentences on top of sentences, scribblings and scrawlings through the margins, it was a wonder they could read their own spells, but perhaps that was the crux. This might be the ideal way to record arcane rituals, and the worst method for literally anything else. "Your potential investment, Shun, was raised among mages, so she already knows the systems, but still applied to you for startup capital."

"Correct. She too sees the inadequacies of capitalism's hungry chains and seeks the greater freedom." Whatever was causing those ripples in Amy's hair had also impacted her mind, clearly, but this was actually one of the more helpful states I'd found her in, so I wasn't complaining.

Double-checking the files again, I shook my head. "That's one explanation. Another is that, whatever her pitch is, it looks like no one was buying. I think you might be her last resort, after everyone else declined."

"Yeah, I figured that might be it, too," Amy admitted. "But she's been the only one to apply, so I also thought, what the hell, let's give her a shot."

The van sputtered as Neil took a sharp turn, a hazard born of poorly marked exits rather than inept driving. With the sun overhead, I had a hard time not tensing at the slightest sign of trouble. For most of the others, a crash would be inconvenient. I was the only one at risk of suddenly lighting up. And this far from civilization, there wasn't going to be any help coming.

We'd gone well off the main roads by this point. I had been reviewing Amy's files rather than watching the window; however, a cursory glance showed me little more than rocky terrain and patches of shrub grass. Whatever we were here to find, it wasn't the type of attraction one spotted from a distance.

"Has no one really applied? I've seen the terms you're offering; to call it generous would do your charity a disservice."

"They're too blind and stubborn to see the gift she's setting before them." Neil laced the words with liberal venom. He'd never been particularly adept at hiding his devotion to Amy. "The existing structures are familiar, so that's what they use, even though she's offering them a lifeline they're too much of cowards to take hold of."

From his side, Amy patted Neil's shoulder. "People are slow to change; mages even more so. We tend to be wrapped up in our projects. Give it time. When the need arises, they'll come, just like Shun."

"Yes, about that. This would probably go much easier if you could tell me *what* it is we're here to evaluate." I held up the clump of pages in my hand, resisting the urge the shake them ineffectually, albeit not by much. "The notes are not as enlightening as one might hope."

That earned me a shrug from Amy, causing her hair-light to ripple faster. "No idea. Shun just said it would be fun. I think the surprise is probably part of it."

"Must be one heck of a surprise." Albert was pressed against the far window, looking out at the vacant landscape. "I can't see anything but rocks."

"We'll find out soon," Neil announced. "According to the directions, we're less than five minutes out."

I dearly hoped our host had some sort of shaded parking system in place. There were contingencies, in case we had to improvise, by which I mean we'd brought along several umbrellas to hurriedly shade me with in a mad bolt from the car to our destination. I'd also slathered on a bit of high-SPF sunscreen. According to Deborah, it wouldn't stop the effects entirely, but it would buy me a few extra seconds. With vampire speed and life-or-death motivation, I'd be able to put that span of time to good use.

Fortunately, we were only a little farther down the road when a new geographic feature popped out: a craggy outcropping of what appeared to be a massive stone formation, with a distinct slope leading downward. Seeing as it was truly the only feature for miles, Neil put us on a direct course, leaving the solid terrain of the road as he pushed into unknown. I expected the van to throw a fit; instead, there was barely a shudder as the ground changed. Whoever had made this thing really had done an exceptional job on the enchantments, or the suspension. Probably both, when I thought about it.

The trek to the outcropping was a short one, and drawing close, it became clear just how large the opening really was. Not only would the van fit, it would do so easily, as if this cavernous maw wanted to swallow as many mobile tributes as possible.

Flicking the lights on, Neil drove further, heading downward and out of the sun's deadly glare. Immediately, it became clear that this was no mere slope: it was a tunnel, something vast and deep, leading into the earth. I tried not to think about the growing pounds of soil overhead, supported by I dared not guess what. It would be fine; even if that collapsed, relatively few of us needed air, and the others could easily dig to the surface before the van filled with carbon dioxide. Then again, if it was only one factor piled onto others, things might not be so simple.

"Sure this isn't a trap?" Strangely, Gregor didn't sound especially concerned about the possibility; his question came out closer to idle curiosity. It was hard to say if that effect was him keeping calm, or hubris about his capabilities, in the moment I was leaning toward the former. Gregor was far from chummy, but then, he also hadn't shown any special penchant for arrogance. The only person he seemed to believe was infallible was Gideon.

"Fairly sure," Amy called from the front. "Be a lot of work to take me out for offering a service no one was using. Unless this was all a ploy to get me to bring Fred along. He does have the kind of scheming enemies who love that bullshit."

That thought didn't make me feel much better, especially when the van rolled to a gentle stop a few moments later. Neil switched the headlights to bright mode, illuminating a dark cave wall into which a single giant door had been carved. Looking at it, I wondered how any human would possibly open such a thing—then realized quickly that the weight was likely the point. Only someone with otherworldly strength or access to magic could get through, a low-tech way to keep humans away.

We piled out of the van, some taking a moment or two to stretch, while others readied themselves in different ways. Neil checked the bags of materials along his waist, along with a dark tome fashioned into a harness at the small of his back. As for Albert, he adjusted his simple, dark armor and checked the draw for his sword. Despite the fact that this wasn't supposed to be a battle, they were Arch's students, and his training went too deep for the situation to matter.

"Should we knock?" If that seems odd, I agree, yet the act of dealing with mages meant that one must often throw sense right out the window. Better to ask a silly question than take a reckless action.

Potentially in response, a loud *clunk* echoed as the door slid away from the wall, revealing a simple room. I started ahead, only to have Gregor grab me by the shoulder. "Bodyguard goes first. Stay near the back."

A protest withered on my tongue, an objection I knew I had no right to raise. Gregor was correct: he should be the one going first, as much for the role he was filling as the fact that he was among our hardiest members present. If attacked by something, Gregor could stop it cold, whereas I'd just be the first victim or a small speed bump as it barreled past. With some effort, I held back as the others went in, joining Neil as the final entrants. Since he had no physical augmentations and lacked Amy's wealth of experience, he too was stuck in a heavily defended position.

"Welcome to the rear," he greeted. We followed the others in, and happily, the door didn't slam shut with a foreboding boom, like I'd been half expecting.

It was a curious room. Arcane symbols were etched into the walls and ceiling, with large, hexagonal patterns swirling through the floor—some sort of magic, or the appearance of it, but we were officially out of my depth. Thankfully, that was why we had actual spellcasters on the team.

"Lots of charms for concealment and containment; that explains why I'm not seeing any residual magic leak out. Nicely done, too. Whoever taught Shun to string spells did a killer job, though her precision could use work. Plenty of inefficiencies here." Amy walked along the far wall, running her hands against the symbols.

Behind her, Albert and Gregor were looking at the ground, probably hoping to have more luck with geometry than magic. Neil gave a cursory glance along the walls, too, but he didn't appear as enraptured by them as Amy.

"Yeesh, she's not wrong. Some of the relays on these are so haphazard, you'd have major timing sync issues if you tried to run—"

Neil's words were cut off by a sudden flurry of activity. The door *boomed* behind us, just as I'd assumed we'd avoided, causing me to jump. While my vertical ascent was higher than a human reaction would have been, the leap didn't explain why my feet refused to find purchase on the descent.

That was when I noticed that the floor had dropped away. What initially appeared as simple geometric patterns were in fact a series of chutes and drops, all triggering at once. We were caught, to a parahuman, tumbling down into the trap. Worst of all, however, was our positioning.

As we slid out of the room, it was clear to see we'd be going to different places. Someone had just managed to split my team. That meant they were dangerous... and we were now vulnerable.

3.

LANDING IN A STRANGE, DARK ROOM WITHOUT explanation is not a pleasant experience. As a human, I'd have been blind, potentially injured, and on the verge of true panic. Thankfully, one of the first, most convenient abilities of being a vampire was night vision. Within a blink, I could see the new room in crisp detail, eyes made to sweep the darkest of nights easily adapting. Rising to my feet, I took a proper inventory of our situation.

The room I'd landed in was at the end of an impossibly frictionless chute. Even using my enhanced strength, grabbing for purchase during the fall had been a vain effort. Magic, obviously, as I rationally suspected would be the case for most of this place. What remained to be seen was whether Amy had been wrong about her potential enemies, or whether it was one of mine trying something new. It was hard to say; I certainly had the larger number of people who'd jump at the chance to wound my clan than Amy had accumulated enemies, but they were all undead. While vampires could wield magical implements, we lacked the power to cast actual spells. Based on just what we'd seen so far, it was hard to imagine any undead successfully putting this together.

As for the room itself, it appeared mostly empty. There was a table covered in items at the far end, a single door on the opposite side, and a few runes etched into the walls at seemingly random intervals.

From the floor, a groan rose. Neil raised his head slowly, tenderly tapping a rising bump on his head. With the speeds we'd been traveling, that was a surprisingly light injury. I knew that he and Albert used protective charms, and clearly with good reason. Even a normal mage would probably be nursing a cracked skull from that headfirst fall.

"By all the nine hells, what the crap was that?" Neil stumbled to his feet, pawing at the air. It took me a moment to realize he was searching for something to grab onto. Unlike a vampire, his vision didn't seamlessly transition between dark and light. Down here, he was effectively blind.

"Seems as though we fell down a trap." Obvious, granted, but someone had to clear the prerequisite hurdles of laying out the basics. "I'm guessing the others wound up in different areas."

"And I, of course, got you." Muttering to himself, not so softly that I couldn't make out a few choice grumbles, Neil wove his hands quickly through the air, clapping them together and causing a glow to flash in both eyes. Moments later, he looked me in the face, no longer impeded by the lack of light. That was the thing about mages; they might not start with as many advantages, yet they could adapt to new situations better than nearly any other parahuman.

Together, we swept the room, searching for any clues or hints. Outside of the table and the door, we came up empty. I even attempted leaping back up the chute we'd come down, only to discover that the frictionless magic still held. There wasn't even the hint of finding purchase. I'd have had better luck climbing a cloud.

By the time I was done experimenting, Neil had set up shop at the table, examining the small array of objects upon it. They appeared simple enough, except I was rapidly realizing not to take much on appearances alone. From left to right, they were a key, a knife, a club, and a feather quill. Neil reached for the quill; instantly, sparks flew between his outstretched fingers and the item. He closed his hand immediately, and the lightshow ended.

"Interesting. It's checking to see if I've already touched one of the objects." Neil flexed his hand, then moved it toward the knife. New sparks appeared, lighting up his face just in time for the satisfied grin to spread across it. "Got it. We're supposed to choose. A single item each is my guess, but just in case we only get the one…" Neil pushed his hand the rest of the way, closing around the knife. There was a crackle of energy in the air, and without warning, the sparks died.

He twirled the weapon once, then made for the quill. Nothing appeared to stop him, yet, when his fingers met the quill, they passed through like it was nothing more than a shadow.

"Crafty. I expected them to use some sort of ward to stop me from taking more. This is smarter." Neil half-looked at me as he spoke; I had a hunch I was here more as backstop than conversational partner. "Someone suspended the objects in a state of pseudo-existence, with an area enchantment that lets someone fully manifest one—but only if they haven't done so already. Stops another mage like me from ripping apart barriers and taking whatever we want."

With every new revelation, I felt more confused. A trap was one thing, but this was a lot of effort if someone wanted to kill us. Whatever the answer was, I didn't expect to find it waiting around in the room. With only three objects to select from, I made the obvious choice, scooping up the key after an identical light display to the one Neil had shown. Once it was in hand, I turned to find the necromancer looking at me incredulously.

"The key? You realize keys are implied to fit a specific lock, which we may or may not find, whereas the club or the quill had other potential uses. You chose a unitasker when we're facing down unknown challenges."

"As opposed to the weapon?" I nodded to the knife in his hand.

"Or the screwdriver," Neil shot back, lightly tapping the blade's narrow tip. "Or the crowbar, if we need to pry something small open. People don't keep knives in their pockets in case they need to do some lunchtime stabbing; they do it because the damn things are useful."

That was a fair, if unexpected, point. However, I wasn't quite ready to yield my ground. "Seeing as we're clearly in some sort of magical trap, I'd hate to make it all the way to the end, only to discover we lack the means to escape. If a key is given, it's usually for a reason."

I felt as if I could see the struggle within Neil, his desire for further debate pushing up against the truth that there was no point to it. We could each make a single selection, and the dice were cast in that regard. Fighting over what we might have done wouldn't get us any closer to freedom.

"Fine, you have the key, I have the knife. It doesn't matter, anyway; we won't actually need to finish this. We just have to find somewhere a little less warded. Once I reach Albert, he can come to us, and after that we're as good as free."

Neil reached up and tapped one of the runes. "These walls are hardy, and reinforced by magic, but they won't stand up to the Blade of the Unlikely Champion. He'll be able to cut his way through this place in no time. We just need to find a way to signal him, and since I don't see one in our current room, I say we press on."

There were times Neil and Albert spoke when I could virtually see Arch's lips moving over theirs, lessons that had been drilled deep into their minds being repeated. But this wasn't one of those moments, despite how competent Neil seemed. Relying on someone else to find you wasn't a very Arch-like move, yet he still spoke with that same assured air of confidence as when he shared some bit of wisdom imparted from his teacher. Perhaps these two had grown even more than I realized throughout their training.

"Safe to say we've seen everything this room has to offer," I agreed. "I should probably take the lead, though."

"Ah yes, because now *you're* the tough one again."

"No, because you can magically repair me if something goes wrong. Whereas I'm not a human-mancer, or whatever the term would be, so you'd just be injured until we found Amy."

I wasn't quite sure how to interpret the look Neil sent my way, but it wasn't an angry one, so I took it to be agreement. Better to act than to wait and risk him dashing out in front. With great care and attention to my surroundings, I inched forward and put a hand on the doorknob. When neither the floor fell away, nor anything huge fell upon me, I felt confident enough to give it a twist. No resistance; it opened smoothly, revealing a new room.

My dark-vision snapped out of focus as a dozen braziers lining the walls all burst with flame, casting our new chamber in flickering, unsettling light. Honestly, I'd have preferred it stayed dark; that was somehow less disturbing than the burning illumination. Some of that may have been instinctual, I can admit, fire being one of the few things that could easily kill me. Finding it in abundance was not a sign I considered to be reassuring.

Finally dragging my eyes beyond the flames, I examined the rest of the chamber. This one was far larger than our landing room had been; a carved cave well below the Earth's surface. Outside the braziers, it was largely featureless, save for the dark pool of liquid looming in the center. It could have been a puddle, or so deep it led to the ocean. There was no way to tell, and the flashes of the flames made it impossible to see beneath those placid, glassy waters. Over the pool were four sets of chains, each leading up to an elevated platform fifty feet off the ground. Although it took some walking to get the right angle, I finally caught the tip of a doorway peeking over the high ledge. That was our way out, apparently.

"So, we climb the chains to get to the top... what else?" Neil too was looking over the situation, brow furrowed as his brain worked overtime. "It can't be that easy. Maybe they have the same charm as the slides we went down, making them impossible to grab. But they don't appear to have anything other than a repair enchantment. What are we missing?"

I knew what Krystal would do in that moment, and while I wasn't going to fulfill her role in quite the same manner, I also recognized its indispensability. Thought and action went hand-in-hand. New data had to be examined and considered, but action was what most often resulted in acquiring such data in the first place. Still, leaping out and climbing the chains was several steps too far for my level of risk tolerance.

Instead, I walked to the wall from which the outcropping jutted and began to climb. Much of that skill comes from training, coordination, and physical strength. I was lacking greatly on the first two, but when one's grip is boosted to vampiric levels, it's possible to lean entirely on the third—for short, well-motivated intervals, anyway.

After three tries to lend some rhythm to what amounted to me scrambling up the wall like some sweater vest-clad squirrel, I arrived at the doorway. Now that I could see the whole platform, it was clear there was more than just an exit up here. Set before the door was a large stone bowl resting on some sort of mechanism. I had a hunch where this was going, but tried the door anyway. Not so much as a budge. While I could try to break it down, it would probably be smart to save such drastic measures as final resorts. Once we made that kind of declaration, there was no taking it back.

"There's a bowl up here," I called to Neil. "Best guess is we have to find a way to fill it with water from that pool."

At least the task was quickly taking shape, rather than forcing us to muddle through some obscure puzzle. Next up was to see if we could even use the chains, as otherwise, I'd have to haul Neil up the hard way. Reaching over from the outcropping, I took one in my hand. No slippage. It felt like a perfectly normal length of chain. I gave it a good shake, just to make sure it bore weight.

The instant the rattle of metal hit my ears, another sound followed: the loud *gloomph* of a giant, brown, slug-like head bursting from the water and swallowing the entire bottom twenty feet of the chain I'd just shook. It oozed back down slowly, leaving the chain intact, but with a quickly drying veneer of mucus.

Right, so I'd been almost correct. Turns out, our task was to fill the bowl, *while* dodging the ravenous monster that lived in the water and emerged at the slightest sound.

4.

"ANY IDEA WHAT THAT IS?"

We both stared at the pool as I skipped a rock across the surface, instantly bringing the giant slug head up to the surface. Its mouth swept the area ineffectually before sinking back below the water, which turned still in moments, hiding its secret below the glassy surface once more. After I climbed down to get a better look and located some stone shards on the ground, skipping them across the surface had been the optimal method we'd devised for drawing the beast out.

"Best guess is it's some kind of custom conjuration, probably homegrown," Neil replied. "Might have started off as a normal slug, but at this point, it's a mystery to me."

Though that didn't help much with our current predicament, it was a clue toward our greater situation. So far, we'd encountered a secret enclosure buried beneath the ground, enchanted slides and rooms, and now a custom-made monster. Far as I was from being a mage myself, I understood enough to realize that such breadth of skill would take specialty knowledge across multiple disciplines. The odds that we were actually here to meet a lone mage seeking aid were getting slimmer by the moment.

Keeping a keen awareness of my distance, I moved closer to the pool. No cups I could see in the chamber, not even up by the door, so we still needed a vessel. There was my flask, but I loathed the idea of throwing away backup blood in our given situation. Plus, it would take at least a dozen flask-worth's to fill that bowl. That was assuming there was any chance we could actually touch the water. It was a hurdle we could put off no longer; one way or another, we had to use that pool.

Every step I took was cautious as I drew closer, ready for the head to burst forth. Nothing happened as I inched along, creeping my way up to the water's edge. There was a small drop between the end of the floor and the pool, perhaps three inches of shorn rock. Seeing it like that, my perspective instantly shifted. This wasn't a small pool at all. There was some sort of massive lake just below our feet, with a hole cut through the stone like its maker had wanted to go ice-fishing.

The surface remained still, despite my being near enough to the water to touch it. There was no helping it now. Hopefully, if things went poorly, Neil had a spell for regrowing vampire arms.

In one movement, I lightly tapped the top of the water and immediately rocketed myself backward with a powerful push of my legs.

It was undoubtedly the right strategy, as even moving that fast, I could see down the slug's throat as the creature shot up, its mouth closing around the air where my limb had been microseconds prior. Flecks of its spit flew onto my sleeve, sizzling the material on contact. I ripped the sleeve off entirely, but not before a few drops ate through and burned my skin. The pain was short-lived—my body healed the damage almost as it came—but now we knew for certain that the slug-of-the-dark-lagoon could hurt us.

"Thing moves fast, considering what it looks like." Neil had watched the entire exchange from a safe distance, a far-off look in his eye as he rubbed his chin. "The moment we dip something in, it'll be on us, and we *have* to dip something unless we want to try brute force.

Given the wards and silver woven into the walls, I expect there are probably traps for those who skip steps. This whole place seems designed to force us to play along."

"Wait, there's silver in the walls?" I gave a tentative sniff and caught nothing. No real surprise; a vampire's nose was good, but whoever built this place had accounted for every detail thus far. They could have easily used the same process the Agency did to mask the scent.

Neil nodded. "Woven carefully throughout. Partially like a circuit, helping direct the magic for this place. Also helps keep parahumans from punching through the walls. That wouldn't work on you, obviously, but the doors are pretty sturdy. Not sure you've got the muscle to force them."

"Likely accurate." There was a barb buried in there, one that I pointedly ignored. We had far larger concerns for the moment than petty personality clashes. "Which means our only real options are fill the bowl, or stay put and wait for rescue."

Turning slowly, Neil spun in place, examining our chamber once more with a critical eye. "I know what I said earlier, but the rescue plan came when I thought we were dealing with a smaller overall area. Considering the size of just this one room, I suspect the whole place might be a lot larger than I initially guessed. The more rooms we clear, the more territory we can search."

There was also the unspoken reason Neil wanted to press on. Seeing this room, stocked with actual danger, he was no doubt worried about how Albert fared elsewhere. We didn't know if he was with the others, or on his own, and while that sword could probably cut through any threat, it only worked if the wielder was willing to draw. Albert was not a man quick to violence, a trait I respected all the more as his power grew, but that could be a hindrance in some fights. Not every enemy would permit Albert to ready himself for proper combat.

"Sounds like we try to get through the door," I surmised. "We just need to find a way to transport the water, and figure out how to get any without getting an up-close tour of a magical slug's digestion track."

"Please, did you see how corrosive that saliva was? We'd dissolve long before we made it to the stomach. That's why the chains are self-repairing; it's all that keeps them intact. There is some good news, though. I found us a vessel."

He clapped me hard on the back. "Seeing as touching the water didn't hurt, we know it's not corrosive. And as you don't have to worry about things like disease or poison…"

I didn't need the full walk; it was clear where this was heading. Worse, try as I might, I couldn't think of a better alternative. We had nothing else on hand to use, and even if we did, any other vessel would take multiple trips to fill the bowl. The fewer times we could deal with the slug, the better our chances of leaving with all limbs still accounted for.

"I take it that means you'll handle the distraction?"

"Already got something in mind." From his back, Neil produced the spell book he'd fastened there. "Amy is a big believer that a mage is defined by their passions, not their specialties, and as such, required me to learn a few spells outside of necromancy. They're not very comparable in terms of scale, but I've still got a couple of tricks I can pull."

Working quickly, we sketched out the bare bones of a plan. Neil would distract our slug while I gathered the water, then I'd rush up to fill the bowl. I *did* say it was bare bones, remember. Keeping it simple was our best shot, anyway; Neil and I lacked the teamwork to coordinate much more complexly.

He moved to the opposite side of the room, book open as words I didn't understand slipped from his mouth. To my surprise, I felt my hair move as a gentle wind flowed past—something that was entirely impossible, since we were in a sealed underground cave. Yet the breeze only grew in strength, whipping at my clothes as it gathered force. I was catching the fallout wind, at that; the true concentration was centered around the chains. Bit by bit, they were moving, swaying in the growing wind. Finally, one gained enough momentum to let out a proper rattle.

In a flash, the slug was on it, mouth gumming around the metal and slowly drifting down its length. The moment I saw it land, I leapt into action, trying very hard not to think about what I was doing. My face plunged into the dark liquid as I opened my mouth and drank for all I was worth. A vampire's stomach, like a human's, could hold a great deal of liquid when fully stretched. The act of expanding my own gut didn't hurt, as vampires were built for liquid gluttony, so I was able to drink far past the point where a human would have cried off. Sadly, amount was not my primary issue. I dared to chug for only a few seconds before physically throwing myself up and back, clear of the pool.

I was roughly two seconds ahead of the slug, which I realize does sound like a close call, but actually felt like a comfortable margin when moving at vampire speeds. It kept groping for me until the siren song of chains rattling pulled it to another, like a fish on a line. When it grew distracted, I dashed back in for another drink.

We kept like that for nearly a full minute, Neil conjuring, me racing in, chugging for all I was worth, darting back, and waiting until it was distracted again. As I neared my stomach's limits, I noticed the wind slowing down. A glance over to Neil showed him sweating from effort; that breeze apparently demanded quite a bit from the caster. Or maybe it was a side effect of casting outside his specialty. I truly didn't grasp how magic worked, which would have bothered me more, except the people who actually studied and used it were often in the same boat.

The writing was on the wall, so I made my last chug a good one, daring to stay for a handful of extra seconds before bolting away. That stunt left me coated in water, as I barely managed to stay ahead of the slug, so close I was caught in its splash. Nevertheless, I was still in one piece as it sank below the water once more, silently waiting for us to return.

Climbing back to the ledge was more difficult with the extra weight throwing off my balance, but with no need to rush, I took my time and eventually made it on the first try. Tottering to my feet, I wobbled up to the bowl and looked down. After several seconds of staring, I finally realized the minor detail that had slipped our minds during the planning process.

"Aw, crud. Hey, Neil, we forgot something. Vampires can't throw up." It was one of our curious, biological shifts that occurred during the change; my best guess was that we were simply meant to be one-track roads for liquids, though there might have been some greater metaphysical meaning in the symptom. None of which changed the problem it presented.

From below, I heard a weary voice rise up. "Are you facing the bowl?"

"I am. What do you—"

Reader, this is where I will take a pause from the play-by-play and simply tell you that, unbeknownst to me, Neil had not forgotten the issue, and in fact had a spell to force an undead to empty its stomach. Useful against a vampire who'd just sucked down potent blood, no doubt, as well as when a bowl needs filling with cave-pool water. The spell was successful, and thanks to some careful aiming, I filled the bowl with a more than adequate amount of water. Curiously, even after a trip in my stomach, it looked the same as it had below: so smooth and still I was half waiting for a smaller slug monster to poke its head out of the bowl and make a bite for me.

The audible noise from the wall confirmed that the way forward was now unlocked. Rather than check it out, I opted to first climb down and get Neil. Whether we liked it or not, we were in this together, and our best shot of making it out was if we worked as a team.

But next time, he was going to have to be the one to chug disgusting slug-water. It was going to take some *very* potent blood to get that taste out of my mouth.

5.

None of it made sense. Secret lair out in the middle of nowhere, sure, that's Magecraft 101. Find somewhere isolated, a place where no one could stumble upon your experiments, be it by accident or intent. Defenses were also an obvious move for a mage looking to protect their intellectual property. The only reason I could get along without a heavily guarded home was the fact that I kept most of the truly powerful stuff in my head—and the obvious politics. Trying to mess with a mage is one thing;

robbing one under Gideon's protection would make a cartel heist seem like a sensible idea.

The lair, I got. Everything else was where it went wrong. Shun hadn't given off any kind of vibes that she was setting us up for something, and after dealing with enough scheming fellow casters, I tended to have a sense for it—to say nothing of the potions I had in use at the time. She read as genuine, which would be more reassuring, except that, with the right spells, it would be possible to falsely convince someone you were telling the absolute truth, at least long enough for a few phone calls. But to what end? Fred seemed like an obvious target, except this was an incredibly roundabout way to get him here. He could have easily elected to send Lillian instead of himself on this excursion, like most bosses would have.

On top of all that, the trap we'd fallen into was ridiculously well-crafted. The room where I, Albert, and Gregor landed was huge, sealed by a large metal door that was manipulated by a complex series of pulleys and switches on the opposite side of the room. There was a puzzle involved, rudimentary as it was, though I was the only one to give the obstacle much attention post-landing. Albert had been methodically walking around, examining all of the floors and walls, while Gregor took a somewhat more... direct approach.

Clang. Clang. Clang.

I tried to block out the noise of strong fists slamming into the door over and over. Were it not enchanted, I daresay Gregor would have cracked through; those blows landed heavy even against the reinforced metal. However, with magic also working against him, it was a vain struggle. Someone had built this chamber to withstand true parahuman power. This wasn't the mortal world, where we were working with cages made to hold humans. Brute force wouldn't see us through.

"Gregor, please stop doing that."

"I will halt once the door is removed, and I have properly resumed my duties."

It was about what I'd expected. The others might not have dealt with gargoyles much, but working with Gideon meant that I'd encountered the Slate-Claw clan a time or two. As a whole, they tended to be literal and—sorry, but sometimes puns are appropriate—stiff in most matters. Gregor was probably the most adaptable gargoyle I'd encountered, which was no doubt why he'd been chosen for the task. They weren't stupid by any means, just direct and stubborn. And *loyal*; by the boiling beakers, were they devoted to Gideon. That meant that while Gregor wouldn't self-direct much, he'd be invaluable if I could find the right uses for him.

"Fine, but if you *do* manage to break it open and trigger all those magical traps, I have a hunch this whole place will come down on our heads. Guess that really only kills me and Neil, though, so keep right on hitting if you must."

While there *were* visible trap-spells woven into the walls and door in case someone tried to skip the puzzle, I doubted the repercussions would be quite that extreme. It would just be a lot easier to evaluate things without the constant clanging.

Halfway through the arc of their swing, Gregor's fists halted, stopping just inches from the metal surface. Slowly, he turned to face me, uncertainty in his eyes. It looked foreign there, an expression he was neither familiar nor happy with. These were not the sorts of challenges he'd been expecting to face as a bodyguard; although, given who he was guarding, perhaps he should have. I'd never been able to figure out how someone as non-confrontational as Fred managed to end up in so many predicaments. It was a curiosity that not even magic fully accounted for.

"From what I can tell, there are no other ways out." Albert ambled over from the last wall he'd been inspecting. The sword clattered on his hip, undrawn, as he walked. Unlike Gregor, Albert hadn't even suggested slicing through the barriers until he fully understood the situation. His training had begun to merge with that sensible head on his shoulders; what they were forming was new, and potentially powerful. "Every part I checked is solid. No breaks, no gaps, no light, no water, no noise.

I think we either go through that door or start building lodging."

Getting out wasn't actually the problem. Our exit was clear: solve the puzzle, and the door would either open or we'd get another surprise. Whichever happened, it was an obvious path forward. The greater dilemma was our situation as a whole. Someone had put a tremendous amount of effort into this place, yet nothing about it was especially tailored to us. Silver and magic in the walls would stop virtually all parahumans, and there were no factors to account for Albert's sword. Nothing vampire-, gargoyle-, or magic-specific, either. Granted, we were only in the first room, but this was also where a target would be most vulnerable: unsteady, not sure of the situation, this would be the place to hide a proper murder attempt. But there was also the slide to consider, and the fact that where we ended up had seemed truly random. It was all based on where we'd been standing when the floor dropped—something that could be timed by an observer, yet not really planned for.

If this was truly a cage, it wasn't one made with us in mind. Perhaps we were a cheap beta-test, seen as easy prey to lure in before the real target was pursued. Or else I was missing something, which, truthfully, seemed like the most obvious answer. Dealing with magic is mostly the art of finding peace with ignorance. To touch it, manipulate it, engage with the fundamental forces of the universe—all took a lifetime of study and effort; to understand it, on the other hand, took the sort of absolute madness only a few had ever dared attempt. Most of us had to simply live with the fact that we wielded a primordial force of creation we would never truly fathom.

After swallowing that pill, admitting that I didn't fully grasp our weird, locked-room situation was a minor concession.

"Sounds like it's the door, then. Just a moment." Given the lack of enough evidence on hand to draw a conclusion, there was only one sensible path forward: to see more of our environment and hopefully gain more data. My hands dug into the bag usually at my side—one far deeper than its shape let on—feeling around for the right bottle. I'd long ago learned that using differently sized and shaped containers let me handle this process by feel, which was much faster. After a few incidents, I also added printed labels as a failsafe, but for the most part, my fingers did the work far faster than my eyes ever had.

A familiar form of glass hit my palm, and I pulled forth the bottle in question. One pop of the top, and down it went. As I drank, my senses expanded. Spells and wards I'd only been able to glimpse previously lit up like Christmas lights in the darkest nights of December. I could taste different nutrients in the air, hear the movements of my friends' bodies, smell the last three meals on my breath, and feel the staleness of the air against my skin.

Useful as it was, I loathed this potion because it was also *disgusting*. Humans are constantly covered in germs, dirt, oils, and other substances that we don't mind because we have the gift of not noticing. In return for such magical clarity, I also had to deal with seeing the constant, nasty truth. That was why I'd mixed a mild sedative into the potion during its original recipe. Made the whole ordeal a lot more bearable, even if my feet did get a little tangled as I made my way over to the system of levers and pulleys.

Behind me, I knew Gregor started forward, and Albert halted him. Just the scuffing of their feet was enough to paint me a perfect mental picture. Looking over the silver panel with my freshly enhanced senses, I saw nothing new of note. There weren't any hidden spells or traps that I'd missed before, but at least now, I could touch the thing without fearing it might steal a finger.

As for the puzzle, it wasn't an especially novel one. Within the panel was a center chamber with a scale. The lever/pulley system would move unmarked weights around, some going directly to the center chamber, while others were on a more circuitous path that would require precise timing. It was clear that I needed to get the center to a specific weight to unlock the door or set off the next trap—whatever would move us forward.

As for solving it… well, not to brag, but in my career, you get pretty good at eyeballing weights for various spells and recipes. Once you add in my exceptional senses, and the fact that I've got a decent brain tucked away, the puzzle really never stood much of a chance. Gregor hadn't even had enough time to lose faith and try to walk over again before a mighty *click* echoed through the entire room, just before the metal doors began to open.

Gregor went right through, not even a moment's glance back. Gargoyles were nothing if not direct, and he had an edict from Gideon to keep Fred safe. I was grateful he'd stopped banging on the door; expecting him to hang back would be asking for a miracle.

"Do you think the others are okay?" Albert was waiting for me, hand on the hilt of his still sheathed sword. Ready to draw, yet not eager. He was shaping up well, indeed.

"Between Fred's risk-aversion and Neil's training, I have faith they would be able to weather any challenges of this level, even if there were dangerous factors in play. I'm sure they're doing well."

Albert nodded in agreement, then looked to the room Gregor had dashed through. "Yeah. I don't like it, though."

"Nor do I. Especially because I still don't fully understand what is happening." Stepping forward, I ignored all the input about the various microbes crawling on and through my skin to put a guiding hand on his shoulder. "Let's go get more information. Once we grasp our situation, we can begin the process of restructuring it."

Albert and I, while friendly, had never spent as much time together as myself and Neil, since the latter was my student. I presume that's why he looked a little nervous at the grin on my face as we pressed forward, deeper into the unknown. Neil, obviously, would have known better.

Neil would have realized that my grin meant he should be a *lot* nervous. I was starting to get interested, and when I got interested, things got fun.

6.

With a thud, the boulder rolled away from the alcove, barreling right past where we would have been standing if Neil hadn't noticed the subtle grooves in the path that betrayed unseen turns in the giant rock's trajectory. This was dangerous room number three so far. After the slug and water had been a complex puzzle surrounded by swinging blades that Neil had easily breezed through, and following that had come the boulder situation. Getting it free was the relatively simple part; figuring out where to stand in the narrow expanse to avoid being flattened, that had been the real test.

As it careened to the bottom and slammed heavily into the door we'd come through, I allowed myself a small measure of relief. This trial, at least, appeared to be over. How many more were yet to come, I had no idea, but it did feel good to be making progress.

Neil started forward, and I darted ahead as I had several times already. He wasn't happy about once more being relegated to the backlines, a sentiment that I could normally appreciate, yet one which made less and less sense with every passing room.

For someone so sensitive about not being a front-line fighter, Neil had proven himself invaluable during our adventure. Not just the magic, either. What really made him so effective were his quick mind and keen eye for detail. No doubt these were necessary traits for anyone working the magical arts, and Arch had sharpened both aspects so fine, it was like he expected them to cut steel.

What was even more ridiculous was that I'd begun to suspect Neil didn't even realize just how competent he'd become. We were coasting through the challenges largely thanks to him, and instead of looking hopeful or encouraged, he only appeared to grow more stressed with each success.

This wasn't the place to try to hammer all that out; such discussions could wait until we were in safer surroundings. Yanking the new door open, I found myself unsurprised to be staring into what would be darkness to normal eyes. For me, it merely appeared to be an empty hallway, and *that* part was actually interesting. We'd gone from room to room with heavy sections of wall separating them, but this was our first transitional area. Maybe it meant we were nearing the end, or that the challenges were going to get harder. Hopefully, no matter what else it conveyed, the hallway was a signal we were heading in the right direction. Not that we had other directions to try, but still, it was a nice touch of reassurance.

"Anything magical I'm missing?" While I might be a fine blockade, I lacked any talents that would let me sniff out enchantments or hidden spells. In the lair of mage, such possibilities were very real concerns, so I was trusting Neil as my mage-eyes, a prospect I'd have found far more worrying at the start of our day.

"Loads, but none of it seems overtly dangerous. Yet. The walls here are crazy reinforced, though; looks like they're warded to reflect back any attack they take. We must be getting close to something. Whoever made this left no chances we'd go exploring off the beaten path."

Taking his position directly behind me, the two of us walked into the dark hallway. Seconds later, as we knew it would, the door slammed shut. That had happened after every room transition so far, and after the first occurrence, it had stopped being such a shock.

Outside the loud noise, nothing bad happened. We just weren't allowed to backtrack, apparently.

"Seeing as we have a few moments of walking, any new theories for what we're up against?" It was partly a sincere question, as well as an attempt to alleviate the oppressive silence of our stone hall. Not even my supernaturally sharp ears were picking up anything aside from us, which made the whole experience more claustrophobic than I'd been expecting. It also reminded me of just how many tons of rock we'd be buried under if any of this came crashing down.

There was some initial grumbling from Neil, but eventually, real words followed. "Nothing I can put a definitive finger on. Every time I think I find an angle, it doesn't make sense. This could be a prison, but then, why let us move around at all? Maybe it's a trap, except the challenges aren't really all *that* hard; we're more at risk of injury than death. That goes double if *you're* the target; these haven't exactly been geared toward killing vampires. Or mages, for that matter. The design appears to account for parahumans as a general entity, which leads back to the prison idea, and 'round we go again. There's more going on here, and we aren't going to know what until we get additional information."

"But if you had to make a guess..." I kept pushing, both because I could tell that Neil actually did have something in mind, and because it beat the continued silence.

"If I were to make an unsupported hypothesis based on conjecture and intuition... it's a test. The whole thing is built to seem like a series of trials, so let's take that at face value. It's some sort of examination. Now who it was intended for, or what the purpose could be, I have genuinely no idea."

Since he seemed content to let the conversation drop there, I picked it up to keep the words flowing. The longer we were in the hall, the harsher the silence grew. "We can make a few guesses, if nothing else. Amy's the most likely, as she was the one specifically requested to come here."

"Except anyone trying to test Amy would know to prepare much harder trials. She'd have breezed through all of these already."

It was sometimes hard to say how much of Neil's devotion came from his not so well-hidden feelings for his teacher versus admiration of her skill, but on this point, he and I were in agreement. Much as Amy liked to hide in the middle of the pack and go unnoticed, I'd been privy to her true efforts and intellect a time or two. Amy had broken a trap powerful enough to hold Gideon. None of these would be a real challenge for her.

"Too true. Amy is our connection, and she doesn't fit. So we expand outward. Who would Amy definitely have with her, in this situation? Those are the next most likely targets."

"You and me," Neil replied. "Given the situation she was presented, her accountant would have had to come along, and it would make a fine teaching opportunity for her student. Possibly Bubba, too, if someone was playing the odds. Those two spend a lot of their free time together; he occasionally tags along on minor mage business, but that one might be a stretch."

Nothing about what we'd seen felt therian-directed any more than it had been designed for a vampire, which didn't tell us much. Neil was right; Bubba was something of a stretch, even if he and Amy were close friends. But that notion got my brain itching as I considered things from a new angle. The only three who would almost certainly be here were me, Amy, and Neil. Except that Neil wasn't really an individual entity anymore.

"This might be crazy, but I wonder if the target was Albert."

I felt Neil jerk to a halt behind me, body stiffening, so I hurried through my theory before he could cut me off. "We just said you'd definitely be here, and who goes virtually everywhere that you do? Albert's your partner for training, adventure, whatever it is that Arch has you both doing; it makes sense to expect that inviting you would also bring him."

This, to me, seemed a theory like everything else we'd been bandying about: interesting, and worthy of consideration, if not necessarily definitively true. We were brainstorming, grasping for ideas, seeing what stuck against the wall. Evidently, to Neil, it sounded a great deal more plausible.

"Shit. We have to hurry. Albert could be in danger." The words were more or less expected. What followed, however, was not. Neil forced his way past me, moving so fast I didn't even think to stop him, attempting to barrel forward into the hallway on his own. While I still felt more or less composed, Neil was visibly rattled. Sweating, eyes bulging, he appeared on the verge of a heart attack.

Despite the impressive breakaway, I was at his side again in seconds. Of all my vampire gifts, the enhanced speed is absolutely the one that has paid off the most, both in the office and the field. It made me a world class champion at running away, as well as helped me plow through some of my more tedious tasks.

"Whoa, calm down. It was just a thought. Why would anyone want to hurt Albert, anyway?"

"Albert wields one of the most powerful weapons known in our world. If someone thinks they can take it, they'll try—doesn't matter if it works. Worse, it could be someone Albert might eventually be set against, some bastard snuffing out a potential threat before Albert can come calling."

The leaps in logic we'd already been forced to take were turning into wild bounds. I was starting to get worried; this was a rapid slide into panic for Neil, especially given how much he'd already seen. This shouldn't be rattling him so much.

Reaching out, I took him by the shoulder, forcing him to a halt. "Neil, pause for a moment. Something is off, can't you feel that?"

With a whip-like strike of his thin arm, he smacked at my hand. "All I feel is you, slowing me down. By the dark moon, Fred, isn't it enough that you hold everyone back in your personal life? Must you stop me from saving my friend, too?"

I almost let go at that, so shocked was I by the vitriol in his voice. Neil and I had never had the same sort of friendship as I had with the others, but we certainly didn't hate one another. He was a member of my clan, and therefore, my family. When my grip didn't loosen, the torrent continued.

"You don't even see it, do you? Krystal would have moved on to bigger, better assignments if she weren't tied to one town. Bubba could be climbing the ranks of a therian hierarchy, except he has this pesky friendship with a vampire holding him back. Richard constantly has to defend his alliance to your house, Amy wastes most of her time pissing around instead of wielding her genius, Lillian once held a real position and is now strapped to a clan that's doomed to fail. The only one you almost set free was Albert, yet even now, you persist in maintaining that hollow friendship to keep him close. Now, let me go, before I remind you that one of us has magical power over the other."

It was the silence that tipped me off. For all the power in this place, nothing so far had neutered my hearing like this. Cutting off the natural noises of the world, the shifting of rock and skittering of bugs—that was nearly impossible from what I'd seen, and I'd dealt with a few mages of potent power. As Neil ranted and I looked over our surroundings, hunting for a solution, I paid special attention to the walls, floor, and ceiling. All the same materials as before, which Neil had described as extremely well-warded.

Well-warded, and *reflective*. That was why I couldn't hear anything. We were in a magical echo chamber: everything reflected back at us in perfect time, hiding the actual noise. The sound wasn't the only thing that was getting turned around on us, I realized.

"Neil, you're a fine young man. When we first met, I admit, I had a poor impression of you. Being chained in silver and threatened will do that. But I've been remiss in letting that image color my perception of the person you've become."

"What are you talking about?" Neil was confused, which was a start. He also seemed slightly less on edge, and I dearly hoped that was a sign my theory was right.

"I'm telling you some sincere truths, because I think this hallway reflects and amplifies everything we put out. Being undead, I don't feel it as much, but you started to grow worried the more we talked about fearful things, even in passing. Since I don't think calming you down with normal methods will work, I'm hoping calm honesty gets you back to being centered, which is why I'm telling you that you've made tremendous growth these past few years. And while I've never said it, which is a failing on my part, I'm glad to have you in the House of Fred. No, scratch that, I'm *proud* to have you in my clan."

His face contorted, red and still sweating, as he turned quickly away from me. For an instant, I thought he was going to cast, which could prove to be serious trouble, given that he was a necromancer and I a vampire. Thankfully, when the words came, they were just that— words, rather than arcane utterings.

"It is... possible that when I look at you, I see that night. My youth, my blind ambition, my stupid ego. Some of my disdain for you could, maybe, be my own shame for who I was."

With every word, his body seemed to come further back under his control, until he finally faced me once more. He was by no means fully restored, but the wild look on his face was tamed for the moment. "And I'm sorry about what I said, about you holding people back. I don't even know where that came from. I just suddenly felt so furious."

"Anger always builds upon itself past the point of reason. I think, in here, it just happens far more quickly. But now that we know the trick, let's focus on putting out positive feelings to echo back. Starting with me saying that I forgive you. For the words, for that night, for whatever guilt still clings to you. I can't make everything right, but you and I are square, Neil."

I extended my hand, which Neil soon accepted and shook. "Thank you, Fred. I think I needed to hear that, somewhere deep down." We held like that for only a moment before Neil continued. "When you're ready, want to very calmly keep going down the hall?"

"I think that sounds like an excellent idea. Well, the best idea we can manage given our circumstances, anyway."

Seeing as we had an honesty vibe going, I saw no reason to mess things up.

7.

WE DIDN'T HAVE A LOT MORE HALLWAY TO clear; part of me still suspects it would have stretched on until we realized the test. Upon reaching the unlocked door, we stepped through into what was immediately evident as the final chamber. There could be nothing else we were looking at.

The entrance let us out in a small alcove at the top of a winding slope. Our position gave us an excellent view of the tremendous cavern that seemed to stretch for over a mile. Along the walls, I saw more alcoves like our own, elevated entrances that I presumed came from other chambers. They were spread out, encircling the rest of the cavern and the enormous maze at its center.

Stone walls rose from the floor, each one at least ten feet tall, twisting and winding round on themselves after only a few steps, creating a gnarled knot of paths that I couldn't untangle even with a partial view. Some sections were obscured by large stone pillars thrusting up at seemingly random intervals from the ground. From up here, it looked quiet and deserted, but I knew that once we drew close, the dangers would reveal themselves. Unfortunately, I also knew that if we wanted to find our friends and make it out of here, that was clearly the only direction to go.

"Seems like it's all been leading to the center of the maze." Neil was wiping his brow on his sleeves, mopping up the last of his momentary panic sweat now that he was free from the hallway's influence. "We just..." As Neil's voice trailed off, his face lit up, relief and joy bursting through his normally sour veneer. "He's here! Albert is probably in the cavern already. I can sense him."

That was a mighty relief, if not much of a shock. I'd more or less expected the others to arrive first once it became clear we were largely dealing with puzzles. Neil had been an invaluable resource in making it through the rooms, but he was still Amy's student. She'd likely cut a much quicker pace through their various challenges than her pupil had.

"Then we shouldn't keep our friends waiting. Before we head down, though, do you see any traps or spells we should be aware of?"

Despite his visible desire to go tearing down the slope, Neil controlled himself, carefully examining the room from every angle our alcove allowed. Only after a full minute and a couple of minor castings did he shake his head. "Nothing I can see. Obviously, things will get crazy once we're down there, but I think exactly how that shakes out is going to be a surprise."

"I'll take the front, you back me up?"

"Might as well. Seems to be working out so far." Perhaps it was relief at knowing Albert was near, or a good mood filling the place of his artificial anger, but Neil flashed me a genuine smile at that. If I didn't know better, I'd have thought he was enjoying himself.

For that matter, perhaps I was too, a tad. With only a nebulous potential threat to worry about and largely non life-endangering stakes, the whole ordeal had been almost fun. It tickled something in my brain. However, before I could fully chase the wild thought down, Neil slapped me on the back, heading toward the slope.

"Let's get down there. No telling if they'll need help."

"Or vice versa." He was right, though. Flights of fancy could wait; finding our friends was the top priority. With more grace than my living body could have managed, and far less than someone like Arch or Krystal would have displayed, I careened down the steep slope, breaking into a run after the first few feet by gravity alone. I could, in theory, rescale this slope if needed, but that would grant me little more than access to an alcove with a now locked door. Everything about this place pushed us forward, driving anyone trapped to the same point.

It was hard not to wonder what we'd find at the center of that maze, especially as my vantage point lowered and I lost my peek ahead to the twisting labyrinth awaiting us. The tradeoff was that I got new details as I drew closer, starting with the arcane runes running up and down every wall in the maze. These were physically present, etched into the stone itself and visible to the mundane eye; I could only imagine what sorts of magical effects Neil could make out. I'd sipped from a mage once during a murder investigation, and it had been curious, seeing magic woven and integrated into our seemingly mundane world. While I didn't miss the distracting displays of sudden color, part of me couldn't help wondering what the show was like.

That is, until the moment I heard Neil mutter from behind me, "Cauldron cocks. This is... whoa." He grabbed me by the sweater vest, yanking me to a halt as our momentum petered out on flat ground. "Fred, that thing is serious."

"By 'thing,' you mean the maze, right? Not trying to be difficult, just making sure there's not some magical monster I can't see."

Neil shook his head, too stunned to even be flippant. "The maze. The walls—the spells, specifically. Everything we've encountered so far has been at a certain magical threshold. Despite the array of what we've seen, there hasn't been anything truly exceptional. With enough time, energy, and materials, Amy or I could have eventually constructed something like this. Well, mine would be worse, hers would be better. The point is that this has all been very doable." He pointed up to the towering walls and the single entrance we could make out near us, though I knew from our prior view that others dotted the maze's exterior.

"*That* is something else entirely. The magics I'm seeing are old, and I mean *ancient*. They go further back than I'm capable of measuring, and as for what they do, I'd barely make a better guess than you. I've never seen spellcraft quite like it."

"Which means we have no idea what happens when we go in," I surmised.

"Except that it has the potential to be on an entirely different level than anything we've encountered so far,"

Neil added. "I'd like to officially update my theory, as well. I think whoever brought us here found this maze, and then built everything else around it. Still no idea on why, and I suspect we're not far from either dying or finding out."

Under different circumstances, it might have been worth stopping to evaluate our other options. While we were stuck underground, Neil had spent the whole day proving just how competent he was. Between a necromancer and a vampire, it wasn't impossible that we might hit on a way to escape. But the simple fact remained that our friends were here, which meant we weren't going anywhere. Terrifying as the unknown was, I'd had to face down far more frightening foes than a bunch of enchanted walls.

"As things happen, keep me in the loop," I said. "If you scream an order, I'm just going to trust you."

"Good call. I was going to offer you some blood so you can see, too, but now I'm wondering if that might be a little... distracting." He paused for a moment, swallowing once. "I think you're better off not seeing what I do."

From Neil, that was more than enough of a warning, even if I'd been tempted by the offer initially. We fell into silence as we crept forward. The looming entrance to the maze waited like a patient mouth, content to let the food wander into chomping range. I hesitated for a moment at the threshold, waiting for Neil to offer some sort of warning. When none came, we pushed on, stepping into the maze proper.

No sooner had Neil cleared the threshold than the flames appeared. Blazing a brilliant white so bright it hurt to look upon, they filled the doorway we'd just stepped through, heat tangible even from several feet away. It wasn't a slamming door, yet it sent the same message quite effectively. There was no turning around: it was forward, or nothing.

"What the... How..." While I'd been staring at the flames, Neil was looking anywhere but. His gaze flittered about, from wall to floor to wall, until he was practically spinning in place. "This is crazy."

"Something I should know about?"

"Yes, but not how you're imagining it. Remember all that magic I was telling you about before?" Neil had stopped spinning, though his face looked a tad queasy. "Gone. All of it. The moment that fire kicked on, I lost everything but my dark-sight. Except all that magic *can't* actually be gone, especially since we see it active with the flames. This place has the kind of wards capable of cutting off even the basic capacity to see magic. I realize none of this is your specialty, so trust me when I say that is *insane*. That's the sort of magic you'd only expect to see from someone on par with a dragon like Gideon."

Setting aside the notion of Gideon being a magical standard of measurement rather than an implied ceiling (because I did *not* have the mental energy to stop willfully ignoring that concept), I tried to pare Neil's statement down to the most immediately relevant pieces. He couldn't see any of the magic at work around us, which meant we were open to ambush and surprise. Worse, the mere fact that the maze had this kind of ability meant that its creator had been crazy powerful. We might be up against very dangerous threats, things far outside our capabilities to deal with. The only silver lining was that the obvious solution already fit with our existing goals.

"We have to find the others. Strength in numbers might be the only advantage we have left. Neil, you said you could sense Albert before. Is that at least still working?"

To my immense relief, he slowly nodded. "Albert and I are bound by the magic that animated him, and the connection was reinforced by all the spells that followed. Limiting a mage's vision is one thing—that's just about manipulating what's visible in the magical spectrum. Severing my connection to a spell is something far more complex and couldn't be done with a generic area enchantment. But it's also not exactly a homing spell, more just a vague intuition."

From his pocket, Neil produced a compass, around which was bound a strand of black hair.

"What are you doing?"

That earned me a look almost—but not quite—on par with the usual Neil glare. "Casting an actual homing spell to find Albert. You've got the right idea, only we need something more efficient. This wasn't useful when we were stuck in our rooms, but now, we're finally in the same place again." Neil waved his hand over the compass, muttering phrases that held no shape or meaning in my ears. The dark hair, one I now recognized as Albert's, lit up and turned to ash in less than a second. When it was gone, the compass arrow suddenly whipped around, pointing toward what it identified as the east.

"Spells still appear to work, so that's something. We can make our way toward the others. When, or if, our paths will join is anyone's guess. Let's take our time and be thorough."

The roar that echoed forth through the cavern was distant, though exactly how far off was impossible to gauge with the way that sound kept bouncing about. What did become instantly clear was that we were not alone, and that our company sounded to be sizable.

"Didn't want to say anything to jinx it, but part of me was wondering if someone went to all the trouble of making a labyrinth and forgot to put in a minotaur." Neil grinned sheepishly, poorly hiding the prudent fear in his eyes. It didn't escape my notice that he produced the knife from the room where we'd landed and had it now gripped tight in his free hand.

I started forward again, cutting a quicker pace this time. "Perhaps we'll focus on speed and thoroughness, for so long as we can manage."

8.

IT BECAME QUICKLY APPARENT THAT OUR greatest asset in the maze would not be Neil's magical compass, nor even my vampire abilities. No, for once, it was our learning skills that were given a chance to shine, as memorization rapidly became the name of the game. There was no figuring out the maze. It was too convoluted to start with, and with magic factoring in to change the natural way some paths wound through the space, trial and error revealed itself as our only tactic for making progress.

"The right leads to a dead end, the left leads here. Time to try center." Neil opened his eyes, dispelling whatever mental map he'd been etching. Trial and error were only as good as one's capacity to learn from them, which was why memory had immediately become vital. Between the unsettling stillness of the maze and the occasional roars bursting forth from seemingly nowhere, we could feel every passing second. Making the same mistake twice would cost time we didn't have to spend.

As we walked, I kept an eye on our overall surroundings, scanning the stone to catch every detail. For the most part, it was uniform to a confusing degree. The only real variance I could find was the arcane etchings, but much like trying to memorize gibberish, they were too unnatural to sit in my brain properly. Occasionally, I would spot some bit of variance: an old buckle, a scrap of leather—at one junction, I even found a torch that had burned out. How long ago it had been left there, and by whom, I had no idea. I felt like a movie archaeologist; if not for the crushing sense of constant danger, I might have even described the process as fun.

"Hang on, this is a new section." Neil brought us to a halt, closing his eyes once more as I examined the juncture. This one was a simple T-frame. We'd been coming up along one path, and now we had to decide whether to take a turn, or press forward. "Barring any magical warping, I think the turn leads back to that section with the half-dozen routes branching out. Let's stay moving forward for now, but we'll circle back if this path dead-ends on us."

"You've got a real knack for that," I noted. With things going well between us for a change, positive reinforcement felt appropriate. Besides, it sincerely was impressive. "I'm no slouch at keeping track of details, and I never could manage to hold so many routes in my mind."

Neil shrugged, but also smiled slightly. "Amy started my education by making me work on visualization. She said the best lab is your mind: do your initial creating there, where it's safe, and only bring it into reality when you've constructed something stable. Also comes up a lot in more complex spellwork, so it's a good foundation to lay. Compared to casting multiple spells at the same time, this isn't all that tough."

I tried not to look as surprised as I felt. It was hardly appropriate given the competence Neil had been displaying. "Didn't even realize that sort of thing was possible."

"Me either, at first. It's part of what makes experienced mages more dangerous. You might get off one spell while they're attacking, defending, enchanting, and summoning all in the same amount of time. I can kind of do two, if neither is especially complex. Amy sometimes goes up to three at once for potion-making, but I suspect she can do more."

My hunch aligned with Neil's. Whatever Amy showed herself capable of, it was a fair bet that it would ultimately prove to be little more than the tip of the iceberg. It also made me wonder about some of the other casters I'd encountered. How many spells could the Clover siblings manage, with their focus on enchantment, versus Cyndi, the archmage who'd helped teach Amy? It was a pointless distraction that helped fill my mind with something other than hypothetical images of what might be waiting for us around the next corner.

That didn't prove to be a long wait to find out, as we soon came to a turn which put us in a larger, open area with multiple paths branching off. It wouldn't have been a point in the journey worth mentioning, save for the fact that this spot appeared markedly different from those we'd encountered so far.

A blade that looked like it was made for someone of Richard's size had been cut clean in half and was lying on the floor amidst cracked stone and smears of what appeared to be old rust. My vampire nose knew better, however. It might be too ancient to put out a scent, but a scratch along the surface of the substance kicked up enough particles to confirm what I already suspected.

Horrifically, I was becoming quite adept at recognizing blood in its various states.

While I checked the stain, Neil examined the walls, running his hands along the cold surface. "Oh… wow. Fred, what do you think the weirdest thing I could tell you I just discovered is?"

"This whole thing is an elaborate ruse constructed by Gideon for his own amusement?"

"Better guess than I expected, but no." His hands refused to leave the stone, slowly inching along. "So, so much weirder. There was obviously a fight here, who knows how long ago. I thought it was weird that something was strong enough to break the floor so easily, yet the walls are left untouched. Except they're not untouched at all. They're scarred. Come here."

Taking my hand, Neil pulled it to the nearest wall, setting my palms against the arcane etchings. "Get a feel for it," he instructed. "While there's no real pattern, you should get a sense of the general texture. Now, check this out."

Moving my hand along the wall, Neil said nothing more. Then, I felt it: a line, moving through the etchings, a break of order in their sea of meaningless chaos. No longer in need of guidance, I moved my own arm, tracing the anomaly. Lighter near the start and finish, most noticeable in the center, the impression perfectly matched what would be left by a bladed weapon swinging in an arc.

"Bizarre. What does it tell us?"

"Potentially, a lot of things. At the very least, that this maze heals itself, which means there's really no way to know how long it's been standing here. On the higher end... it's possible we have another Charlotte situation, though I'd have expected some display of sentience by now if that were the case, so call that one a long shot."

The roar that split the silence was unlike any that had come before. Those were too distorted to track, which was a blessing I only recognized once it was gone. Being closer meant that we could tell the noise was nearby, which meant the sound's source was, as well.

"I guess the other thing you could take away from this scene is that there's something in here strong enough to break swords and scar stone," Neil added, his tone barely above a whisper.

"Oddly, that isn't the part that scares me. I'm more worried by the fact that it's gotten closer. If that's not a coincidence, then it means that thing can track us."

It wasn't a roar that reached my ears this time, rather the noise of something big and heavy thudding along the stone. I had no idea if my hearing was at its normal levels; between Neil losing his magic sense and the lack of anything but roars, there hadn't been a chance to test it. In a general sense, it didn't especially matter, but in a specific sense, it was the difference between a few minutes of forewarning and a few seconds.

No reaction from Neil meant I wasn't working in the human spectrum, or he was very much distracted. Since the lumbering was moving toward us, though, my response was the same either way.

"Neil, I think I'm going to have to carry you. Minotaur or something else, this creature is big, and can presumably cover a lot of ground. We need undead speed."

I was braced for all manner of pushback on the concept, yet none came. It could have been our improving dynamic, or the fact that death was a real concern, but he nodded grimly rather than dismiss the notion out of hand.

"Let's do a piggyback instead. I'll be a second set of eyes, using the compass to steer us."

That was the extent of the discussion, as the sounds of movement were getting near enough for Neil to make them out, as well. The effort took a moment of coordination, but soon we had him clinging to my back while I carefully locked his legs in with my arms. It was unwieldy, and as a human, I'd have gone toppling over immediately. Poor a vampire as I might be, lifting a young mage was still within my realm of capability. Neil picked a direction, and I took off, moving as fast I could without making a racket.

Unfortunately, no sooner had we started to gain speed than the noise behind us picked up in volume.

Our pursuer was getting louder, no longer showing even a cursory concern for the concept of stealth, if it had ever had one in the first place. My guess about it tracking us also appeared correct: the ruckus was definitely following us.

In a pure sprint, I felt I'd have had a relatively easy time. It's hard to beat a vampire in a footrace, as our enhanced speed and lack of need for rest or air make for a potent combination. The trouble was that, running or not, we were still navigating a maze. Dead-ends popped up, forcing backtracks, to say nothing of the paths that led us in perfect loops, burning up our precious lead.

It was one of those loops that proved to be our folly. A particularly circuitous one burned several full minutes, sending us on a pointless circle. As I returned to the juncture where we'd gone off path, I smelled something new. That settled it: whatever was affecting Neil had definitely tamped down my own senses, as well. There was no way I could have missed a stink like that otherwise. It was the equivalent of a thousand years of musk combined with wet dog. I barely made it to the turn before the creature stepped into view.

Neil had been correct in his guess: this was certainly a minotaur, more or less as I'd imagined them from myth. Huge, hulking, with giant horns and an axe that looked like it could cleave through fully grown oaks, he stamped a meaty leg ending in a hoof down one time only, and then charged.

There was no question or inner debate. I immediately knew what my course of action had to be. Run, obviously. For a fleeting moment, I was tempted to do the same loop I'd just finished. If the minotaur pursued, then I could sprint at top-speed to widen the gap. Except I had to assume the minotaur actually knew this maze and would realize that if I did take that loop, this room would be the only place I could return to. Better the unknown than certain doom, so I pointed myself down the route we hadn't taken and pumped my legs.

Two quick forks in rapid succession had me making snap decisions. Pressure on my side from Neil's leg was his input as I veered right, then left, dearly hoping we were nearing either an exit or our friends. This was one of the times I actually wouldn't have minded having a bodyguard nearby. Sadly, I didn't suddenly run into the rest of our team.

What I did encounter, however, was a long, straight run of stone hallway. No turns, no ways off. I could already hear the minotaur gaining; the forks weren't slowing it by even a moment. It was definitely tracking us, which meant that it would be here any moment.

It seemed I was going to test direct vampire speed against a minotaur, after all.

9.

WERE I IN A LESS FRANTIC STATE OF MIND, I might have mulled over the humor of an undead man dropping into a dead sprint, but the giant axe-wielding monster giving chase kept mirth to a minimum. Instead, everything I had went into running, all my vampire strength that went unused the majority of the time finally having a proper outlet. My feet were a blur as I tore ahead, bounding toward the end of the hall, where I could put some turns between us.

Except... the end of the hall didn't seem to be drawing close as fast as it should, and I could hear the minotaur gaining. I'd thought myself largely free of ego, yet seeing my skill at fleeing fail did feel a tad deflating—that was, until my eyes darted low and I noticed the way the floor was shifting. Every time I laid a foot down, the stones shot backward, robbing me of the vast majority of my progress. It was the equivalent of trying to run up an escalator, or backwards down one of those moving walkways at an airport. Doable, especially with my speed; however, it did slow the effort down substantially.

Worrying as that was, my larger fear was whether this was an existing trap we'd been herded toward, or one the minotaur had somehow caused to happen. The first notion was worrying; the second meant we were as good as chopped. Seeing as I had no insight, whatever the truth might be didn't change my options in the moment. Fighting that thing was a no-go from the start. In these narrow quarters, it would rob me of even my ability to dodge or run. This had started as a contest of speed, and it was going to be resolved as one.

Setting my jaw, I ran harder, though I didn't have a lot left to give. The giant minotaur hadn't exactly put me in a state of mind to hold back. Yet, to my surprise, my progress suddenly increased by a noticeable margin. And, now that I was paying attention, there was something else to notice: the sound of Neil's voice whispering arcane gibberish. I didn't mind it one bit. He was resting a hand on the back of my neck, and with every passing syllable, I felt my body growing stronger. It wasn't comparable to the time I'd had a drop of Gideon's dragon blood, but this was the closest I'd come since that time.

The efforts of the floor to drive me back were no longer adequate. I was making real progress again, which was good, because the minotaur was definitely gaining, the floor offering it no resistance in the least. I chanced a single look back to see it thundering along, the teeth in its vast snout smashing against each other like it was trying to take bites of us even from that far away.

If I'd needed more motivation, that certainly did the trick. In truth, I think it was less my terror and more Neil's spell that moved us forward. Great as the mind might be for some challenges, there were times when magic was called for, and in those moments, a necromancer shined brightest with undead at hand. Granted, his normal partner might have actually been able to fight our attacker, but the mark of good support was that it made everyone's strengths all the more powerful, while also shoring up against their weak spots. My talent just happened to be running away.

Unfortunately, it was turning out that our minotaur was no slouch at the sprint, either. I'd have expected it to tire or slow eventually, yet it refused to lose so much as a step. Maybe it was more magic of the maze, or maybe I'd deeply underestimated its cardiovascular system. Regardless, the end result was that, as the end of the hallway finally drew close, I could almost feel the minotaur's breath. I actually *could* feel the wind from a swing of its axe, which mustered an extra burst of terror-speed I hadn't even known was in me.

Gripping Neil for all I was worth, I lowered my head, ignored everything else about the world, and gave every last bit of effort I had to my legs. Nothing else existed or mattered: only the steady rhythm of my feet slamming against the traitorous ground. At the last minute, I caught the flick of metal catching the light. Neil had thrown his knife into the ground, just between sections of sliding tiles, offering me a stable point to push off from. Stepping lightly to put as little weight as possible on the metal implement, I finally found an instant of solid footing and pressed off it with maximum force.

I was so lost in the act of running that I actually missed the point where we cleared the hallway. That proved troublesome, as the moment I was on normal ground that didn't push back against me, my rate of advancement took a tremendous leap upward before I'd registered the change. Neil was smart enough to hop off my back before I careened headfirst into a wall, so at least I was the only one momentarily hindered. The knock on my skull had the walls spinning and my brain a bit cloudy, even as I struggled to my feet. Which is why I was just as able to be surprised by what came next as the minotaur.

"Now."

That wasn't Neil's voice, and it certainly wasn't mine, so unless the minotaur had learned to do a flawless Amy impression, there could only be one source of the order. Turning around carefully, I found myself looking at Albert and Gregor as they dumped a pair of Amy's potions onto the ground, right where the hallway let out. Amy stood nearby, streaks of light, like falling stars, running along the surface of her skin, watching with a careful eye. At the last moment, she spit out a single word, and the mixed potions on the ground exploded into a cloud of smoke.

Her timing was perfect, as seconds later, the minotaur barreled directly into what I'd taken for a distraction. Except our pursuer wasn't getting lost in the smoke, it was getting... tangled? The cloud was glomming onto the minotaur's massive body, solidifying wherever it made contact. My closest equivalent would be to compare it to watching spray-foam insulation harden, though even that woefully fails to describe the terror of a creature realizing that the very air had turned against it.

Strong as the minotaur was, it only got three steps past the hallway before it collapsed to the ground, completely entrapped by Amy's alchemy.

"See? Smarter, not harder." Her smug expression was pointed at Gregor, who I could only imagine hadn't been too keen on a plan that required waiting around and trusting us to arrive. But then, he didn't know what Amy's apprentice could do, so it was hard to blame him for being worried.

Albert and Neil had embraced one another in a quick, strong hug, and then immediately fallen into hushed discussion, most likely comparing notes and deciding how to proceed. While they caught up, I shook the last of my mental fog away and examined our new surroundings.

Unless this was some sort of false victory, it seemed like we'd made it to the center of the maze. One clue was that all the exits from this circular area were identical to the one we'd come down: long hallways that I had a hunch were enchanted to keep folks out in the same manner as mine had been, or perhaps each with their own challenge. The other major hint that we'd reached our destination was the elaborate stone jutting up in the exact center of the room.

It resembled a much sloppier, smaller, and darker version of the Washington Monument, a five-foot-tall obelisk with strange lines and notches etched all over it.

Leaning in close, I noticed that some of the parts had visible give, and that all the decoration formed some sort of pattern. One last puzzle, then, if we were lucky. Find the pattern, move the bits around until it worked, and go from there. My main problem was that the more I looked at the obelisk, the less I could see any breaks in the pattern to even solve. I wasn't just failing to see a solution; I couldn't even find the problem.

Mercifully, I eventually hit upon the obvious explanation after a few moments of intense study.

"Hey, Amy, did you already solve this while you were waiting on us?"

"All but the last switch. Didn't want to risk getting yanked out of here without you." Amy barely paid the question any mind; she was examining the pinned minotaur, which had gone silent since tumbling down. The most it would do was glare, most often at me, a fact I neither understood nor was particularly comfortable with. "There's also a keyhole on the other side. I guess this place has different ways to clear it."

I was thankful Neil was occupied with Albert and unable to claim his rightful "I told you so" about my item selection. It might have been useful in other contexts, just not with someone like our alchemist to handle tests of intellect.

While Amy worked to satisfy her curiosity and the two friends caught up, I made my way over to check on Gregor. "How did you hold up?"

It probably was significant that I saw the annoyance fight to rise on Gregor's face, given how stalwart he was by default. "That woman is as chaotic as she is effective."

In my bones, I had no idea if that was meant as a compliment or an insult. Not that it mattered: Gregor might have just more accurately encapsulated Amy Wells than anyone else had previously managed. "I think she may put that on a crest or a shirt, if you tell her. But things went okay? No major problems?"

Another strange look before he shook his head slowly. "Only that I failed in my duties and was separated from my charge."

Part of me had been braced for that sort of reaction, so I had a rebuttal locked and loaded. "Look, when it comes to parahumans, nobody sees every trap coming. Even Gideon has to go rescue Sally sometimes. What matters isn't that we got split up, it's that you stayed safe, kept calm, and made it back. I'll never ask you to be so good you don't make mistakes; all I request is that you try to learn from them."

More staring, some that might have led to eventual words if Amy hadn't chosen that exact moment to stand up and clap the minotaur fur from her hands. "Okay, everyone, if we're all feeling nice and ready, I should probably solve that last puzzle. In about thirty seconds, the binding foam will start to dissolve, so we'd best be gone by then."

A loud *crack* came from the dark foam near the minotaur's hooves as the first section began to break.

"Or maybe twenty seconds; never held something that strong before." With a casual ease that somehow made my own anxiety worse, Amy strolled over to the obelisk, motioning for us all to gather close. Whatever this triggered, we didn't want to be split up again. Behind us, more cracking sounds arose from the struggling minotaur.

Bending down, Amy ran her hands delicately along the stone, fingers dancing from notch to notch. "Where was that little turd... no, no, no... ah, here we go."

A thunderous cacophony rose from behind us, the foam fully breaking apart as the minotaur rose steadily to its feet. As it reached for its axe, Amy took a socketed chunk of stone and wiggled it forward, completing the last anomaly in the winding pattern. For a fleeting moment, there was nothing, and I feared she'd made a mistake.

Then, as we all *really* should have expected, the floor fell away. Again. Only this time, we weren't split up. The entire area around the obelisk popped down, forming half a sphere that sent us all to a single hole in the center. The obelisk stood above us, floating magically in place, tethered to nothing. I wondered if this was what it felt like to be flushed as I flew into the dark opening, falling through darkness for several seconds before coming to a surprisingly soft landing.

I was seated on a couch, along with the rest of my friends, in what appeared to be a slightly less-than-contemporary living room. In front of us was a coffee table with various refreshments of the mundane variety: chips, beer, soda, and cookies, but no blood or anything of the like. Overhead was a large, wrinkled banner, bearing the single word: "Congratulations!"

Confusing as it was, I forgot all about the room as soon as I heard a new, unfamiliar voice pipe up behind us.

"Looks like somebody made it through my maze."

10.

MY EYES WENT WIDE, ALBERT LAID A HAND on his sword, and Gregor started to rise from the couch, shoved back down by the dainty, yet forceful hand of Amy Wells.

"Everyone, I'd like to introduce you to Shun. Shun, you might want to speak quickly. While I realized what you were doing, the rest of the group still thinks they were being attacked."

A new form stepped into view, a woman not too far from Neil's age. Her black hair was a wild mess, the sort that hadn't even seen a comb in years, and she wore robes that were simple and well-used. The most noticeable facet of her was her smile, which was small but warm as she excitedly examined our faces.

"Attacked? They think I'd try to kill a vampire and a gargoyle with puzzles and slugs?" Shun shook her head, laughing slightly off-harmony. "That was my pitch! I've been working on it for years. Humans have these escape rooms that are all the rage, but to most of us, they aren't scary or challenging. I want to make attractions catered to parahumans, and this is my proof of concept."

With that, it clicked. I'd even thought to myself several times that if our lives hadn't been in peril, the whole experience might have been fun. Now, it made sense: I'd been on a roller coaster without knowing there were security measures in place.

"Hang on, you built all of this *alone*?" Neil looked skeptical, if not outright incredulous. "In just a few years? Even if you have the skill to weave all those spells, there's no way you could do that; the construction, the hollowing out of sections of pure rock, and everything else required to create something like this is too much work. Especially that maze section."

Shun's smile dimmed a touch, a sheepish look darting across her face. "Sorry, I phrased that poorly. I didn't make the center of the attraction. I found it by chance while I was out here doing research on areas of magical anomaly. After I defeated the maze, I won power over the entire area; that's how I was able to do all the hollowing and building. Everything within a certain range of that structure is malleable to me."

With a single wave of her hands, a stone chair shot out of the ground across from us—a chair onto which Shun took a seat. In the meantime, I was mentally flipping back through the adventure, hunting for any detail that didn't mesh with the story we were getting. None of the traps had seemed especially deadly, and even the scarier ones might have had worse bark than bite.

Although, one notable exception did stand out.

"What about the minotaur trying to murder us?"

"He only puts on a show," Shun replied. "If you fought him, you'd find he always *just* misses, or stays a little behind you during pursuit. Adds stakes to the last session. Be thankful: when I did the maze for real, he actually *was* trying to kill me. It's how the last person in control set him. I had to dissolve him in acid before I managed to get the controls figured out."

That was both horrifying and confusing. Thankfully, Neil leaned over and explained to Albert, purposely raising his voice so the rest of us could hear. "Some minotaurs are creatures of their labyrinth and bound to them. You can't kill the guardian—for good, anyway—while the maze still stands."

"And if you control the labyrinth, you control the guardian." Amy took a long sip from one of the provided beers, the lights on her skin speeding up and slowing down. "Is he sentient?"

"Not so far. Artificially created—reforms from the labyrinth's material within a day or so of being destroyed. Follows orders and instructions well, but I don't think the designer intended for independent thought."

Spinning her beer bottle by the neck, Amy watched the liquid slosh within its container. "Good thing. Controlling a creature with will of its own would be a very different proposition than using an automated defense system. Break it all down for me, Shun. Tell me about this place."

Fascinated as I was by the prospect of such a discussion, it became clear almost immediately that the knowledge would be lost on me. The conversation veered directly into the sort of complex, magical equations and practical discussions where I didn't even understand enough to know how much I was missing. It was akin to them switching into another language, so I took the time to examine our new surroundings.

I rose from the couch and walked around through the large room, one big enough to comfortably hold twenty plus people without anyone feeling cramped. This was obviously going to be the success room, a spot where people who'd finished the challenge would be able to bask in the satisfaction of their achievement. Refreshments were good, though given how long we'd been down there and the metabolism of many parahumans, such snacks would be woefully inadequate to slate any true hunger.

Near the back of the room, I found a secluded section with more couches stacked and tucked away—extra seating in case of larger groups. I started to wonder how Shun had moved these around and stacked them so casually, then the image of her stone chair returned. If you could control the very shape of your environment, these sorts of chores were probably quite minimal, which meant changing things could also be accomplished on the cheap.

The idea as a whole was a neat one, and had legs, but to my mind, Shun's biggest obstacle was the maze itself. First off, the remote location put it much too far out to draw in any casual traffic; people would have to make a pilgrimage for this experience. Then, there was the sheer size of the thing. With a brilliant mage on each team, we'd made it through the entire game over the course of several hours. A team less puzzle-oriented could be down there for days. Like many parahumans, Shun had grasped the concept of a mortal creation without understanding the smaller details that led to a successful business.

It was while I was investigating a shoddy bar set up by the rear wall that Albert wandered over, also evidently weary of the magic discussion. Gregor stayed put, his eyes never leaving my location. I was impressed he hadn't turned into an eager shadow, but maybe he just didn't want to tip off Shun if he still expected a surprise attack.

There was no such worry in Albert, not that I'd expected to find any. He strolled up casually, hand near the hilt of his blade without touching it. It was a stance he'd nearly perfected over the years: ready without being threatening. While I was positive he'd never say it, I was even more sure that Arch had to be proud of the progress Albert and Neil had made.

"How was everything?" For Albert, it was a delicate touch; he didn't even glance over to Neil as he posed the question.

"Good." I realized a moment later that he didn't want to articulate what he was truly asking and shifted to the topic for him. "Neil and I bonded rather well, in fact."

"Happy to hear that, and also a little surprised. The two of you have never... well, some of us get along better than others." Albert's diplomatic skills might not have grown as quickly as his combat ones, but he'd managed to find a polite, if honest way of describing my interactions with Neil.

Unlike Albert, I did look over to the couch, taking a long look at our necromancer. It was amazing how much Neil had grown up when I wasn't noticing. Even now, it was easy to still see that mad gleam in his eye as he cackled before his captives. But that Neil hadn't been around for a very long time, and it was well past time to acknowledge that difference. We'd both become locked into that dynamic by habit and resentment, but the silver lining to being shaken up was that things didn't always settle back down in the same shape they'd been before. Whether today was a blip in our history or the start of a new dynamic for us would depend on the efforts we each made moving forward.

"I think we just needed a little time to better see each other. Being thrust into what we thought was a near-death experience certainly helped with the team building."

Albert laughed at that notion. "Maybe we should use this place for all new company employees. Start them off with a bond."

I felt like someone had just thrown a hammer through a glass wall of my own blind spot. That was it. "Albert, you're absolutely correct."

The panic on his face was crisp and immediate. "I was joking. I don't think Al's going to be happy if you drag her out here for a first assignment."

"Not about us, specifically, about the team building." Rather than explain myself twice, I walked back over to the couch with Albert following close behind.

No sooner had I drawn near than Amy looked up. "Good timing. We were just about to call you over.

I think I've got a good, general sense of how Shun managed most of this, and while it is still a marvel, having magical control of the area explains most of my larger logistical questions. Next question is, how viable is this as a business?"

"For an escape room? It's a non-starter. You have no other attractions nearby, you're miles from major roads—to say nothing of foot traffic—and you don't even have lodging where people who wanted to come could stay. Unless you made a gate from somewhere more accessible using spatial magic, which I'm given to understand is quite difficult, this place would be unlikely to even sell a ticket, let alone recoup a profit."

With every word, Shun's face had fallen, her smile growing dimmer and dimmer, until it threatened to fall away entirely. Just before we reached that point, I swung around to the rest of my assessment.

"That said, there *is* a viable business model here. Don't bill it as just an escape room: it's a parahuman corporate team-building exercise. Human businesses do versions of this constantly. The simulated danger and need for cooperation force people who might not normally get along to work together, perhaps even overcoming their own issues in the process." My gaze darted to Neil, who rolled his eyes but couldn't stop himself from chuckling a little.

"How is that better, though?" Albert, despite it technically being his idea, was having trouble seeing the bigger picture. "Aren't all those other issues still problems?"

It was Amy, funnily enough, who'd already seen the answers. "Nope. Corporate retreats are supposed to last for at least a weekend, so the longer time frame isn't an issue. Nor is travel; most of these things take place some distance from centralized society. Lodging might be a problem, but I'm guessing Fred and I both see the same easy fix. Not hard to make more space when someone can shape this whole area at will. Form a small village up top, and we've even got somewhere for them to relax if they finish early."

The dim grin flashed back to full strength as Shun looked back and forth from me to Amy. "I could do that. I could make changes to the maze, as well, turn it more team oriented." There was a familiar hunger in her eyes, a look I'd seen on both Neil and Amy's faces when a new ambition had their attention. "Does that mean you're interested in investing in my project?"

"The magic is sound. Since my money guy thinks there's potential, and I'd love to see more of what you can do, it seems like it'll be cash well spent. Let's start small, work on a new room design and a sample lodging unit, then we'll go from there."

To my surprise, Shun shot out of the stone chair and wrapped Amy in a hug. She'd been so reserved in her body language that only now did I realize it had probably been the result of nerves. While they embraced, I made my way back over to the shoddy bar at the rear of the room.

Digging around, I found a few cold bottles tucked away and brought them forth into the light. Once the tops were popped, I headed back and began to hand them out. Since Amy and Shun were still talking, I set a pair of bottles down near them and moved on. Gregor accepted his drink with a nod, Albert looked uncertain, while Neil drained a quarter of the bottle immediately after touching it.

"Should we toast to the new business?" Neil proposed, after noticing that no one else had drunk yet.

"That's a good one." I lifted my own drink and tapped it against the others'. "To new ventures, and old friends."

That earned me another eye roll, though this time, it was paired with a smile. We weren't the best of friends, or suddenly bonded for life, but Neil and I had definitely found a new footing with one another. If that didn't convince me this place was magical enough to invest in, I couldn't imagine what would.

A PLACE OF BLUE

1.

WITH ONE WEEK LEFT UNTIL THE WEDDING, we were officially hitting crunch time. Between Krystal and me, we were beginning to feel like we had no time at all. We still had to finish clearing our plates for the honeymoon, planning the final touches, and putting logistics in place for our convoy to drive down—we were bringing far too many things and people to fly. Thankfully, our friends had been pitching in to pick up the slack.

On the afternoon where this part of the tale begins, we were seated in the living room of Charlotte Manor, going over cake samples. While we'd ultimately decided to use Boarback's catering in general, Charlotte had graciously offered to create our wedding cake. Given her culinary skill and ability to conjure food seemingly at will, she was an ideal fit, even if it did mean one more item to bring in the car. I'd have to ask the Clovers about purchasing some sort of stabilizing enchantment to prevent slippage, or else ask if they had anything like a magical Mary Poppins bag.

"That one predominantly uses chocolate, coconut, and espresso." Charlotte was in what I thought of as her usual form, except she'd swapped the dated dress for a chef's coat, white pants, and one of those white poofy hats you see more in cartoons than in actual use. Sometimes, I wondered how much of her appearance was for our sake versus just amusing herself.

"Bleh, not a coconut fan." In spite of her words, Krystal jammed a fork down and took a taste. "Although *you* almost make it palatable."

"I like coconut, and the cake, but it's certainly something of a controversial flavor choice. We should lean toward things more people will enjoy."

Our eyes turned to the next hunk of dessert in the lineup: a white cake with orange frosting that I was quite curious to try. Before we had a chance, June appeared in the doorway.

As Krystal's maid of honor, June's presence had become increasingly common in recent weeks. The closer the wedding drew, the more she was around for support and help, to the point where I'd rented out a room for her with Charlotte. It was truly the least I could do to repay all of her assistance, which was varied, numerous, and included the swatch of fabric draped over her arm.

"Yo, Krystal, quick interruption. I finally got a hold of Umar to go over designs for your rehearsal dinner outfit. He says the fabric you wanted won't stand up to having that many enchantments layered on. Either lose a function or resign yourself to scratchier fabric."

"Fine, tell him to drop the deflecting enchantment. Probably overkill on top of the durability boosts, anyway."

No sooner had Krystal said the words than June gave a thumbs-up and darted back down to wherever she'd left her phone. Before I had a chance to even ask, Krystal turned to me and explained. "Sometimes, there will be an idiot who decides to take a run at an agent when they're having one of these major life events. Company policy is to minimize such chances by making sure we're ready to fight, even while metaphorically dressed to kill. Obviously, since our event is in Boarback, good fucking luck to any idiot who tries something, but I never turn down a chance to get a new outfit on the company dime. Mostly going to use it on missions after this, anyway."

The strategy seemed slightly counterintuitive, given what I knew of Krystal's power, which appeared to engage whenever she was hurt or in peril. A person with those innate skills seemed like they would warrant less defense, not more. However, I acknowledged that my understanding was limited: I wasn't involved in that world, nor did I want to be. Whatever Krystal's tactics, they existed for a reason, and I'd be an absolute imbecile to think I had a better grasp on the demands of that job than the people actually doing it.

"This next cake is white chocolate, with chunks of it throughout the icing. You'll also note vanilla, hints of caramel, and a few other flavors I'll let you try to suss out."

Whatever the hidden flavors were, I didn't catch them. After a quick first bite, I took my time on the second, and by the time I looked up, the rest of the cake sample was gone. Even Krystal looked somewhat surprised at the suddenly empty plate and incriminating fork in her hand.

"*Damn*. Just found my front-runner."

"If you'd like further samples, I can have more brought out," Charlotte offered.

I could see Krystal was ready to accept the offer and so hurriedly spoke first. "How about we take you up on that after we finish the tasting? Can't ruin our appetites for cake before we've tried all our options."

There was a slight pout in my fiancée's expression; although, paired with a playful wink, it wasn't too melancholy. She perked up even more when the next cake proved to be peanut butter based with no coconut. It didn't vanish like the white chocolate selection had, yet the plate was cleaned all the same.

Just as we were moving on to the final sample, June dashed into the doorway again. "Sorry, sorry, Umar wants to know where you'll hide the gun on this outfit. He's going to pad the fabric and add concealed pockets so you—"

Without so much as a flash of light for warning, June was suddenly gone. All that remained was a flurry of snow that landed on Charlotte's floors and immediately melted. It was quite the impressive trick; I'd never seen her teleport like that. Only when I looked at Krystal's face did I realize that something was amiss.

"June?" Krystal rose from the couch, looking around. "Not funny. Not the time." A slight edge crept into her voice, the reality she was trying to ignore forcing its way through. "Where are you?"

"A man is coming up the walk," Charlotte informed us. "He employed some manner of cloaking magic; I didn't notice him until he was already in the parking lot."

Magical concealment at the same time one of our friends vanished didn't take much math to put together, and the absolute fury building in Krystal's eyes told me she'd finished the equation. Leaping to my feet, I placed myself between her and the door. "Hold on, let's make sure the two things are connected for certain before we make any bold decisions. There's always the chance it's a coincidence."

"Bullshit," Krystal spat back.

"Then how about the chance that someone timed June's disappearance like this on purpose, so we'd be tricked into attacking a potential ally?" Though it was true that I hadn't gained much experience in Krystal's world, I did have the advantage of having seen quite a few films about espionage. To me, the suggestion seemed convoluted and impractical, yet Krystal steadied herself, halting her powerful march toward the front door.

"Probably also bullshit, but not impossible. Especially since the Turva clan still holds a grudge." Her fingers flexed against her palm, nails trying to pierce her flesh. "If those bastards have hurt her…"

"June is an agent. I highly doubt that if they had the means to steal one of us from inside Charlotte Manor that she would be the choice, especially knowing how much Petre would love to get his hands on me. Let's answer the door and go from there."

Moving as a unit, we exited the living room and headed down the hall. Before we reached the door, I noticed the sizable form of Gregor standing nearby, as well as Al, who was seated in a large chair reading one of the many accounting books I'd given her to study. I started to wonder how Gregor had known about the guest, then noticed Charlotte's old woman form standing behind the front desk. She could be anywhere and everywhere in this house at once; of course she'd alerted my bodyguard, as well.

"Expecting trouble?" The question didn't seem worried, more like Gregor wanted to know what kind of work this would be.

"I sure fucking hope so." That was, obviously, Krystal.

The knock came then, crisp and sharp, two quick bangs. At my side, I felt Krystal go stiff. It meant something, but there wasn't time enough to ask what. Gregor opened the door, carefully using his bulk to shield both Krystal and me from a potential surprise attack. Anyone who wanted to get to us would go through Gregor, and what a trip that would be.

"Good day. I have come to deliver a message to the betrothed couple, a missive from Hellebore of the fey lands." The man standing there was inhumanly beautiful, somehow both masculine and delicate at once. I might have stared more if June's presence hadn't inured me to the appearance of those with fey blood. It also didn't hurt that I'd already seen this particular man before, albeit briefly.

Before us, holding a silver letter, stood September Windbrook, June's brother and Krystal's former betrothed.

Which effectively torched any chance at all that this was a coincidence.

"What did you do?" Krystal started forward, a look in her eyes that genuinely scared me for a moment. I had no idea what the rules about agents fighting amongst themselves were—or whether such rules even existed at all—nor did I suspect Krystal cared one bit about them in that moment. "Tem, where the living shit is June?"

"If you think *I* had the power to rip her from this place, especially given the house's magical protections, then you've truly lost your footing. Center yourself. While I dared not open the missive, I have no doubt you'll want to be on top of your game. Hellebore is not one to send idle correspondence."

Tem held up the letter, and in better light, I saw it wasn't actually silver. It was white, with the intangible glitter of freshly fallen snow. Gregor reached for it, and Tem's hand darted away. "With apologies, I was ordered to deliver this to the couple. My fingers won't release it to anyone else."

In spite of Krystal's anger, I wondered how happy Tem was about the situation. His sister had just vanished, and I was beginning to have a solid hunch as to where; plus, it sure sounded like he was being forced to play a role whether he liked it or not. Since Krystal was still processing her best friend's disappearance, I stepped forward. Gregor started to block me, but I halted his movements.

"September Windbrook is an agent. He's not going to kill me in plain view of another agent and several witnesses." I looked from Gregor to Krystal, then over at Al, who'd popped down to her tiny form at some point and appeared to be hiding behind the book she'd been reading. That was odd. Maybe she didn't want anyone else from the fey realm to see her? It was a curiosity that could wait until we had less pressing matters. For the moment, I moved Gregor aside and accepted the letter.

No sooner had my fingers touched it than a jolt went through me, and Tem appeared to relax, if momentarily. Whatever grip he'd been in had clearly lessened now that the task was completed. Wordlessly, he turned and started to walk off.

I couldn't follow—outside the shade of the porch waited the midday sun, ready to roast any vampire that wandered into its path. Instead, I merely called out, hoping for a response I knew I wouldn't get.

"Is there anything you can tell us? Any advice?"

"Not allowed." Tem called the words over his shoulder, feet compelling him forward. It appeared he wasn't entirely free just yet. "But be careful. I've only seen Hellebore like this a few times. It almost never ends well."

Then he was gone. Out in the sun, his pace picked up, turning into a sprint. He vanished not long after clearing the parking lot. Since there was little point in leaving myself exposed to the world, I shut the door and held up the letter.

"Guess we should see what this is about?"

2.

"TO THE ESTEEMED AGENT KRYSTAL JENKINS
and Fredrick Fletcher, founder of the House of Fred, I
must send my dearest apologies for the inconvenience.
Unfortunately, a problem has arisen in our lands, and
June Windbrook was deemed best suited to dealing with
the threat. As you no doubt are aware, while half-fey may
serve as agents, they are forever connected to their true
homelands and the duties carried with such a heritage.
While it is my right to recall any of those under my authority, I am not a being without compassion. Should

you wish June returned as soon as possible, this letter will allow only those named within passage to our realm. She must stay only until the task is completed; whether you wish to speed things along is up to your discretion."

I lowered the page, fearful of what look would be waiting on Krystal's face. "The only other thing is the signature. She signed it, 'Hellebore, Seer of Winter,' which doesn't mean much to me."

Krystal was, to my surprise and worry, both silent and seated. The look in her eyes was anything but, however. I watched her forcefully control her rage, shaping it into something useful. It wasn't often I got to see Krystal's agent side in action; I had a nagging hunch that this day would be an exception.

Thankfully, Al was still around, and back to human-size. I hadn't pressed on why she shrank down; there were far too many more immediate issues to tackle, and besides, she was entitled to her privacy. I was just appreciative for the information she did choose to share.

"Seer of Winter is her title. The fey lands don't have weather in the traditional sense, but we do have it. The seasons, the lands, it all exists in a shifting spectrum. There are fey from lands you'd more traditionally think of as having spring and summer climates, but the fey would just say those are the static conditions of specific lands. Same for fall and winter. If you go far enough into their lands, you can find their major cities and kingdoms, which is where the great royalty dwell: King of Summer, Lord of the Fall, Empress of the Winter, Guide of Spring."

Even with the tremendous amount I'd just been forced to absorb, I did manage to pick a few key points out of there. "So, she's associated with the Empress of the Winter, which we probably could have guessed from her running the Court of Frost, but she's not at the top. Also, Guide of Spring seems the odd man out in that title scheme."

Al shrugged, and behind her, I saw a cup of coffee change in hue as its contents appeared to gain cream and sugar. "He's what the mortal kids today would call 'chill.' You're also correct: Hellebore is not at the top of winter hierarchy, but it makes little difference. She is one of the Empress's Hands, empowered to act on behalf of her ruler in most matters, and second in power only to the true royals, who use cats' paws largely because, when they fight, entire regions of the fey lands are destroyed."

"Doesn't matter." Krystal had finished her long sit and risen from the chair. We'd gathered in the living room to hear what the note had to say, and while Gregor was sitting calmly, Al was pacing. Both made a stark contrast to Krystal, who moved slowly and deliberately, like every step had the potential to start, or end, a fight. "I'm getting her back. Fred, you wait here. This won't take long."

"Um, hi. So, we haven't really gotten a chance to know each other, and I realize that this is not the kind of situation where you want a stranger correcting you—"

"Spit it out," Krystal snapped. She took a moment, forcing her eyes closed and drawing in some deep breaths. "Sorry, Al. Just… on edge. But if you have something I need to know, tell me. Always better to know."

Though still appearing nervous—Tem's visit had really knocked her off-kilter—Al quickly found her words. "You can't leave Fred. She names you both in the opening, and then specifically mentions that *only* those named in the letter get passage. Read the top: she didn't say Krystal or Fred, she addressed it to Krystal *and* Fred. Whatever magic she wove, it works for both of you, or neither. Specifics are vitally important in formal fey matters."

"I'll go." It didn't seem prudent to waste time bickering about on whether or not it was smart to take me along. This whole ordeal was hitting Krystal hard, and with every blow, it became more and more clear that was the intent. They'd stolen her best friend, sent her ex-fiancé to deliver the news, and now had saddled her with a non-agent tagalong to slow her down. Much as I might have liked to stay, we weren't leaving June in the middle of whatever pretense they'd found to steal her away.

"Fuck…" I could hear the "that" forming on Krystal's lips, yet refusing to fall. She couldn't kick back on the idea entirely without giving up on helping June. What had been raw fury before was now tempered by turmoil. She didn't want to risk my safety to retrieve June, and was no doubt also aware of how very trap-like this all felt. "Fuck... just fuck."

Much as I wracked my brain, I couldn't think of an easy fix. Arch might have had something, but he was off somewhere with Neil and Albert doing other things. Amy and Bubba were at Richard's, not that neither of them had ever indicated they possessed much knowledge about fey. Gideon could be around, but getting in to see the King of the West was no small feat, and I'd never actually heard him speak on the fey. I didn't even know what relationship dragons and fey had. The more I thought about it, the more I realized just how little on the topic I really knew.

Gregor pulled himself solidly from his chair. "I will keep Fred safe."

"You're really not getting the detail-specific magic, are you?" Al poked. "Best guess, the 'passage' she mentioned will take both of them to somewhere specific. Even if I grabbed you and went through the nearest pathway between lands, there's no guarantee we'd be anywhere near Fred and Krystal. Not that it matters, because if Hellebore wants them alone, we'll never get within ten miles of their location. The roads would betray us."

It was a sound argument, or at least as logical as one can hope for when magic is the topic at hand, yet it was one that still drew a rare expression of frustration to Gregor's brow. "When the King of the West, in his great wisdom, told me you would be difficult to guard, I did not yet understand his guidance. You have a habit of making yourself hard to protect."

"Welcome to *my* life," Krystal muttered. "Freddy, I can't take you along on this."

"You aren't taking me. I volunteered."

That earned me a look that was half-anger, half-appreciation. "That doesn't change anything. You're not trained for this. Depending on what she's setting up, *I* might not even be trained for this. But seeing as one of us has a sealed devil that offers tremendous power, healing, and durability, that's the one who is charging blindly into the Stronghold of Winter."

I nodded. "Yes, you are, and I'm fully aware that nothing I say can stop you. Just as you need to be aware that I'm coming along. Not because I intend to get in the way; I'm going along solely to get you there. I'm not some macho idiot who will try to prove himself in a fight. We go, I stay low, we find June, and you remind them why nobody out there messes with Agent Krystal Goddamn Jenkins."

Despite the heavy mood that had fallen over the room, Krystal let out a snort of a chuckle. "Whoa, not every day you go busting out the big-boy curse words."

"It's not every day someone manages to actually hurt the woman I love." The words were bolder than my usual fair, but Krystal wasn't the only one feeling a bit stirred up. Someone had reached into Charlotte Manor, the home for most of us, and snatched away our friend. The very idea of it made me scared, which in turn lit a small flame of anger—a flame that burned hotter every time I saw the pain and frustration in Krystal's eyes.

"Very good answer." Krystal examined me coolly, taking gauge not as my betrothed, but as an agent who'd have to be carrying the weight of protecting me. "If we do this, which I'm still not signing off on, then we do it smart. You reach out to the Clover twins and see if they have anything that can surprise a fey, then Cyndi to ask if she's got any fun toys we can borrow. I'll touch base with Arch and the Agency, see if there's any level of support they can offer. Fey deals are fairly ironclad, and I know they do have the authority to recall their people, but there's always some sort of clause or red tape. Let's call it two hours: long enough to change, handle our due diligence, and see what our options are. If there are goodies to grab, we scoop them up, then head to wherever we have to go for passage."

"I was looking for that, actually, and having no luck." I turned the paper over in my hand, checking to see if the back offered further details. There was clearly passage promised in the letter, yet no method to be found for how to utilize it.

Krystal came over to my side, looking at the letter with me. "Weird. She definitely extends the offer, and they can't do that falsely. Maybe if we rub a corner?" Her hand reached forward, taking hold of the edge opposite where my hand held the missive aloft.

The cold hit instantly, albeit more as a factor brought to my attention than any sort of discomfort. Frosty temperatures didn't hold much hindrance for a being already partially dead—at least, not ones animated by vampire magic. A far larger issue was the fact that we were no longer in Charlotte Manor or anywhere close to it.

Together, Krystal and I were standing in the center of a frozen field. Gorgeous flowers of every shape and color grew around us, each made entirely of ice and more lovely than the one before. I could have gotten lost in those colors, the shifting hues catching the light of the fading sun. I blinked, having momentarily forgotten that the sun of the fey lands didn't burn my kind the way ours did. Nobody I'd asked seemed to have any idea as to why, though that tended to be the rule more often than not when dealing with the fey—as well as their lands. They worked by their own rules, and evidently, that included the methods of transportation.

"Of course, it was the letter! What in the hell is wrong with me? That was so obvious." Krystal kicked the snow several times, her sneakers not having the same impact as the boots she normally wore into battle. At least we'd been dressed and wearing shoes; had the letter come at breakfast time, we could be even worse equipped.

Finally, her stomping ended, she wiped a stray fleck of sweat from her forehead. Weather wouldn't be an issue for her, given her parahuman abilities; not that I'd expected otherwise.

"Sorry, mad at myself for being so tilted I didn't see the obvious. But we're here, and since I'm pretty sure that letter turned to snow when we arrived, we've got no easy way back. Stay close to me, Freddy. I truly have no idea what's in store for us, or what Hellebore is planning."

The lovely flowers made a tinkling sound when they moved, their vines creaking and shifting as a path appeared through the frozen foliage. Unlike the letter, there was nothing puzzling about this setup: follow the path before us, or try to charge out into the unknown. Terrifying as Hellebore was, the idea of being lost in the world of the fey seemed like an even worse scenario.

Hands intertwined, Krystal and I walked down the path, deeper into the heart of winter.

3.

IT DIDN'T TAKE LONG FOR US TO SEE where we were going. After less than an hour, we rounded a bend and a new sight of wonder came into view: a castle, coated in ice and snow, gleamed in the distance. While it wasn't actually made of frost, the entire structure appeared cloaked in winter's frozen elements—and that was no small feat, given the size of the thing. The structure sat atop a mountain, towering high in the sky, then rising even farther, its jutting spires seeming to pierce the atmosphere. I couldn't even see what lay beyond the castle—only a large cloud of swirling white, which I suspected to be a snowstorm raging on the other side.

Krystal's hand tightened on mine as we saw our undeniable destination. "Be careful. The closer we are to Hellebore, the more danger we're in."

Only as we made our way along the snowy road did I realize I'd never bothered to ask Krystal if she was stronger than a fey like Hellebore. It certainly wasn't a prudent query to pose when I had to assume we were being watched. Fey, like most parahumans, tended to have a prideful streak; no sense in making an already tense situation worse. The answer had no real impact on our plans, anyway. We were pressing forward to find June; if Krystal decided to try to fight our way out, I had to trust it was because she knew she had a shot at winning.

My own hope was for diplomacy, yet with every new facet this situation unveiled, I suspected more and more that such a thing wouldn't be in the cards. Hellebore was setting us up like pawns on a board; we just didn't yet know the game we were playing. Until we did, there was no telling which moves suited her interests, ours, or both, and given the utter dearth of information we'd been provided, Hellebore seemed content with our ignorance.

Soon after spotting the castle—much *too* soon, in fact—we arrived at the terminus our road had guided us toward: a small door in the side of a stone wall that opened as soon as we approached. My guess was that this was some sort of servant's entrance, but when we stepped through, our eyes were greeted by an enormous hall, decorated predominantly in blue with swaths and accents of silver and white. Banners hung from the walls with torches bearing blue flames interspersed among them. The whole scene matched nicely with the chandelier, floor runner, and other elements dotted around the vast hall. The pale blue of ice from the coldest of environments had been chosen as the central hue around which the rest of the décor was built. The choice struck me as odd, not because they hadn't made it artful and elegant, which it was, but rather I found the color to be a bit cheerful for Hellebore. She seemed more suited to winter's darker hues.

A glance behind me showed a different door than the one we'd entered through, which at least explained why a side entrance opened into a receiving hall. Dealing with mages proved to be excellent practice for navigating the fey lands; I allowed my mind to stop trying to puzzle over such a detail. The rules here were different: I didn't need to understand them, only accept and adapt.

"Hellebore!" Unlike me, Krystal wasn't quite so spellbound by the decorating or shifting doorways. She took several steps forward, visibly wanting to shake a fist and stymied by having nowhere to direct it. "What the hell did you do with June?"

282

"Down to business so soon? Shall I not treat you as guests, offering you first a chance to dine, rest, and recover from the journey through the wilds?"

It would be wrong to say Hellebore appeared. From my perspective, limited as it was, she stepped away from the nearest wall, like she'd been camouflaged there all along and was only now revealing her presence. I nearly gulped in reflex at her arrival; last time we'd met had been at a distance. Up close, she was even more terrifying.

June and Tem were beautiful to the point of seeming nearly inhuman. There was nothing "nearly" when it came to Hellebore. From her pale, unmarred skin and icy eyes to her sharp yet subtle features, there was no denying Hellebore's breathtaking effect, but it wasn't akin to human beauty. Hellebore would best be compared to the summit of a mountain, or a still sea with a full moon hiding its depths: lovely, yet inherently dangerous.

"I didn't come for a snack, and you well know it. Where. The Fuck. Is June?" Krystal actually managed to step up to Hellebore, though not quite to the point of getting in her face.

Our hostess merely stared at her in response, blinked a few times, and then turned to me.

"What say you, Fredrick Fletcher? Do you wish to make use of my hospitality?"

Tempting as it was to rush things along, that word pricked something in my head. Hospitality was important; I did know that the fey had rules for how they could treat guests. Granted, I didn't have the training to know what most of those rules *were*, and Krystal wasn't in a state where I could expect much diplomatic support. Best to wing it and split the middle.

"Would it possible to revisit that later, after Krystal has spoken with you? I don't wish to be rude or ungrateful as a guest; however, neither of us will be at ease until we know June is safe."

For some reason, that earned me a longer stare than Krystal. It hadn't felt like especially adept social maneuvering—barely covering the basics, really—but it seemed that was enough to warrant consideration. "Very well. We can reserve refreshments and rest until after you have been made aware of the situation. If you please will follow me."

She didn't even make a motion: as soon as Hellebore stopped speaking, a section of wall slid aside. Behind it was a new hallway with a distinct slope and curve, a ramp leading to the castle's higher sections. Without even a glance to see if we were following, Hellebore led the way, Krystal and I close on her heels. No way were we getting left behind to jump through even more hoops.

"Sure as I am that the timing was quite inconvenient, it was, unfortunately, equally inevitable. You see, recently something wandered in from the deepest parts of winter. There are a few wilder beings out there, so old and strong that they will obey no one save the empress herself. Even my authority is insufficient. As such, the standard way to remove our intruder is to drive it back with more aggressive means."

As we made our way up the curving ramp, I noticed that we kept passing doors lining either side of the hall. Most were open, showing new turns or rooms to explore, all matching the same aesthetic we'd seen thus far. A few of the doors were closed, however, large stone obstacles that I was sure had more than just heft and locks keeping them sealed.

"And June Windbrook was the only one who could do the job?" Krystal demanded.

"Of course not. But she's the one who was selected." Neither an apology nor an explanation. Something told me Hellebore would have had an excellent career in human politics. "The Windbrook family has long been loyal servants of the empress. It is customary for those of their line, when they are ready, to undertake a great task on the behalf of winter, proving their devotion and capability to handle harder deeds."

"Except June doesn't give a shit about any of that."

This time, Hellebore smiled, and there was something in it that nearly made my legs go briefly numb. "The June of now is not the June of always. One tries many paths before the one meant for their feet. And we fey are as bound by our bargains as those we make them with."

Even with minimal context, it wasn't hard to put together. June had agreed to something when she was younger, maybe before she had been quite so soured on whatever this whole scene was about, and that agreement allowed Hellebore to call her in. Much as I wished it were a trick, most of what we'd witnessed so far indicated that it had to be accurate. Hellebore had already demonstrated that she had power over June the moment she'd brought her here.

Krystal apparently arrived at a similar conclusion. "So, you're using an old deal to yank my friend over, all in the name of fighting some monster. Is that really the story you're pitching?"

"I have no idea what you mean. Is it not my duty, as an emissary of the empress, to drive encroaching threats from our lands? Should I not offer such tasks to those who have come before me and made oaths to undertake such challenges in service to winter?"

"A threat that just happened to encroach a week before my wedding. Which you all are apparently still salty about."

While Krystal and Hellebore were arguing, we passed a new door that piqued my interest. It was unique, in that it was the first one I'd seen completely frozen over. Even odder was that this door seemed more ornate than the ones we'd previously passed: larger, for one, with engravings along the edge. I couldn't make out much more detail than that through the thick sheet of ice, plus, we didn't linger there long. It might have been my imagination, or Krystal's aggression, but it felt like we picked up the pace as we approached that door.

"Do you truly imagine that this is about me being miffed at you for not wedding a half-fey? Agent Jenkins, while you would have been a useful ally once wed, we can both see the window for such an opportunity has passed. There are already other plans for Tem, ones that will better suit him and us in the long term. I assure you: I hold no grudge against you for breaking things off. You won your freedom in the Court of Frost under *my* supervision; it would be quite strange for me, of all people, to then be angered by the outcome."

At last, we arrived at the end of the curved hall. As we rose into a vast chamber, one I suspected could be a throne room should royalty deign to visit, we also got our first view of what was happening beyond the castle through a set of wide windows. It still seemed to be a storm, only now, we could see the center instead of just the periphery. For a moment, I thought we were looking at another mountain, until it lifted its head and belched what appeared to be a half-melted slush. The liquid exploded on impact, creating more snow and ice over whatever it met.

"A blizzard behemoth, the aforementioned threat to our lands," Hellebore continued. "As you can see, it is quite disruptive, and this is the creature in a relatively calm state. When properly angered, they can destroy whole cities. This one must be stopped here, before it can move inward toward civilization."

Whatever else Hellebore was up to, she hadn't fudged things when it came to the threat. The creature was enormous, with a blocky, almost square head and a long body that branched off into three sets of legs. Between the size, the breath, and the hungry look in its eye, I had no trouble believing this was a threat that would require an agent's abilities.

"Are you kidding me? Are you *fucking* kidding me?" Krystal whipped around, and if she'd had her gun, I genuinely think she might have drawn on Hellebore, usefulness be damned. "June doesn't have the right skill set to take on something like that. She's speed and precision; that requires raw power to stop."

"Yes, I'm afraid she hasn't performed as well as I'd hoped. Dear thing got frozen solid within the first hour she was down there. I'm sure she'll free herself eventually, though the blizzard behemoth's ice is no mean feat to crack. With apologies, there is a strong chance she might still be detained when your wedding rolls around, but you can hardly put one social event over the safety of an entire region." This time, there was nothing subtle about the danger in Hellebore's smile.

Krystal lowered her head; I had no idea what to expect next. One thing I certainly wasn't prepared for, though, was laughter. It rang out from her throat, half-sincere, half-insane, and how much of it was pageantry, I've still never fully assessed. When her eyes rose again, Krystal no longer looked worried or frustrated. No, now she was sporting a toothy smile and the kind of glare that would send anyone with sense running for the hills.

"That's it? That's what this is all about? One little petty bit of bullshit and having someone come clean your mess on the cheap." Krystal walked to the edge of the room, where a thin sheet of ice ran from floor to ceiling, our window and only protection from the outside world. "That's fine, Hellebore. You want animal control? I'll be your wrangler. Because I want you to watch and see exactly why my reputation is what it is. Then I want you to think about this, the next time you get an idea to kidnap my best friend."

She started to reach for the frozen window, then paused. "Hellebore, you've invited us here as guests, correct?"

"Was that not implied?"

"Very implied, just not explicit." Krystal's eyes moved from the nightmare outside, shifting to me, then Hellebore. "So why don't you go ahead and say it, in no uncertain terms. Since I'm here to help the lands and all."

It seemed I'd been wrong about Krystal's state of mind. She'd clocked the same details about hospitality I had, only she'd chosen to wait to pounce on them. In some ways, it was one of the most impressive things I'd seen her do. This wasn't some parahuman power granting enhanced observation; it was her, refusing to let anger lead to mistakes. Even knocked off-balance by the sudden loss of a friend, it was never wise to underestimate Agent Krystal Jenkins.

"As I recall, you are here to help June Windbrook," Hellebore countered. She did give a little ground, too, at least. "Very well, at your request, I recognize Agent Krystal Jenkins and Fredrick Frankford Fletcher as my formal guests. You should know, however, that the protections afforded by such niceties won't apply if you step into battle."

"Wasn't me I was worried about." Krystal shot me a meaningful look from her place by the window. "Freddy, stay here, no matter what. Hellebore recognized you as her guest, so she is bound to keep you safe and return you home, unless you took a dump on the floor or something else disrespectful. Don't make any deals, don't offer any favors, and if you can avoid talking to her at all, I would."

With that said, she looked to Hellebore. "Little help, or you want me to open it up myself?"

No sooner had the request been made than the ice window slid upward, exposing all of us to a freezing draft that blew inside. Pausing only long enough to blow me a kiss, Krystal took several long steps back, and then ran, building as much speed as she could. When she reached the edge, she leapt out from the tower of the castle to where the ground would be waiting for her quite some ways below.

I raced to edge, only to find the ice window back in place. From my vantage point, I could only watch as the woman I loved plummeted through the air, disappearing into the snowstorm before she could land.

4.

EVEN KNOWING WHAT I KNEW, IT WAS HARD not to be afraid as I watched the swirling white vortex below. This had clearly been a trap laid by Hellebore, and we were in an entirely different point in reality. What if the healing didn't work? What if the fey had found a way to limit Krystal's power, cut her off from the source, and this was how they took her out? Eyes against the cold pane, I waited, reminding myself exactly *who* it was I was fretting over.

For all the faith I had in her, it was still a relief when I saw the sudden flare leap up from the ground, sailing through the sky to land on the blizzard behemoth's lower front leg. It was hard to make out Krystal's small form from so far up; however, her burning hair gave away that she'd once more tapped into the power of the devil sealed within. It was an inherited burden, one passed from mother to daughter through generations, but it was also what kept her safe. To kill the host was to kill the creature sealed within, and devils apparently weren't keen to go down easily. I only knew that from reputation—I'd never actually met one, thankfully. They were the sort of problems that arose rarely and were on the plate of people far more capable.

"Would you care for a better view?"

In watching for Krystal, I'd forgotten Hellebore was even there. Turning around, I found that we were no longer alone. A host of small fey had appeared, each moving too quietly for even my ears to have picked up more than the barest whisper, carrying an array of foods and liquids. They set the smorgasbord down on tables that rose from the floor, usually halting their growth mere seconds before the plates were set down. It was what I imagined a ballet set in a restaurant would look like.

While the others prepared the tables, Hellebore's attention was on the large pane of ice lowering from the ceiling. Massive and smooth, I realized its purpose only seconds before the picture flared on.

Despite Krystal's warning about chitchat, the floating pane of ice was a bit too much to resist. "You made a magical flat-screen?"

The device put the highest of definitions to shame. I could see Krystal perfectly while she clung to the giant creature's leg, slowly climbing upward. Flaming hair, nails and teeth like obsidian, she was far past human. It had been years since I saw her this way, and I was a bit surprised to realize it didn't scare me like it had the last time. I'd learned too much about what people were versus how they looked; to me, this was nothing more than an aesthetic shift.

"Or humans made a technological versions of a simple ice-screen," Hellebore replied. "The truth is a bit of both. We've used the screens for ages, but it required humanity's predilection for excess to utilize the idea in some of its newer fashions."

I genuinely had no idea what to make of that reply. Was she making small talk? Offering an olive branch of conversation while Krystal fought to save June? The whole situation was so turned around and convoluted, I had no real hope of cracking into Hellebore's true motivations. In a fortunate twist of fate, this meant my only real option was just to play everything straight and treat the conversation like it was just that: idle chatter.

Unthinking, I reached for a plate with what looked like slices of steak, save the scent did not match any meats I'd encountered before. There was always the chance it was some sort of wild game, but as my fingers drew close, they suddenly halted before picking a piece up. A flood of tales about the danger of eating foods in other realms had just burst through my brain, giving me second thoughts about casual snacking.

"The food is safe, Fredrick Fletcher. You are my guest, and it is offered freely. There is no debt incurred by hospitality already granted." Despite the words, Hellebore hadn't actually looked in my direction; she was still watching the screen.

On it, Krystal was climbing the leg, her searing claws carving handholds into its flesh. Unfortunately, the pain was drawing the creature's attention. I could already see the enormous body shifting as its head began the long journey of swinging around. I really hoped she had some sort of power or plan for dodging, because there was no way she'd get all the way up before the blizzard behemoth could blast her.

While part of me was hesitant, I also didn't think it was a good idea to belittle or ignore the graces of a fey host, so I picked up the slice of meat, which was lain atop some toasted bread, and chomped down. It was both incredibly good and definitely not any animal I'd ever had before—I could tell by something about the tang of the meat and the chew of the fat. Good, delicious, but off in ways I couldn't quite articulate. Taking another piece, I also helped myself to what looked like the clearest water I'd ever seen in my life, held in a goblet of exquisite ice. Not a lot of variety in the theme, go figure.

"You really sent one person against that thing?" I wandered over to the screen, where whatever magical camera was in use had pulled back, giving a wider view of the trouble heading Krystal's way.

"Certainly not. That would be suicide for all but one of the royal blood. I sent an *agent* against the blizzard behemoth; surely you know how fearsome their reputation is." Maybe it was because Krystal was gone, or she just didn't care what I thought, but there was practically an aura of satisfaction around Hellebore as she landed that line. Perhaps the reputation of the Agency bothered her for some reason.

This was probably where I should have let things lie. In another context, I very well might have, too. But Krystal was out there fighting a giant monster to save our friend; at the bare minimum, I could conjure the courage for conversation in the hopes of uncovering something useful.

"It didn't have to be June."

For the first time since Krystal had left, Hellebore's eyes flitted briefly in my direction. "You think I have a list of agents that can be summoned to serve at a moment's notice?"

"I think anyone cunning enough to gain a favor from the Blood Council has the wits to obtain plenty more from other, less challenging sources. Meaning that yes, Hellebore, you probably do have a list of people you can fetch at a moment's notice, some of whom I presume are even stronger than agents."

I was not blind to the hint of accusation I was presenting, which was why I'd been sure to frame it all as a compliment. Hopefully, she wouldn't find a way to take offense at me praising her intellect and resources.

"That would depend on the agent, I suppose." Her eyes were back on the screen, and mine soon followed.

The blizzard behemoth was glaring down at Krystal like a dog spotting a tick. It was clear what was coming—to us and, apparently, to Krystal, who adjusted her position, putting the bulk of the leg between herself and the head. As it swung around, she leapt up and over, gaining height and a fresh position of cover as she clawed her way onto new patches of flesh. On a normal creature, it would have worked, forcing the animal to try from another angle as it reoriented. Unfortunately, the leg began to rise, lifting up along the blizzard behemoth's body, free of any joints or spinal structure. It was more like a growth, apparently, one that could be moved around the body as needed. The whole thing started to spin, putting Krystal in point-blank range for a blast of slush.

There were limits to her power—we'd talked about that before. In this form, she could die for real. If something was strong enough to overwhelm her, she'd be gone for good, along with her unseen prisoner. I had no idea what those limits were, or where a blizzard behemoth fell on that scale. Sure, it was huge, but Gideon lived as a child. Looks weren't everything in the parahuman world.

"Is this what you wanted? Krystal facing defeat, humbled for some slight against the fey?"

"You must be mistaken. I summoned June Windbrook for the task; Krystal Jenkins joined of her own free will." For a moment, it seemed like Hellebore would stick to the story—until she kept going. "One could certainly invent their own, were they so inclined. Wild, slanderous accusations, such as that I knew Krystal would follow when June was taken and was prepared for the two of you. As to what purpose, now, that is where your conjecture falls apart. The blizzard behemoth is a challenge and a danger, but it would be hard-pressed to actually kill either June or Krystal, so my intention cannot be murder. A more charitable theory, also clearly an incorrect one, might be that this was all set up as a wedding present, of sorts."

I'd been keeping up with her obfuscation for the most part; however, that final sentence momentarily stalled my brain out completely. "A wedding present?"

"Every partner should see the other as they truly are before binding their lives together."

In spite of her best efforts, Krystal couldn't keep up with the moving leg; the creature she was fighting controlled the very "ground" she was clutching. It waited until she'd jumped to the side and landed, twisting the leg as her grip caught. There was no chance to dodge this time: Krystal vanished in the vomit of slush, and the explosion of snow and ice that followed.

"Hang on, that's what this is all about? Seeing her devil form? I did that forever ago. Back when we first started dating." I waved at the screen, truly hoping we'd just hit upon a misunderstanding that could put everything to a halt. "None of this is necessary, if that's your aim."

As the recent wave of snow cleared, I could see a huge chunk of ice tumbling down the behemoth's body. I'd have known it was Krystal from context, even without the wisp of steam rising from the surface and small trickles of water running down the side. She was still in there, trying to melt her way out. But as the ice chunk tumbled, I noticed that the water quickly refroze. The very environment was against her out there, making the job of escape all the more impossible.

"You really think *that* is the form that earns Agent Jenkins such a reputation?" Hellebore looked as though she might actually break out into laughter. "She is called in when force is demanded most, when raw power is what is needed to deal with a threat. Given all you've seen of the parahuman world, does fast healing, burning hair, and deadly claws truly feel like they warrant that much reverence?"

"What are you saying?"

"I am saying that today, by sheer happenstance, you may get to see the true form of your betrothed. The one she can let out when there is nobody else around to endanger. Once you do, only then will you have proper insight into the woman you intend to marry. If nothing else, you'll have a better appreciation for why it's so silly that you're actually worried for her."

I'd have asked for clarity from Hellebore, save for the fact that it wasn't needed. On our screen, steam stopped rising from the Krystal ice-container. Instead, something inside the frozen prison was glowing with a dark, unnatural light. The ice cracked once, a massive split running at a diagonal across the surface, then exploded outward into burning, quickly melting chunks.

Standing there, wreathed with purple-black flames, stood a being that was almost recognizable as my fiancée. The wings and horns certainly didn't help, though.

5.

THE DARK, OBSIDIAN MATERIAL OF HER claws and teeth now coated the majority of Krystal's body like armor, culminating in a pair of sharp horns that jutted from her forehead. Around her, the snow was burning off at a rapid clip, no amount of cold capable of matching the heat rippling off of her in this form. Her purple-black flames danced across the armored body, flaring and contracting, obliterating everything they touched. Despite how dramatic the transformation was, it was the wings that stole the show.

Each was the same color as her flames, four wings extending from her back, forming a rough "X" across her figure. They flapped a single time, and a wave of heat eroded the snow in a line in front of her. As she got comfortable, her flames grew. Brighter, larger—she wanted to attract the behemoth's attention. I had a hunch this round wouldn't go the same way.

"Well?"

I realized that, inadvertently, I'd been ignoring Hellebore's attention, too focused on the screen to notice she was waiting for something.

"Well, what?" I turned, the edges of my patience fraying slightly. "Did you expect wailing and gnashing of teeth? Sudden remorse? Terror? Did you think for one actual second that I have even the slightest of concerns about what Krystal is? Let me put it plainly, then. I love that woman, regardless of what forms she can change into, or what sorts of abilities she has. Krystal uses that strength to stand up for people who can't protect themselves, and that will always matter worlds more to me than some powers she possesses. The life she lives tells me who Krystal is; *that* is nothing more than cosmetics."

I jerked my thumb to the screen, where Krystal had begun to take flight, lifting from the ground slowly as an expanding circle of melted snow grew from her epicenter. "And what really gets my goat is you already know that,

Hellebore. Whatever game you're playing, this obviously wasn't your real goal."

"Whatever makes you say that?" Her eyes weren't on the screen anymore. Being under her stare was heavy, but no matter how much I wished they might flit away, one glance to the enchanted pane of ice showed me what Krystal was dealing with. I could push my way through an uncomfortable conversation, at minimum.

"Because it's a stupid plan, and you are much too wise to have formed it."

Her smile showed me more teeth than needed, white and sharp and perhaps just a hair too long. "You're dancing on a line."

In for a penny, in for a pound. I was fairly sure that, so long as I kept things polite, my guest status would protect me. To an extent. "Then I apologize for any implied slight. I was complimenting your intelligence, not belittling it. What I've seen paints you as a brilliant thinker, capable of playing both the Agency and the Blood Council to your own gain. That doesn't sound like the sort of mind who would expect something like this to genuinely derail our wedding."

The smile closed a tad, and her eyes went back to Krystal for a merciful reprieve. "It certainly would be surprising if you were scared away so easily after how far you've come, but you'd hardly be the first to run from what was hidden. Many parahumans have revealed their actual selves only to be abandoned, or worse. Yet you speak truth, Fredrick Fletcher: I had little expectation that this would change your mind. Still, did you not deserve to see it, to make this commitment fully informed? A marriage is a contract, and by now, you should have realized how seriously the parahuman world takes those."

A roar brought my eyes back to Krystal. She'd risen higher in the sky, and from the dripping sear on the blizzard behemoth's flank, the first attack had gone well. It attempted to bite her out of the air, enormous jaws slamming down so hard I felt the castle shake. Not that it mattered; like a fly dodging the swatter, Krystal was fast and nimble as she blazed through the sky. Zipping in close, she raked its skin with her claws, opening up steaming wounds wherever she struck. The burns didn't subside, either; purple-black flame continued to sizzle on the surface.

Changing tactics, the behemoth let loose a torrent of slush, aiming for Krystal and its own back in the same shot. The material hit one target, kicking off another storm of flurries and ice, but the dark wings carried Krystal out of range. She rolled through the sky, lining up another angle of attack. While she'd avoided getting frozen again, I did notice the lingering fires were extinguished. How smart was this creature, anyway?

While Krystal circled, I turned the situation over in my head again. What had we missed? Hellebore stole June, had Tem deliver a message, brought us here, and was now making me watch Krystal fight some snow monster. How did this benefit her? What possible goal could there be? The ones she'd stated were a flimsy pretense—an excuse, if I was generous. Fey didn't move without reason, and nothing about Hellebore suggested a grudge toward Krystal. There had to be some part of the game we'd yet to catch.

"If all you wanted was for me to see Krystal in her full-power form, then we've done it. I see her, I accept her, and I have no regrets or doubts about my upcoming wedding. Does this need to drag on?"

"What a thing to say. Is there not still a blizzard behemoth on the steps of my kingdom? Obviously, Agent Jenkins will need to drive it off before she can pronounce the job completed, no matter how long it takes."

She wasn't being subtle, but I'd needed the help, so was in no position to complain. "How long? Seems to me, she has a clear upper hand."

On the screen, Krystal had launched into a dive, falling low and striking for the creature's face, only to hit neck as it twisted at the last moment. Her attack left visible wounds, yet I now realized they were only surface level. She was hurting it, not injuring it, and that would make for a much more protracted fight.

Hellebore ran her fingers along one of the ice tables still holding refreshments, a new hue of blue washing over from the point where she touched. It was darker than the shade decorating most of the castle, more somber. "Ordinarily, Agent Jenkins would be raining hellfire down to burn that thing away. Such a technique would be dangerous with Agent Windbrook frozen somewhere below, so I suspect she's been forced to use slower methods. Even with that, this invader seems to be particularly strong, almost like it's drawing power from another source. All told, I still expect she will win this fight, given a month or so."

Was that it? Did she want Krystal to miss the wedding? No... this piece was the leverage. Just like pulling June had been all about drawing Krystal in, holding our next month hostage gave Hellebore power. Why she needed more, I couldn't possibly imagine. She already had every part of the situation in hand. Outside of killing us, Hellebore could more or less do what she wanted, and if she did want us dead, there were no shortage of options once we left. What did this give her that she didn't already have?

"You know what, Hellebore, I give up. I can't play these kinds of games, not while watching Krystal out there fighting. How about instead of all this dancing around, you just tell me what it is you want from us?"

"Impulsive child, did you never imagine that some of us like to dance?" As Hellebore spoke, Krystal dropped in for another dive, narrowly dodging a stream of slush-vomit that the blizzard behemoth had held waiting. They were both adjusting to one another's style, meaning that this actually might prove to be a more prolonged battle, not that I'd really doubted Hellebore. She was the sort to make sure her threats carried weight. "Besides which, the first rule of negotiation is that power comes from knowledge. Were I to reveal my true designs, it would just make you haggle all the harder on those points."

"Or I might just give it to you so we can be done with all of this," I countered. "Not that I'm sure what I could offer. You don't seem the type for white-collar crime, so I can't imagine you want my clients' records, and there's no item or access I have that you don't. Unless this is a Gideon thing; though, in that case, I should tell you upfront that I'm not a particularly valuable hostage."

No change in Hellebore's face; if not for the occasional shifts of her gaze, I might not have even known she was listening—until I got to Gideon's name, which earned me a slight raise of an eyebrow. "Few have the gall to so casually use the King of the West's name without a proper title attached. However, this has nothing to do with him. There are channels for those of our stations to communicate."

Then what? My condition might make me slightly interesting as a prisoner—as a novelty, if nothing else— but I had a hunch Deborah and the Blood Council would take umbrage with that, at least until I'd been fully studied. The longer this drew on, the more I loathed the entire thing. Calling us out, forcing Krystal to fight, toying with us under her thumb because she could… it felt like I was dealing with a more competent version of Quinn, my sociopathic sire.

At the thought of him, pieces began to fall into place. Outside of a vampire specific condition, there was nothing special about me from Hellebore's point of view. Anyone I had alliances with, she could reach. Any item I might have, she could obtain. But Quinn… Quinn was something different. He'd made a lot of enemies on all sides of the parahuman tracks, and was so good at hiding, not even the Agency could find him. The only thing he'd consistently shown up for was a chance to torment me. It was a wild swing in the dark, no question, which made me all the more grateful vampires could see even without light.

"It is impressive that you've made her show this much strength." I had to approach this very carefully: my guest status was all that kept me safe, and I wasn't entirely sure what level of slight would rob me of its protection. "Been a long time since she had to try like this. The last one to pull it off was my absolute bastard of a sire, a man named Quinn."

No reaction, not that I'd expected one to come that easily from someone like Hellebore.

"He used kidnapping, too, actually. And a unique location. No giant monster; just a bunch of ghouls. Did the dirty work himself, so that's another difference. Still, lots of similarities in the plan. I guess you two must tactically think ali—ACK!"

I had expected this to be the start of a long, drawn-out process by which I would slowly attempt to elicit some manner of reaction from Hellebore. Instead, before the end of my sentence, I found my whole body spun instantly through the air, stopping only when my head pressed hard against the icy floor, Hellebore's hand tightly gripping the lower half of my skull. Her eyes bore down into me, the horror and savagery of winter on full display. In that moment, I saw the storm inside her, and realized for the first time that I'd gotten the entirely wrong gauge on Hellebore.

She wasn't calm at all. She was a furious sea buried beneath a thick sheet of ice. The placid demeanor and constant control was a mask to hide whatever was fueling this rage.

"You *dare* compare me to that vile, slithering worm. I should tear out your tongue and hang it over my bed— with the others."

On a positive note, I'd definitely found Hellebore's sore spot, and the likely reason we were in this mess. The downside was that I might not survive long enough to make actual use of it.

6.

THE ROOM WAS SILENT AND TENSE.
Ultimately, it was a roar from the blizzard behemoth—
coming first through the enchanted ice screen, and then
rattling the castle itself, albeit slightly—that broke the
stillness. Not much, but enough to shake Hellebore's
mind back to the actual moment. I saw the shift in her
eyes, that hard wall sliding back into place as she reas-
serted her control. It was also of note that even as her
demeanor changed, her grip never lessened. My cheek-
bones felt like her fingers were leaving dents, and without

magic, I suspected the floor under my head would have cracked, if not shattered. Her strength was incredible, and this was her just casually throwing someone about.

"It seems we have both come very near to crossing a line today, Fredrick Fletcher. You flirted with the idea that I am equivalent to Quinn, and I almost tore your head off for the slight. However, as neither of us quite went that far, it seems my hospitality is still in effect. I would caution you not to test it."

Finally, Hellebore's grip vanished. In the time it took me sit up, she was already back across the room, watching the screen as Krystal created a sphere of flame the size of beach ball between her hands. I took my time rising, rubbing my neck slightly, but whatever damage she'd done was already healed. At least I didn't have to choke or gasp for air; one of the perks of breathing only out of habit.

"I hate him, too, you know. He turned me, abandoned me, then tried to kill me and my friends because I failed to live up to expectations. There's no loyalty, no connection. If I knew where he was, I'd tell you."

"Of that, I have little doubt. You complimented my intelligence earlier, do not underestimate it now. I am fully aware of the relationship you have with your sire." Maybe it was because of the slip, or maybe I was starting to see past the flawless features to the emotions hidden beneath, but Hellebore seemed slightly stiffer than before.

I had to pick my words carefully here. Another slight, and that was probably it. Hellebore was clearly off-balance when it came to the subject of Quinn. From the hatred, it was evident they wouldn't be in league together, though perhaps that had occurred in the past. She knew I couldn't contact Quinn, and that we hated one another, so I had no value as a hostage. My only value...

When it clicked into place at last, I felt like an absolute buffoon. It was all there: the connections, the intelligence, even why she'd go through all this trouble just to get me alone, with leverage over the person I cared most about. In a way, it was comforting. It answered a question I'd been carrying with me since Quinn's last attack.

"You know, a few years ago, someone had me put out in the field on an assignment I wasn't really suited or needed for, which just so happened to lure Quinn out from hiding. I've been wondering for a while who within the Agency would want Quinn bad enough to use me as bait. In theory, I suppose it also could have been someone from the outside, the sort of person with clout to spare and favors to burn. But I dismissed that idea, because if someone from the outside had set it up, they would have sent some forces to see the job done."

"One might have assumed that drawing Quinn to a domicile with four active agents and Arch would have been enough to handle a single rogue vampire. Or, perhaps, the force was not permitted to act directly."

I really hadn't been sure if Hellebore would rip my heart out for that or not, so getting a soft confirmation that I was on the right track nearly tipped me over with relief. Rising to my feet, I shook off the last of her attack, steeling myself to press on. I could see Krystal hurling her orb of flame, catching one of the blizzard behemoth's legs and blowing off a visible chunk of flesh. A massive roar of pain rattled us once more, giving me time to prepare my thoughts.

That last bit had been an obvious hint—more a signpost, to be honest. Hellebore couldn't act independently to go after Quinn for some reason. She had to use pawns. My only role in her plans would likely be as bait; Quinn had consistently proven a willingness to show up for any chance at taking me out. She needed to make me play that role at any point and time that best suited her next scheme. All of this, stealing June, maneuvering Krystal—it was designed to make me offer the one thing Hellebore couldn't just take. I didn't know much about the fey, but I'd gotten a crash course on their rules regarding contracts and favors.

"While I do recognize the difficulty in halting such a large monster as a blizzard behemoth, seeing the tremendous power you possess, I have to wonder if things might not resolve faster with your aid. Is that the sort of negotiation you were looking to enter?"

Hellebore tapped the bottom of her chin, as if she were actually considering this bold new idea that had been brought to her attention. "Since you suggested it, I suppose that could indeed be possible, were I willing to significantly exert myself. Of course, there must be recompense for such aid, wouldn't you agree?"

On screen, the blizzard behemoth fired a torrent of slush across its wounded leg. Seconds later, it swung the appendage around, revealing a hunk of ice that had formed in the missing section. It hadn't healed, precisely, but it had avoided losing any mobility, and even caught Krystal by surprise. She narrowly avoided a different leg's claws, soaring between them at the last moment.

"You want a favor. I get it. And I'll give you one, with conditions. I won't do anything illegal—that includes both human and parahuman laws—and I won't do anything immoral."

"Strange, you value such trivial distinctions over your beloved?" Needling as her tone was, I didn't fall for it.

"Absolutely. You're not actually threatening either Krystal or June; you're just stealing time from us. Yes, changing a wedding at the last minute will be a bear, but Krystal would far rather deal with that than have to

DREW HAYES

hunt me down for a crime or watch me do something unforgivable. Not illegal, not immoral. Oh, and toss in that you can't use the favor until after our honeymoon. Let's make sure nothing else potentially conflicts with the wedding. I know how specific these conditions *can* get, so I'm perfectly aware that this is cutting you a good deal."

Another set of roars—Krystal was apparently going for the eyes again, this time staying close even as the behemoth snapped for her. She managed to land a few wounds at that, despite the constant need for dodging made attacking quite the challenge. I lingered on that image of her fighting, watching the monstrous form, still fairly sure I could make out her signature wild grin on the obsidian-armored face.

For her part, Hellebore's attention lingered there only briefly. "Not so good a bargain as you might expect. Fredrick Fletcher is known for a few things among parahumans already, and one of them is his sense of ethics. The law is defined; morality less so. What is immoral to you might be perfectly normal to me, so you can see how such a nebulous definition leaves you with all the power. You could claim moral objection to any request, and I would have little recourse."

The point wasn't completely irrelevant; at the same time, there was zero chance we were going to use Hellebore's ethics as our gauge. No sooner had the problem been posed than I saw the solution. In fact, it came so fast, I immediately questioned it, wondering whether this had been Hellebore's design all along. Maybe it was; she was someone who schemed on a scale I couldn't even begin to fathom. Whose idea it had been didn't change the validity of it, however, so after a few more moments of consideration, I made my pitch.

"Then I propose we use September Windbrook as the judge of morality. If I oppose the favor you request, he will give us his best, honest ruling, free from any other favors or obligations he may owe to either of us. Should September rule it to be moral, then I'm bound to comply. Immoral, and we change the request or cancel it entirely, using the favor at a later point."

There was something in Hellebore's expression, too fleeting to identify—though, with her, any break in controlled expression was worth noting. "Interesting. Might I ask why you nominate September, of all people?"

"He seems like the best middle ground. Part-fey—of the winter region, at that, so he has personal loyalty to you. Add in the fact that I'm marrying Krystal, and we can agree that he's probably not disposed to liking me. At the same time, September Windbrook works for the Agency, which means he also has some sense of duty and ethics."

"Not quite the same as personal morals," Hellebore pointed out.

"No, it's not. But whatever else about September Windbrook might be true, he also won Krystal's heart for a time. Even in the state she was back then, Krystal is too perceptive and smart to be taken in completely. September might have turned out to be a jerk, but Krystal could never love a monster. I trust her, and I trust her judgment."

A long pause stretched between us, until Hellebore's hand dipped into an unseen pocket on her shimmering dress. From within, she produced a single metal disc with a small divot on each side. It reflected the light strangely, the rainbow hue of spilled gasoline, as she turned it around in her fingers. "Your conditions are acceptable. In return, I will lend aid to Agent Krystal Jenkins in defeating the blizzard behemoth."

"Hellebore, I think it's safe to say I've been a pretty good sport about all this. I'm not even fighting on giving you what you want, merely laying out some basic rules of protection. Do we really need to go through the back and forth of me getting you to commit to meaningful help, rather than a nebulous promise?"

She clucked under her tongue at me, as though I was a child caught reaching for the cookie jar. "Yes, we really should, but I did slip up earlier when I laid hands upon you. It was a minor incident, yet I can already feel the effects. I'll make amends by granting your request. Frankly, I'm about ready to be done with all of this, too. Very well: in exchange for the favor as outlined, I will aid in defeating the blizzard behemoth, then return Fredrick Fletcher, Agent Krystal Jenkins, and Agent June Windbrook safely to Charlotte Manor before day's end. Specific enough?"

I couldn't see many ways that might go wrong, and betraying us didn't make much sense from Hellebore's perspective. Sure, I might now be under her thumb, but she'd have a pissed-off Krystal to deal with—which, as the blizzard behemoth's back could attest, was no small amount of trouble. Krystal was currently running along the top of the creature, leaving as many burning wounds as she could. Hopefully, her battle was nearly done.

Walking over, I looked down to the metal disc. "It sounds like we've got a deal. I'm presuming that plays some part in it?"

"Just something to keep the official record. While the magic of our agreements empower themselves, when one in my station makes such a bargain, record must be kept. It is not unheard of for one to attempt renegotiations down the line, arguing about the spirit of the terms when wording has multiple interpretations. This preserves the bargain as it was struck, words and meaning, so that such cases can be immediately resolved."

Sure as I was that this served more than just that one function, I was effectively out of wiggle room. Besides, I didn't see Hellebore giving ground on this one. As I watched, she lifted the disc by the edges with her left hand, then put her right thumb on the divot at the bottom. It stayed perched there, no matter which way she angled her hand, and she extended the arm toward me. The other divot faced up, implication clear.

Hoping with all my might that this wasn't a huge mistake, I pressed my own thumb onto the disc.

There was a tingle, a prick, and then the entire disc changed color. It went from reflecting that odd, rainbow-like sheen to a simple, dull golden color, which vanished into Hellebore's dress as suddenly as it had appeared.

"The terms are set. The deal is struck." Hellebore looked not at the screen, but through the ice-window that Krystal had leapt out of, past the swirling storm to the giant monster swatting ineffectually at its flying foe. "I suppose that means it's time to deal with my little yard pest."

7.

I WAS EXPECTING HELLEBORE TO GO leaping out the window like Krystal had, or maybe vanish and reappear on screen, inches away from delivering a devastating blow. Instead, I was treated to watching a simple snap with a crystal clear harmony that echoed off the castle's frozen walls.

"While I trust you to uphold your end of the bargain, would you mind terribly explaining what you just did?"

Hellebore motioned to the screen, where I saw Krystal lobbing another orb of purple-black fire, this time causing an explosion on the monster's rear left flank. Unlike the prior attacks, this one wasn't ignored or quickly patched. Instead, the behemoth let out a horrendous wail that thundered against my ears, even from so far off. Rather than trying to chew Krystal from the sky, its legs scrambled to find purchase as it began to move rapidly away from her.

"Remember how I said it seemed as if this particular nuisance was drawing power from somewhere? I forcibly severed such connections, returning the creature to its natural state. Aggressive though they are, the nuisances are also smart enough to avoid fights they can't win. It has already noticed the change."

She was right. The blizzard behemoth wasn't just repositioning for a better attack angle; it seemed to be gaining speed, large claws gripping the peaks of mountains as its long body dragged across the range. Krystal flew after it at first, not striking, but staying in close range. After ten seconds of pursuing her enemy, who was solidly sprinting away from her as fast as its legs would go, she circled back to the area where the two had been fighting. While I might have momentarily forgotten what this was really about, Krystal never had. Her burning body dropped low as she presumably searched for June. With her opponent fleeing and no more slush streams clouding the air, it should be a much easier process.

"Hypothetically speaking, had this been organized by someone, it would be quite an intricate plan. Enhance a strong enough creature to make a viable threat, have it assault your lands, use your own people as pawns to draw us here, coerce Krystal into joining the fray, all to get one favor out of me. A lot of trouble and ways to go wrong, yet the outcome speaks to the planner's genius."

"If you think that hypothetical constitutes much of a plot, you should really familiarize yourself better with fey culture. What you just described would be our equivalent of a puzzle with only four corner pieces." Hellebore didn't sound like she was kidding—not that her tone ever told me much. It was probably a mix of both truth and hyperbole. I had a hunch that this endeavor represented a bit more effort than she might want me to think, but I also knew these were beings of incredible power who lived for untold centuries. Lots of time to practice thinking ahead.

With the snowstorm steadily clearing, I could once more make out Krystal's flames on screen as she flew around, searching the ground. Every flap of those four wings (that really shouldn't have supported a human's weight) turned more flurries to steam, bypassing the material's liquid phase entirely. She worked methodically, checking each area up and down before moving on to the next section. I doubted she even noticed the fading storm; everything she had was focused on hunting for her friend.

Looking away from the screen, I turned my eyes to the window, where I could still see the blizzard behemoth running deeper into the mystical mountains, to a place I imagined was even colder than here. I'd only seen pieces of the fey world, and was only now beginning to understand just how huge it could really be. For entire species like that to exist, in balance with the world around them, meant we weren't just in a place where the rules of sunshine worked differently. This was truly another ecosystem, an entire new world, not some mere reflection of our own.

"Forgive me if this is rude or some manner of kingdom secret, I really don't mean to pry, but my curiosity demands at least an attempt. What's the connection between our two lands? Why can we walk between them? Are they just neighbors, or are they more interwoven than that?"

Now that I'd finally gotten the gumption to pose a few queries, the questions burst forth. Hellebore seemed unbothered, for all that was worth, so I'd hopefully managed to avoid more offense. "If those answers are a secret of our kingdom, then they are known only to the empress and other rulers, not to ones such as myself. I am old, Fredrick Fletcher, old beyond what most mortals would dare to imagine, yet not even I have been here from the start. Yours is only one of the realms we can reach, as is ours to you. Do not forget where your beloved's power comes from. Why such passage is possible and varies between realms is either the domain of those beyond ourselves or simply the nature of existence."

Right. I'd forgotten about the fact that devils did occasionally break over into our world, along with demons, fey, and other assorted beings I'd probably never heard of yet. Every time I thought I had a handle on how dangerous the parahuman world was, I got a fresh look to show me I'd barely scratched the surface. Even with years to adjust, I was still slowly growing accustomed to living on the same planet as beings with Gideon's power. Now, I had to start grappling with whole other worlds right on top of ours, places where a blizzard behemoth was considered a pest.

A whoop of triumph stole my mind from such unproductive thoughts. On the enchanted screen, I could see Krystal, now standing over a familiar chunk of ice. It looked much like the one that had bound her, and as she sank her dark claws into the gleaming surface, the miniature prison melted away. Within seconds, it was weak enough to rip apart, which was precisely what Krystal did. In fact, she yanked so hard that chunks went flying through the air, crashing in the snow quite a distance off.

From within the now shattered ice, Krystal arose, carefully holding June Windbrook, whose face showed her to be a touch dazed, but otherwise unharmed. She leapt up from the ground, moving so fast the screen lost her. Moments later, I realized the item would no longer be necessary. Hellebore removed the ice-window once more, just in time for Krystal to come barreling through. The divider was back in place moments later, though I wondered how long it would hold with the heat Krystal was throwing off.

Seeing her at a distance had been one thing; up close and personal, I could appreciate how terrifying this new form really was. The armor was more than dark and hard, it was sharp, like any attack would hurt the striker more than the one receiving it. It didn't help the general sense of menace that there was a sort of unnatural red shimmer that came and went, almost following one's gaze. Her wings were still the show stealer, some parts so dark they looked like an abyss that had been sliced into reality. I felt like, the longer I looked at them, the easier it would be to fall into that space.

Yet before my eyes, the whole veneer was fast fading. Her wings shrank, the fire dimmed, and most of the armor fell away in cracking chunks, crumbling to what looked like ash upon hitting the floor. By the time the room was no longer capable of serving as a makeshift oven, Krystal was back to what I'd previously considered her devil form: claws and teeth, burning hair, glowing eyes.

I never thought I'd be so happy to see that shape.

"Very well done, Agent Krystal Jenkins. You have successfully driven off our invader, assisting Agent June Windbrook in her task. While you did so of your own volition, and thus have no right to claim reward, I do send you on with the thanks of winter, and this small token." Before any of us could move, Hellebore was next to Krystal, leaning into kiss her delicately on the forehead.

The room spun for an instant, and when it was done, Krystal was back to normal. Human form, clothes unsullied by snow, ash, or blood: it was like she'd never jumped out the window in the first place. Usually, Krystal needed a few hours to fully downshift; I hadn't even realized it was possible for a fey to aid the process. Was Hellebore flexing her power once more to drive the message home?

"You have been refreshed." After a moment, Hellebore placed two fingers against her own lips, and then lowered her hand onto June's forehead. This time, there was no immediate spin or change, but June's half-opened eyes fully fluttered shut. "Agent June Windbrook will recover, as well, given some time to rest. Her injuries were more severe than your own."

"That's because she never should have been put against that thing in the first place," Krystal snapped. Unlike me, she wasn't quite so concerned with keeping things polite. "I still don't know what this was about, but I'm going to find out, Hellebore. And if you get any fresh ideas, feel free to remember the sight of me sending that big old bastard running for the hills."

I almost missed it. The moment came so fast, a simple point where assumptions and misunderstandings could create a secret. Luckily, my brain caught the snag, and I saw the trap laid out, plain as day. Hellebore expected me to keep the favor a secret, to protect Krystal from knowing the deal I'd made to help, preserving her pride in winning the day. There wasn't even a need for me to lie: Krystal was already heading toward the expected conclusions without a word of input on my end. It was a cunning trick, cloaked in concern, yet giving Hellebore one more piece of leverage over me.

"It didn't run on its own. Hellebore agreed to help drive it off, sooner than the weeks it would have taken, in exchange for a favor from me." For all of Hellebore's planning, she'd erred in expecting me to keep something secret. Krystal and I didn't always see eye-to-eye—we'd had our share of disagreements, and even a few outright arguments—but we'd made it through everything we had by trusting and relying on one another. Keeping the truth from her wouldn't make our predicament better; it would just mean we couldn't face it together.

To my utter shock, Krystal stayed calm. Perhaps flying around in devil form had worked off some excess aggression, or holding her unconscious friend would make a second fight harder. Whatever the case, she took a deep breath as understanding set in, then set her jaw.

"I get it now. I mean, I don't *get* it, but we'll have time to figure that part out. This was all a ruse to squeeze you, and they used me to do it. Well, used June to use me, and I think now, maybe you're seeing why I'm glad I didn't marry into a fey family. Hellebore, anything to add?"

"He spoke no mistruths. When presented with the timeframe of your task—information you never thought to request—Fredrick Fletcher grew concerned for your upcoming wedding. In return for my aide, he offered recompense: a favor, with some limitations. The deal was fair and agreed upon by both sides." From her pocket, Hellebore produced the dull gold disc.

The sight of it pulled a frown to Krystal's face, but she retained her composure. "I see. That is something we'll definitely need to discuss at length. For now, I'd like to get June home and resting. Unless there is something else, we request passage home."

"As a guest, such is your right." Hellebore raised her hand, only to be stopped by Krystal a moment later.

"Hang on! Sorry, almost forgot. Since we're here, and I have the opportunity, I would like to extend a formal invitation for our wedding. Please inform the Empress of Winter that she is welcome to attend our modest celebration, and the invitation extends to you, as well, Hellebore. We of course understand the time demands placed upon those of royalty, but one must always leave the door open should they choose to grace us with their presence."

For a reason I couldn't even begin to guess at, Hellebore's face twisted in begrudging annoyance. Something passed between her and Krystal, a look I lacked the context to interpret. "I shall pass all official correspondence along, as is my duty. Now, as you have said, my time is short."

She clapped her hands, and suddenly, the castle was gone. Instead, we were sitting on the front porch of Charlotte Manor, looking out onto the dark sky of a new evening, the sun having vanished from the sky for an hour, at most. We'd been gone for the majority of the afternoon, despite how long the ordeal felt.

I heard rustling as Krystal gently lowered June into a rocking chair, then walked over to my side.

"So, you owe the fey a favor?"

"I didn't see another way out," I admitted.

"They're pretty good about setting things up like that." Her hand landed on mine, fingers intertwining.

"At least you were smart enough to put in some limits. We'll go over those in a bit. I need to rest first. Throwing around that much power takes a toll."

Tempting as it was to let things fall off into peaceful silence, my curiosity refused to stay mute on one point. "I'm fine with that, but I have to know: why did you invite the empress and Hellebore to our wedding?"

That drew of chortling snort of laughter. "Oh man, that was a stroke of last-minute genius. Fey pride themselves on manners, procedure, all that crap. By inviting one of their royals to our wedding, through one of their *official* attendants, we have shown deference. Anyone who tried to move against that wedding, then, doing crap like what Hellebore just did, would be seen as disrespecting their royals. It's convoluted as crap, but that's politics. Hopefully, it will keep her from throwing up any hurdles just to prove a point or something equally dumb. Also, I'm pretty sure they now have to send us a gift."

"It's going to be ice-themed, isn't it?" I asked.

"One hundred percent," Krystal confirmed. "Thanks for doing what you did, by the way. Not sure I agree with the move, but I get where your heart was."

The fallout from this day would echo for unknown time to come; I now had a fey-made sword hanging overhead, and no idea when it would drop. However, in that moment, we'd won. The day was saved, the wedding was on, and our future looked bright, evening sky be damned. Not every scuffle would end this way, so I was making a point to savor the victories when they came.

I kissed Krystal, and she kissed me back, a tender moment interrupted by a hacking snore from June. Though the spell was broken, we lingered on one another's lips a bit longer before heading inside to face our friends, along with their armada of concerned questions.

TRUST, FRIENDSHIP & LOVE THAT'S TRUE

1.

PART OF ME KEPT WAITING FOR HELLEBORE to act again: another vanished friend, perhaps a loophole to call in my favor early. But as the days wore on, and we drew closer to our wedding, only a keen sense of unease crept up on me. Some of it was in regards Hellebore, but honestly, she was only one piece out of many. The more I thought about the fey, the more I realized she was probably laying groundwork for a much longer term plan. It seemed her way to be slow and deliberate, like a glacier.

No, Hellebore had only been the rock that started the avalanche of worry. Much as I tried to deal with everyone fairly and respectfully, I had made a few enemies throughout the years. The Turva clan stood out the most, as they were a constant pain in my side. There was also the serpantiles I'd helped keep from stealing a magic jewel, a rogue vampire hunter I'd gotten captured, dracolings from whom I'd won Bubba's freedom, and a myriad of tiny conflicts that had the potential to create grudges. That was without even getting into the larger threats, like my sire's occasional attempts on my life.

It was a train of thought I had to work hard to keep from my mind during the final week leading up to the wedding. Mercifully, there was plenty to do. While we'd ordered much of what we needed at the wedding in Boarback, we had still ample left to prepare and haul down. Krystal's dress had to be specially made, the Clovers were working on some enchanted displays, and Amy was whipping up a keg of something she promised would hit every parahuman like wine, regardless of their physiology. Amidst all of that, I was fielding calls to Boarback, wrapping things up with clients before the break, and giving Lillian everything she'd need to hold down the fort while I was gone.

By the time the day we were finally set to head down arrived, I'd managed to work myself to near exhaustion. Keeping busy had helped me avoid the fear of something going wrong. A few weeks prior, I'd have been anxious about bad weather, or shorting the catering order. After a full week of worry, I'd just be happy so long as everyone survived the event.

For the trip down, we had to split into multiple cars. Krystal and I, as the happy couple, rode down in my hybrid, despite Krystal's protests that her truck was roomier. I won that fight thanks to the fact that we were taking a terrestrial route into Boarback, which meant, as the honored couple, we needed to blend in. She countered by pointing out that a truck in Texas was far less distinctive, at which point, I gestured to her bumper sticker—"My only brake is breaking my foot off in your ass"—and the debate was settled.

Following us in Krystal's truck, doing the bulk of the hauling, were Asha, Amy, Bubba, and Gregor. There had been some complaints from Gregor about being in a different car, but even he seemed to understand at least this much situational context. Lillian had gone down early to see the town; Arch, Neil, and Albert were all flying in, since they had a job to do first, whereas June and Al had both said they'd take their own route. They'd been gracious enough to take the model of Charlotte Manor with them—the same one we'd used to bring her into the fey world to visit the Court of Frost. With Charlotte stuck in place by nature, it was a rare chance for her to do some sightseeing, and since I suspected

June and Al would be moving through the fey realm, Charlotte would see quite the sights indeed.

As the roads rolled by and Colorado faded into New Mexico, I slowly started to relax. For all my worrying, no one else had attacked us or stolen one of us away. Now that we were out on the road and harder to find, I felt a tad more at ease. It also didn't hurt that we were heading toward a place Krystal considered to be absolutely safe. I might never find out just what Sheriff Thorgood was, or what his powers were, but if he made Krystal feel unneeded in a fight, then it had to be impressive. Hopefully, a day in Boarback would unknot my stomach before the ceremony.

The closer we drew to our destination, the more at ease I felt. It was strange, sitting in the sunlight filtered through my enchanted windows, watching the world roll by, to know that I was so strong in darkness, yet popping open the door would set me instantly alight. That was the hard adjustment to the parahuman world too many people skimmed over. It made you stronger, yes, but also more vulnerable. It put you on the radar of far more dangerous creatures, took away your ability to pretend monsters weren't real; sometimes even changed the way you could live entirely.

My hand frequently found its way into Krystal's on the drive, a reminder that not all vulnerability was negative. Before I'd met her, my life was quiet and peaceful. Ever since... not so much. Yet I wouldn't have traded my time with her and the others for anything, not even a return to my human body. Seeing June used to manipulate Krystal had been an excellent example of how the people we loved could be wielded against us. By the same token, however, Krystal's willingness to dive in and fight proved how we were stronger when we had one another to depend on.

Thanks to an early morning departure, we managed to limit the entire journey to a single day, minimizing our need to deal with roadside motels or potential ambushes. Normally, I'd have been far more concerned with the former than the latter, though I was grateful to skip the ordeal entirely. We also made excellent time thanks to Krystal's heavy foot and some apparently enchanted dashboard trinket that kept cops from noticing us. Sometimes, I was very glad indeed for the Agency; others, I wondered just how much useful, incredibly dangerous stuff they were sitting on. In this case, I could certainly see why those items were not just given to the public at large.

Near the final stretch of travel, once the sun had dipped below the horizon, we pulled over to a roadside diner to wait for Sheriff Thorgood. Since we were going in by road, he had to escort us. The ways to Boarback were secret, and most of them would be blocked off by one seemingly natural phenomenon or another if we lacked guidance. It was one of the many layers of protection used to keep humans from accidentally wandering into an openly parahuman town. Boarback was among the very limited places in the country where supernatural beings could exist without hiding; no normal person was prepared to walk in on that scene.

As we filtered into the diner, I wondered how many parahumans took this route. The faded '50s facade felt like any other roadside eatery across the nation, yet no one blinked an eye as our party of six—two of whom were pale, two of whom were huge—ambled through the entrance. Granted, there were maybe seven other people in the entire establishment, and it was a bit late, so perhaps they were dealing with their own distractions.

We gathered around a table probably built for parties of eight, the extra space just enough for Gregor and Bubba's shoulders. Looking at the pair, it dawned on me that perhaps we should have added another car to the convoy. There was no way those two could have been comfortable in the same vehicle, even one as spacious as Krystal's truck.

The menu was simple, essential fare one would expect from such a venue. Krystal ordered a pot roast, while Bubba and Gregor chose to consume multiple burgers each. Amy, who was wearing oversized sunglasses and a hair-concealing hat despite the late hour, asked for two milkshakes and a packet of saltines. Asha opted for one of the few salads on the menu, and I got a club sandwich. It didn't really matter what I chose, as my real nutrition came from blood, but I had a hunch it wouldn't go to waste. Between Bubba and Gregor, there was no shortage of appetites to go around.

Once orders were placed, Asha lifted up her water glass, the only drinks we'd all been served so far. "Before we dig in, I just wanted to say thank you once more for letting me come along. I know I'm not technically in this club, but it means the world to me to get to cheer for you on your special day. Fred, Krystal, cheers to your upcoming nuptials. And thanks for hiring me to do the paperwork—that really helped my billable hours."

That drew a few chortles from Bubba and a snicker from Krystal, a sure sign that I needed to know more about what we were discussing. "I'm guessing that entails more than a standard marriage contract?"

"Not all the time, no," Krystal explained, keeping her voice low, for her. "Depends on the situation. Since treaties usually apply to a type of... condition, they split up easily. But where things get sticky is when people merge their families, such as in marriage. The treaties cover those outlined, and usually their families, for obvious reasons. So when you have people with different conditions getting hitched, you're also effectively merging the rules and protections of two treaties. Now, factor in my job and all the perks that come along with it, which also apply to spouses, and you can see how it gets a little thorny. The hard part is done, though; I hired Asha to knock out the legal work a few months ago."

I wasn't sure which part of it floored me more: that Krystal had thought ahead regarding paperwork, or that she'd actually gone to the trouble of hiring a lawyer. Either way, I leaned forward and gave her a kiss on the cheek in a rare case of me initiating public affection.

"You're an amazing woman, and I can't wait until we're married."

That earned some uncomfortable fidgeting around the table, as well as a brief blush on Krystal's face. "Geez, Freddy, save a little romance for the altar."

The sound of a chair skidding scraped along the floor as Asha rose to her feet. "Since we've got some time to kill until dinner, I can go grab the contract and start running Fred through the particulars. Krystal, you have the copy I gave you?"

"Packed in my suitcase—top of the pile in the back. But you don't have to bother." Krystal tossed over my car keys, in spite of her offer to let Asha sit. We both knew she wouldn't, not when there was work to worry over, but the offer still had to be extended. As the person usually in Asha's shoes, I appreciated it when others at least tried to help me relax.

In a surprisingly graceful move, Asha snared the keys out of the air. "I've been to enough weddings to know how hectic things get once we're at the venue. I'd rather use our downtime well, then enjoy myself the rest of the trip."

"Ahhh, work first, then on to full party mode. I respect it." Krystal offered up a high-five, which Asha accepted.

As she ran out to grab the contract, I turned my attention to the rest of the people in the diner. While my fear was largely abated this close to Boarback, it wouldn't do to falter in my caution in our final mile. At least with everyone together, there wasn't much fear of being overwhelmed. Even if everyone in here was an enemy, I doubted they'd be able to get past the combo of Bubba, Gregor, and especially Krystal. I forced my eyes away, out to the window, where my anxiety wouldn't have as much to latch on to.

That twist of the head was why I witnessed it. The others only heard the boom, saw the windows crack and the plates rattle. I witnessed the actual explosion. I saw as Asha lifted the key fob and double-clicked to open the rear door. I watched the bloom of red, the sudden flash that sent her delicate, all-too-human form tossing through the air.

I was numb, unable to process what I'd just watched. In my moment of dumbstruck terror, I happened to glance down at the table where my phone was resting.

Displayed on top was a new text from an unknown number, crisp, concise, and like a blade to the gut.

"Hurt that I didn't get a wedding invitation, but I dropped off a gift, anyway. Hope you enjoyed. —Quinn"

2 .

KRYSTAL MOVING BROKE THE SPELL,
freeing me from my helpless fugue as she leapt over the
chairs, barreling for the door. The others were on her tail,
but the moment my feet hit the ground, I was already
past them. Vampire strength means our leg muscles are
enhanced, as well, so I was built for speed, but I couldn't
recall ever moving this fast before. As I briefly registered
the tickle of the front door's glass breaking on my skin
as I sped through, I realized it was because no part of me
was holding back. In that moment, I didn't give a damn

what any of those people thought or figured out. All that mattered was our friend.

I could smell the blood before I saw it, and there was plenty to whiff. Something else, too, something potent, but nothing sang to my senses stronger than blood. Reaching Asha's side, I surveyed the damage. The diagnosis was bleak. Asha's small bit of distance from the explosion had unquestionably saved her life, for the moment. Shrapnel tore up her torso, and the landing had cracked more than a few bones. I'd never had much talent nor penchant for the medical field, but as a creature who lived off blood, I knew that she was losing too much of it.

"Oh shit. Oh shit." Amy skidded to halt, dropping to Asha's side while Krystal kept coming. Gregor and Bubba took up defensive positions, which was smart. I hadn't even considered that this might only be the opening volley of an attack.

"Amy, tell me you've got something in that bag to stabilize her," Krystal barked.

"I'm sorry, but nothing I have will work. Not against that." Amy still dug into her bag, despite the hopeless expression on her face.

On the ground, Asha was struggling to breathe, grabbing my hand as she rasped. Every gurgling breath was a countdown to the end, and it was only coming faster. She was going to die. There was no doubt about it, given how far we were from the nearest hospital. There was only a single hope for her, slender as even those chances were. I looked at Krystal, who stared straight back. Bless this woman, she'd reached the same conclusion as me.

"Two per year, right?"

"Right, Freddy."

I looked backed down to Asha, one of my oldest friends, a person who'd actually known me in my human days. Part of me wondered if it would always come to this, if humans simply couldn't exist in the supernatural world. I hoped I was wrong about that; however, this wouldn't be the day to find out.

"Asha, you're dying. I am so sorry, but there's no use in hiding the truth. We've got one shot that I can think of to save you. I can try to turn you into a vampire. Odds are low you'd survive, but they're..." Deborah's words haunted me from the past, reminding me that this was yet one more inevitability she'd long seen coming. "But they're a lot better than your odds if we do nothing. It has to be your choice, though. I won't force this on someone else."

Despite her ravaged body, Asha mustered the strength to squeeze my hand once more and nod, albeit weakly. She wheezed out two lone words—"Trust... you..." before coughing spasmed in her lungs once more.

That was as good as we were going to get, and she didn't have time to spare. Leaning over, I sank my fangs into one of the unbloodied patches on her shoulder, around where the pavement had torn at her skin. I drank for as long as I dared, making sure to get enough. After that, I sank my fangs into my own palm, producing a bright pool of blood.

For a moment, I feared Asha was too far gone to drink as my hand pressed to her lips. At last, she managed to slurp down a few gulps before shuddering and falling still. I heard her heart fall into the same unnaturally perfect rhythm I'd heard in Sheri. The process had begun; how long it would take with a victim in this state, I had genuinely no idea. I looked up and noticed that the diners were starting to gather around outside. Bubba and Gregor had blocked their view as best they could, but people were getting curious.

The blare of a siren and flash of lights startled everyone; we'd been so focused on Asha and the flaming wreckage that we didn't even notice Sheriff Thorgood's truck pull up. He hefted himself out of the cab, took in the entire scene with a single glance, and then leveled his eyes at the patrons.

"All of you, back in the diner! Can you not see the damn car still burning? Sit tight until the fire department gets here. I'll have someone in to take statements shortly."

It was the same genial Leeroy tone I'd come to expect, only this time, there was a little bit more to it. A flicker of force, an iota of willpower, barely even perceptible, yet every single person did exactly as he instructed. Cheerful and kind though he was, the man held together an entire town of parahumans and commanded the respect of agents. Nobody managed that without serious power to back it up.

With the crowd handled, he strode over, sucking in a breath as he saw Asha. "Sweet mercy, what happened?"

"Quinn, my sire." I spat the words, and only then saw the surprise on the others' faces. "I got a text when the bomb went off. He wanted to make sure he got the credit, I assume."

"In just the time when we were inside? That means he's still in driving distance." A very dangerous look appeared in Krystal's eyes, one that had to be nipped in the bud.

"Or he used pawns again, which Quinn loves to do," I reminded her. "Either way, Quinn doesn't matter right now. Asha does. My first turn attempt worked; that's no guarantee that this one will, too. I might have just gotten lucky. Amy, is there anything you can do, any alchemic additive that will increase Asha's chances of success? Anything: a tenth of a percent is fine. We just have to give her a fighting chance."

There was a long pause before Amy spoke again. When I looked up, I realized that she had removed her glasses and hat, showing her eyes and hair to be both a fizzing purple. "No such potion exists to my knowledge, or the Blood Council would have huge standing orders for it. She's in the hands of your power now, Fred. That has to run its course. My larger concern is what happens if it succeeds. None of you have even noticed yet, have you? Why none of my potions could have helped? Not all the shrapnel in her is from the car."

At her words, the second scent finally clicked. "Silver. That bastard made a bomb and stuffed it with silver."

"If he was expecting to hit a vampire, that would do a lot more damage," Bubba concurred. "Also means Quinn doesn't know your secret yet."

Silver was bad. It weakened us, limited our healing, turned us back to the non-magical corpses we were meant to be. Having it stuck in her torso would be a living hell, assuming Asha was even able to survive the change with that metal still inside her. Given how weak she was, we couldn't very well go hacking around for the pieces out here in a parking lot. Even if we could find them all, there was no way we could manage in time, not at the rate her heart was fading.

"Oh god, I didn't even realize..." I shut my eyes, thinking hard. "We are not bringing Asha back just to see her die again. There's got to be a way." My mind darted back to my first attempt, and how Deborah had brought along specific blood to regenerate Sheri. "What about blood? Is there any blood out there that gives a resistance to silver, if not an immunity?"

Krystal shook her head. "Only the rarest and most powerful grant even a resistance. Dragon blood, some versions of refined fey blood, certain ancient beings that are as much myth as history, none of which we have on hand."

I heard the tinkle of glass and knew it instantly. From his pocket, Sheriff Leeroy Thorgood produced a vial with a small amount of blood in it. I'd seen that vial once before, when we first visited Boarback. He'd offered it to me as payment for services, though in truth, that was just a pleasantry. The real reason had been that it would make me strong, powerful enough not to fear the threats I'd been facing. When I turned it down, I'd expected that to be the end of things. Never had I been so glad to be mistaken.

"The hell is that?" Krystal asked.

"Wedding present," Sheriff Thorgood replied. "I thought you might want to keep this around, just in case a real bad day ever happened."

"Holy shit. Something made *you* bleed?" Krystal reeled; her reaction to this admission of Sheriff Thorgood's slight fallibility at least explained why she hadn't originally counted him as a possibility for donating blood. "Did you fight the director?"

Sheriff Thorgood shook his head. "Just found something old that felt like moving into town. We disagreed about what proper conduct was. I won, but it was tough enough to draw this, so I saved it, just in case."

"Great as all that is, it doesn't tell us dick about what that does, or even what you are," Amy pointed out. "I'm not sure if the rest of you are tracking her deterioration, but Asha is fading fast. She's either about to be dead, or in a whole lot of pain, so how about less backstory and more telling us what effects your blood has."

To that, she received a simple shrug. "No idea. Never given my blood to a vampire before, nor have any of my kind that I know of. I was a little curious myself to see what would happen if Fred drank it."

Evidently, that was Amy's last straw. Her eye and hair color changed to crackling red as she stepped up into the sheriff's face. "Then why in the living shit would we give it to our dying friend? This is not the fucking time for experiments!"

The fact that it was Amy, of all people, who was saying that truly drove home just how dire the moment was. Sheriff Thorgood, on the other hand, remained completely calm.

"I don't know what it will do, exactly, but I do know it will help." He shook the vial, then tapped it once. "That is *my* blood, which means it carries within it my willpower and intent. I offer this freely, as a gift meant to aid, so that's what it's going to do. I just don't know the shape that aid will take."

Asha's breath was so thin even I could barely hear it now. She'd gone a lot faster than Sheri, then again, Sheri hadn't been bleeding to death. The end would come soon, and she couldn't make the decision about the blood. The pain would be far too intense, and there might not be time even if we could explain everything. Asha had put her fate in our hands, *my* hands, as her sire.

My eyes went to Krystal once more. "You trust him with your life?"

"More. I'd trust him with yours."

"Then, for Asha's sake, let's hope we're both putting our faith in the right places." I held out my hand. "Sheriff Thorgood, if you don't mind, I think I'd like to accept that wedding gift."

It was in my palm near instantly. I could feel the power coming from within the vial. One day, I was going to have to learn more about what this man was and what it was he could do. Gideon's blood was the most powerful I'd ever tasted, and something told me that this would be an experience on an entirely different level. I hated that I was making Asha take the plunge with something untested, but there was simply no time for anything else.

Her breathing stopped. The end was here. I held on, realizing for the first time that we'd all been assuming I would succeed. There was an incredibly real chance that Asha would stay dead, as most who tried to become vampires did.

Seconds ticked by, each one representing more and more risk that Asha's eyes would never open again. My anxiety tried to overtake me, images of what would happen if it failed flashing into mind. I could picture her funeral, the looks on her friends' and family's faces, never understanding what had truly taken her from them. With every passing instant, the doubt threatened to swallow me whole, but I remembered that Sheri had required a bit of time, as well. I couldn't give up. Not yet. Not until we were sure she wouldn't—

Asha's eyes flew open, a scream rising through her throat. I could already hear the sizzle of flesh where the silver pierced her now enchanted body. It would be like getting stabbed by burning metal from the inside, and I had no desire to see her suffer any longer than necessary. I gripped her face firmly, turning it to mine, hoping to cut through the pain and panic.

"Asha! You have to drink this to stop the pain. Focus on me, on the blood." With that, I flicked the cap from the vial with my thumb and pressed it to her lips. I saw her entire body recoil; it was trying to fold in on itself, pain overriding reason.

But Asha Patel did not force her way into the parahuman world and build a successful law practice without potent willpower. Hands curled into fists, she bit back the screams and tipped the vial into her mouth, spilling the meager number of droplets along her tongue. With a look of defiant triumph, Asha swallowed hard, and then crumpled to the ground.

Now the screams did come, harsh and guttural, but mercifully short-lived. As we watched, Asha's body changed. The sizzling stopped, her wounds healed, but it was more than that, too. The few bits of metal I could see poking from her body were dissolving, rivers of silver running along her flesh, interweaving with the repairing skin. She lay there, shaking, as her body rebuilt itself, some sections more extensively than others.

After the first minute, she stopped screaming entirely. After the second, her body had more or less become whole. By the time Asha got to her feet at the end of minute three, she looked much like her old self: an old self wearing a half-shredded outfit, but an old self nonetheless. Her eyes were different, though. Previously brown, they seemed to glimmer with a faint, metallic twinkle.

Looking at all of us, then herself, Asha took a deep breath from habit. She clearly noticed it felt slightly off, and I could relate too well to the storm of emotions that raged across her face. None it came through when she spoke next, the false cheer in her voice working to stamp out her terror from moments prior.

"I'm really never going to get away from the bloodsucking lawyer jokes now, am I?"

3.

THE TRIP TO BOARBACK WAS LARGELY
silent; we were all more or less in shock from what had
happened. Krystal, Asha, and I all rode with Sheriff
Thorgood, while Bubba, Amy, and Gregor followed in
Krystal's truck. I tried to focus on a bright side, but the
best one I could find was that Krystal and I had packed
very little of the wedding necessities in my hybrid due to
the limited space.

I could have counted Asha being alive as another
silver lining, which I was certainly grateful for; however,

that felt more like we'd narrowly avoided a worst case scenario. I wasn't sure how she was handling the shift; despite her flippant remarks upon rising, I could see the terror in her eyes. Much as I wanted to comfort her, to tell her there were great things about this change, I also wasn't sure how to even do that. I opted instead to give her space while I figured out what to say.

Rather than head to the Bristle Inn as intended, Sheriff Thorgood took us to his office. I didn't even notice the destination change until we'd arrived and begun unloading, my mind lost in its concern for Asha. No sooner were we out of the car than a figure ran out from the building, pale and familiar as she darted through the night. Lillian arrived at our side in seconds, much to my confusion.

"Sheriff Thorgood radioed ahead. He told us what happened and had Nax grab me from the hotel." That was all I got by way of explanation before Lillian's full focus turned to Asha. "Now, I understand there's a new member of the clan I need to talk with."

Was Asha a member of my clan? I hadn't considered that, but this wasn't like Sheri, where the Blood Council had laid out her future before the change had even happened. Maybe Asha was automatically entered since I was her sire, or Lillian was just using creative language. It was something I had to investigate, though. Turning

Asha might have been unexpected, but that wasn't an excuse to blunder through the rest of her adjustments.

"I'm fine for now," Asha assured her. "Not like I haven't known you all for years. I've got a pretty good grasp on the reality of being a vampire."

"Well, obviously." Lillian leaned in conspiratorially. "But you don't think we give away *all* the cool secrets to the public, do you? You're in the club now; that means I can walk you through the really fun stuff. We'll go grab a drink and have a talk while they deal with the paperwork. For once, that's not on you."

Asha started to protest again, but the words died somewhere between her throat and lips. Instead, she merely glanced back toward Krystal's truck, which was pulling up. "I guess I'll go grab my luggage."

"Nah, just hop in the truck. They're heading to the hotel with us," Lillian explained. "Well, Gregor will probably wait around the station, but the rest of us are heading back. I'll join you shortly."

We both watched Asha walk off, legs unsteady as she would occasionally move with more power than intended. She'd need time to adjust to her new body, along with whatever potential side effect the sheriff's blood had. I waited until she was next to Krystal's loud, idling engine. Her hearing wouldn't be that good yet, not until she got the knack for focus, so I risked a few words to Lillian.

"How do you think she's holding up?"

"Asha is tough as hell and has nerve to spare. She'll probably make it somewhere private before she has the full weeping breakdown we all go through." Lillian paused, making sure I'd taken note of her words. "She just died, Fredrick. She needs to mourn that loss before she can start her new life. But don't worry about her. I've got this."

My sense of responsibility bucked immediately. "As her sire, shouldn't I be the one to help?"

"Sure, if you want to fuck it up," Lillian countered. "You know how you wouldn't have thrown me into a client meeting when I first started? Same thing. Having met some of the Turva clan, you have an idea of how diplomatic they are. It often fell to me to handle our new recruits, easing them into their new situation. Do you want Asha in the hands of someone who has done this dozens of times before, or in those of a new guy poorly suited to the task in the first place?"

"A fair assessment, if a tad harsh."

"Not enough time to be gentle. Besides, you've got bigger concerns." Lillian looked around briefly, scanning for unseen presences. "Two successes in a row."

"Doesn't mean it will work every time." I knew where she was headed; it had been lingering in my mind, as well.

Lillian shook her head. "Won't matter. That's already better than anyone I've even heard rumors of in millennia. Before, you had good odds. Now, you have the kind of success they can't ignore. I don't know how that will impact things, just be ready."

"Thanks, but I've got Krystal. Take care of Asha."

Since Asha had made it into the truck by then, Lillian hurried over, barking a few words to Bubba before hopping in. Sure enough, Gregor leapt out heavily, and I gave him a brief nod before following Sheriff Thorgood and Krystal into the building.

Boarback's sheriff's office looked much the way I remembered it: like a well-preserved artifact from a bygone era. They'd upgraded their television set, and I spied a new microwave in the break room, but otherwise, the place felt just as we'd last left it. Except for Arch sitting in the middle of the station; that was an addition that hadn't been around last time.

"Sit." He pointed at the two chairs across from him, which Krystal and I filled. Sheriff Thorgood stood over in the corner, watching with his arms crossed, but saying nothing for now. Gregor waited in the door, silent and watching, determined not to be cut from the action once again.

Once we were seated in the proffered chairs, Arch continued. "The Blood Council probably doesn't know yet, but they will soon. The turn-attempt was reported to the Agency as soon as Leeroy called it in, and while the Blood Council might not have a direct line on our operations, they pick up enough. Besides, legally, we have to notify them within twenty-four hours, as they also track the turn-attempts. There's no hiding this one, if that was even what you were considering. Beyond that, the Agency also realizes the danger Fred's numbers are posing. They are sending representatives to discuss the matter, since Fred is technically one of our freelance assets."

It was a lot to absorb, though the part at the end caught me by surprise. "Sending representatives? Between you, Krystal, and all the agents here for the wedding, how many more do they want? I'm hoping that's not code for them trucking in an army."

"If it were, they'd never make it into town," Sheriff Thorgood tossed in from the side.

"Correct. To my knowledge, they'll only be sending in three additional assets." There was something off about Arch: he was showing the smallest hints of nerves. For Arch, it was the equivalent of pacing and ranting. He wasn't a man who let much slip through. "What should be of concern is who those assets are. Or rather, one of them, really. Krystal, the director is coming to oversee this matter personally."

Everyone in the room went still. Even Sheriff Thorgood seemed temporarily dumbfounded. Since no one but the perpetually quiet Gregor was around to ask the obvious question, I opted to get it out of the way early in the hopes of moving on briskly. "Pardon, but who is the director?"

"The Director of the Agency. The head of our entire organization." Krystal's face had taken on an uncharacteristically severe expression. "Why would she come all the way out here over this?"

"That might be my fault," Sheriff Thorgood admitted. "Didn't expect her to care that much, but technically speaking, she does have a stake in seeing what happens to Asha. I'm the first of any of us to give blood to a vampire."

After a moment to piece his words together, understanding dawned. "She's like you."

"Even worse. She's my sister. Well, our version of what you'd think of as siblings, anyway. We fight approximately the same as you, so the word works as well as any other."

There was so much to deal with, so many hurdles facing us, but for some reason, that was a bridge too far. The mystery had been a neat curiosity before, but now, my friend had this being's blood coursing through her. It was time to get a concrete answer.

"What exactly are you, anyway? With all due respect, I'd like to have some idea or warning of how best to watch over Asha."

I expected to be rebuffed or ignored, but the truth was, Sheriff Thorgood had never been the one refusing to answer; I just never found the gumption to outright ask. He tapped his bicep for a few moments, giving the question some proper thought. "How can I put this? The terms you had for us never conveyed all that much, so they'd probably just make things more confusing."

Finally, he extended his arms. In the right, there was suddenly a pile of dirt; in the left, a floating orb of clear water. "Let's say the soil represents reality, the physical, natural world as you know it. This is what humans are made from. Simple, uncomplicated, uniform bits." In his hand, the pile of dirt took on a humanoid shape, standing up and giving a small wave. "Whereas the water is magic: powerful and malleable, yet ultimately shapeless. A human turned parahuman, then, is earth that has been infused with a few drops of water."

Three droplets floated over from the sphere, landing in the dirt. As the liquid soaked in, the dirt drew together, becoming a more stable mass. "Add in that little bit, and suddenly, it can take new shapes, hold sturdier forms— you get the metaphor. Now, natural parahumans, like fey, dragons, and the like, those are different. They're creatures of both reality and magic, born in balance."

As he closed and opened his right hand, the dirt reset. This time, it flowed upward along with the water, joining in the air between his arms to form a figure made of mud. "Natively, these are more powerful than the first version, but there's also a limit here. Normal earth has more room to absorb, more opportunity to grow, whereas these must maintain a balance. They can't absorb greater amounts of water the way humans can. It's why you don't see things like vampire dragons, or therian fey. Their natural magic prevents them from absorbing those enchantments."

This time, Sheriff Thorgood closed both hands, resetting both the water and the dirt. "Which brings us to your question: what am I? Well, there is one scenario we haven't discussed yet. What about creatures born on the other side of the equation?" The orb of water shifted, turning into a humanoid form. From the right hand, a few blobs of dirt rose up, about the same size as the droplets of water earlier. "If you take a being made almost entirely of magic and sprinkle in a bit of reality, you get something that's mostly unreal, but can still interact with the physical world."

As the dirt swirled into the figure, it changed once more. It swelled outward, taking on a hugely muscular form, then shrank down into a diminutive frame. Out again, then tall, then short, a parade of forms until it finally halted on the shape of a muscular, heavyset man, identical to the form of the sheriff holding it.

"That's what I am, put as simply as possible. It's also what my sister is, which is why those two are so worried."

My head felt like it might crack. This day had already been far too much. What he was describing spoke to entire systems of power I didn't yet understand, one of which I'd just fundamentally connected to Asha. Tired as I was, ignorance did me no favors. Whatever we were about to face, the more I knew, the better the chances we'd actually make it through.

"Arch, tell me everything I need to know."

4.

"AT LEAST MY DRESS WASN'T IN YOUR CAR."

In spite of what happened to Asha, Krystal and I were still here for our wedding, and after spending several hours with Arch getting briefed, we found ourselves thrust suddenly back into that reality. With Asha getting the introduction into vampire life from Lillian, and most of our friends needing actual sleep, we'd begun the process of inventorying what had been lost in the explosion and would need to be replaced.

Sitting in our suite at the Bristle Inn, going over my spreadsheet, it was hard to imagine the scene in the parking lot from mere hours earlier. My nerves still hadn't settled down, nor did I expect they would for quite some time. Most people are already on edge about the act of marriage; I now had a homicidal sire and an interested Agency to worry about, as well.

Krystal held the plastic package, carefully hiding the garment inside. Getting it custom made by an Agency tailor meant that it had come down with Arch, sparing us the ordeal of finding a last-minute replacement. Honestly, outside of the car itself, there was relatively little that needed immediate substitutions. I was borrowing Lillian's computer, but thanks to cloud computing, a few sign-ins had me up and running again. Asha's contracts were toast, though those were obviously just copies. Truly, the only real loss would have been Asha herself, and while part of her had undeniably been killed in that explosion, we avoided having to say a final goodbye.

None of which dealt with the larger problem of Quinn. This wasn't the first time he'd gotten another person involved in his schemes, but last time, it had been Krystal, which ultimately worked to his great disadvantage. Tonight was a reminder that he had no compunctions about bystanders, as well as just how vulnerable my friends truly were. We were going to have to do something to protect ourselves, maybe even employ more bodyguards—though, for the moment, I'd settle for not having to try turning anyone else on this trip.

"I hate to even ask this, I do, but Krystal, is there *any* chance—"

"None." She didn't even need the full question. She set her garment bag on the bed. "He struck outside Boarback for a reason. These places aren't just hidden from plain sight. There is old, powerful magic woven around these towns. I'm not saying Quinn couldn't break in; he's definitely proven to be that capable. I'm just saying that if he did, Sheriff Thorgood would know immediately, and that would be the last time Quinn made trouble for us or anyone else." Her expression lightened. "Maybe he'll be dumb enough to try."

Unlikely, given that Quinn had proven very adept at knowing when to fight and when to flee. While I still didn't know a lot about Sheriff Thorgood, after watching a few drops of his blood neutralize Asha's torso full of silver, I felt no need to question Krystal's assessment of his power.

"Sorry, I just had to know."

Krystal made her way over to my chair, putting a gentle hand on my shoulder. "It's okay to be rattled, Freddy. I'm a little shaken, too, and I deal with this kind of thing a lot more frequently. Our friend almost died, and you had to do something you feel conflicted about to save her. I'm not upset you wanted some extra reassurance that we're safe. Just wanted you to understand how reassured you should be."

I gripped her hand, thankful all over again that this was the person I'd soon be marrying. "Truth be told, I actually didn't feel all that conflicted. It was just like Deborah told me: in that moment, I knew with absolute certainly what would happen if we did nothing, versus giving her some kind of chance if I tried. Once I knew what Asha wanted, there was nothing to hold me back."

"I'm glad you feel that way, because now that you've succeeded twice in a row, the Blood Council is going to double-time those extra turning attempts."

My gut reaction was to reject the idea entirely; however, I was slowly beginning to see that this didn't have to be an entirely negative aspect of my life. "I figured. But I still have to choose to be the one to do it, right? They can't compel me?"

Krystal raised her hand in the air, palm parallel to the floor, and shook it a few times. "Sort of? Legally, no, they can't, but there's also bribery or manipulation, which we both know Deborah can wield effectively."

"Good."

"That's good?" Krystal asked, forehead crinkling in confusion.

"I hope so. Deborah knows me well, so she won't bring in the sort of people I'd refuse to turn." I looked down at my hand, pale and thin, yet shockingly powerful. For a long time, the change had been about what I'd lost. Seeing Sheri and Asha make the turn had shown me an aspect I'd overlooked. "There are people out there who are sick or injured, people for whom vampiric powers would be a second chance. I never gave it much thought before because I went from a relatively functional body right to undeath. But if I really can turn people more effectively than other vampires, then that means I can use that gift on the people who need it, give it to those for whom it would be only a blessing."

The crinkles on Krystal's forehead faded as her expression shifted to one of affection, hand brushing through my hair. "Most people wouldn't see getting more responsibility as a silver lining."

"You get to save the day all the time. For me, the idea of making such a substantial difference is still pretty novel," I replied.

She sighed, then kissed me for a long, lingering moment. "Honestly, you really are the strangest vampire I've ever met."

"I really don't try to be."

"I know. That's what makes it endearing." One more kiss, then she started sorting through our pile of items once more.

Before she'd sifted far, we heard a sharp knock on the door. Instantly both alert, Krystal pulled the gun from her hip as she quietly moved to look through the peephole. Given the night we'd had, there wouldn't be many reasons to come calling short of an attack or emergency, and by that point, I genuinely wasn't sure which I'd have preferred.

At least it wasn't a long wait to find out; after one glance through the peephole, Krystal threw open the door, allowing Lillian and Asha inside.

"Hey, you two, what's shaking?" Though her tone was flippant, Krystal pulled them both in quickly, then checked the halls before shutting the door.

"I thought you weren't worried while we were here?" I asked.

"That was before I found out the director was coming. Plus, someone from the Blood Council won't be far behind." Krystal motioned for Lillian and Asha to sit, which they did.

In our time apart, Asha had changed into a different set of clothes—simple slacks and a blouse that was much too dressy for lounging around in; I imagined she'd just grabbed whatever was on top of her luggage. Her face didn't betray much crying, but then, vampires weren't known for getting red faces or puffy eyes. There was worry in her expression, though, a fear that hadn't been there before.

I leaned closer to both of them while Krystal was getting settled. "What happened?"

Lillian didn't respond initially. Instead, she rolled up one of the dark sleeves of her black sweater, showing a small series of wounds in her forearm. That was curious, indeed. Wounds to a vampire healed fast; shallow ones like that, almost instantly. The obvious exception being injuries made with silver, of course. Which was exactly what these punctures looked like, except I wasn't sure why someone would wield a silver weapon that small.

"We were going through the basics. Past how sleep works, drinking blood, all of that, getting to some of our offensive capabilities. I explained how our teeth and nails are unnaturally sharp and was working on teaching Asha how to angle your fingers to use them as claws. She got a little too close on accident, which is no sweat off my steer, happens all the time. Except it *hurt*, Fredrick. It hurt like silver."

The room fell silent. I understood what Lillian was telling me, as did Krystal, but the idea of it was too much to digest in one go. I had to break it down into pieces, grappling with not only the possibility of what this could mean, but also the implications if it were true.

I decided to start with the obvious beginning. "Let's get the most essential test out of the way. Asha, would you raise three fingers, please, nails as extended as you can manage."

"Really hoping this gives us some answers; it's already been a pretty stressful evening." Asha had her game face on, somehow fighting through what already had to among the worst nights of her life.

Krystal didn't need me to tell her what we were doing. No sooner was Asha's hand up than ours were both moving forward. My index finger pressed against the nail of Asha's middle finger, whereas Krystal took the ring finger. Catching the implication, Lillian moved to tap the last unclaimed digit.

As we all pressed down, Lillian jerked her hand away. Krystal was unbothered, moving her hand a few seconds later. For me, there was no noticeable pain. However, I did feel something: the familiar tingle along my skin that silver had produced ever since my experience with Gideon. No doubt about it: Asha's nails were acting as though they were made of silver. My mind darted back to the parking lot and all those rivers of metal flowing out from the shrapnel.

"One last check. Asha, with sincerest apologies for the insanity of this, would you please put your teeth against my arm? Or I can poke them, if you prefer."

"Nope, for some reason, that sounds even weirder," Asha replied. She leaned in, delicately biting the side of the hand that I'd pressed into her nail. Not strong enough to break the skin, yet with adequate proximity for me to feel the telltale tickle of silver once more.

After nodding that she could let go, I composed my thoughts as best I could. "The conclusion seems obvious, right? Sheriff Thorgood's blood didn't get rid of the silver, it integrated the foreign material into Asha's body. Her teeth and nails—and perhaps even bones, since Lillian wasn't hurt by when they touched skin to skin."

Krystal rose from her seat and walked over to a black bag in the corner. I knew that bag well; it was one I took care never to touch without good reason. From inside, Krystal produced a blade she quickly unsheathed. Unlike normal silver, the blades agents used were treated to hide their scent; though, this close, it was hard not to catch at least a small whiff or two.

"Sorry, but we have to check this. From here on, the fewer surprises, the better." With great care, Krystal sat down next to Asha and pressed the blade to her left forearm. It eventually cut in, drawing a thin ooze of dark blood, only to heal up seconds later. "Guess that makes sense. If you were still weakened by silver, you'd be showing non-stop symptoms."

From her chair, Lillian rose, walking to my side. "I already put word out to the Blood Council, letting them know we had a new clan member. Figured with so many witnesses around, it made the most sense to do this one purely by the book."

"It was the right call. I was worried about whether Asha would actually be automatically in my clan or not."

"The ones you sire are automatically added unless there are preexisting arrangements in place. It's part of how vampires are kept accountable. They have the right to leave later, technically, though most clans work hard to eliminate those options. None of which was my point," Lillian added, her voice getting more forceful. "Fredrick, given what you told me about the last person you changed, it seems likely the Blood Council will want to check over Asha, as well."

"And when they do, they'll discover that there are now exactly two silver-immune vampires in the known world, both of whom are part of the House of Fred," Krystal finished, not bothering to look away from Asha.

As the meaning sank in, I fell heavily back onto my bed, dumbfounded. While I didn't know exactly what the ramifications of this would be, one thing was certain. The Blood Council was absolutely going to be interested, and the attention of the Blood Council was a very dangerous thing to have. I had to get Asha protected first: properly logged into the clan, added to alliances, everything.

"Everyone, grab a computer and a piece of paper. We have to dot every 'I' and cross every 'T' before anyone else knows about Asha. They can't change a matter that's already been settled, so let's make sure there isn't so much as a single loophole or technicality they could use to challenge Asha's status in this clan."

For the first time since the explosion, something like her old self settled on Asha's face, an expression of excited determination as she pulled a phone from her pocket. "I might not know much about drinking blood or stalking the night, but if it's a paperwork battle we're in for, then we're going to kick the technical shit out of them."

5.

WALKING INTO THE LUXURY GUEST HOUSE, where, to our utter lack of surprise, this hastily called meeting was being held, felt somewhat akin to how I imagined striding into battle would be. There was probably a fight ahead, one I'd geared and armored myself for as best I could. At my side were Krystal, Asha, and Gregor, whom I'd expected to be held at the door, but apparently, bodyguards were allowed in for this kind of thing. I must not be the only one who was employing one, because there was certainly no chance they'd made such an accommodation solely for me.

Upon arriving in the main foyer, an agent I didn't recognize, but who greeted Krystal by name, was waiting for us. He was squat, with mottled skin and a laughing grin, the sort one might see in a thousand nameless bars while holding a captivated audience. Some agents stood out; others specialized in blending in. Whatever this one's standard task, on this particular evening, he served as our guide. While we'd seen much of the building during my previous testing, that didn't mean we knew where everyone had elected to set up shop.

Once we arrived, I realized I could have guessed. They were using the vast ballroom where Claudius had housed his equipment the last time, only it had been cleared out and restocked with several tables and chairs. The largest, a massive conference table that appeared to have once been a solid piece of tree, already had a few people seated around it.

I recognized them immediately. Not their names, for we were as much strangers as the man who'd pointed our way; no, what I knew at once were their roles. They were the support staff, the ones handling details and paperwork, people digging into the nitty-gritty while their leaders made grand, sweeping decisions. Multibillion-dollar corporation, secret government supernatural agency, or ten-person office run by a single boss, the job was the same all over: head down, always offer solutions, never get too in-depth on problems leadership doesn't have the expertise to understand.

Despite the kinship, it wasn't seeing fellow drones that lightened my heart. They gave me hope, because if they were here, then however good this director was, she didn't do the detail work herself. Any information she needed, any clarification required, it would require her to stop and ask her people. There was a limit to how often most leaders would go to that well in public. It wasn't much, especially considering all the barrels I was over, but any tool that gave us a bit more leverage might make a difference. We had a newly made vampire to protect.

Footsteps from behind us came only an instant before I noticed a new presence standing beside me. I turned to find Deborah waiting, Claudius trailing several feet behind. Evidently, he didn't care enough to bother with the fast-moving surprises. Or maybe he couldn't, now that I thought about it. Deborah's blood diet, while potent, might not be what was most useful for Claudius. The versatility of vampires was part of what made us so dangerous; I could never forget that if I didn't want to be taken off guard. Not that I was expecting a fight—at least, not until further into the meeting.

"I must say, I was surprised to hear you reached out and invited us," Deborah greeted. "Almost as surprised as I was to hear you'd already done another turn. Although, seeing who it was, the situation makes a lot more sense." To my surprise, Deborah slipped over to Asha's side, taking her hand gently. For a moment, I almost tensed, afraid she'd brush those dangerous nails, but instead, Deborah leaned forward, kissing Asha once on each cheek.

"For your loss, I offer my condolences. For your gain, I offer my congratulations. While we may not be clan, we are kin, and I pray that you one day find more joys in the night than the sun could ever offer."

Asha held it together well, managing a small "Thank you" before carefully taking her hands back. There was no reaction from Deborah; then again, I imagined most newly turned vampires probably needed time to adjust.

While we'd been talking, Claudius went on and took a seat, not bothering with so much as a single greeting. Deborah, on the other hand, hung around as we made our way into the ballroom proper. "So, back to the main subject: why *did* you invite us personally down?"

"You were going to come to examine Asha, anyway, and given the circumstances of her turning, we felt it best to have the Blood Council represented in the initial discussion, alongside the Agency. Minimizes the chance for misunderstandings down the line." My words were honest, though they pointed to something Deborah didn't yet know about, which led her to make the assumption I was hoping for.

"Ah. You know our feelings toward Quinn, and this is a vampire crime, so by having us here from the start, we cannot say we were denied our proper chance at retribution. You're doling out all the information to both organizations at once, rather than risk being caught between them."

"You have correctly devised my tactic," I confirmed, because she had. She just didn't yet know what piece of information I was dumping in both their laps at once.

Before we could get any deeper into our discussion, a door on the other side of the room burst open and the director walked in. I wasn't sure I'd have known who she was on the street; I might have assumed CEO or high-profile attorney. She walked with the purpose of one in charge, a powerful stride aided by her exceptionally long legs, her height approaching nearly that of Richard. Unlike Sheriff Thorgood, nothing about her appeared gone to seed; she was lean, focused, and dressed impeccably in a white suit the likes of which I couldn't even begin to venture the cost of. The moment she appeared, every eye turned to her, unable to look away as she walked right up to the table.

Only when she stopped did I notice the helpers tagging along after her: two men with phones and tablets, both working frantically despite not a single order having passed through her lips upon entering. They either knew their roles well, or had standing orders; whatever the case, they hung back as she laid her hands upon the back of her chair and formally addressed the room.

"For those of you who do not know me, my title is Director of the Agency. You can call me Director Waxwood, if the lack of a surname is bothersome, but as I am the only director at the Agency, clarification is superfluous. Now then, my understanding is that we have a new development in the case of Fredrick Frankford Fletcher, the vampire-variant caused by the King of the West."

Crisp, concise, no-nonsense; if I didn't know how different those from the same family could be, I'd have never believed she and Sheriff Thorgood were of the same ilk. Part of me appreciated the willingness to get down to business, however. The sooner we got into this, the faster Asha's future could be properly protected.

"That's correct. If everyone would like to sit, I'll run us through a debrief of the situation as it unfolded." Krystal took the lead, stepping in at the agreed upon moment. As an agent, she had the best understanding of what information should be conveyed to these people, and how to do it efficiently. The plan centered on playing everything as by-the-book and upfront as possible, so it was vital that no detail got skipped over, regardless of how hard they might be to say aloud.

"—and after Asha gave her permission, Mr. Fletcher repeated the turning process as he'd been taught." Krystal stopped, looking around the room with more apparent nerves than I knew she really felt. "Director, with apologies to our guests, I'm afraid I have to ask for a momentary pause. While you know what comes next, I wanted to be sure that information wasn't classified in any capacity. Forgive the blunt setting, but there was no chance to ask beforehand, and I presume you would prefer this to me speaking plainly without checking first."

"You're right," Director Waxwood agreed. "That does present complications."

That got Deborah's attention instantly, and even Claudius appeared to momentarily check in when she sprang to her feet. "Beg your pardon? I thought we were brought in specifically so there wouldn't be any secrets kept?" Her eyes went to me, my hands already up in the air.

"We're doing our best, but obviously, we have to comply within the limits of the laws set by the Agency. So long as the director says proceed, Krystal will happily continue." We had to set this up right, remind them that they weren't necessarily on the same side.

"Might I make a suggestion?" Asha piped up from the table, much to the surprise of most of the guests. They were anticipating a more quiet, shaken Asha, the one they'd seen since arriving. But she didn't need vampire powers to be dangerous in this setting: Asha was already one of the sharper minds I'd ever encountered. Motivated to protect her own life, not even an explosion hours prior was enough to put her off her game.

When no one objected, Asha rose to her feet, slow yet steady, the eyes of everyone upon her. "As one of the few people here with full knowledge of what occurred and an outsider's perspective, I think I can see the issue. Director Waxwood is afraid the Blood Council will try to assert some claim over me, challenging my place in the House of Fred, stealing me into your service. If you recognize my status, officially acknowledge that I am part of Fred's clan without challenge, it would remove any such risk. I've certainly read enough to know you can't go poaching clan members without good reason and due process."

Deborah's inscrutable expression softened instantly. "My new child, those are plainly your fears, not ours, though I don't fault you for them. But rest assured. We have a positive relationship with the House of Fred that benefits all parties involved. We have no plans to challenge your placement."

"That's not quite the same as recognizing it here and now," Director Waxwood said. "In truth, I hadn't really given the possibility much thought; however, I can't just leave it on the table now that she's spelled it out. Give the woman to the clan she wants, and you can listen to what comes next. You'll hear about it eventually, anyway." That last line lost some of the authoritative power; for a moment, I could see the exasperated sister cleaning up what seemed like yet another of her brother's messes.

Deborah drummed her fingers along the polished wood of the table for a few seconds. "I don't like that you're trying to shove me into something, but I'm willing to meet in the middle as a show of good faith. I will recognize Asha's placement in Fred's clan, on the condition that should good cause for removal be found, the Blood Council reserves the right to formally raise the issue with the Agency. Highest levels, no red-tape."

"Agreed," Director Waxwood said. "Agent Jenkins, you may continue."

I watched Deborah as Krystal detailed Sheriff Thorgood's arrival. For the most part, her expression remained neutral. Only when we got to the part with the vial of blood did she suddenly come alive, flickers of emotions coming too fast for me to catalog. It had definitely gotten her interest up, a feature that grew exponentially as we reached the end of the scene, when Asha successfully regenerated despite a body riddled with silver.

"I see." Director Waxwood was silent at the end, a powerful kind of quiet that radiated off her, infecting the rest of the room. No one spoke, shuffled, so much as adjusted their hands in that long stretch where she sat unmoving, taking in the entirety of the tale. "And, to your knowledge, have any other symptoms manifested from exposure to Sheriff Thorgood's blood?"

This time, it was my turn to stand. Krystal had the expertise to do the debrief, Asha added heart and insight, but this was where the clan leader needed to speak. "Yes. In the course of her evaluation, we discovered that Asha's body appears to have acclimated to the silver, perhaps even absorbed it. She no longer suffers the effects of exposure; she reacts to it like any other metal."

Already, Deborah and Claudius were animated, whispering to themselves, but we hadn't even reached the biggest shock yet. "There's more than just an immunity. For the moment, Asha's nails and teeth appear to have the same effect on undead flesh as genuine silver. In effect, she not only has no weakness to silver, she now wields it as naturally as her own limbs."

With that, more or less exactly as we'd expected, the room devolved into chaos.

6.

MOST OF THE AGENCY CONTINGENT WAS yelling amongst themselves, frantically discussing a myriad of technicalities and precedents I hadn't even the slightest bit of context for. Claudius was excitedly yammering away in Deborah's ear, who was silently staring at the room, taking everything in. Amidst it all, Director Waxwood remained unmoving, unbothered, her face creased only in thought.

After a long stretch of loud, unprofessional behavior, she finally spoke.

"Enough."

Instantly, the entire room fell silent. Even Claudius slammed his mouth shut; quite possibly the first time I'd seen him acknowledge the order of anyone who wasn't Deborah. The director's voice hadn't been loud, or even all that forceful. It simply carried the weight of unchallengeable authority.

"Before we have a complete tizzy, let's go ahead and confirm this wild, frankly unbelievable claim. Fredrick Fletcher is a young vampire—mistakes in the evaluation of Asha Patel could have been made."

"There certainly might be more going on. We're too early on to be sure of much," I agreed. "Her silver condition is rather undeniable, however. If Claudius would like to come experience the effects for himself, we will happily permit a test to confirm."

Claudius moved so fast I had to mentally reevaluate whether or not he was consuming the same speedy blood as Deborah, after all. Perhaps it was just a matter of properly motivating him to action. In no time, he was at Asha's side, Deborah intentionally trailing some distance behind. He looked over Asha with unabashed interest, rolling up one of his oversized sleeves and offering a surprisingly muscular arm.

"Push the nails in to different depths; it will give me a better idea of the effects." That was the only request he had before getting raked by Asha's new, completely natural weapons; the more I saw of Claudius, the more I saw that he'd been a mage before the turn. Only they had that kind of reckless passion for discovery.

Extending her hand the way Lillian had instructed, Asha formed her fingers into claws, pressing them down easily into Claudius's unprotected skin. There were actual gasps from some of the Agency underlings as the wounds appeared, thick blood oozing out along the lines Asha left. No sudden surge of healing followed to stitch them back up; the injuries remained even as Asha's hand moved away. Before she could rest, another hand appeared in her line of sight—this one, next to her head.

"The fangs, too," Deborah said, wiggling her arm. "Have to be sure, you understand."

Without protest, Asha carefully bit down on the side of Deborah's forearm. Just like the nails, her fangs slid in easily, leaving behind lingering wounds as she pulled them free. While she didn't wince, Deborah did examine her own arm at length, staring hard at those twin holes that had been left behind.

"Claudius, to the best of my assessment, their evaluation was accurate. These feel and behave like injuries inflicted by silver. Tell me your conclusion."

"Conclusion?" Claudius looked as if she'd ordered him to defecate on the floor. "We have barely even begun to test, yet you wish for a conclusion? There are too many variables to evaluate, materials to test, subjects to bring in—"

"None of which is happening tonight." Director Waxwood had evidently run out of patience now that the testing was done. "Tell us what you can discern based on the information available."

"Very well." Something in Claudius seemed to shift. His expression turned stern as the overall ambivalence melted away, replaced by a keenly engaged mind. "Based on what we know, the likeliest explanation is that Sheriff Thorgood's blood did indeed allow Asha to fuse with the silver in her body, acclimating her to it and even incorporating it into her bones. However, we cannot even take Asha as a true sample of solely the effects from the sheriff's blood due to the complicated nature of her sire."

Though Claudius wasn't looking my way, I felt more than a few eyes shift over while he continued to speak.

"It's possible that this transformation only worked because of some potential for silver immunity passed down in her sire's blood. Recreating the experiment with another vampire might yield wildly different results. That's to say nothing of her state at the time of absorption, when her body was going through the shift to undeath, a factor that might well have played a key part in her survival. Frankly speaking, my assessment is that we have far too many factors at work to know with any certainty which were essential and which were superfluous. We're dealing with a second-generation mutation while still struggling to understand the first."

The moment served as a good reminder that no matter how eccentric a member of the Blood Council might be, they hadn't gotten their positions by chance. He'd just broken down the situation completely, with only a minute or two to process, and brought up factors I hadn't even thought to consider. His words landed heavily on the audience, silence and thought following his findings.

Taking his arm, Deborah led Claudius back over to their chairs, but not even the physical and metaphorical removal she was inflicting could stop the curious, evaluating glances he was throwing at Asha. When they were once more seated, all eyes slowly turned to the director. We were clearly in uncharted waters, ones that concerned her directly. In the long-term, her choices could be questioned or worked against, but for tonight, what she said would be law. To us, to the Blood Council, to the Agency itself. We just had to hope that that law fell in a way that kept Asha safe.

"Given the circumstances of the attack, and the appropriate procedures used, I do not find fault on the behalf of Fredrick Fletcher in the turning of Asha Patel. While he did do so in sight of humans, her condition easily qualifies as a medical emergency. I would, however, remind Mr. Fletcher that he is now out of legal turn-attempts for the remainder of the calendar year, and that should he overreach, there will be consequences."

Her gaze fell upon me, and after a moment, I realized that she was waiting for a response. "I can say with absolute sincerity that I have no plans or desires to turn anyone else in the near future. In truth, Asha was one of the few humans I still interact with, so there wouldn't even be candidates."

"For now. Humans, para and otherwise, have a tendency to form bonds quickly. But so long as you stay within the law, that means the Blood Council has several months to continue testing you and Asha. A vampire with a higher than average turn success rate is dangerous enough; if the vampires you create have the potential to mutate further, gaining unseen abilities, that represents a power that could cause a great deal of trouble."

To my surprise, Deborah stood, interrupting the exchange. She wasn't one to jump in, preferring to wait and strike, which was my warning that this concerned something serious. "Director Waxwood, the Blood Council has already begun the process of transferring additional turn-attempts to the House of Fred. By next month, he'll legally be empowered to turn about twenty per week."

My mind reeled at that number, even as I noted it was only the maximum. Luckily, before I even had to contemplate the possibility of such an arrangement, Director Waxwood made her own thoughts known.

"Denied." She met Deborah's gaze, staring the elder vampire down, and finding her undead opponent more stubborn than expected. "What he could do was already skirting the line; this takes it a step too far. Mr. Fletcher gets two attempts per calendar year according to the treaties, and that is all he's going to be cleared for in the foreseeable future. That said, the Agency is not unreasonable. With your steadily increasing sample size, you can continue testing. Once enough data is present to convince us that Fredrick Fletcher can consistently create normal vampires, turn-attempts can again be moved to his house. Until then, we will take things slowly, just in case his line is more dangerous. This way, it can be contained before it becomes a true threat."

There was no way Deborah would take this lying down. I was sure she had political schemes already turning in her head while Director Waxwood gave her edict, yet not so much as a frown touched her face. Deborah was perfectly gracious as she accepted the judgment, nodding and returning to her seat, sitting silently at Claudius's side.

"Which brings us to you, Mr. Fletcher." Director Waxwood's full attention fell on me entirely, a weight I hadn't been prepared for. Had I needed air in my lungs, I truly think I'd have struggled to breathe. "Although there is no crime to charge you with, I'm sure you must realize how this complicates matters. Putting aside the specifics of Ms. Patel's condition, a great deal of which can likely be laid at my own brother's feet, the fact remains that you have now succeeded on two vampiric turning attempts in a row. That you have better chances of success when acting as a sire is now undeniable, and we must consider the possibility that you will have *no* failures. You are, potentially, capable of turning any human into a member of the undead, a fact that would make you into one of the most valuable political pawns of this century."

The weight left as Director Waxwood split her focus, sharing it now between me and Krystal. "While it pains me to say this, I'm afraid at this point, there's really no other choice to be made. Just like the Blood Council must wait and do proper investigation, so too must you both wait and see where Mr. Fletcher's position and value shakes out. With apologies, I cannot allow a person of such consequence to be bound in Agency treaties and protections, not even those to be offered to a spouse."

I felt Krystal stiffen, even as I was sure I'd misunderstood. "What are you saying?"

"I am trying to tell you that the marriage is off. For now, at the very least, your wedding has to be canceled."

7.

"CAN THEY REALLY DO THAT?"

Even after the meeting, I felt dumbfounded. Things had wrapped up quickly once Director Waxwood finished laying down her edicts. The agents all left; Deborah stopped by to say a few parting words to Asha that I barely heard, and to give me a gentle pat on the back. I'd been so worried about the Blood Council being our biggest obstacle, and in the end, they'd been the ones who made the least trouble.

"Yes and no." Arch sat down in a desk chair that squeaked even at his slender frame. "The contracts are signed, the paperwork submitted—from a mortal perspective, you'd be fine. But they're all only good for one day, which is tomorrow. If you two aren't wed by the end of the day, it goes void like any other unfulfilled document and has to be resubmitted. The trick is that, to actually be married, you need someone to perform the ceremony. Someone with the right standings and authority, the sort of people who would never think to go against the head of the Agency. Even if you did find one to start it, the ceremony itself is magical, meaning that, as soon as it began, you'd have the director and other agents coming to stop you. None of which even mentions the consequences of Krystal disobeying an order."

We'd come to Arch's room in the hopes of finding some sort of recourse; nobody knew Agency bylaws and procedures as well as he did. He was kind enough to find us seats and offer drinks, which everyone save for Gregor accepted, before he hit us with the news.

Asha looked up from deep within her scotch, eyes narrowing slightly. "Did it have to be phrased as a true command? Because all she ever said was that the wedding had to be canceled. No one actually ordered Krystal to do that directly."

"Hmmm." Arch considered the point, turning his glass in his hand as he kept touching the pocket where his cigarettes lived. "A minor technicality that might shelter her from fallout, but it doesn't address the larger concern. The one where you can't actually manage to *get* married."

In a flash of serendipity, at that very moment, Arch was interrupted by the sound of a crisp knock at the door. Gregor opened it, blocking the entrance bodily, before we were treated to what sounded like the sound of stones slamming roughly together. I leapt up, looking over his shoulder, only to find Gregor fist-bumping with another stiff-faced man of similar proportions.

"The King of the West invites you to his suite, presence requested immediately." He even sounded like Gregor—in tone, if not actual voice. A fellow gargoyle, then; one who stood there waiting patiently.

It took me a few seconds to realize that he was going to escort us, because of course an invitation from one in Gideon's position wasn't something that could be turned down. Given that whatever he had in mind couldn't be worse than licking our wounds in Arch's room, there was no reason to deny the request. With a sense of resolution, we flowed into the hall, following the new gargoyle as he led us to the elevators.

These were, on the surface, normal elevators that we'd been taking regularly since our first arrival. Yet on that night, I saw something new. Our gargoyle guide tapped a claw above the buttons on what looked like a blank metal panel. Green light rippled outward, and the elevator rose. Higher than any other floor. Higher than the building actually reached into the sky. Then, with a ding, it stopped, doors parting to reveal a massive foyer.

We were in a suite that took up roughly the same size as an entire floor of the hotel: huge, sweeping ceilings, polished marble floors coated in the thick, furry hides of animals that didn't look even remotely familiar. The furniture was mostly oversized—a decorating standard when one dwelled with therians, especially ones like Richard. Most surprising of all, the scene was already bustling, and with familiar faces, at that.

Albert and Neil were over near a buffet line that was piled high with shrimp, crab, and other things they weren't hurriedly shoveling onto their plates. Al, Lillian, and June were sharing drinks by a roaring fireplace, while Lillian held the enchanted model of Charlotte Manor. Amy was standing over a punch bowl, staring like a master chef as she held two different-colored potions in her hand, adding them a drop at a time. Richard and Bubba sat on a vast couch, with Richard's daughter Sally seated next to him, looking a tad drowsy. It was late into the evening, after all. Slowly drawing near midnight, in fact; the start of what was supposed to be my wedding day.

"What's going on?" I asked.

"Come on now, Freddy, even you can recognize the start of a party when you see one." Krystal put a hand on my shoulder, leading me deeper in. "Though, I'm not sure what the occasion is anymore."

The voice came from behind us, despite the fact that there was no way he could have snuck around. "Kings do not need reason for revelry. But if you must know, Sally was promised a party, and it seemed you two would be unlikely to throw one any longer."

Gideon stepped forward into sight at last. I hadn't really noticed day-to-day, but he looked older than when we'd first met—no surprise, since his form was made to match Sally's growth. They were nearing their teenage years, a concept I didn't even want to imagine when applied to an ancient dragon with Gideon's power. There was something else in his expression that was unfamiliar, a trait I wasn't sure I'd seen before. It wasn't until he spoke again, with voice lowered this time, that I finally recognized the pity in his eyes. "For what it's worth, I find such bureaucracy ridiculous. My condolences on your ceremony."

I was momentarily taken aback, as no part of me was expecting sympathy from Gideon. "Thank you. It's deeply disappointing, obviously, but I'm trying to take a longer term view of things. In a few years, when all the political stuff settles down, we can get it handled."

A snort that was a tad more dragon than human escaped Gideon's lips as he shook his head. "Honestly, parahuman or true mortal, you all make the same mistake of thinking that time is some endless resource. I have lived for millennia, watching lives as long as my own and as fleeting as a mayfly, and each one seemed to believe it would go on forever. In comparison to this world, our time is incalculably brief, and of that limited slice, there will only be a small section in which we are truly happy. Do not take it for granted, do not let it be pried easily from your grasp, and never assume our time with anyone or anything is endless. A piece of wedding advice, for when you do decide to try."

Then he was gone, walking over to Sally, Richard, and Bubba. I turned, only to realize that Gregor and our escort gargoyle had both been bowing the entire time Gideon was present. Only when he'd moved on did they lift their heads, Gregor taking a position at my side while our escort went back to the elevator.

As the group we'd arrived with broke up, I found myself shifted to the side of Asha, who carefully led me over to the bar. Krystal aimed for the buffet, and Arch all but ran toward the nearest balcony, cigarettes already in hand. (I was pretty sure none of the rooms of the Bristle Inn even had balconies, though neither was this the time to get bogged down in dragon magic.)

"I don't know if I said this or not, with everything that happened, but… thanks, Fred." As Asha reached for the nearest bottle of scotch, no attention paid to the label, she kept talking. I had a feeling she needed to do it all in one go. "This night has been totally batshit, which I only realized after saying it is kind of a pun for us, and I think it's going to take me weeks before I've fully processed everything. But I'm still here, alive in a sense, and that's thanks to you. Wanted to make sure I told you I appreciate it, especially in light of what it cost you."

"Asha, if I could go back in time… well, I'd stop you from getting hurt, possibly set a trap for Quinn in the process. Taking that off the table, though, there's nothing I would do differently. Krystal and I can reschedule a ceremony; there's no second chance on saving a friend. If you asked her, she'd tell you the exact same thing, only with more cursing."

"You sure? She was pretty excited about all of this."

"Without question. No one cares more for the people in her life than Krystal. It's one of the many reasons I fell in love with her."

"Have to admit, it's a real bummer to hear they've stopped your wedding. We were all pulling for you two. Would have been nice to see you tie the knot." Asha removed two glasses from the bar and filled both with more scotch than we knew I would drink. Nevertheless, she slid one over to me, lifting the other into a toast. "Well, here's to love, and eventual marriage."

While my glass met hers, there was no true spirit of cheers in the gesture. I'd accepted Director Waxwood's declaration without question, because she was in charge, and that was that. But the more I turned it around in my head, the more troubled I became. She didn't actually have the legal right to bar our marriage, not with the paperwork having already been submitted. That was the joy of bureaucracy; it rarely had provisions for last-minute intrusions from outside parties.

"Asha, this is more your area of expertise than mine, but in theory, what sorts of people can perform legally binding parahuman weddings? That is to say, what titles or authority do they need to be recognized?"

"Well, you need another parahuman off the bat. Mortals can't get the magic moving. Then, it either has to be someone recognized for the role by your culture's ruling council, or an Agency-approved asset open to those from any heritage. There are also provisions for those in positions of high leadership, sort of the same way we used to let boat captains hitch people at sea. Technically, if your clan was bigger, you'd qualify. Not that you can do the ceremony yourself, has to be an external party." Unlike me, Asha put away the entirety of her scotch, downing it all in a single gulp. "Hey, no more burn. I'm finding perks to this undead lifestyle already."

Even after the day she'd had, Asha was as reliable and knowledgeable as ever. Better, her answer left me with options. I started first toward Richard, but then thought better of it. While he would be essential to the plan, if he was willing, there was someone who had to be talked with first. The entire point of this ceremony, of the marriage overall, was becoming a team. Whatever came next, we had to make that decision together.

I made it to Krystal between plates of shrimp, sparing me from having to wait while she speed-chewed prawns. Instead, I took the plate from her hands, and then her hands in mine. Krystal instantly keyed that something was up; for me to show blatant affection in public was a telltale sign that things weren't normal. "What's up, Freddy?"

"What's up, is I have an idea." No, that didn't capture it properly. "A bad idea. A ludicrous, dangerous, insanely mad notion of an idea. A Krystal idea, if you will."

The glint of dangerous curiosity sparked in her eye. "And what's that?"

"Let's get married. In half an hour, when the day rolls over and it becomes midnight, everything we turned in becomes valid. Director Waxwood didn't order you not to get hitched; she only said the wedding was canceled. But a marriage is so much more than the wedding itself. Who cares if she cut that ceremony? We'll just hold another."

"You know there are hurdles, right? Arch broke them down for us." A slow smile parted those bright red lips. "But you don't miss a detail, so there's no way you didn't clock those issues. Does that mean you've got a plan?"

"Plan is much too good for this; it's an idea, at its very best." Despite the situation, I was grinning right back at her. Maybe we were biting off something beyond us, maybe it was a stupidly big task, but we were doing it hand in hand. Context be damned, it felt good to be in the thick of trouble with the woman I loved.

I winked at her once before continuing. "As I see it, when faced with a problem, your first recourse is to break the rules, whereas mine is to run away. Seeing as tonight is all about our marriage and partnership, I thought we'd do both. Let's break some rules *while* running away."

8.

"SINCE YOU'VE DECIDED TO PROPOSE something reckless and impulsive, I guess that means it's on me to point out the obvious logistical hurdles, starting with the fact that we don't even have anyone who *would* marry us. Everyone with proper authority is going to listen to the director." Krystal didn't sound especially defeated; she likely suspected I had something in mind, but it was still a valid point to raise.

"About that…" I turned, locking eyes with Richard from across the room. "According to Asha, the head of a pack Richard's size would have a high-enough position to legally oversee the ceremony. Much as I hate to impose—"

His massive hand was waving through the air to silence me. "Don't worry about it. Now that I know you two want to push on, if you didn't ask, then I would have proposed that I perform the wedding."

"And I second," Gideon added.

It was a surprising show of support, but one we didn't dwell on long as Richard continued. "However, if you want it to be proper and binding, in the magical as well as legal sense, then you we can't just do it in a hotel room. Has to be at a place where power gathers; venues like churches usually work, thanks to all the concentrated faith in one spot."

There had to be more than a few areas like that scattered throughout Boarback, but my mind instantly flew back to our original wedding site. Remote, hard to reach, and so magical I could almost taste it in the air when we'd stood there. "Krystal, do you think the grove would let us through without Sheriff Thorgood?"

"I doubt it," she admitted. "Not that it matters. If we do this, we have to bring him in on it."

For a moment, I wondered if that was wise, and Krystal sensed my hesitation. "Freddy, this is *his* town. Your idea is totally crazy; I want you to understand that out of the gate. The Director of the Agency is here, along with the dozens of agents who came for the wedding in the first place. The only way we have even an outside shot of this working is if Sheriff Thorgood wants us to succeed. Besides, he has to be there. He's giving me away."

I'd almost forgotten that part. It still seemed like a risky venture, given that the director was his sibling; though, it wasn't as if family never fought. Ultimately, I had to put my faith in Krystal, whose certainty never wandered where the sheriff was concerned. If she said he'd help, then I counted him as an ally.

"You do both realize that it's not as if they won't consider this possibility." Arch came in from the balcony, waving to clear the last of the smoke from his face. While I didn't know precisely what type of parahuman Arch was, I did know he always managed to hear more than it seemed like he should be able to. "In fact, I already spotted two agents in the street, keeping tabs in case you decide to do something exactly that crazy." He shook his head and tsked slightly. "Which means, those two are also getting a fresh round of stealth training the next time I'm in the office."

"Then we create a distraction. Heaven knows, if there's one thing this clan is good at, it's causing a scene." I looked around at my friends' faces and saw that they were unsure. Perhaps they, not unreasonably, thought this to be nothing more than a thought experiment, or the venting of steam through fantasy. Time to get my people on the same page, because this would take a lot of teamwork if we wanted even the slenderest shot of success. "Everyone, let me be explicitly clear right now. I am not kidding, joking, or in any way messing around. I'm discussing violating a direct order from the Agency. Anyone not comfortable with that, or the fallout it could have, should probably enjoy the view from the balcony for a bit."

Slowly, the room fell silent as the severity of the situation set in. It was Krystal who moved forward, speaking what I imagined was no doubt the question on a great many minds in the room. "Are you sure about that, Freddy? I'm mad, too—spitting nails angry, in fact, so I get the impulse. But even if this isn't technically illegal, it's going to piss some dangerous people off. It's kind of hard to wrap our heads around the idea of *you* being the one who says, 'Fuck the rules, let's do what we want,' when you go to great pains day-in, day-out to not ruffle feathers or break any rules."

"The rules never tried to stand between me and you before."

Admittedly, it was a bit of a clumsy way to express my sentiment, yet the message got through, as I saw Krystal be momentarily taken aback. While I still had her by surprise, I took her left hand—the one wearing her engagement ring—carefully in both of my palms.

"Krystal, please look at my expression, because I want you to truly understand how much I mean these words."

She leaned in, slightly, enough that I could have whispered, if not for all the other prying ears.

"*Fuck* the rules. Let's do what we want." The smile that broke across my face, nervous, half-mad, was one I suspected bore at least a fair resemblance to the grin Krystal often sported when diving headfirst into trouble. "And what I want is to marry you. Tonight. Up on that hill, overlooking the town. How about it?"

"Well, I did go to all the trouble of buying a dress. Seems like a waste of effort not to use it." Krystal darted in as her words finished, kissing me hard and brief before spinning around to face our friends. "Okay, folks, this is officially not a drill. While what we're pitching might not come with legal consequences, expect the director to react to being defied the same way most powerful people do: that is to say, poorly. Anyone who wants to bail out here and now before they know enough to feel like an accessory should feel free to walk away. There are jobs and alliances in play, most of you have duties that extend beyond yourself. No hard feelings if this is a step too far."

Not so much as a single person in the room moved, with the lone exception of Amy, who continued piling her plate high with cocktail shrimp, pausing just long enough to acknowledge that a speech was occurring.

The first non-eater to actually say something was the one I'd expected the least. Tapping the closed pack of cigarettes, Arch glanced wistfully to the balcony, then sighed. "Since this will inevitably go bad, and agents are likely to get involved, I'll have to be part of it. I think the director overreached, so I'll back your play, but we have to make sure the kid gloves stay on. I'm not putting any of my people at risk; if someone needs to delay the agents, I'll be the one to do it."

"Not alone. I've survived quite a few of your 'training camps,' so I think I can help run the basics," June offered. Her eyes turned toward Krystal. "You know I've got your back, especially after what you pulled me out of to be here."

I barely even noticed June's heartfelt sentiment; my mind was still boggling over the idea that the ones Arch was saying he'd protect were the agents, not us. That seemed excessive, until my gaze wandered a few feet over, to where Gideon and Sally were seated by Richard. Right. When a powerful dragon who did what he pleased was in play, it was probably best to leave the agents to Arch.

"I've got a few ideas for a distraction," Amy offered. "Going to need some muscle, though. Bubba, at the least. I'd like another therian, but you'll need Richard with you guys for the ceremony to work."

"What about Gregor?" I asked. Instantly, I saw the gargoyle open his mouth in protest—that is, until

Gideon moved to speak, at which point Gregor's jaw slammed shut so hard I swore I heard the sound of rocks smashing.

Gideon nodded at my idea, touching his chin lightly as he considered it. "An excellent substitution. This will be my first opportunity to see one of the Slate-Claws functioning in a new role. I expect to be suitably impressed."

In that moment, if Deborah and Director Waxwood had walked through the door, Gregor probably would have tried to take them both on singlehandedly. He looked as if someone had turned a switch, flipping all of his energy to its exact opposite polarity. Energy poured off the man; he was starving for a fight now that he knew his king's attention was upon him. Whatever Amy needed, she now had quite possibly the most enthusiastic helper imaginable.

"Happy to pitch in if there are legal issues. Not too sure how good I'd be with these yet." Flexing her hands, Asha's newly enhanced nails caught the light of the fire, making them look even more dangerous.

"Hopefully, it won't matter. We're not trying to assault anyone, break in anywhere, or otherwise court violence. We're just using the venue that we paid for, on the day we booked in, for the ceremony we scheduled. Granted, it's on the wrong side of the sunrise, but it's not like the contracts had timetables."

As I was speaking, the others in the room were rising slowly to their feet. Lillian joined up with Albert and Neil, stealing a few bites from their plates, leading them both to where Asha was standing. Al made her way over to Amy, whispering quietly while still keeping an eye on us for more cues. Bubba took a spot near Richard and Arch, ready and waiting. As one, the clan and our allies moved, readying for the next adventure.

I was temporarily dumbfounded. Part of me had expected at least the agents to bail on the discussion entirely; instead, they were offering to help. Seeing these people leap to my aid, I couldn't help remembering my life before Krystal: keeping to myself, laying low, subsisting only on bought blood and classic movies. Back then, I could never have imagined a life like this, and that was without including a single supernatural element. No matter where she went, Krystal shook things up, and for a moment, I silently thanked the universe that I was such thing to be shaken. Terrifying and crazy as what we were planning was, I wouldn't have traded the chance at marrying her for a thousand years of peace.

"I am touched to see all of you on board, and it is dearly appreciated. We have less than an hour until the day turns over. Before then, we'll need to reach out to Sheriff Thorgood; might as well get his help as early as possible. We also have to figure out transportation logistics for everyone—"

"You may exclude myself and Sally," Gideon informed us. "This seems the sort of journey fraught with peril and chaos. I will take her a safer route."

I hadn't even considered the idea that Sally would come up with us, although Gideon was absolutely right that whatever trouble we were getting into would be no place for a child. "Excellent thinking. That means we need transportation for everyone else, plus Sheriff Thorgood, presumably. My car is burning wreckage, and Krystal's truck can only fit so many."

Cackling filled the air, unmistakable for anything else. All eyes slowly swiveled to the laughing form of Amy Wells, who'd just finished the last prawn on her formerly heaping plate. She dropped the dish to the carpeted floor, rubbing her hands together in glee, unrestrained excitement bursting forth in literal sparks of light.

"I have *just* the potion I've been waiting to try out for such an occasion."

That should have horrified me to my very core. For a person with sense, there was really no other plausible reaction to have to such an outburst, especially knowing Amy's overall capabilities and joy for experimentation. Instead, my chest swelled with hope. Sure, this meant Amy had some sort of high-level insanity in mind, but that was—somehow—heartening. Maybe, after all these years, I was turning as mad as the rest of them, or perhaps I always had been, but never saw cause to let such inclinations loose. On this evening, however, I had uncovered ample motivation. So long as no one was hurt, I didn't especially care how insane Amy's ideas were.

The time had come to show the parahuman world just how big a mess the House of Fred could cause when we tried.

9.

IN THE END, WE HAD TO SPLIT UP. THERE was no other way we had even an outside chance of making it to the grove, and no single vehicle that could fit all of us in the first place. The distraction team, consisting of Bubba, Gregor, Amy, and—surprisingly enough—a volunteering Al, had left the rest of us earlier to prepare for their task. Ideally, if all went to plan, they'd follow up behind, likely trailing the agents who gave us chase.

As for the rest of us, we were piled up in Krystal's truck, parked in the shadow of the sheriff's station. We hadn't hidden our commute; the two of us walked over in plain sight of the agents keeping watch. There was nothing especially suspicious about her turning to a mentor after a trying day, so we didn't pretend there was. Acting as if we had nothing to hide seemed the natural tactic.

The others had come over through more covert means. I didn't know the exact route they'd taken, but given that they'd had Arch in the lead, I wasn't particularly worried about them being spotted. The truck was a tight squeeze as Arch, Neil, Albert, and I crammed into the back, while Krystal, Richard, Asha, June, and Lillian piled into the cab. Resting in my hand was a vial of swirling purple liquid, so active it nearly seemed alive. While I wasn't entirely sure what it would do, I had specific instructions not to use it until we were on the move. Amy refused to tell me more than that, which either meant that it was so dangerous she knew I wouldn't use it with full knowledge of its effects, or she was merely tickled by the notion of our surprise.

We said nothing as we waited, too aware of the prying parahuman ears throughout the town. Between the Blood Council and all the agents around, there was no shortage of people who'd be quite surprised to see us geared up for a sudden trip. I was tense, yet strangely absent of any nerves. There was nothing to feel conflicted about; this was what I wanted. Despite knowing the endeavor would likely end in failure, it was more important to try than to just give up. Even *my* predilection for cowardice had a limit.

As we began to hear noise rippling over from the center of town, we readied ourselves. Right now, the townsfolk were no doubt confused by the sudden appearance of Amy and Gregor, especially since they were hauling in a large wagon of wares—probably interested, more than worried, given the nature of the goods. Just as Gregor was unloading the haul, their attention would be stolen by—

A loud boom echoed through the air as the first firework exploded overhead, forming the shape of a bat before fading into smoke. Amy's plan of distraction, as it turned out, was to do the same job she'd originally been tasked with, only in a more aggressive manner. We'd booked her to put together the reception, given that we'd have a myriad of different parahumans and Amy's business was built on being able to get anyone buzzed. I hadn't expected her to also make custom fireworks, nor was I sure the process for that had been in any way safe, but as a wolf and a cauldron formed from sparks of airborne light, I took a moment to appreciate the effort.

Anyone searching for the source of the display was in for a tough time, because the explosives weren't being launched at all. Al was up in the sky, darting down to store roofs and resupplying from the stashes of explosives she'd dragged up there. She would light the fuse, let it burn, then simply toss it a few feet up and zip away. One more element of confusion, albeit minor, but this was distraction by a thousand cuts. We had to pile every element on we could in order to buy ourselves a modicum of breathing room.

A cheer rose up from the town, meaning that Amy had begun to tap the kegs and Gregor would be unloading inventory, keeping her stocked despite the sudden spiking demand. With fireworks drawing people out and free refreshments to lure them in, it would be downright irresponsible for the agents not to go investigate. I even caught sight of a pair moving down the street, bickering between themselves about what to do. For an instant, part of me feared they'd pop in to the sheriff's office. Here, they would find only Nax, who was already abreast of the situation. Sheriff Thorgood hadn't stuck around, nor had he jumped in the truck with us. Instead, he's simply said he'd do his part and meet us there, then wandered off down the street. Thankfully, the agents never came near enough to discover our truck or the sheriff's absence, rather pushing onward to the source of the commotion.

Across the bed of the truck, Arch had his eyes trained on his watch. Our timetable had come from him, based on his estimate of when the most agents would likely be gathered up in one central location. They would run in to see the issue, then expand outward to check for other threats. It was crucial that we hit them during the point where their numbers were contracted into one spot.

In the distance, my ears picked up the sound of hoof beats. From the soft nod Arch gave to what I suspected was himself, it seemed Bubba was right on cue. While I couldn't see our therian friend, I knew he'd been burdened by a pair of wooden casks, each punctured in one single spot. Every drop that hit the ground sizzled briefly before blooming into a bright, airy mist that wafted up into the air. His legs were carrying him around the center of Boarback, where everyone would be starting their revelry, and this would only make things *more* fun. Originally, I suspected this was some of sort of high-end product Amy had planned to use for toasts or those who truly wanted to touch the sky. Apparently, it was based on the same stuff she'd used the night we met Al and Gregor, though I'd been assured this batch was more "grounded" than the last.

What surprised me most in that moment was not the sound of Bubba, however. It was the sudden shift in the wind. Without warning, the breeze adjusted, blowing now directly toward the party and away from us. Looking off at the trees in the distance, I could see that they were moving as well, except the direction didn't quite line up. They moved as if the wind was blowing toward the center of town, just like every other marker I could spot indicated. The air itself was helping us, sending the magical mist directly into our crowd of merrymakers.

The surprise must have shown on my face, as Neil leaned in and whispered, "Krystal did say this was *his* town."

"To the point where the winds are his ally?"

"It is never prudent to underestimate one of those beings, be it the director, the sheriff, or the other," Arch informed us. "I'm not sure we've ever seen the limits of what they can do—only the boundaries they impose on themselves."

Much as I wanted to dispute such an idea, largely for my own sanity, there was no denying the increasing wind at my back. More importantly, there wasn't time for such discussions. With Bubba on the move, the trap had been sprung. Everyone in the center of town was about to care a whole lot more about where the food was and a good deal less about my impending nuptials. Those who tried to flee would only go deeper into the chemical mist that had been poured around them. Some might have the willpower or resistance to break out, but this would dramatically cut down on our potential pursuers without any risk of someone getting hurt.

Arch slapped the side of the truck twice, and Krystal fired up the engine. As the only one of us to ever actually reside in Boarback, she was the obvious choice to drive, especially considering her aggressive vehicular nature. Despite the massive coat covering most of her body and weighing her down, she didn't miss a step once the signal came. We jerked into motion, our combined weight substantially slowing the acceleration. If we'd been trying to work with just the mechanical advantage, we'd have been sunk. Even I could have outrun us at our initial pace, to say nothing of someone like Deborah.

Taking each movement carefully, I leaned over the side of the truck bed, popping open our gas tank. For a flickering moment, part of me tried to hesitate, to question whether it was wise to toss some untested potion into a combustion-based engine on a vehicle where we were well ensconced inside the blast radius. Then, I shook off the notion. *Of course*, it was a bad idea. Rational choices were for other clans: this was the House of Fred. We survived by leaning on each other, no matter how insane a path that led us down.

With minimal flourish, I dumped the entire vial into the gas tank, then slammed the lid back in place. At first, there was only the struggling groan of the truck's engine as we putted down the road toward the nearby forest. Then, I heard a growl. Not a growl, as in the engine was suddenly cranking more aggressively:

an actual, literal growl came from underneath the hood, and with it, a new burst of speed. We were picking up the pace—substantially, at that—yet there were more differences to be observed. The hard metal of the truck's surface began to segment in spots, forming plates like an insect's carapace. Its shape contoured in, turning more organic and less boxy, even as the bed swelled in size. On the ground, I saw something shiny and viscous reflected in the moonlight. Was it leaking oil? No, oil wasn't clear. This looked more like... drool.

Albert clapped his hands, a look of pure joy on his face. "A monster truck! Amy turned Krystal's ride into a literal monster truck."

The roar from up front seemed to confirm his suspicions, as did the tufts of thin metal, almost like hair, that were sprouting between the cracks of its newly plated segments. Whatever else was happening, we were definitely picking up speed. Despite being loaded down with a basketball team's worth of people, we were racing along now, cutting a breakneck pace as we left the main roads and entered the woods.

Nice as it was to have cover, we were far from in the clear. There was still a long trek up to the grove, and I was sure the Agency had access to faster options than even our alchemically amplified vehicle. That was to say nothing of our larger threats, such as the director. While I was glad she'd yet to appear, it was hard not to imagine her popping out from behind every tree or bush, suddenly putting a halt to our efforts with casual ease.

As it turned out, my instincts were correct, except I'd chosen the wrong threat. Our journey through the woods was going well, Krystal dodging swerves in the dirt road that would have sent other drivers right into an ancient trunk. She knew this whole area by heart, despite the years away. As such, I found it confusing that we began to slow. There were no expected obstacles in our path so soon, no hairpin turns or downed trees to avoid, yet our pace dropped more and more rapidly.

Inside, I could see Krystal slamming on the gas, so she wasn't the cause. I momentarily feared that Amy's potion had ended up destroying the engine; however, a soft whimper from up front added new clarity. Albert hadn't been off base: the truck was functioning as if it were alive and capable of animal-level intelligence. That meant it had senses, ideas like self-preservation, the concept of predator and prey. Things that even a creature born moments before would have the capacity to feel. Hunger, fear, these came with us from the start.

The truck shuddered to a halt just before a small clearing, sinking low on its front tires in what I imagined to be a submissive position. In truth, I didn't really blame the truck for such a reaction. As a being less than an hour old, I could only imagine the terror it felt coming upon a pair of ancient, powerful vampires.

Standing in the clearing, with obvious intent to bar our path, waited Deborah and Claudius.

10.

"FRED, HOW DO YOU WANT TO PLAY THIS?"
Arch was looking at me, as were the others. It was a fair question; even if I hadn't been the one in charge of the clan, I'd certainly had the most dealings with the Blood Council, out of anyone.

My initial reaction was one of despair; however, my pragmatic side quickly quelled such notions. This wedding had little to no impact on Deborah or the Blood Council; they'd been willing to sign off on it already. True, she'd caught us in a compromising position, but that didn't mean we were sunk. Deborah was nothing if not reasonable. Negotiation was still very much on the table, so long as we didn't open by doing something stupid.

I rose in the truck, looking over the top and meeting Deborah's gaze. "Have you come to wish us a happy wedding, or to try stopping us?"

Deborah lifted an eyebrow artfully. "Try?"

"You are a mighty opponent, indeed, but there are quite a few of us, and you know my clan can be rather surprising when pressed. Escape is not impossible."

The fact that I was referring to getting away, rather than victory, appeared to mollify her ego, which I wasn't entirely sure existed in the first place. "I suppose one my age knows better than to assume we've seen everything. You do have a knack for the unexpected, though I'm afraid, tonight is not such a case. Anyone could have seen this potential move coming, so I'm sure you know that the director is already aware. Every moment you spend with us allows her to organize her forces, or perhaps give chase herself."

"Which is your way of putting a clock on this to keep me under pressure."

Deborah looked momentarily off-step. She'd evidently forgotten that this was one area where my business training came into play. I, too, knew the choreography for the dance of negotiation. The mental stumble took up less than a second. She recovered instantly, moving closer to our truck.

"Did I put the clock on? Funny, I don't recall founding an Agency, installing a director, and then ordering her to block your wedding. Seems more like I was merely laying the situation bare. Time is vital, you clearly need to be on your way, and I gain nothing by stopping you."

Pleasant as that sounded, I knew the difference between the windup and the pitch. One was a lot more dangerous than the other.

"However," Deborah continued, along with her slow advance. "We did hear the head of the Agency make it explicit that this was not allowed. As the Blood Council, it would reflect quite poorly on us if we merely let you pass. Now, if you were to use some sort of distraction on us, the kind of thing we couldn't resist, that might offer up a viable explanation as to why we didn't block your progress."

I was still unraveling her intent, but I'd forgotten that I was not the only one present with this sort of experience. The passenger door popped open as Asha emerged, looking still slightly shaken, but steadily more and more like herself. "I get it. You want me. Because if you have the chance to test a new type of vampire or stop a wedding, the Blood Council would of course choose the former."

"Absolutely no—"

"Fred, I make my own deals." Asha never broke eye contact with Deborah. "Is this the same battery of tests you made Fred go through on his last visit?"

"Close to it, with a few obvious exceptions. No terminal patients on hand for you to try turning." Deborah paused, pondering for a moment. "We also might do some light combat testing, just to get a sense of where you're starting out. I would handle that personally, though, so I can assure you it would be perfectly safe. In fact, I'll go so far as to promise no lasting harm will come to you during any of the tests."

The sound of a door opening once more surprised all of us. Part of me expected to see Krystal emerge, gun in hand, ready to put an end to this discussion however she deemed necessary. Instead, I found myself looking at the final vampire of our clan. Lillian strode forward, failing to conceal her rattled nerves. Not much scared her, but the Blood Council was a notable exception. Her general policy had been to stay far away, only living in the same house as Deborah had softened the terror slightly.

"She's not going alone," Lillian declared. Asha and Deborah both started to protest, so Lillian denied them the chance. "Hey, guess what? That wasn't a question." She whirled toward Deborah, pointing a finger. "There is no chance in hell I'm leaving someone in your position alone with a newly turned vampire who doesn't know diddly about how our society works." Not done, her glare turned to Asha. "And I know you're the bee's knees at the law, but there's a *lot* more to learn when you actually become part of a parahuman species. Treaties, customs, rules of manners, so much more than you're picturing. Seeing as I'm the only member of this clan who also has extensive practice actually *being* a vampire, that means I'm her chaperone."

I'd seen many an amazing thing since becoming undead; however, watching someone actually compel both Deborah and Asha Patel into momentary silence was one that shone through as truly remarkable. After a few seconds to consider the idea, Asha spoke once more.

"How 'bout this? I'm on board with doing tests, so long as they are the same ones Fred did. Anything variant, we negotiate, but I'll go with you now as a show of good faith."

"As well as getting the car moving again," Deborah pointed out. "But I'm certainly not going to argue with getting my way. The deal is acceptable. We will run through only the tests conducted on Fredrick Fletcher in his last visit, where viable, and all others are subject to separate negotiations." She grinned, the barest hint of her fangs peeking through in the moonlight. "I think I'm going to like having someone with your talents among our kin."

Smoothly as it all seemed to be going, I couldn't help myself. "Asha, are you sure?"

In spite of having been through literal death and back in less than a day, Asha still managed to look almost bored by the question, as if she were truly unbothered by it all. "They're going to insist on this eventually; it can either be an inconvenience, or a way I help. I like the helping version better, especially given what you've done for me today." Asha tapped the hood of the truck, eliciting something like a wag for those of us in the bed. "Go get hitched. We've got this."

My eyes turned to Deborah, who was waiting politely. "Should I even ask why you're doing this? I'm sure there's at least five more motives I'm not seeing."

She feigned shock, placing her hand over her heart. "My dear man, you wound me. When have I dealt with the House of Fred in anything less than clear, honest, fair terms? Aside from the times I tricked you, of course—those were part of the testing." We stayed looking at each other, and the mock humor slid away. "Long-term view, remember? What you are is unique, and now there's another one-of-a-kind vampire in your clan, as well. To my thinking, the Blood Council is far better served by an ally I aided in his time of need than by one I angered on his wedding day. Especially one who is keenly aware of just how easily I'm letting him off the hook. On top of which, I did say I would make up for Claudius's rudeness to you, and I loathe having a debt overhead."

No arguing with that. If Deborah wanted to stop us, we'd be sunk. Testing Asha wasn't great, but she'd also promised to keep her safe. Given who were going up against tonight, not even those of us moving on had that guarantee.

"I take your point, but I'm not sure I'd call stealing two of my people giving us aid."

"No, the aid is when I tell you that there's a series of traps just up ahead, lining the woods. However, some incredibly powerful vampire going for a stroll must have accidently triggered a few. If you follow the direction the broken branches point, I daresay you could wind your way through the obstacles without any further delay." The gleeful twinkle in Deborah's eye said it all. She'd walked in with all the cards and was leaving with exactly the prize she'd had her sights on. Tonight, it was helpful, but part of me feared what would happen on the day she decided to play for keeps.

With Asha and Lillian at her side, Deborah shifted toward the tree line, motioning for Claudius to come, too. I'd almost forgotten he was even there; the guy had been completely absorbed in whatever he was typing on his tablet. My best guess was notes and testing ideas for Asha, who was in for a tiresome next few hours. By the time I looked back over, the trio was already gone. Seconds later, Claudius gave chase.

No sooner had the last of the Blood Council left than our truck roared with vigor once more. Krystal gripped the wheel like it was the reins of a bucking bronco. "Hold on! Going to try to follow those branches, but it might be a bit of a crapshoot."

We lunged forward; the truck had only gotten more animalistic in the time spent idling. Had we been thinking about it, moving someone inside might have been smarter from a space-allocation standpoint, but Deborah had taken up enough time. Even though the exchange had been relatively brief compared to our overall trip, each passing second felt like it brought the Agency closer to our heels.

I assumed that was me being worrisome and paranoid—my standard mode when trouble was about— until Arch muttered under his breath and adjusted his position. For most people, that would have meant nothing, especially as we clung for dear life to the bed of a magically animated truck. But Arch was not most people; his only tic was the cigarettes. Other than that, he rarely wasted movement, and never words. Something had his attention, and there were a limited number of potential options for what could manage that.

Sure enough, as we tore through a section of forest, swerving in the direction indicated by a massive branch snapped into an awkward angle, my nose caught the whiff of other bodies. I couldn't catch a single sound or sight; however, a vampire's nose is an extremely potent detection tool. Even with that advantage, it soon became clear that I was the last to notice our pursuers.

"Here's how it's going to work," Arch said, talking loud enough to be heard through the open glass by those in the cab. "The agents are expecting one of the traps to take out our vehicle, after which point, they'd converge on us. To do that, they're spread out, capable of reacting no matter which point we're at. When we break through the end of this area, they'll need to regroup. That's when June and I hop off."

"You going to fight them?" Krystal called from behind the wheel.

"Certainly not. But it has been some time since I held a teaching session on the subject of ambushes. Let's see who's been keeping up with their training, and who gets to spend some practice time with me next month."

Despite knowing they were on our heels to halt our wedding, a piece of me felt a great swell of sympathy for any agents who failed Arch's exam—which I had to assume would be most of them.

A sudden bump nearly tossed us out; only good reactions and keen grips saved us as the truck literally jumped over a small pit we'd almost careened into. Nearby was a smoking husk of ground and a tree trunk

432

that looked like it had been punched over. This must have been their final line where the traps were piled thick. Deborah had torn a hole right through their defenses, and thanks to her guidance, we threaded the needle by the thinnest of margins, the truck's right side taking scratches from a tree we were pressed against.

Then, we were through, breaking into another small clearing. It was a momentary respite as Krystal eased off the gas, slowing us down to allow for the departures.

"Don't bother. I heal, and June is nimble." Arch spat the command literally the moment he jumped over the side. There was a disconcerting bump, like we'd hit something human-sized, yet Arch was unbothered as he used the momentum of his roll to spring to his feet. A soft *thud* came seconds later as June hopped out, landing light and easy.

The next two sounds of landing were far less graceful. With one, came the rattling of a scabbard and the ancient weapon held within. From the other, a selection of "oofs" and grunts, along with the jangle of countless unseen tools below his robes.

Arch and June stood, waiting for the assault of agents as planned. Only, they weren't alone. Without any warning or discussion, Neil and Albert had leapt out of the truck, too.

11.

"**KRYSTAL, STOP!**" **I GLANCED INSIDE,** noticing that her wrestling match with the steering wheel had only gotten more violent.

"Not really an option! I'll slow us down and try to run in a circle." With a forceful effort, she jerked the wheel to the right, putting us on a loop back toward Neil and Albert. I didn't actually need to get close to hear their argument with Arch; my keen ears had been on that since the moment they'd touched the ground.

It wasn't often Arch was caught off guard, and he was visibly annoyed about the anomaly. "What do you two think you're doing?"

In response, Neil pointed in four directions, one after the other. "We were tracking the pursuers, too. There's four teams converging, meaning the numbers are too high to effectively delay, at least according to the way our instructor taught us to analyze combat situations."

"Your limits and mine are not the same."

"Arch, the kids aren't wrong. Even for us, this is still a lot." June was stretching, though her standard daggers were nowhere to be seen. This was, after all, the equivalent of a sparring match, a surprise training session thrown by the Agency's top teacher. "You've been drilling them for years. There's no way they aren't semi-competent. We could use the help."

In a rare display, Arch appeared uncertain. He shook his head, hand touching the pocket with his cigarettes once before dropping to his side. "It's not about them being able to help. Right now, you boys are a side project, a novelty the Agency lets me spend time on because I've earned that much leash. If you do this, word will travel back. I'm not saying you'll be drafted into working as agents, but there's no more flying under the radar. Once you show people what you can do, it's out there for good."

"I can't speak for Neil, but I haven't spent all this time training to *not* help when my friends need me." Albert's cheery smile was in place, and his sword was sheathed. This had nothing to do with his enchanted blade: it was merely the kind of man Albert had grown into, even as his body remained largely unchanged.

While I couldn't imagine any of us expected differently, Neil remained planted at his best friend's side, even laying a hand on Albert's shoulder. "Same here. Besides, I can't leave Albert to show off on his own. The show really works best as a two-hander."

As this conversation was occurring, we were drawing ever closer to them; however, the fight inside was growing more difficult. Richard reached over across the now vacant seats, gripping the wheel and adding his substantial might to the struggle. Just as the pair got control, Arch signaled for them to go.

"Is he serious?" Krystal asked.

"They're all serious," I replied. "And I don't think there's any changing of minds to be had on this one."

She hesitated briefly, then nodded to Richard, and together, they yanked the wheel back around, aiming us toward the approximate area we needed to go. The escape was on once more, and sincerely, not a second too soon. Since I was in the bed—the last remaining person there, in fact—I could look back at our four defenders as they held the line. Without sound or warning, the trees around them suddenly boiled with motion. Darkness seeped out; moments later, I realized it was agents dressed in black clothing, moving with such synchronization that they genuinely appeared to be one entity.

None of which was especially helpful when Arch dropped a flash grenade to the ground, drawing a huge spat of cursing and yells as half the agents were suddenly blinded. Anyone without natural night vision would be using tech or spells, both of which increased the eyes' sensitivity to light.

I could just make out Arch's words, carried over on the Texas winds.

"I see some of you ignored my advice to master the art of moving without sight and are still relying on rudimentary tools. Let us hope you took the blind-fighting lessons more seriously."

One of the agents stumbled over, and like flowing water, Arch eased past him, coming away with a gun and the knife from the man's belt. "Oh my, not even properly securing our weapons? Capleson, that's going to be a week of extra training."

Another agent made a real attempt for Arch, coming at him from behind, only for him to easily step aside during her lunge, sending her sprawling to the grass. "Avels, that's a week of stealth work for you. I heard those heavy steps before you were even close to attacking."

Funnily enough, it seemed like the agents were a lot more interested in Arch now that he'd presented himself as a target. After watching for only a few seconds, it wasn't hard to figure out why. Between the prideful ones looking to prove themselves and the vengeful ones he'd put through training, there were no shortage of agents happy to take a swing at Arch. And he was only warming up.

"Neil, Albert, why don't you take the group near you through defensive maneuver seven? It should be familiar for the ones who paid attention at my last lecture."

Curious as I was to see those two in action, just as they were moving, we broke into the trees, my vision once more obscured. Turning to the cab, I was struck by the emptiness that remained. Only Krystal and Richard were still inside; everyone else had traded their seat for a chance to buy us a little more time. With every step forward, the goal seemed more and more unreachable. We were shedding allies at a rapid pace, and at this point, the next one we lost would sink the entire venture. We couldn't very well get married without two partners and someone to perform the ceremony.

The upside was that we had actually managed to make substantial progress. I was even starting to pick out a few familiar features of the landscape from our initial trip. Had we been in a more traditional vehicle, I suspected functions would have begun to fail; this was close enough to be inside the discouragement field. Either by the sheriff's will or Amy's potion, the truck was holding together; in fact, it was picking up speed as we bounded through the trees.

For a fleeting second, as the branches whizzed by and the entrance to the clearing grew closer, I permitted myself to wonder if we'd actually managed this impossible plan. It was a ludicrous notion. The whole thing had been a Hail Mary from the start, yet it was hard not to hope. That idea was brought to an immediate halt at the same time as our truck.

This was not like with Deborah, a gradual decline in speed. No, the truck dug in so hard there were tracks in the ground, half tire, half claw. It stopped with all its might, lowering to the ground and whimpering. Only my vampire strength kept me from flying out over the cab. There wasn't a clearing this time, not that we needed one to see who were up against. If this entity was more instinctually terrifying than Deborah, there were only a few contenders to choose from.

"Agent Jenkins, your uproarious nature is not unknown to us. In fact, we sometimes count it as an asset. There is certainly a place in this organization for those who take to trouble with gusto; however, one must be capable of recognizing their limitations. I believe I made my feelings on this clear."

Director Waxwood stepped into view from behind a tree. She looked exactly the same as she had in the meeting. I had a hunch she hadn't even taken a break since then—habitual workers can smell our own. There was no anger or malevolence in her expression. She had the same look of bored detachment worn by any manager enforcing a company rule they had no stakes in, which was odd, given that she *was* the one who'd blocked our wedding.

"You show me the official, treaty-backed, legal loophole that lets you cancel a wedding on a whim, and I'll turn myself in," Krystal countered.

"Technically speaking, all I have done is pull my support. But Agent Jenkins, please don't act as if I'm some mad monster here. You know what Fredrick Fletcher represents, should his abilities pan out. To the Blood Council, to vampire kind as a whole. Connecting him to our protections, however tangentially, creates an immensely complicated matter. I'm not wrong to insist we consider the situation thoroughly before making such a bold decision."

"No, you're not wrong." This voice belonged to neither Krystal nor Director Waxwood, and it held far too much confidence to be mine. From behind an entirely different tree, one that was much too small to conceal his bulk, Sheriff Thorgood stepped into view. "But that's your problem to deal with. Responsibility comes with position and power; they're just a couple of kids in love."

Director Waxwood's eyes narrowed. "I might have known you'd be involved. You never were good at keeping a macro view of things. Too prone to getting hung up on individuals."

"I know. That's why you took a country, and I took a town," Sheriff Thorgood replied. His jovial tone dimmed slightly, and I caught a stern look in his eyes. "A town that I'll remind you we are still inside the boundaries of. Just because I've been playing nice doesn't mean I can't get serious. One must be capable of recognizing their limitations, right?"

"You think to mock me?"

There was a playful shine in Sheriff Thorgood's expression; that was hard to deny. "I think to remind you that not everyone says 'how high' when you say 'jump.' Sometimes, it's good for you not to get your way. Builds character."

In truth, I'd expected the director of the Agency to be above such simple barbs and taunts. More evolved. But regardless of how magical or powerful a being was, family was still family, and nobody gets under our skin like those we love. All of her focus seemed to have left us as she stared daggers at Leeroy. Overhead, clouds I was sure hadn't been there previously swirled, momentarily blocking out the stars.

"For that, you insist on taking the mortals' side, yet again. I'll never understand what compels you to this. What madness drives you to make such poor choices? Or is it truly nothing more than overdeveloped sentimentality?"

"The answer could be a lot of reasons. Depends on the situation." Sheriff Thorgood was moving now, his bulky frame ambling along at the same casual speed as always, heading in the direction of our truck. "In this particular case, it's actually your fault."

I hadn't thought Director Waxwood could look much more bothered, but the fact that several patches of grass near her suddenly wilted definitely added to the overall effect. While she fumed, Sheriff Thorgood leaned down to the driver's window, winked, and mouthed five brief words. Krystal began to tear up, but there was no time for a reply. Director Waxwood had finally found her voice.

"And how, pray tell, is you inserting yourself into Agency business without due cause my fault?"

"Because a long time ago, the person these beings would call my big sister taught me to always keep my promises. I gave my word to Agent Jenkins that I would her give away, you see. So that's exactly what I'm going to do."

There was no warning, no time to react. For all his gentle movements, it turned out Sheriff Leeroy Thorgood was beyond fast when properly motivated. He lifted the truck off the ground with both arms, no visible effort or strain on his face as he looked around just once to take aim.

"Pretty sure this isn't how the job is supposed to work, just playing it by ear. I'll hold her off, but don't dilly-dally. We can only play so much before the town would be demolished."

That was the entirety of our warning before Sheriff Thorgood hurled our entire truck over the trees and into the sky. A bit of extra push from his right hand in the launch put us in a spin once we were airborne, forcing me to direct my entire focus into clinging to the side of the truck. Our vehicle was whining from my hands digging into its metal/armor, though that just as easily may have been my own terrified screams ringing in my ears. It was a very real mercy that vampires are incapable of vomiting, or my stomach's contents would have stained many a treetop.

Something hitting my leg nearly tore me loose from the ride as we cleared the last of the treetops. I initially assumed it to be a rogue branch clinging to my slacks; unfortunately, a single look down afforded to me by the rotating truck was more than enough to see the actual source. One of the drawbacks to being massive and muscular was that standardized items, such as seatbelts, rarely fit.

That was likely why Richard had been thrown free in the chaos, or perhaps the nausea had been too much. Whatever the reason, I got a good look at the man who was supposed to be performing our ceremony, clinging onto the top of a tree as we spun off through the air on a crash course with our wedding venue.

12.

UNTIL THE MOMENT WE CAME DOWN, I WAS sure that we would crash. That would be more annoyance than issue; I healed from such injuries and Krystal would only grow more dangerous from a would-be lethal accident. As it turned out, I should have had more faith in Sheriff Thorgood, as well as remembered that the grove was no mere assembly of trees.

Just as the truck came plummeting down, branches shot up from all directions, catching us and carefully killing our momentum. In seconds, we were moving steadily along a river of shifting branches. They carried us along, finally depositing Krystal's transformed truck onto the ground. The enchanted vehicle collapsed, panting like a hound after a run.

Happy as I was to be uninjured, in that moment, I was more struck by how lovely the venue truly was. In the time since we'd left, there were new buildings grown, and the flower-lights had increased in number and spectrum of colors. There were no decorations, those were scheduled to go up later in the day, yet I could picture how they'd have looked, and it was dazzling.

Shaking off the effects of the fall and the surroundings, I hustled down to the driver's side door, just in time to watch Krystal force it open and come tumbling out. I caught her by chance, the two of us standing in the light of the trees, finally at our venue. She looked up at me, smiling despite the fact that we'd unequivocally lost.

"Richard caught a bad spin and went flying out. Doesn't look like we're getting hitched tonight."

"You never know. Maybe there's an online certification I can sign up for quick."

"No cell service out here; although, Douglas could have WIFI." Krystal looked a bit surprised when the trees around us shook, almost as if they were laughing at her joke. "We came really close, though. Even making it this far is crazy."

She wasn't wrong, especially when I thought back to all the powerful pursuers on our tail. Nevertheless, we had made it. Whatever the fallout, we were here. Might as well enjoy it while we could.

Stepping back, I offered the crook of my arm. "Want to go walk down the aisle? Call it practice for next time."

"What the hell. We at least deserve a taste of it." Undoing the belt of her oversized coat, Krystal allowed the garment to fall away, revealing her wedding dress to me for the first time. It was surprisingly normal—at least in appearances. No sheathes or gun pouches, just a beautiful white dress elevated to gorgeous by virtue of its model. She was a vision, a living dream who stepped gracefully to my side.

Wordlessly, we walked, arm in arm, through the section of the grove where we would have set up the chairs. It wasn't far from a fictional buffet table and a hypothetical dance floor, to say nothing of the planned bar. So many hours of effort to create a single night that had ultimately been in vain. Yet my heart was light as we reached the point where the aisle would have begun. Even if it wasn't the result we'd wanted, I'd still made it here with the woman I loved. It was hard not to be a little happy in the moment.

"Pissed as I should be, and I'm still pretty miffed," Krystal clarified, "I have to admit, I'm starting to get over Director Waxwood stopping our wedding."

"This is a heck of a time for cold feet."

She swatted me in the arm with her free hand. "Not like that. Like… I guess tonight reminded me that no title defines a relationship. Married people break up all the time. But you and I have each other's backs. We're on the same team, and when shit goes down, we get through the thick of it together. Married or not, we're in it for the long haul. Far as consolation prizes go, I can think of worse."

Our trek down the imagined aisle continued, the backdrop of foliage all that we could see. It made for a peaceful, serene setting, like we were the only two people in the world. Much as I would have loved for the walk to be observed by our loved ones, there was also something special about this stolen moment just for us.

"I agree wholeheartedly, with one caveat. Even though we failed tonight, do not think for one moment that you have seen the end of my resolve. I know my nature where conflict arises, but on this subject, I will not yield. I'm going to keep trying to marry you, Krystal Jenkins, until you change your mind or we pull it off. If you'll forgive a favorite job-related pun: you can *count* on it."

That earned a snort, which bubbled over into a chuckle as she laid her head against my shoulder. "Don't expect any argument here. Also, you might be the only person I know who could sincerely make a joke that bad after the night we've just been through."

"No wonder you're trying to put a ring on it," I replied.

Our solemn walk came to an end as we reached a modestly sized pulpit that had grown since our last visit. Clearly, this was where the one performing the marriage would stand, which meant that Krystal and I had arrived at our destination. Evidently, we weren't the only ones to mark the arrival, either. All around us, the trees began to shift.

It had probably been planned as effect for once we both were at the altar: the backdrop of foliage that the crowd would be facing began to part, revealing once more the breathtaking view of Boarback. Even knowing it was there, I was still taken back by the sight. That might have been due to the colorful smoke rising from the center of the town, or the flashes of light coming from within the forest.

Then again, maybe I was simply awestruck by the sight of an enormous, copper-scaled dragon soaring through the night. My jaw quite literally hung open as I watched the creature that *had* to be Gideon float on the winds. I'd never encountered a dragon in its natural form, let alone one who held a ruling title. He was massive, with a wingspan that only added to his prodigious size. The long neck and tail meant that he had incredible reach, and that was without considering the massive magical capabilities Gideon was packing. Had he been so inclined, a single swoop and bite could have ended me, or almost anyone else in Boarback, with a few notable exceptions.

A blast of wind washed over us as Gideon flapped his wings, slowing his momentum once he neared the newly formed opening in the trees. As he approached, he appeared to ripple with light, shrinking down to fit his landing space. Now, instead of blotting out a chunk of the sky, he was merely as large as a few buses lined together. With two more flaps that nearly took me off my feet, his claws settled lightly in the grass. Lowering his head, Gideon allowed his neck to rest on the ground. Only then could we see the seat rigged up just behind his head, keeping the rider safe from the winds and in easy earshot. With visible practice, Sally unhooked herself from the contraption and climbed down, looking around, confused.

"Where is everyone?"

"They got caught up in other business along the way." I'd expected Gideon's voice to sound different, but it was just the same as always, even if his gigantic mouth wasn't moving. Then again, seeing him change size so easily, it was likely that his voice was the same, a setting that he could alter with minimal effort.

At least I didn't have to bother asking how he knew that; the aerial approach meant he'd have had an excellent view. "I'm sorry you came all this way—wait! Gideon, you have wings! Richard fell into a tree not long ago. Maybe there's still time to fetch him."

That earned me a mighty scoff, all the more impressive on a dragon's face. "He fell near two beings it would be unwise for me to trade blows with. Such altercations leave lasting damage, and while Richard is too weak to be of concern to them, I am not."

It had been a briefly lived hope, yet only when it was fading did I realize just how strong the disappointment was. Fortunately, Gideon wasn't done speaking.

"Aside from which, there is no need to fetch him. Richard has become unable to fulfill his duty, which means it falls upon me to complete. I'd expected at least *you* to have some appreciation for the proper meaning of words."

I was truly dumbfounded by that one; however, Krystal didn't have such an issue, smacking herself in the head. "Son of a bitch, he's right. When Richard offered to marry us, Gideon said he seconded. I thought he meant the idea, not in the literal sense."

Comprehension dawned at last. "Oh. Gideon was volunteering to be Richard's second, like in a duel."

"Or a great many formal parahuman ceremonies where one might offer support to their long-term host.

We're nothing if not prepared for things to go wrong."
Rearing up, scaly head somehow looking more regal,
Gideon stared directly at us. "Time is short. Do you wish
to proceed?"

Together, Krystal and I met one another's eyes.

"With pleasure," I said.

"Fuck yeah," she declared.

"Very well, then. Given our limited window, I will
be holding a prudently abridged ceremony." Somehow,
the dragon's face grew momentarily vexed. "There is only
one issue to solve first. A ceremony such as this needs
witnesses, and Sally's youth means she doesn't qualify.
As I agreed to wed you, fixing that issue falls upon me."

Gideon's lavender eyes, so huge now in his new skull,
flashed with copper light. Seconds later, a mist began
to rise up around us, right where we'd planned for the
chairs to go. I could catch shapes in there, nearly faces
occasionally. It was so mesmerizing that I didn't notice
Gideon preparing to speak once more, which meant that
his voice caused me to leap a foot in the air.

"Attention residents of Boarback and all current
visitors. I, Gideon, King of the West, do hereby call
upon you to witness the joining of Fredrick Frankford
Fletcher and Agent Krystal Jenkins in marriage. We ask
the oldest magics to seal this unity, to bond your souls
past the grip of even death."

The longer he spoke, the more I could feel the electricity in the air. My neck hairs were standing like I'd rubbed them with a balloon. I'd been warned that marriage was a magical ceremony for parahumans; I just hadn't expected it to be so... potent. It was building, flowing all around us. Perhaps, in other venues, those not presided over by a dragon, this was a slower process. I had no objections to speed, though. Frankly, I was sick and tired of not being married to Krystal.

"You have fought to stand here, in this place, harder than most could or would have been capable. Speak now your words to one another, your vows, your promises, the deepest truths of your heart."

Strange a situation as it was, this part was mercifully clear. The time had come for vows. In the original plan, Krystal had wanted to go first, and this one bit, it seemed, would actually go as intended.

"Fred, for a long time after my change, I felt like reality itself was spinning. Losing my mom, learning what I was, getting betrayed... it started to feel like I had nothing real. I drifted through life, barely more than the job, afraid to let anyone in close. Then, I met you again, and for the first time in years, I remember what it was like to have solid ground underneath my feet. You are the kindest, most honest, most lovingly sincere person I've ever met. For all the amazing things I've seen in my life, your unwavering ability to see the best in people wows and humbles me to this day. I want to spend the rest of my life with you at my side, growing together and making one another better."

What had started as ambient magic was now flowing through Krystal, winding its way around her in a series of infinite, invisible knots. It was an interesting tidbit, something I focused on largely because I'd suddenly discovered a boiling case of nerves at the prospect of having to speak. On this occasion, though, it was a relatively minor hurdle. After staring down tonight's challenges, my own cowardice was a paltry opponent.

"Krystal, I am a vampire, standing on a hill overlooking a town of supernatural beings, at a wedding being presided over by a dragon who is also a king, and by far, the most incredible thing about this moment is the woman I'm sharing it with. Your courage, selflessness, loyalty, and determination all inspire me daily. Being with you has shown me how messy, chaotic, dangerous, and *fun* life can truly be. Our time has changed me in ways that I'll never be able to articulate, nor stop being thankful for. I want to spend the rest of our lives together, seeing the world through one another's eyes, offering support in times of struggle and cheer in times of need. Not to mention, always having each other's back." I winked on the last line, which earned me a slight grin from Krystal.

"Ride or die."

"Dying hasn't technically stopped either of us," I pointed out.

"Guess we're in for a long ride, then."

Tempting as it was to get lost in her eyes, I could feel the magic winding its way through me now, as well. It didn't feel bad, really. Didn't even have much of a feeling. It was more like noticing a breeze from a vent that had been blowing on you for hours that only just happened to catch your attention in the moment. The magic was primed and ready, waiting to be engaged.

"By my authority as King of the West, I have heard your vows and recognize them. From this day henceforth, you shall be joined, two minds, two souls, two bodies, yet with a shared bond that unites what was once separate. Seal this ceremony with a display of love and connect your magics."

While the phrasing was a bit odd, I'd seen more than enough films and general pop culture to know what came at the end of a wedding. The magical part was interesting and made me wonder if perhaps humans had taken the tradition from supernatural ceremonies. It was an idle, short-lived curiosity, as I had far more pressing matters to attend to.

Taking Krystal in my arms, I dipped her slightly, giving a dash of theatricality to our special moment. With no more delay than that, our lips met, and together, we shared the first kiss of our marriage. In some ways, that kiss actually *was* the marriage, as the instant our lips connected, all of the built-up magic came alive at once. I could feel the crackle along my skin, hear snaps and pops in the air, and I paid all of it absolutely no mind. In that moment, there was no magic, no dragon, no spectators, no woods, no town, none of it.

For that brief moment, the world consisted solely of myself and my wife, kissing one another in triumph.

13.

THE PARTY WAS STILL GOING BY THE TIME
we got back down to town. Outside of a momentary
dragon-induced vision, it had never stopped. To the den-
izens of Boarback, all they knew was that someone had
wheeled free refreshments into the center of town, put
on a show, and then dropped a magical mist to put everyone in the festive spirit. The agents had either gotten
out or been swept along in the celebration, meaning that
all our conflict happened out in the woods.

Part of me expected to be stopped as we rode down in Krystal's truck, after it had recovered. Gideon and Sally left the way they came, not bothering to offer us a lift. I'd dealt with dragons enough to know that riding was an extraordinarily rare event, reserved only for dire situations and those they held in the highest of esteem.

We almost literally ran into Richard not too far down the hill; he'd been chasing after us since getting thrown and was cutting a good pace until we nearly crashed into his torso. Thankfully for the truck, we swerved just in time.

He hopped in as we started to explain what had happened, until Richard told us he'd gotten a magical view of the whole ceremony—as much of the town likely did also. None of it had surprised him, anyway. Unlike us, he'd clocked Gideon's original meaning from the start; evidently, the King of the West frequently acted as Richard's second as a part of their alliance. It made challengers even more hesitant to try to tackle the alpha therian, because success only meant a dragon would be waiting instead.

Passing through the swath of woods where we'd met Sheriff Thorgood and Director Waxwood was surreal. Neither was anywhere to be seen, but what remained terrified me to my core. An entire section of the woods was devastated: shattered trees, huge grooves cut in the earth, mini-craters like a blast had gone off. Even stranger, the destruction was perfectly contained in this one area, with zero spillover. This was no full-on brawl— we were seeing the results of playful sparring, at best. I was finally beginning to appreciate why Krystal always felt at ease in Boarback as I gained a greater grasp on the sheriff's capabilities.

Arch's team was also gone by the time we arrived, a more traditional battlefield left in their wake. I could understand things wrapping up quickly; once Gideon showed us getting hitched, there wasn't anything left to fight about. We continued down through the woods, past where Deborah and Claudius had been waiting, out onto the actual streets of Boarback.

Most of the mist had cleared, lost to either lungs or the winds, giving everyone an unimpeded view as we approached. Doing some quick movements, we had Richard take over the wheel to act as a sudden chauffer, driving us to where the bulk of the crowd was gathered. I had no idea if we were walking into our own arrests or a strong talking to. Either way, we'd take the consequences head-on. Whatever the cost, it was worth it.

As it turned out, we were greeted by a thundering cheer the moment Krystal set foot outside the truck. I'd almost forgotten that she spent years here; to the townsfolk, Krystal was one of them. That set a firm standard for the night's mood. Even the few agents I spotted sulking around seemed to register that this was going to be a party. It was either that, or be set against the entire population of a supernatural town, including their sheriff, and the agents were all much too smart to make that basic an error.

Stepping out of the truck, I was relieved to see our friends had also joined the revelry. Neil and Albert were standing with June, talking to a clustered group of other agents. Though I was sure they'd just been facing off in the woods, everyone seemed animated and cheerful, clearly enjoying the conversation. Something told me the Agency had gotten a taste of what those two could do, and the recruiting attempts were about to get serious.

Amy and Bubba were manning the makeshift bar, Bubba doling out drinks that Amy would "spice up" with a few drops from an array of bottles, depending on the parahuman in question's needs. I spotted Gregor with a few other blocky fellows, recognizable as fellow gargoyles once I knew what to look for, chatting with the most excited expression I'd ever seen on that stoic face (which is to say, he looked mildly interested). Al had turned back into her larger form and was hunkered down with a bunch of locals, playing what appeared to be a dice game, only the kinds I knew of didn't call forth miniature illusions.

I also spotted many of our older friends, people who'd come to town for the wedding, only to find it all happening a day too early. The Clovers were having a chat with Cyndi not far from where a familiar pair of satyrs were chewing the fat with a small cluster of goblins. I even noticed Sheri, looking far more composed than at our last meeting, talking to agents I suspected were fellow vampires. Who I couldn't find was the only one that might shed insight into what came next. My eyes kept probing as I stepped out of the truck, searching the crowd that mobbed Krystal.

The smell of smoke from behind me worked better than a theatrical cough could have. Arch was there, stamping out his cigarette in the ash box he always carried. "You look like a man with too heavy a mind for an occasion this happy."

With all attention on Krystal, I took the opportunity to motion for Arch to follow. Together, we walked a bit out from the crowd, putting the truck between us and them for a small modicum of privacy. There was really no getting around potential eavesdroppers—parahumans in open air just inherently came with that risk—but we also weren't going to be talking about anything exactly secret. The entire town had just seen what happened; they all knew we'd bucked an order from the Agency.

"I suppose my main question is what sort of fallout should we expect? Even if we didn't break a law, we disobeyed Krystal's boss. I know there's going to be retribution."

"Unquestionably, though most of it will fall on her," Arch said. At my expression, he seemed to realize his choice of wording and mercifully added some clarification. "She ignored a directive, if not an order, and ours is a system that punishes such actions. Part of the job. Don't worry about it—not Krystal's first or last time. The punishment is annoying, not painful. Worse jobs, extra shifts, maybe a few weeks training with me if you've *really* pissed somebody off, but they're not going to hurt her. We still have an HR department."

While I wasn't in love with that response, I also didn't see many avenues for protest. Short of becoming an agent myself, there was no way to share in her punishment, and that gesture would open *far* more problems than it solved. Also, it ignored the fact that I'd never make the cut, because I was in no way suited to such work. If all we got in payback for our marriage was Krystal having crappier assignments for a while, then that was manageable.

"The larger concern for you is what sort of message the House of Fred just sent the entire parahuman world," Arch continued.

That seemed like a bit of an exaggeration until I really considered our situation. There were representatives from all manner of species and clans here: therians of Richard's tribe, the Clover twins and Cyndi were all mages. Obviously, there were vampires thanks to the Blood

Council, to say nothing of the countless diplomatic-necessity invites we'd sent to Krystal's agent connections. Arch was right. There was all sort of parahumans here, and we had to assume they'd all gotten the show thanks to Gideon. Word would spread; there was no stopping that.

"To me, I'd say we showed the world we don't roll over on matters that are important to us. I'm guessing you have another take."

Arch offered a single nod. "Believe it or not, I've basically got the same one, with an important distinction. You didn't just show an unwillingness to quit; you also demonstrated just how powerful this clan is."

"We barely pulled it off. If not for Gideon, it would have been a bust," I protested.

A hand touched the pocket with his cigarettes, then pulled back. "Fred, let me explain something. We, being the Agency, said you couldn't do something. You said 'fuck you' and tried to do it, anyway. Happens a lot; people push limits, especially parahumans. What makes your case special is that you succeeded. You got your way. Tonight, you metaphorically slapped the Agency. That also happens; most of us have been at this long enough to know you can't win all the time. The larger concern is that, as tale of this spreads, others will take note. It's not often anyone wins against us, even in a low-stakes scuffle. No one is going to underestimate the House of

Fred anymore. People will know your name, will count your clan as a player in the games of politics."

I'd never considered that possibility. My mind had been entirely occupied by dealing with the Agency and making it to the venue. Oddly, I found myself less bothered by the revelation than I might have expected. I suppose that, deep down, I'd known this was inevitable. Even if it wasn't happening the way outsiders thought, my clan *had* slowly been accumulating unique, powerful individuals. With the addition of Asha and her condition, I'd known we'd end up on a bigger radar eventually. If sooner than later was the cost of tonight, it was one I'd easily pay all over again.

"Thanks. I'll keep that in mind moving forward." I paused, mentally rerunning through the evening's events. "Also, I'm not sure if I ever said it, but thank you for helping stall the agents. I'd have understood if you weren't on our side in this one, and I'm grateful that you were."

"The smart call would have been to side with the agents." Arch looked away, up to the night sky, where the stars were still shining with all their might, fighting against the dark until dawn's inevitable arrival. "But even after centuries to learn better, I still have the same weakness that got me into this mess in the first place. I'm a romantic. Living as long as me, you see a lot, but I never stop rooting for real love, when I find it."

A roar came from the crowd, and I heard music start playing. Seemed as though we were moving into the dancing portion of the reception, the simple road filling in for our planned dance floor. I'd be needed back soon, as Krystal and I would be expected to open things up. Arch caught the implication, as well, nodding to the party.

"You should head back. I'm going to have a quick light, and then I'll join."

Perhaps it was the boldness of the evening, or my curiosity spilling over; whatever the case, before leaving, I looked to Arch and posed a question that had been burning in my mind for quite some while.

"You don't age, you don't die. You're not weakened by silver or any other metal. Despite appearing to be human, you make of habit of defeating parahumans that should be much stronger. I've only been able to think of one potential mythical being who could explain all that. An utterly crazy one, but knowing what Krystal is has forced me to keep a very open mind. Just on the offhand chance my guess is right, I have to know this much. Arch... short for archangel?"

That earned me the first outright burst of laughter I'd ever gotten from Arch. It exploded from his lips, quickly dissolving into quiet shaking and a few light coughs, before he shook his head.

"Not even close. Archibald just isn't a name you hear in use much anymore. Baseline: I'm human. That's what I started as, same as you. Then, life happened, but it isn't a story we have time for, and definitely not one I would tell on a wedding day."

A high-pitched whistle got my attention. I could now see Krystal with her fingers against her lips, preparing to fire off another call if I didn't get in gear. Good as it was to get a sense of what was to come from Arch, I wasn't going to miss the night we'd worked so hard for.

Strolling up, I walked past a town's worth of supernatural beings, my clan, an assortment of agents, allies, and other various strangers. Near the back of the crowd, I could even spot Sheriff Thorgood, who was grinning from ear-to-ear despite the shiner already growing on his face.

I walked past them all and up to Agent Krystal Jenkins, my old friend, my hero, my wife. Together, we took each other's hands as the music began to play, falling into a rhythm that was clumsy and awkward, yet quickly took shape into something coherent as we found each other's tempo. Our first dance of so many more to come. Some would be awkward, some could be graceful, others would be chaos incarnate. And we would face them all together.

This was only the beginning. Hard as it had been to reach this point, it was merely the first step on the path of our lives together. Yet, in that moment, dancing with Krystal, surrounded by strangers and loved ones alike, I could hardly wait to see the adventure we'd encounter next.

Perhaps the future wasn't so scary a thing, after all. Not with a partner like her at my side.

ABOUT THE AUTHOR

Drew Hayes is an author from Texas who has now found time and gumption to publish several books. He graduated from Texas Tech with a B.A. in English, because evidently he's not familiar with what the term "employable" means. Drew has been called one of the most profound, prolific, and talented authors of his generation, but a table full of drunks will say almost anything when offered a round of free shots. Drew feels kind of like a D-bag writing about himself in the third person like this. He does appreciate that you're still reading, though.

Drew would like to sit down and have a beer with you. Or a cocktail. He's not here to judge your preferences. Drew is terrible at being serious, and has no real idea what a snippet biography is meant to convey anyway. Drew thinks you are awesome just the way you are. That part, he meant. You can reach Drew with questions or movie offers at NovelistDrew@gmail.com Drew is off to go high-five random people, because who doesn't love a good high-five? No one, that's who.

Read or purchase more of his work at his site: DrewHayesNovels.com